Praise for
BECOMING MARIE ANTOINETTE
and
DAYS OF SPLENDOR, DAYS OF SORROW

Novels of Marie Antoinette by Juliet Grey

"This engaging voice, coupled with vibrant descriptions of clothing, palaces, masques, and dinners, really thrusts the reader into the story. . . . Exceptionally well done!"

—Historical Novel Review

"Grey has the gift of truly bringing Marie Antoinette to life. Many authors have written about the Queen of France, but no one has managed to give her such a voice as Grey." —Examiner.com

"In her richly imagined novel, Juliet Grey meticulously re-creates the sumptuous court of France's most tragic queen. Beautifully written, with attention paid to even the smallest detail, *Becoming Marie Antoinette* will leave readers wanting more!"

—MICHELLE MORAN, bestselling author of *Madame Tussaud*

"A thoroughly enjoyable novel, brimming with delightful details . . . Grey writes eloquently and with charming humor, bringing 'Toinette' vividly to life as she is schooled and groomed—molded, quite literally—for a future as Queen of France, an innocent pawn in a deadly political game."

—SANDRA GULLAND, bestselling author of
Mistress of the Sun and the Josephine Bonaparte trilogy

"A great read that is sure to be requested by lovers of historical fiction, especially those who enjoyed Michelle Moran's *Madame Tussaud* and other novels about the French Revolution."

—*Library Journal*

"Everything is so vividly described that you feel as though you are right there experiencing it all. This novel is very well written and it captivates you from the very beginning."

—Peeking Between the Pages

"A sympathetic and engaging read that presents the French queen in a manner seldom found in other novels . . . Readers will see Marie Antoinette in a whole new light. Anyone interested in French history will savor every page of this novel."   —BookLoons

"A lusciously detailed novel of Marie Antoinette's rise to power and the decadent, extravagant lifestyles of eighteenth-century Versailles."
—Shelf Awareness

"Well researched and lovingly written with sparkling details—this new trilogy is not one to be missed by any lover of historical fiction."
—Stiletto Storytime

"This novel was by far the best I have read that tackles such an interesting and misunderstood queen. Grey weaves fun scandals into the history we all know."   —Mostly Books

"A lively and sensitive portrait of a young princess in a hostile court, and one of the most sympathetic portrayals of the doomed queen."
—Lauren Willig, bestselling author of the Pink Carnation series

"Wonderfully delectable and lusciously rich, an elegant novel to truly savor. Juliet Grey's Marie Antoinette is completely absorbing."
—Diane Haeger, author of *The Queen's Rival*

"I really appreciate that Juliet Grey has decided to take a trilogy to tell Marie Antoinette's story, instead of simply a single novel, because it really helps readers understand how and where her world went so terribly wrong. Not only are Marie Antoinette's motivations—particularly for her party girl ways early in her queenship—more easily understood, but so are the reasons for the French Revolution. In fact, I think only in nonfiction have I seen the causes of the French Revolution so well laid out."
—Devourer of Books

"This is a beautiful novel that opened the gilded gates of Versailles for me. More important, it opened the gates of Marie Antoinette's soul. . . . A vibrant novel that illustrates the blindness of politics and tradition."
—A Writer's Life: Working with the Muse

"Highlighting Marie's strengths and her weaknesses, Grey paints a sympathetic portrait of France's last queen, successfully showcasing how she matured as both a person and a monarch."

—Confessions of an Avid Reader

"Juliet Grey has a way of making this period new and exciting for me."

—The Maiden's Court

"Grey leaves no detail to chance and combines impeccable research with an easy and enjoyable writing style. . . . This was the first time that I felt that [Marie Antoinette] was presented as a human being, rather than a one-dimensional character."

—Luxury Reading

"Ms. Grey has captured the essence of who Antoinette was. A figure that has been much maligned in history who was actually a caring soul and someone who was loyal to her husband and to the country to which she became a transplant. While reading, I was transported to that time and place. The book really makes the reader feel as if she is part of the book. The characters are so engaging and the dialogue is natural."

—The True Book Addict

"This second book of Juliet Grey's Marie Antoinette trilogy exceeded—by far—all my expectations. In the author's first book, *Becoming Marie Antoinette,* we read about Antonia and how she, at a very young age, becomes Queen of France—a most delightful read from beginning to end—so much so that I named it my favourite read of 2011. So how was *Days of Splendor, Days of Sorrow* going to compare, or better yet, give me more to get excited about? Every little detail in this book is delectable, and I savoured it thoroughly. Written in good taste, nothing is amiss, and everything is possible. A work of fiction, yet written with such precise historical details, *Days of Splendor, Days of Sorrow* is much more than just another Marie Antoinette story! I can't wait for the next and final book of this amazing trilogy. Excellent!"

—Enchanted by Josephine

CONFESSIONS *of*
MARIE ANTOINETTE

By Juliet Grey

Becoming Marie Antoinette
Days of Splendor, Days of Sorrow
Confessions of Marie Antoinette

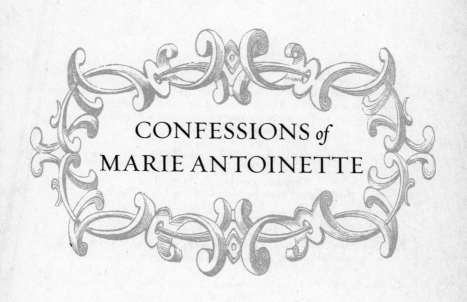

CONFESSIONS *of*
MARIE ANTOINETTE

 A NOVEL

JULIET GREY

BALLANTINE BOOKS TRADE PAPERBACKS
NEW YORK

A Ballantine Books Trade Paperback Original

Published in the United States by Ballantine Books, an imprint of The Random House Publishing Group, a division of Random House, Inc., New York.

BALLANTINE and the HOUSE colophon are registered trademarks of Random House, Inc.
RANDOM HOUSE READER'S CIRCLE & Design is a registered trademark of Random House, Inc.

LIBRARY OF CONGRESS CATALOGING-IN-PUBLICATION DATA
Grey, Juliet.
Confessions of Marie Antoinette : a novel / Juliet Grey.
pages cm
"A Ballantine Books Trade Paperback Original"—T.p. verso.
ISBN 978-0-345-52390-7 (paperback) — ISBN 978-0-345-52391-4 (ebook)
1. Marie Antoinette, Queen, consort of Louis XVI, King of France, 1755–1793—
Fiction. 2. Nobility—France—Fiction. 3. France—Fiction. I. Title.
PS3607.R4993C66 2013
813'.6—dc23   2013004316

Printed in the United States of America

www.randomhousereaderscircle.com

2 4 6 8 9 7 5 3 1

Book design by Casey Hampton

Pour mon mari, Scott, for making everything possible.
Bisous!

Tribulation first makes one realize what one is.

—Marie Antoinette to the comte de Mercy-Argenteau

Posterity should pay no heed to those secret legends which are spread about a Prince in his lifetime out of spite, or a mere love of gossip, which a mistaken public believes to be true and which, in a few more years, are adopted by the historians who thus deceive themselves and the generations to come.

—Voltaire, *Éloge Funèbre*, written during
the reign of Louis XV

CONFESSIONS *of* MARIE ANTOINETTE

ONE

Adieu, Splendor

❧ OCTOBER 5, 1789 ❧

"We will take the queen dead or alive!"

Louison's voice is hoarse. Small wonder. She has been chanting the slogan for the past few hours. But she is as impervious to the sting at the back of her throat as she is to the rain that lashes against her cheeks and spatters her only good skirt, now heavy with mud, as she trods along the unpaved road from the center of Paris to the palace of Versailles.

"I want a thigh!" crows the *poissarde* behind her, broader and beefier, brandishing an axe, her apron already stained with blood.

A deep voice cries, "I'll fashion her entrails into a cockade!" Louison turns, expecting to see another fishwife, or perhaps one of the prostitutes from the Palais Royal who had joined their sodden march, now six thousand strong. For the first time, she notices the Adam's apple, and a faint hint of stubble on her confederate's cheeks. Now she comprehends why the *"poissarde"* has been able to wield a pikestaff as if it were a mere baton for so many miles. "Pardon, monsieur," she says, elbowing him. "*Votre perruque*—your wig is askew." Sheepishly, the man adjusts the ratty hairpiece. It looks as if it had never seen a comb. She would have used it as a prop to sculpt Medusa. Whoever the disguised man is, if one doesn't peer too closely, he resembles any number of the bedraggled army marching on Versailles.

He catches Louison by the wrist, taking her by surprise, then puts a finger to his lips. "There are many of us here," he says. His accent is cultivated, like that of an educated man.

"I want the Austrian bitch's heart!" shrieks a female from deep within the crowd, her voice emboldened with alcohol. Four leagues on an empty belly in the chilling, relentless rain requires fortification; many of the ragtag mob have stopped at every tavern along the route. By now, their aprons and wooden sabots are caked with mud as thick as pig slop. It is clear from their cherry-hued cheeks ·and noses that their guts are as full of brandy as their spirits are imbued with hatred.

Now that she has discovered a lion among the lambs, Louison glances about her to see who else comprises this unusual citizens' army. She is astonished at the presence of many women with fashionably powdered heads, dressed all in white the way the queen had done when she, Louison, teetered on the verge of womanhood. She had girlishly dreamed of dressing in such flimsy, flowing gowns and attending *fêtes champêtres* on the verdant lawns of Versailles. These ladies who sing while they march with such gaiety— despite the rain, despite the mud transforming their pristine frocks into sodden rags—are no market women; Louison imagines them to be the sort who might frolic at the palace.

The drummers at the vanguard commence a new tattoo, this one more urgent and energetic than the slow and steady rhythm that has accompanied the march for the past six hours. "We must be nearing the town," someone shouts. Thousands of weapons that had begun their lives as agricultural implements—pitchforks, scythes, and mattocks—are thrust into the air as the news makes its way toward the rear of the mob. Ahead of the drummers, the four cannons in the van are fired; the hollow explosion of the twelve-pound guns reverberates through the early autumn air. Dozens of muskets are discharged, as if in response. "I see the gates!" comes a cry, and Louison shivers involuntarily. Her calloused palm closes more tightly about the handle of her chisel, the tool of her trade.

"I'm afraid," she murmurs to the man striding alongside her. His body smells more of civet and pepper than of sweat, the fish guts and chicken blood smeared so artfully on his muslin apron that they might have been painted there. His lank wig is now firmly in place, secured with a triangular red cap—a liberty bonnet, they are being called, loaned to him by one of the drunken *poissardes* who mistook him for one of her own.

"Think of the gorgon and you will have nothing to fear," he reassures her.

The young sculptress wonders aloud whether hunger is her greatest nemesis at this moment, but her companion hastily reminds her that there is only one reason her belly is empty. Louison shakes her wet skirts and draws in her breath. Reinvigorated, she resumes her battle cry. "We will take the queen, *dead or alive!*"

I have taken to walking in the rain. The fine mist feels like falling tears. There are no visitors in the palace gardens today and the emptiness lends the vast parterres an eerie aspect. I walk where my slippers take me. Inside my mind a solo cellist plays a nocturne. I have no companions as I enter the gardens of Trianon and no bodyguard has shadowed me. Along my path the leaves cling to the dirt, shining wet and golden, pasted there by the gentle rain.

I clutch my skirts and climb the rocky outcropping that leads to the grotto, lured by the sound of rushing water over a fern-covered cliff. And there I sink to the granite-colored ground and gaze upon the water for several minutes, shoving my hands through the slits of my gray silk gown to warm them in the pockets. I close my fingers around my father's timepiece, enjoying the weight of it in my hand. This watch on its slender chain is all I have left of Francis of Lorraine, the only possession I was permitted to take across the border when I left Austria forever to become dauphine of France. Removing it from my pocket I glance at the hour: nine past two. A slate-hued cloud rolls past. In sunnier days I reposed in this very spot with Count von Fersen. We would speak of anything and everything, unburdening our hearts. He came to me last week to say that he had taken a house in town here in Versailles in order to be nearer to me every day. I cannot fathom what I would do without him. Life has been unbearable enough these past few months. There have already been too many good-byes: *mon cher coeur* Gabrielle Polignac, all but banished from France. In July, after the Parisians stormed the Bastille, they cried out for her blood; what else could my husband do but tell her family to run? The comte d'Artois, too, and his family. I weep for Gabrielle, but can hardly begin to imagine what it must have cost my husband to exile his youngest brother, so detested by the populace, in order to appease their thirst for guts and thunder. My dear abbé Vermond, who had tutored me since childhood and accompanied me from Vienna; my reader, and a confidant of fifteen years. He, too, had hastily packed his belongings and taken one of the coaches for the border in mid-July.

Autumn has descended on Versailles, thanks to the Revolution. The companions of my past, like Gabrielle and Vermond, have become their victims by virtue of their exile. Most of my beloved Trianon *cercle,* such as the princesse de Lamballe, have fled for their own safety. Days of green and brightest blue are now gray and brown. As I gaze at the waterfall I see the face of an innocent, taken by God just as the crisis was beginning. The first dauphin Louis Joseph's soft brown hair curls about his shoulders, his soulful eyes are still so large and blue. In the rushing water I hear his voice, a reassuring plea: *Sois courageuse. Don't despair, Maman.*

"Je te promets, mon petit—I promise," I whisper. I finally begin to feel the dampness in my bones and wonder how long I have been sitting here. As I take Papa's pocket watch out again, I hear a distant "Haloo!" and glance toward the sound. One of the palace pages, a tall boy in royal blue, practically canters toward me. *"Votre Majesté!"* He points frantically toward the château, and beyond it the town. "It is requested that you return to the palace at once. Thousands of women are marching toward Versailles—all the way from Paris. Some say they are armed!"

My first thought is Louis and the children. "Where is His Majesty?"

"Still hunting at Meudon, *Majesté,*" he says breathlessly. "Several messengers have already ridden out to fetch him back. Please, you must come—now." He looks as if he is about to cry. He cannot be older than twelve, no matter his height. I give him my hand as I ask who sent him to find me.

"Monsieur the Minister of War, the comte de La Tour du Pin. He is quite agitated, *Majesté.*"

I try to calm the boy as we make our way back to the château, asking his name and inquiring about his family. It is a little more than a mile to the palace from the gates of le Petit Trianon, and Daniel and I must return on foot. In his haste to locate me, the page had not thought to request a carriage in my name.

I enter a scene of near chaos. Since the frightening news reached Versailles, the State Apartments had grown more crowded with each passing hour. With such a crush, one might have thought there was a ball about to commence in the Galerie des Glaces. The Oeil de Boeuf is thronged with ministers and courtiers, offering as many opinions as there are souls. "Messieurs, we can make no decisions until His Majesty returns from Meudon," I tell them. While all about me are feverish, I feel strangely calm. "There is nothing to do but bide our time," I inform the ministers. The former Finance Minister, Jacques Necker, who was given his congé in July after disagreeing with the king over how to treat the rebels, has returned, only to bicker, it seems, with the comte de Saint-Priest, who had been dismissed under the same liberal cloud. The comte de La Tour du Pin shouts to be heard above the pair of them.

The hundreds of courtiers who have remained at Versailles after the purge in July are in a panic. And yet even as fear stains the dove-gray and salmon-colored silk of their suits, their morbid curiosity has gotten the better of them. They rush to the tall mullioned windows of the Salon d'Hercule, hoping to spy the mob as it approaches.

With as much grace as I can muster I retreat to my private rooms, tucked away behind the enfilade of State Apartments. "Make sure we have plenty of firewood," I tell Madame Campan. She casts me a glance, immediately knowing my mind. Abandoning her book on the little marble side table, she joins me beside a carved tallboy. Taking a ring of keys from my pocket, I open the lock. Together, we remove four weighty chests and carry them to the hearth. "Burn everything in them, Henriette," I instruct her calmly. My memories turn to ash and cinder as the smoke rises up the flue. While the bright flames incinerate years of precious correspondence with my mother and brothers, I sit down to pen a final letter to my beloved duchesse in exile.

I dip my quill and write in fluid, even strokes, although my hand is not much finer than it was when I was a child, and bore endless corrections from my indulgent governess. Remembering the words I imagined my son uttered to me this afternoon from the waterfall, I inform Gabrielle de Polignac of our circumstances, adding, *You may be sure, however, that adversity has not lessened my strength or my courage. These I shall never lose. My troubles will teach me prudence; and it is in moments such as these that one learns to know people and can finally distinguish the difference between those who are and those who are not truly attached.*

God alone knows when—or whether—this missive will reach her.

I return to the Oeil de Boeuf where the comte de La Tour du Pin is insisting vociferously that our best course of action is to send the Flanders regiment of mercenary soldiers to cut off the road to Paris. "What good will that do?" argues Necker, who has too often been accused of being a man of the people. "When the floodgates are already open and thousands of angry citizens have been on the move for hours?"

I remind the comte yet again that he cannot take such an initiative in the absence of the king. De La Tour du Pin regards me, his heavy jowls quivering in an effort to tamp down his rage. "And so we pace and wring our hands like helpless maidens? *Sacré Dieu!* We may as well be lined up like waterfowl waiting for the hunter's blunderbuss to pick us off one by one. By God!" He gestures about the grand salon, thrusting his arm toward the Hall of Mirrors where the anxious countenances of France's nobility are reflected in multiples. "Every one of those peacocks wears a decorative sword that might just as well have been dispensed by your *Intendant des Menu Plaisirs.* They are little more than jewel-encrusted stage props, no sharper I am sure, than a butter knife. And I'll hazard that among those who have seen combat, few remember how to wield their weapon against an adversary. Were we at the gaming table, *Majesté,* I would place my money on an angry fishwife from the Paris Halles rather than on the marquis de Noirmoutiers or any of his ilk."

Although in Louis's absence the comte remains powerless to dispatch a regiment, he can take measures to protect us within the palace walls. He orders the great iron gates outside the Ministers' Courtyard to be shut. The occasion carries significant portent: Never before has the Château de Versailles been closed to the public. With brisk efficiency de La Tour du Pin dispatches a detachment of guards to close the heavy doors that separate the grand chambers of the State Apartments, portals that have not met since the time of the Sun King. "Barricade all passageways!" he shouts, as the members of the royal bodyguard shrug their shoulders and demand "With what?"

Soon, dozens of our periwigged guards in their blue coats with white facings, begin to stack gilded and brocaded furniture. As armchairs are precariously perched atop tables and heavy sideboards are rolled into place, blocking doorways, the comte de La Tour du Pin thunders, "We will not let ourselves be captured here, perhaps massacred, without defending ourselves!" Amid the mass of blue uniforms heaving furniture to and fro is a tall figure in a bottle-green coat, his light brown hair barely powdered.

"Axel," I murmur under my breath, wondering how I have been unaware of his presence until now. I cannot greet him without drawing attention to the act itself. But knowing each other as we do, the mere fact that he is the only courtier—and he is not even a Frenchman—who is willing to aid the soldiers in their efforts to safeguard us is enough to demonstrate the depth of his feelings, not only for me, but for Louis as well. I pray that he will turn around so that I might catch his eye and convey the contents of my heart, but Axel is intent on his task. He balances an armchair upholstered in sea-green brocade upon an inlaid chest, which already sits atop a table, and orders a trio of guards to help him push everything against the closed doors.

I am concerned that the children of France will be frightened by the commotion, so I hasten to my library, retreating into my private suite of rooms through a doorway cleverly concealed by the damasked wall covering. I find the four-year-old dauphin Louis Charles happily sprawled on the carpet, playing with his older sister Madame Royale, under the watchful eye of their new governess the marquise de Tourzel. My son has nicknamed her Madame Sévère.

Louise de Tourzel rises when I enter the room.

"Maman!" The dauphin looks up and grins at me, gripping a yellow wooden ball in a chubby fist. Mousseline frowns and, now that I am in the room, pointedly turns her back on her brother. Nearly eleven, my daughter makes it clear that she would rather not be cooped up with a little boy.

Catching the look of concern in my eyes the marquise approaches and I take her hands, drawing her close enough to whisper, "Who can say what will happen, but the children's routine should not be disrupted, unless of course—"

There is a scratching at the door. Madame Campan opens it to admit a footman who pauses breathlessly at the threshold. Spying the royal children, he whispers urgently, "*Votre Majesté*, the king has returned!"

I sweep my son and daughter into my arms and press my lips to their sweet brows. Campan and Tourzel curtsy to me as I head to the door, placing my finger to my lips as a reminder not to unduly alarm the children. But how much longer, I wonder, can I shield them from the events that threaten our doorstep?

I glide through the State Rooms, entering the Salon de Mars to see Louis, still wearing his tall hat, his hunting suit of olive-hued velvet spattered with mud. His ministers cluster around him like colorful lichens on a stone wall. I spy the powdered head and incongruously dark eyebrows of the loudest speaker, Jacques Necker, who strains to be heard over their raised voices. The council chamber now honors its celestial namesake; it has become a war room.

"You *must* stay here, Sire." Necker glares at the comte de Saint-Priest, Secrétaire d'État of the royal household. "Think of how it would appear to the mob if you were to flee!" he insists.

What have they been discussing in my absence?

"I was not the one who suggested that His Majesty abandon the throne," Saint-Priest retorts hotly. "I merely said that—for their own safety—the *queen* and the *children of France* should be taken under escort to Rambouillet. If you were listening, you would have heard my proposal that the *king* ride with his bodyguard of eight hundred men and the two hundred troops of the Chasseurs des Évêchés to meet the advancing Parisians. A force of a thousand men is confrontation, messieurs, not retreat!"

It would not be a long ride to the Île de France; Rambouillet is not far. Still, I worry about making the journey. Six years earlier Louis had purchased the château, a medieval fortress in its early days, for its location at the perimeter of a lush game forest. There, the children and I would be secure, at least for the time being.

The comte de La Tour du Pin clearly agrees with Saint-Priest; however, being Minister of War, he sees ahead, as if everything is an enormous game of chess. "But it is, said that there are some six thousand on the march. When a thousand men stand to be outnumbered, you have only two alternatives: to attack with the element of surprise and then fire upon them, and to have another plan, should the first one fail."

"I will not order the blood of any Frenchmen shed—especially on my account," Louis says bluntly. "And you tell me these are disgruntled *women*. Under no circumstances will I give the order to fire upon women!"

The War Minister inclines his head. "With your permission, *Majesté,* these are very *angry* women. Now, if by some misfortune the rebels will not turn back, nor will they heed reason, then, as you will be under heavy guard, you will have adequate time to withdraw to Rambouillet. From there, you and the royal family can set off for Normandy, placing greater distance between yourselves and the disturbance."

I spare a beseeching glance at the portraits of Louis XV and my late mother, Empress Maria Theresa of Austria, suspended on opposite walls of the vast salon, gazing at each other from a sea of blood red damask. What would they do in our place: Louis the monarch who would dither and delegate and my autocratic Maman, always so certain, so decided about everything?

"I don't want to compromise anyone," Louis insists. Does he refer to our safety, to the ministers' conflicting advice, or to the goodwill of the people? Within the enfilade of State Apartments hundreds of courtiers murmur amongst themselves. Marquises and duchesses hide behind their ivory-handled fans, snapped open and fluttering nervously. None dares address me.

The men continue to debate the subject as the hour strikes four. At the sound of the chime I turn my head to look out the window toward the parterres where the topiaries are silhouetted against the encroaching dusk. What will the end of day bring? A tingling creeps up the small of my back and I shiver.

Suddenly Louis's voice rises above those of his sparring ministers. "Messieurs, I will make no decision unless Her Majesty agrees." The Mars Salon grows suddenly silent, the hubbub diminishing to a hush in an instant. All heads turn as one.

I have but one thought at this moment. I look across the room at my husband, my gaze meeting his, although with his shortsightedness I doubtless resemble no more than a silvery gray blur. "I do not wish the king to incur a danger that I cannot share," I say.

"Then for the nonce we remain," says Louis with finality. "And remain together." The comte de La Tour du Pin emits an exasperated roar.

In every room the clocks of marble and gold tick and chime as the hours inexorably proceed. By five o'clock we receive word that the mob, fortified on brandy, had stopped at the National Assembly, the entity formed by the Third Estate this past June. They call themselves a people's government, but thus far all they preach is hatred and intolerance and all they seem to wish for is blood. Not one of them knows how to govern; none has formed an acceptable solution to the nation's ills, and yet they loathe the monarchy, blaming it, and us, for their every misfortune.

News arrives from the mob's effort to meet with the Assembly. Evidently we have been misinformed. There are men amid the rabble as well, including an anatomy professor from the University of Paris, a Docteur Guillotin. Not every marcher is disenfranchised and impoverished. Someone has goaded them into this act of rebellion; each footstep taken by a fishwife in wooden sabots is shared by an intellectual in buckled shoes.

"What more do they desire?" Louis asks the messenger from the National Assembly. "They now have freedom of the press. The Church has been forced to forgo lucrative rents and revenues. The perquisites of the nobility have been abolished—all within the last three months. And now this new hubbub about the 'Rights of Man'—what more do they want?" he repeats, bewildered.

It is incomprehensible. Everything is moving so fast. Yet for the rebels, the world cannot change quickly enough.

"They are hungry, Your Majesty," replies the messenger. "They believe the Assembly contains enemies of the people who are the cause of the famine. They say wicked men are giving money and bonds to the millers so they will not grind their grain. When the president of the Assembly demanded specific names, they told him that the Archbishop of Paris was one of them. At this, the deputy from Arras, Monsieur Robespierre, urged the women to climb upon the benches and shout for bread." The messenger casts a desperate glance in my direction. "It is not good for the queen, Sire. One of the fishwives pulled a hunk of black bread from her filthy apron and announced to everyone that"—he pauses, and inhales a gulp of air.

"*Continuez, s'il vous plaît, monsieur,*" I say softly.

His eyes dart anxiously about the room. "She said she wanted to make *l'Autrichienne* swallow it before she wrings her neck."

The room falls silent again, but only for a moment. Then the uproar begins anew as every courtier sputters in outrage and every minister tenders his opinion at the top of his voice. But they are drowned out by a clamor at the gates.

Outside, darkness is falling and a heavy mist blankets the sky. A member of the royal guard informs us that hundreds, if not thousands, of women are pressing up against the iron bars, demanding entry. Regardless of their cries, I know that what they really crave is my blood. I would be a fool not to fear them.

"I cannot ignore them," Louis insists. "A king is the father of his people, and even the rebellious are my children. If they are merely disgruntled market women, I see no present reason for panic." He agrees to meet a delegation of five of them, chosen from among the mob. They are to be escorted to the Oeil de Boeuf by deputies from the Assembly. I pray that none conceals a weapon that will not be detected in advance by our bodyguards.

Yet when the delegation arrives I fret that perhaps there was more to fear from the deputies. The man from Arras, introduced to Louis as Maximilien François Marie Isidore de Robespierre, seems a stranger to smiles. His face is as insolent as a rat's and his bearing and manner of dress are more fastidious than that of many courtiers. The spills of white lace at his throat and cuffs are pristine, as are his hose, and his shoe buckles are polished to such a sheen that they glimmer in the candlelight. As he crosses the vast hall, Robespierre's dark eyes dart avidly, if not enviously, about the Galerie des Glaces, as if to make note of the magnificent trappings of the monarchy he so despises. And yet he dresses like a marquis. It is enough to convince me that he cannot be trusted.

Scurrying alongside Monsieur Robespierre is one of the more moderate deputies, Monsieur Mounier, who takes a moment to bow to me when the man from Arras is looking elsewhere, most likely at his own reflection in the myriad mirrors. "Robespierre is piqued, Your Majesty," Mounier whispers loudly, "because word reached the Assembly this afternoon that the king has refused to ratify the 'Declaration of the Rights of Man.'" He speaks as he trots along the parquet, struggling to keep pace with the rest of the delegation, even as he lags behind to communicate this turn of events. "After all, the Assembly ratified it on the twenty-sixth of August and they have been waiting more than a month for His Majesty's imprimatur. Their patience has reached its limit. But I do believe that violence may be averted if the king can be persuaded to sign it immediately."

I blanch. I have read this document and recall with clarity what the people demand: Sovereignty residing not within the monarchy but in the "nation," whatever that means? Citizens determining of their own accord whether or not to pay taxes? "Today?"

"You must convince the king, *Majesté*. It may be the only way."

"Monsieur, I would never attempt to persuade my husband to do something that runs contrary to our sacred belief. Louis Seize rules by divine right. The members of your National Assembly are nothing more than self-anointed usurpers, and if the 'principle of sovereignty,' according to the 'Rights of Man,' resides in *every* man and woman, then you have nothing but anarchy. *Who* therefore *reigns?* I will tell you, Monsieur Mounier: Chaos."

We reach the end of the Hall of Mirrors and round the corner into the Oeil de Boeuf where Louis, surrounded by guards, permits the market women to have their say. I hear him asking each of them about their métier, their husbands and children. He speaks kindly to them, without condescension. Instead he offers paternal solicitude. There is genuine concern in his pale blue eyes. A pretty young woman in a leather apron smeared with mud, her brown curls spilling out of a *tricolore* tied about her head like a scarf, tells him her name is Louison Chabry. "I am a worker in sculpture," she says, putting the lie to the rumor that we have been set upon by thousands of *poissardes*. "We are hungry," she adds, clutching her chisel. I eye it warily, fearing that she might prove a madwoman who at any moment might attack him. My thoughts are not so unfounded; Louis XV was nearly assassinated by a deranged man right in the Cour Royale.

"The millers are not grinding," the girl says. "We have no bread. I have not eaten for two days." Mademoiselle Chabry's gaze darts around the Oeil de Boeuf, taking in the grandeur of the salon, the vast marble pilasters, the unusual ox-eye window that gives the anteroom its name, the enormous chandelier fashioned from thousands of glittering crystals. "Your head, Sire," she murmurs. "The same profile I see on every coin!" She is clearly overwhelmed in the presence of the monarch, by his own majesty and by the splendor of Versailles. Her eyes roll back in her head as she sinks to her knees and a moment later she is lying on the floor, supported by her sisters in rebellion.

It is the king himself who calls for smelling salts. As the courtiers look about helplessly, no one wishing to be the first to offer a vinaigrette to the young sculptress, the hubbub of raised voices carries all the way from the courtyard. One cry pierces the air so distinctly that it feels as Damiens's dagger must have done to the heart of Louis Quinze. "We will bring back the queen's head on the end of a pike!"

All eyes turn from the fallen mademoiselle to me. I stand up straighter and hold my head high. I do not want these market women to see that I am afraid. They do not see me bite my lower lip. Louis sighs with the weight of all France upon his broad shoulders and turns back to the woman collapsed on the floor. "Have you come to harm my wife?" he asks her pointedly. I do not hear her reply.

I hear Louis promise the delegation of women that they shall have bread—they shall *all* have bread—from the palace stores. We have plenty of it, he tells them. Let it not be said that the king of France does not comprehend his subjects' pain.

One of the marquis de Lafayette's aides-de-camp presses his way through the audience. During the American colonies' revolution against the British the redheaded marquis had been a general in their Continental Army serving under George Washington, the man who has just been elected the infant nation's first president. Regrettably, Lafayette returned with the rebellious fire still pulsing in his blood. After the Bastille was stormed in July he answered the call, not to help the crown, but to aid our enemies instead, accepting the appointment as commander in chief of the Garde Nationale, the militia formed by the citizens.

Elbowing his way to the king, "A word, *Majesté*!" he demands. Louis holds up his hand, but the adjutant insists, "Sire, it cannot wait." He announces that the commanding officer of the Paris Garde Nationale is marching on Versailles with thirty thousand men at arms, including the former French Guards, soldiers once loyal to the crown.

As the comte de La Tour du Pin demands the immediate removal of the market women and the Assembly deputies, Saint-Priest reiterates his recommendation for the royal family to remove to Rambouillet. Maximilien Robespierre and I cross paths as he exits the antechamber and our eyes lock. His are black and cold, like those of a fish. Someone jostles me and presses a paper into my hand, but I cannot, dare not, read it in the middle of a crowd.

The king quits the Oeil de Boeuf leaving a sea of confused courtiers in his wake, and the two of us repair with the ministers to his private apartments. In the quiet of Louis's library, Saint-Priest actually throws himself at his sovereign's feet and passionately urges a decision. "If you are taken to Paris tomorrow, *Majesté,* you will lose your crown!" The clock atop the mantel strikes the hour of eight. For the second time today, my husband looks to me for advice before he will commit to a course of action.

There is no thought of leaving him, especially as the peril draws even closer. "We go now," I say. I kiss his cheek and turn, racing downstairs to the children's apartments where I instruct Madame de Tourzel and one of their *sous-gouvernantes* to pack as much as they can. "*Vite, vite!* We depart in a quarter hour!"

By the next chime of the clock the family, including the king's sister, the princesse Élisabeth, are gathered in the hall below the Salon d'Hercule by the foot of the grand marble staircase. My son and daughter are wrapped in cloaks of inky blue wool and cling to the skirts of their gentle aunt. Madame Élisabeth's lower lip trembles with fear. Thinking first of the safety of my children, I usher them outdoors into the night. As we set foot in the Cour de Marbre, a jeer rises. The Place d'Armes just outside the gates is crowded with market women. They raise their weapons in the air, holding aloft scythes and pikes. I am grateful that the king's eyesight is so poor he cannot see these implements raised against us.

We scuttle along the edge of the buildings like rats, headed for

the royal stables where our carriages await. "A fugitive king, a fugitive king," Louis mutters, as if the phrase is the most distasteful to
ever leave his mouth.

But no sooner are the gates to the stables thrown wide than the
mob cries as one hysterical, furious voice, "The king is leaving!"
They surge toward our coaches and hurl their bodies upon the carriages, cutting the harnesses and leading the terrified horses whin-
nying into the night. We are trapped. Saint-Priest and the comte de
La Tour du Pin, who have come to see us depart, offer their own
carriages as a last resort. They are harnessed beyond the gates of
the Orangerie. If we can manage to make it there without hin-
drance, we can hope for a more discreet exit from Versailles.
But the mob now presses toward us. The regiment of Flemish
mercenaries—the only thing that stands between us and this sea of
human vitriol—does all they can to keep them in abeyance without firing a single round, for Louis still forbids any attack upon his
subjects. There is nothing for us to do but retreat.

Back upstairs, in the State Apartments, my heart beats beneath
my stays, but I betray no emotion. I must be strong for everyone.
They have enough fear of their own. Every candle is lit, as if to
stave off the demons of the night by creating a perpetual day. Some
courtiers pace the Galerie des Glaces, their red heels echoing upon
the gleaming parquet. Others sit in the Games Room, playing
hand after hand of piquet or écarté, laying their cards and markers
upon the green baize with eerie deliberation, as if by prolonging
the game they forestall whatever fate lies in store for us.

At eleven o'clock Louis and I receive a number of courtiers as
well as a handful of officers, among them Count von Fersen. Axel's
chin juts angrily and his eyes, their color so changeable, are steel
gray tonight, conveying much, even as he speaks little.

"Give me an order, Your Majesty, authorizing us to take horses from the stable so we might defend the royal family if you are under attack," he insists.

I look at my husband but he is deep in conversation with deputy Mounier, who is still pressing him to sign the "Declaration of the Rights of Man."

"I will consent to give the order on one condition," I tell Axel. "If His Majesty's life is in danger, you must use it promptly. But if I alone am in peril, you will not use it." Count von Fersen gives me an inexorable look and tears spring to my eyes. "Those are my orders," I repeat.

I had already informed the marquise de Tourzel to convey the dauphin and Madame Royale to the king's private apartments, should she feel the slightest cause for alarm.

"But where will you spend the night, dear sister?" Madame Élisabeth's blue eyes are red-rimmed from crying. Her *dame d'honneur,* the marquise de Bombelles, seems powerless to comfort her. "Won't you be safest with the king?"

I know what these market women want. By now I have read the anonymous note I was passed in the Oeil de Boeuf. YOU WILL BE MURDERED AT SIX IN THE MORNING. But the *poissardes* and their confederates still trust Louis. I feel my chest constrict within my stays. "I know they have come from Paris to demand my head," I tell Madame Élisabeth. "But I have learned from my mother not to fear death and I shall await it with firmness. I prefer to expose myself to danger, if there is any, and protect His Majesty and the children of France. I shall sleep alone tonight."

Yet sleep remains a long way off. His eyes brimming with tears, Louis reluctantly agrees to sign the "Declaration of the Rights of Man" and deputy Mounier watches each stroke of the pen like a vulture eyeing fresh carrion. I have never seen my husband looking more defeated. I stand behind his chair and wrap my arms about his shoulders, pressing my lips to the top of his head. Although his face betrays no perspiration, his scalp is damp, sticky with fear.

Shortly after the clocks strike the hour of midnight, the mud-spattered marquis de Lafayette arrives at the palace, so exhausted from riding posthaste from Paris that he limps into the Salon de Mars. His face is drawn, drained of its customary ruddiness, and he struggles to remain on his feet. With a dramatic sweep of his arm worthy of the great Clairval he announces to Louis that he has left his men in the Place d'Armes. "Sire, I thought it best to die here at Your Majesty's feet than to perish pointlessly in the shameful light of the torches at the Place de Grève."

"Are you turning your coat yet again, *monsieur le général*?" I inquire of the commander of the Garde Nationale. "Have you abandoned your citizens' militia and come back to offer your assistance to your king?"

Lafayette shakes his head. "They want to be heard," he tells Louis. "They want to know that you have listened to their concerns and that action will be taken."

My husband splays his hands. "They demanded bread and I have already promised it from our own stores. It seems imprudent to dispense it in the damp dead of night. At daybreak there will be bread aplenty. You may reassure them of this." He looks imploringly at the general. "I have always been a man of my *parole*. A man of honor." He lowers his voice to a whisper that could still be heard on the stage of the Comédie-Française. "But they must promise not to think of harming the queen."

"Tell her to set her mind at rest and go to bed," Lafayette says to the king. He has convinced Louis to entrust him with the security of the palace. The French Guards will resume the posts they deserted a month ago. Is this wise?

Louis retires for the night as well. I cannot imagine how he will sleep. I do not wish to endanger my women, so at two o'clock I urge them to leave me. My first waiting woman, Madame Thibaut, and Madame Campan's sister Madame Auguié are in attendance this night, along with their own maids. But they will not depart even after I insist that they go to the room where my other ladies have gathered. Madame Auguié is weeping. She looks to Madame Thibaut for reassurance as she reminds me that there are thirty thousand troops and ten thousand brigands, with forty cannons mustered outside our gates. "Once upon a time they would have protected Your Majesty. Now the world has turned upside down and it is just the four of us," she sobs, indicating Madame Thibaut and their maids. "*We* are your only *sauvegarde* now. It would be wrong of us to desert you."

We compromise. I will not place their lives at risk by allowing them to sleep in my bedchamber. And so they drag four armchairs outside my door and prepare to spend the night in these *fauteuils*. The muffled sound of tattoos beaten on sodden drumskins reverberates from the Place d'Armes where the market women and soldiers are encamped, a hoarse, frightening call to protest that has lasted without surcease through the night. I do not think I will be able to sleep after all.

I lie upon the featherbeds gazing at the underside of the pink and gold brocade canopy. With no comprehension of how much time has passed, suddenly I bolt upright, my eyes blinking open, my heart pounding. Below my windows, a commotion seems to be coming from the direction of the Orangerie. A single chime strikes and I look at the clock. Half past five. My feet bare, I rush to the bedroom doors, clutching the thin cambric of my night rail to my breast. Madame Thibaut jumps out of her chair, then swiftly rearranges her skirts and sinks into a curtsy.

"Did you hear that?" I ask her. The other women are now wide awake.

"Some of the marchers must have made their way to the parterres," she answers. "With nowhere else to sleep, perhaps they sought refuge on the terraces." The regiment of French Guards, so newly reinstated, had been assigned to patrol the gates and entrances to the parks. But are they to be trusted, despite the *général*'s assurances? Had Lafayette been naïve, deceived, or an outright liar? "I think it is safe to go back to bed, *Majesté*," says Madame Thibaut. "In any case, the men of the *gardes du corps* are stationed in the hall. Try to sleep, madame," she adds gently, closing the heavy wooden doors.

As the clock strikes six I hear a fearful pounding. My ladies throw open the doors to my bedchamber. Their faces are drained of color. Madame Auguié is hysterical. "Rise, Your Majesty! They are coming up the marble staircase—hundreds of them—armed with pikes and muskets and broomsticks and knives. They are headed through the Galerie des Glaces, making straight for your bedchamber." The two maids cry for help and frantically wave their arms to simultaneously stave off the stampede and summon the royal bodyguard.

"It is as if someone has given them a map of the palace," adds Madame Thibaut. "Otherwise, how would they know exactly where you sleep?"

Fractured phrases reach our ears. "Kill! Kill!" "No quarter!" ". . . make a *cocarde* from her entrails!"

"There is no time to dress, madame!" urges Madame Auguié. "*Vite, vite*—you must make for His Majesty's *petits appartements*."

They open the doors to my wardrobe and pull out the first petticoat they find, along with a wrapper or *lévite,* a loose-fitting dressing gown of pale yellow and cream striped silk. There is no time to search for stays. From a drawer I grab a pair of white stockings and a fichu but cannot stop to don them. Madame Thibaut pulls a black velvet hat with a white plume from the top shelf of the wardrobe and thrusts it in my other hand, while Madame Auguié shouts "Shoes!" and gives me the first pair of black satin heels she finds.

The din of the approaching mob increases, their resounding footsteps augmented by guttural shouts, bloodcurdling screams, and the sounds of splintering wood, shattering glass and porcelain.

I remind myself to keep my wits, though my bedroom threatens to become a blur of rose and gold. My hands are full of accessories and so I use my shoulder to press against the secret panel beside my bed, thrusting my weight against it as I fumble for the hidden latch that will release the door.

"We must have the bitch's heart!" "Where is she?" I hear, the voices growing closer. My women are now right behind me and we disappear behind the door into the passage that connects the queen's bedchamber to Louis's rooms. What a stroke of brilliance the comte de Mercy had to have suggested its construction all those years ago! Who could ever have foreseen that the secret passage intended to facilitate the *creation* of life, that of the children of France, would one day play a role in *saving* mine?

I finally reach the heavy door to the Oeil de Boeuf, but find it locked. My breath is ragged and my heart pounds beneath my breast. The intruders have reached my bedroom. I can hear them through the wall. I must find Louis—and safety. I race down the corridor to his apartments and, dropping my garments in a heap, I begin to pound upon the first door I come to, flailing upon the wood with both fists. "Save me, *mes amis*!"

From the direction of the State Apartments I hear the rioters' shouts and the crash of an axe shattering wood. They are breaking down the door to the Oeil de Boeuf. Only Providence has saved me. Had the door not been locked from the corridor, I'd be in the antechamber now, torn to ribbons by a mob that is baying quite literally for my blood, my entrails, my head.

Finally, after what feels like an eternity, the door to Louis's bedroom opens and a tiny face peers out. It belongs to a frightened page, who apologizes for not having heard my frantic entreaties for entry. "The noise has been so great, *Majesté*." He is trembling.

I scan the room. Madame Élisabeth is there already, along with Madame de Tourzel. But where—where are my children? Finally I spot them. Madame Royale is standing on a chair, looking out the window. The dauphin is clinging to her skirts. I throw my arms about the pair of them, clutching them to me. Then the dauphin says, "Papa?" and I realize something is horribly wrong.

Where is the king?

"He went to search for *you, ma soeur*," says Madame Élisabeth. Her face is as white as parchment. "You must have missed each other in the corridor."

Merciful God! Was Louis inside the antechamber when the mob . . . ?

My ladies-in-waiting urge me to finish dressing as I continue to ask the empty air, "Where is my husband?" Realizing the door remains open, I run to tug it shut, only to hear a familiar voice shout hoarsely, "*Attends!* Wait, *ma chère*!"

I fall weeping into Louis's embrace, never so happy to see him as in this moment. But it is impossible not to think of the future as well. Choking on ragged sobs, I tell him, "They will kill our son."

TWO

Mayhem

Louison Chabry finds herself swept up in a tide of teeming . . .
Amid the chaos, her mind freezes helplessly. One could never refer
to this clamorous mass as "humanity." There are so many people
that she is lifted off her feet and borne on the tide of rioters through
the most magnificent rooms she has ever seen. Is she the only one
to gawp at her surroundings? The palace is almost as wondrous as
a cathedral! She cranes her neck to admire the ceilings with their
gilded copings and breathtaking murals, and marvels at the fluted
marble pilasters that stretch as high as the eye can see, ending in a
spray of perfectly carved acanthus leaves. She envies the sculptors
commissioned to create such beauty, and wonders if any of them
might have been women. And as her comrades-in-arms rampage
through the gilded halls, Louison's cheeks grow wet with tears at
the willful destruction of it—Chinese vases that must have cost a
king's ransom, bronze figurines decapitated with a cry of "Kill the
queen!" and chests and chairs inlaid with porcelain, marquetry,
and mother-of-pearl, representing untold hours of painstaking

craftsmanship, smashed to bits in a matter of moments. And for what? For bread? Her belly rumbles as loudly as those of her confederates, as hollow as the sound of their wooden sabots against the scuffed parquet, but what did the devastation of all this splendor have to do with their empty stomachs?

The king had promised them bread. She was there when he said the words—well, at least before she had fainted from hunger. But she had believed him. His eyes, so large and pale, had been full of genuine concern. Someday she would like to sculpt his head as she remembered it: noble and kind. She could never exhibit her creation, though, for fear of being tarred as a royalist instead of a realist. But the man she saw was a figure who commanded respect and awe, not terror. This—this clamor for wanton destruction, this stampede of people who smell of body odor and urine, of fish and decay, even more so now that no one has washed in at least two days, *this* is terror. And Louison is caught up in its midst, unable to turn back if she wanted to, even though she is having second thoughts. Even though she had been inclined to credit the king's promise.

All through the night, some of the protestors, many of whom revealed themselves to be men dressed *en travestie,* had gone among the rioters and begun a whispering campaign. "His Majesty lied to you," they said. "The Austrian bitch has him by the balls and she has told him not to give you so much as a stale crust. The king was playing us all for fools. But we will show them who is ruling France now!" They distributed coins with their propaganda. In every hand outstretched for bread they placed a silver image of the king's head, the same profile Louison had envisioned creating with her chisel from a block of solid marble.

Bribes and rhetoric had fired up the crowd, as drunk and wet as they were sleepless. By dawn some members of the French Guard whom the king had naïvely permitted to resume their former em-

ployment had opened the gates leading to the terraces, and many of
the protesters had rushed onto the broad parterres as though the
gates of Heaven had been flung wide and Saint Gabriel had blown
a fanfare on his trumpet, welcoming them to paradise.

"This way!" someone shouts as the mob surges along the Hall
of Mirrors. Louison has never seen a room so grand. She tries to
imagine what it must have been like filled with dancers instead of
rioters brandishing mattocks, pikestaffs, axes, and knives and calling for the queen's beautifully coiffed head. Although she had not
detested Marie Antoinette with the fever pitch of the women on
every side of her, Louison has never felt sorry for *l'Autrichienne*
until this moment.

The clamor has an unearthly musical accompaniment: the cacophony of countless freestanding candelabra being toppled like
a row of dominoes to the sounds of shattering crystal. Rioters
swing their pikes and broomsticks overhead in an effort to bring
down the enormous chandeliers, and massive pendants rain down
upon them like icicles of faceted glass and strings of diamonds the
size of hen's eggs.

Someone steps on Louison's toes when the entire throng rocks
back as one unit, their progress halted by two of the royal bodyguard who stand at the end of the vast hall, their halberds crossed,
denying entry.

"Traitors! You cannot stop the people of France from obtaining
justice!" a woman shrieks. She waves her arms furiously.

Another picks up the cry. "We will take the bitch dead or
alive!" Louison hears the crunch of weapons, wood against steel,
bloodcurdling cries of pain and bone-chilling shouts of triumph.
Too petite to see the action at the far end of the Galerie des Glaces,
she can barely make out what is going on by jumping up and down
and peering between the shoulders of those in front of her. She
gasps when she sees the outcome of the skirmish, for the trophies

of victory are raised high enough for the entire mob to witness: the severed heads of the two brave men of the *gardes du corps* spitted upon the ends of a pair of pikestaffs, their eyes wide open and mouths agape in an eternal expression of fright.

Nothing can stop the rioters now. The enormous doors the decapitated men had given their lives to safeguard are hacked apart with the same fervor that separated the bodyguards' heads from their shoulders.

Someone points the way to the queen's bedchamber and the mob presses ahead. As Louison reaches the doorway where the guards met their gruesome ends, she is forced to step over the legs of one of the dead men, twisted like a broken doll's. His boots have already been stolen. She holds her hand to her mouth to stifle her urge to vomit. *I am not like these people,* she thinks, of their murderers. *I want bread, not blood. There will never be bread, now.*

The queen's bedroom is a grand formal chamber; inside each niche of the high ceiling is a painted allegory. Like Furies, Louison's confederates begin to destroy the room from top to bottom, shredding the sumptuous draperies with their pikes, breaking open the wardrobes and stabbing visciously at the luxurious brocade coverlet, bed hangings, bolsters, tester, and featherbeds, searching for the consort herself. If the queen had been hiding beneath them she would have been pricked like a wild boar with the deadly spears of relentless hunters.

The sculptress cannot bring herself to participate in the destruction but is nonetheless caught up in this blizzard of flying feathers and silken upholstery wrought by hundreds of women and a small number of men who are still wearing their muddy skirts and aprons, ratty horsehair wigs, and red liberty caps. Not finding the queen in her bedchamber, they vent their anger and hatred on her possessions. Mirrors are shattered with musket butts, spraying shards of glass about the room. With a sick crunching sound, the rioters smash tall wardrobes painted with delicate roses, yanking out the queen's garments and tossing them playfully from hand to hand—stays and chemises, lavishly trimmed bodices, petticoats and skirts, silk stockings and kidskin gloves. *Poissardes* and market women fight each other for the clothing, stripping to the waist or pulling the consort's elegant clothes over their own filthy rags.

"*Regardez, mes amies!*" shouts an aging fishwife, nearly toothless. She brandishes a set of stays, a heavily boned corset fashioned in the current style, with shoulder straps, though constructed of finest damask. As she tries it on over her bare breasts, a shout goes up among the crowd as they discover the secret the Austrian bitch has cleverly concealed from them until now. The left shoulder strap is heavily built up with the addition of quilted padding. The only reason for such an unusual alteration is to correct a physical defect. Beneath the garments that had bankrupted the nation, as the women now agreed they had suspected all along, was a fraud— a false, pretty doll, dressed up to trick the people.

Louison watches the women fight over the queen's clothing. The mob has lost sight of its purpose. What had begun as an assassination attempt has metamorphosed within moments into wanton destruction of everything connected with the sovereign, and then into a ferocious melee, as the protesters tear each other's hair, and scrabble and claw at each other's skin and eyes, all for the possession of a garment, or even a shred of one, owned by the despised queen of France. The victors parade their spoils, mincing about in a mockery of the monarch's walk, tilting their heads to acknowledge the presence of their "inferiors," as the queen so famously did when she greeted courtiers, government ministers, diplomats, and other visitors to Versailles. Everyone knew that with a single artful tilt of her evil receding Hapsburg chin she could acknowledge a dozen people at once, her lecherous eyes conveying a different message to every one of them.

A new cry arises from the heart of the crowd. "Where is the vicious bitch?" It is clear from the demolished bed, the furnishings in the chamber reduced to thread, rubble, and sticks, that the target of their hatred isn't there.

She must be called to account for her sins, the market women decide. If Saint Peter could not judge her this dawn, we will be her jury.

THREE

The Bakers' Procession

"Maman, j'ai faim." The dauphin looks at me with wide blue eyes.

"Do we have anything in here for him to eat?" I whisper to his governess. Madame de Tourzel shakes her head.

"I'm sorry, *mon chou d'amour*," I coo, snuggling him to my breast. "You will have to be a big boy and be patient."

"I'm hungry, too," says Madame Royale.

"Let's pretend we all have a sweet inside our mouths," I say gaily. "And we each have a different flavor. Mine is horehound. What flavor do you have, *ma petite?*"

Before Mousseline can respond, Madame de Tourzel's little daughter Pauline proclaims her preference for peppermint.

"I don't want to play silly games," Marie Thérèse replies sullenly, shoving her thumb in her mouth, a habit that she persists in, even at the age of ten, when she wants to end a conversation with me. Madame Royale goes to the window and I anxiously follow her, only to tug her away from the sill when I see a troupe of rag-clad harridans, some nearly bare-breasted, having stripped to the waist in the autumn chill, parading beneath the window. They are accompanied by sinister-looking men brandishing pikes.

Despite the tumult outside, we can hear a scratching at the door. Louis assumes it is friend, not foe, for it is the time-honored protocol at Versailles to use the nail of one's pinky, rather than to knock for admittance. Nonetheless, I urge caution. If the mob had been given directions straight to my bedchamber by someone who knew the plan of the château, then it is just as likely that one of the assassins has been informed of the age-old etiquette.

The door opens and a large man enters the room, impeccably dressed and groomed, his hair powdered and coiffed. One might have thought he had come to attend a meeting of government ministers on an ordinary morning.

"More than friend—*mon frère!*" Louis exclaims, clasping his brother the comte de Provence—known as Monsieur—to his chest. This embrace of these two ample men would be comical, like a moment out of an *opéra buffa,* were our circumstances not so desperate.

Monsieur announces that he has just come from the Oeil de Boeuf, where the destruction is severe. It seems odd to me that he has been utterly unmolested by the rioters. But before I can question my brother-in-law, there is a furious pounding upon the door.

"*C'est moi! Lafayette!*" The voice indeed belongs to the commander of the Garde Nationale. He bursts into the king's bedchamber as though he has been shot from the mouth of a cannon.

"There is no controlling them any longer, *Majesté,*" he says, without bowing to the king. "I threw my hat upon the ground before them, pulled open my coat and bared my breast"—he illustrates his words by grabbing his lapels—"and dared them to kill me on the spot. They have already murdered two of the royal bodyguard, Your Majesty. Lieutenants de Varicourt and Deshuttes." Lafayette lowers his bare head; his hat, embellished with the revolutionaries' detestable tricolor cockade, remains in his hands. "I am genuinely sorry," he says. "A general is supposed to know his troops, but I did not expect this. 'I do not wish to command cannibals!' I told them. 'If you wish to take the lives of the *gardes du corps,* then take mine as well.' My dare turned the tide, for the next moment, they cried, '*Vive le roi! Vive la Nation!*'"

More of the bandits have gathered outside our windows. "The king! The king! We wish to see the king!" they roar, demanding that he appear on the balcony. Louis looks to Lafayette. After nineteen years of marriage I know my husband well enough to see that he fears the rabble, aware that they have both betrayed and abused his trust. After meeting with the delegation of market women, moved particularly by the poor young sculptress who had fainted from hunger in his presence, he had ordered the grain stores to be opened and bread disseminated among the sodden hordes, but their storming of the château at daybreak had prevented his plan from being brought to fruition. With the greatest effort, Louis surmounts his trepidation, not wishing to appear craven in the presence of his brother and Lafayette. I wonder whether the pair of them enjoy his trust as well, for neither merits my confidence.

The king throws open the mullioned doors and rushes onto the balcony. Raising his arms, he cries, "My good people, your sovereign craves your mercy—not merely for myself, but for my faithful defenders." He refers to our pair of unfortunate bodyguards who have paid the ultimate sacrifice. They were brave young men, with families. "Let no more blood be shed on this or any other day."

After hearing a resounding cheer, followed by, "The queen! The queen on the balcony," *"Allons, mes enfants,"* I say, taking each of the children of France by the hand. "We will greet our subjects as a family."

The crowd grows ominously silent, as if a dark cloud has passed over their heads. "The queen alone!" shouts a single voice, high and shrill. "No children!" My shiver passes all the way through my arms into the small warm hands of my son and daughter. At the sight of so many fearsome people with their weapons raised against us, the children both burst into tears. Madame de Tourzel appears at the window and I usher them indoors, safely into her care.

Below me, a sea of angry faces wear frowns that only moments before were smiles prepared to welcome their king. A cry pierces the morning air announcing that I am an agent of Austria. "Just look how she's dressed!" the woman adds, and not until this moment do I realize what she means. From where they stand my striped silk *lévite* appears to be yellow and my hat is of course black—the colors of the Hapsburgs. The plume in my hat is the white of the Bourbons and the point where it is affixed is embellished with a black cockade, an emblem worn proudly by France's aristocracy.

Among the thousands of *poissardes* and market women are a fair number from other walks of life, and I venture a guess that a good many are shop girls, although some of them are arrayed more expensively, if not flamboyantly. Demimondaines. Streetwalkers from the area around the Palais Royal, I assume. Yet others, similarly dressed in gowns of fine white muslin, with tricolor scarves artfully draped like banners across their chests or tied like bandeaux about their curled and powdered locks, convey the impression of wealth. The salons of Paris have been emptied of intellectual women seeking an adventure. These *petites bourgeoises* stand before me, amid their inferiors, including women who troll the coffeehouses and arcades, wearing without irony the same type of gown that just a few years ago the entirety of France derided me for favoring. My *gaulles,* the *chemises à la Reine,* were described as the ultimate luxury for their fragility, and now they are the frock of choice for these harpies who claim them as the ideal garment to denote classical purity and simplicity, a denouncement of the trappings of wealth by the gown's distinct lack of embellishment.

I am shocked by the harridans' brazenness, but mask my emotion from my enemies. They will not know what I am thinking, will not so much as see my lip tremble, or my eyes dart about. It is one of the virtues of a queen. This is what being regal is. Instead, with every ounce of will, I endeavor to transform their hatred to love by acknowledging them and giving credence to their right to assemble here. Despite the fact that they have cried out for my blood. Despite the fact that they have demanded in great detail various parts of my body as though I were a calf they were driving to the slaughterhouse.

And so I sink to my knees in a deep court curtsy, inclining my head in a show of profound humility. The roar diminishes to a murmur. And when I rise, I lay my arms across my bosom and raise my eyes heavenwards, offering a prayer to God to spare my husband and children as well as myself. Out of the corner of my eye I spy a man in the crowd raising a musket to his shoulder and peering over the barrel. I can even see him squint as he takes aim at my breast and I pray with greater fervor. The crowd falls silent. Will this would-be assassin pull the trigger?

But when the moment comes, he cannot bring himself to commit regicide in the presence of thousands of witnesses; he is unprepared to become a martyr to the Revolution.

It seems to take an eternity, but he lowers his musket. My armpits are wet with perspiration. For another few moments the mob remains hushed, but then the spell is broken by one, then two, then a chorus of ragged cries of *"Vive la reine!"* Soon the courtyard reverberates with resounding applause. I shut my eyes and thank heaven, and a moment later, am sensible of someone beside me. Lafayette has stepped through the doorway onto the balcony. With tremendous deference he makes a great show of raising my hand, bringing it to his lips and kissing it as the approbation continues.

"Madame," he murmurs, for my ears alone, "what are Your Majesty's personal intentions?"

I am no fool. "I know the fate that awaits me," I reply softly. "But my duty is to die at the king's feet and in the arms of my children."

With one hand the general raises my arm to indicate that we are united, while with his other, he calls for silence. "Men and women of France, the queen has been deceived," he tells them. At this, one cannot hear so much as a hairpin fall. "But she promises that she shall be misled no longer. She promises to love her people and to be attached to them as Jesus Christ was to His Church."

The applause crescendos again, to cries of *"Vive la reine! Vive le général!"*

My cheeks are now wet with tears. The people think they are tears of shame.

But before the clapping peters out, a lone voice shouts, "The king to Paris!" Within seconds, dozens of others have taken up the call, transforming it into a chant, and once more I am frightened. "To Paris! To Paris!" they cry. His hand on my elbow, Lafayette guides me inside. The crowd's admiration is so fleeting that shots are once again being fired from the courtyard. I shudder and look to Louis to see what he thinks we should do next, but he is deep in conversation with Monsieur Necker. Necker's wife and daughter Germaine, Madame de Staël, are in the king's bedchamber as well, witnesses to the scene on the balcony just now.

I approach Madame Necker. "They are going to force us to go to Paris with the heads of Messieurs Deshuttes and de Varicourt on pikes at the head of the procession, just to prove that our bodyguards are useless. We are prisoners of the people, now." I glance at the Provences, Monsieur and Madame. For they, too, will be compelled to accompany us to the capital; if the mob is to be appeased, the entire royal family must depart Versailles. Marie Joséphine looks terrified, her complexion more green than usual. But my *beau-frère*'s sangfroid is admirable, unless of course he has no reason to be afraid.

The comte de Saint-Priest is shaking his head. If only we had fled to Rambouillet as he had urged, we would not be in such a predicament.

Out of Général Lafayette's earshot, Louis confides in his family. "I feel we must go," my husband says heavily, his voice barely above a whisper. "Although I have never been fond of wagering, if I were to stake one bet this day it would be that my cousin has something to do with this attack. If I—if *we*—do not acquiesce to the people's demand, there is a chance they will try to place the duc d'Orléans on the throne in my stead. There will be no more shedding of blood; the Salle des Gardes is already red and reeking with the sacrifice of two brave souls and many more guards are dead and injured."

My husband rises from his armchair and makes his way back to the balcony. Addressing these vicious insurgents as his friends, he tells the mob, "I will go to Paris with my wife and children. I confide all that I hold most dear to the love of my good and faithful subjects."

They have won. And so they cheer him.

We are lost.

My ladies help me pack what I can, but there is not much I can salvage. My bedchamber has been gutted and it is probably unwise to bring too much from the royal wardrobe. Général Lafayette's word to the people of France that I have seen the error of my ways would appear to be worthless if I continued to dress as opulently as ever. And so, in this grandest of shams I must play a role, feigning humility before those who hate me and wish me dead, no matter what I wear. But if it will keep my children safe and my husband alive, I will do it.

"Do you think we will ever return?" I ask Louis, as we reach a small staircase which leads to the Cour de Marbre. We cannot even exit the Château de Versailles the way we entered the palace in June of 1774 after my husband ascended the throne. There will be no descending the grand marble stairs in the manner of monarchs—because the treads are slick with blood. Instead, we flee like refugees.

The king makes no reply. At least he makes no pretense of sweetening a bitter cordial by lying to me. I swallow hard, not wishing the ministers and courtiers, nor even my attendants to see that I am on the verge of tears. I wonder in this instant what my late mother would have made of this moment. Would she chide, "I warned you many times, but you never heeded," or would the corners of her mouth, usually set in an expression of formidable determination, soften and her eyes dim with tears, fretting over the fate of "the little one," her favorite child?

By the time we are ready to depart, the clock has struck one P.M. The carriages that will convey us to Paris wait in the courtyard, yet we all must run a gauntlet of sorts to reach them. Lafayette and his Garde Nationale clear a path and we make our way through the rabble as their jeers and curses rain down upon us. An old woman clears her throat and spits upon the dauphin, the gobbet landing on my son's smooth pink cheek. He begins to cry and I wipe the spittle away with my handkerchief. I immediately turn to say something to the harridan, but we are surrounded by raised weapons, so I remain silent instead.

The mob chooses not to fire the cannons in a celebratory salute announcing our departure because drunken women have clambered upon them and are riding astride the black iron barrels as though the guns are war horses. Soldiers from the Garde Nationale open the gates and our coach begins to roll forward, the horses scarcely moving, for they have nowhere to go. We are surrounded on all sides by harpies who continue to hurl insults at us through the closed windows of the carriage. At the front of this procession of two thousand carriages, conveying not only the royal family but our courtiers and household goods, the severed heads of our body-guards are carried aloft on pikes, macabre trophies of the people's victory.

And so, we leave Versailles, after being trapped within the car-riage for twenty-five interminable minutes. I consider turning around to look back, but I would see nothing of the palace that was my residence for nearly twenty years because we are mobbed on all sides. They call me *l'Autrichenne*—the Austrian bitch—but I have been a Frenchwoman since I was fourteen, for longer than many of the rioters are old. They crowd the coach and peer into the win-dows, pulling ugly faces and frightening my children.

The king cannot bring himself to brave their leers. He is weep-ing but dares not let the *canaille* see his disgrace, so he buries his face in his handkerchief. He does not see the marchers use their scythes and knives to slash the branches from the trees as we rum-ble by, weaving tricolored ribbons through the golden leaves. Bran-dishing these colorful trophies they dance alongside our coach as if they are performing a pagan ritual about a bonfire, taunting our family with increasingly offensive slurs. I do not have enough hands to cover my children's ears.

We travel at the pace of a funeral cortege, passing through one village after another on the twelve-mile journey to Paris. With so much time in the company of my thoughts I recall the velocity at which the reeking corpse of Louis XV made its final journey to his sepulcher at Saint-Denis. He had been *le Bien-Aimé*, yet at his death was so despised by his subjects that they taunted his hearse as it flew by them on the road. My husband and I, seated side by side as we were that day in May so many years ago, were cheered as our carriage followed the former king's. *"Louis le Désiré!"* our people cried. As quickly as we sped that spring afternoon in 1774, today we crawl, to the accompaniment of *"Louis le Détesté,"* shouted lustily by those old enough to know what they parody.

The coach lurches forward as we come to a halt. The dauphin, who had fallen asleep on my lap with his thumb in his mouth, awakens and looks about like a turtle poking his head from his shell. "Where are we, Maman?"

I look to Louis, who lowers the handkerchief from his face and tries to peer through the crowd of people surrounding our carriage. He replies, "We're in Sèvres."

Whatever for? I wonder. I am certain the rabble has not paused to purchase porcelain. I take my father's gold watch from my reticule. It is easier to focus on the motion of the minute hand as it slowly makes its way around the dial than it is to give consequence to the hordes outside who taunt us.

The dauphin goes back to sleep, the slumber of the innocent. Madame Royale is hungry, and from a pocket of his coat Louis produces a handful of nuts and shares them with our daughter. She nibbles them slowly, taking care to savor each one as if she doesn't know when she will eat again.

After a delay of an hour or so we are treated to the reason. A pair of *friseurs* are paraded past our coach, their faces pale with fear, mouths grim, and no wonder, for the blade of a knife is pressed against their respective throats. With their eyes they direct us upward, but we have no need to slouch in our seats in order to obtain the view. What we are meant to see is shoved in our faces. The hapless hairdressers have apparently been forced upon pain of death to coif the severed heads of our bodyguards. The remains of Lieutenants Deshuttes and de Varicourt have been further desecrated, dressed to resemble the famous *poufs* worn by myself and my ladies in our most frivolous and verdant days, teased and frizzled as high off our foreheads as possible, then pomaded and heavily dusted with powder. But the mockery and the insult do not stop there. With such outlandish coiffures these two brave men have been feminized—even more so with the addition of ribbons, pearls, and feathers. The hideous impression is that the sovereigns had been under the protection of raddled, overdone women, a message not lost on the mob.

One of the pike-wielding ruffians cavorts about our coach, poking the chassis with the butt of his staff, then thrusting Monsieur Deshuttes's head against the window. He has jettisoned his *poissarde*'s disguise to reveal loose, long pants that reach his scuffed leather shoes, the mark of a man of the lowest social order. Each time Deshuttes's head bobs in front of us, my daughter screams, which engenders no end of malicious cackling from our tormentor and only incites him to further torture. This day will bring her nightmares enough. I clutch Madame Royale to my breast to shield her vision and shout through the window, "Get this *sans-culotte* away from me!" After one more swipe at the window with poor Lieutenant Deshuttes's head, the laborer disappears into the crowd, laughing like a madman.

Their gruesome trophies newly embellished, the mob parades them upon the pikestaffs toward the vanguard of this hideous cavalcade and, accompanied by the sort of dancing one expects to see at a country fair, a new chant commences. *"Nous vous amenons le boulanger, la boulangère, et le petit mitron*—We are bringing you the baker, the baker's wife, and the little baker boy!"

Madame Royale stares glumly out the carriage window. "They do not even mention *me*."

FOUR

The Tuileries

It is ten in the evening by the time our carriage rumbles up to the courtyard of the Tuileries Palace. In the coaches that have traveled behind us are six hundred and seventy exhausted and frightened attendants.

It is so dark that there are not enough torches to illuminate the vast façade. The château is little more than a ghostly shell. It has remained formally unoccupied by the court for 124 years, although for some time a small apartment has been kept furnished for me and a few of my attendants. If I stayed later than usual at a masquerade ball, we would retire to the cavernous Tuileries for the night.

I expect a footman to open the steps and hand me down from the coach. Instead, Count von Fersen and the comte de Saint-Priest are there to greet us. My eyes meet Axel's, and our unspoken exchange, conveyed only through our eyes, is noticed by the Secrétaire d'État of the royal household. "You should go," Saint-Priest murmurs to Axel. "There are too many people who know. And if they do not know, they suspect. And if they do not suspect, now is not the time to give them reason to do so."

We have not been able to say a single thing. I extend my hand to Count von Fersen and he raises it to his lips, softly kissing my knuckles. I feel the heat of his mouth through my glove. "I will visit you," he says quietly. "Tomorrow." With a toss of his dark blue cloak about his broad shoulders he disappears into the night.

I look back toward the coach. The carriage bearing Madame de Tourzel, her daughter, and the princesse Élisabeth has arrived and the governess has been reunited with her charges. She smoothes the hair off their foreheads and asks them if they are tired.

Louis is conferring with Monsieur. They speak in low voices, inaudible to the mob that has waited through the brisk October night for our arrival. The king's brother still looks less perturbed by our enforced *déménagement* than I believe he should be. My husband is approached by the mayor of Paris, the astronomer Jean-Sylvain Bailly, the selfsame delegate to the National Assembly who in June refused to allow the king to grieve for our firstborn son because he required his attention to the meeting of the three Estates General. The men exchange a few words, their faces masks of cordiality, and I hear Louis say, as much for the benefit of his audience of thousands of citizens, "It is always with pleasure that I find myself amidst the inhabitants of the good city of Paris." If I were to utter those words I would be lying, but Louis really does love them. In his heart he believes the citizens are unhappy and misguided but can be swayed back to the right path when they are made to see that it is their sovereign, and not the Assembly, who cares about their needs and wants.

The royal family is escorted through the entry by armed guards. "Kings who become prisoners are not far from death," I murmur under my breath to Madame Campan.

Torches and candles illuminate the grand entrance hall. Like many French châteaux, the main building is a cavernous rectangle, but the Tuileries' windows are smaller than most, so even on the brightest days, but most especially late at night, one gets the feeling of being trapped inside a large dovecote. The furniture, dating from the distant reigns of the Sun King and Louis XV, is out-moded and the furnishings are coated with dust.

"Maman, it's very ugly here." The dauphin's words are blurted in a child's burst of honest appraisal.

I chuckle in spite of myself. "The great Louis Quatorze lived here, *mon petit,* and he was very comfortable. We must not be more demanding than he." We climb the stairs to my little apartment and pull the covers off the furniture, coughing from the clouds of dust. For the time being, we will stay here until apartments can be renovated for us. Madame de Tourzel and I tuck the children in with the linens we have brought from Versailles. The dauphin curls up on a daybed, aslumber within moments. There is nowhere for his *gouvernante* to lay her head, and so the marquise de Tourzel passes her first night in the Tuileries in a chair beside his bed, after first creating a makeshift barricade around the room with all the furniture she can find, as the chamber is open from all sides and none of the doors will shut.

Madame Royale lies down upon a sofa, her only admission of fear being her request to sleep with a doll named Lamballe that she had recently deemed herself "too old" to enjoy. Louis and I bed down together for the first time ever, as matrimonial beds are not comme il faut in France, each spouse maintaining separate sleeping quarters. Madame Campan tries to turn the locks but finds that none of them work properly, if at all. As I fret over our safety, my husband declares with tremendous equanimity that if every lock in this palace of thousands of rooms is in a similar state of decay or disrepair, he and his tutor Monsieur Gamain will have a project to last out his reign. With the prospect before him of indulging in a favorite hobby, the king is the only one of us to locate the crumbs of birdseed in this gilded cage.

Morning breaks and in the lemon-yellow light of day there is much to do. First, we must decide where to set up our permanent residence within the vast, labyrinthine palace. Monsieur and Madame, wishing to have nothing to do with the Tuileries, elect to move to the Palais du Luxembourg. Good riddance, I say. The immediate royal family, however, hasn't the luxury of a further *déménagement*. We must make the best of our dark surroundings, for it is clear that *we* have no other option.

Louis chooses a suite of rooms on the first floor overlooking the Seine, and does not mind mounting the stairs to reach his *appartements* even though he has become tremendously rotund. When he becomes anxious, he eats even more than usual. We are determined to hold court as if nothing has changed. Our formal *levers* and *couchers* will continue. What is deeply unsettling, however, is that no matter where any of us goes, we are followed, shadowed by one or more of the Garde Nationale. They are not here to protect us, but rather to monitor our movements. "How are you managing?" a member of the Paris Commune deputation asks me, receiving a glare from his superior officer.

"I've seen everything, known everything, and forgotten everything," I reply, my voice hollow.

However, to my utter astonishment, I have a most unlikely friend who tenders the royal family a remarkable offer. That afternoon I receive a letter from a man in yellow livery.

Votre Majesté,
     Two of your wounded *gardes du corps* managed to escape the awful carnage of the sixth and as soon as I saw who they were and in what dire condition, I opened the doors of

Louveciennes to give them sanctuary and to see that they received medical attention. I hope you will not reproach me for taking it upon myself to nurse them at my château as their families would have done, had they been near. My home is at your disposal, Madame. Everything I possess is due to the kindness and largesse of the royal family. If you recall, I once offered you my treasures, during the Assembly of the Notables. I offer them again, knowing how great your expenditures are. *Permittez-moi, Majesté,* to render what is Caesar's unto Caesar.

Jeanne du Barry

I refold the note very slowly and place it in my pocket. My eyes grow moist with tears. We had once been rivals, oh so many years ago, when she was vain and jealous and I was stubborn and naïve. Twenty years ago I was certain we had nothing in common. Who then could have imagined that the comtesse du Barry would one day offer me her unswerving loyalty?

A half dozen of the guard, fully armed, are assigned to follow the king, even during his strolls in the Tuileries Gardens. They are in the employ of the National Assembly. What have they been instructed to do, should the king try to elude them? Will they draw their sabers or raise their muskets against their own sovereign? Would they fire?

The National Assembly have themselves become our wardens. Lafayette tells us that next month they intend to move into the Tuileries' disused riding school, the Salle du Manège, as it is the single most capacious space within the palace precincts. How fitting, I think, that these animals who see fit to govern France in our place will occupy a practice ground for horses! I hope the lingering odor of manure haunts the hall, even after it is renovated to suit the needs of this fledgling legislative body.

Louis spends our first morning at the Tuileries meeting with deputies from the Assembly. Yet it would seem that the comte de Mirabeau—a mountain of a man whom I had thought more rational than the other revolutionaries, and who *au fond* is a monarchist—wishes to demonstrate his republican sensibilities and his weight in the new legislature by parading before the king all manner of human detritus. These delegates to the National Assembly are ragged and unwashed, their hair uncombed and unpowdered. Nearly every one of them is a *sans-culotte*, wearing *pantalons* of unhemmed slubbed textiles rather than knee breeches and hose. In a deliberate affront they keep their hats on in the presence of their sovereign, bloodred liberty bonnets modeled after the ancient Phrygian slave cap. Are these truly the men who represent the new government? Or is this a mockery, intended to demonstrate to my husband that any fool can rule France? I am disgusted, but Louis calmly listens to their petitions and entreaties even as they seek to strip him, bit by bit, of his monarchical rights.

Later that day I, too, am visited, or should I say confronted, by a deputation of sorts. In the company of my *belle-soeur* I am taking coffee on my balcony, still in my bonnet and negligée—the dressing gown I wear when I receive courtiers during my toilette. Below me, dozens of women have gathered. I can't say if they are the same *poissardes* from Les Halles and prostitutes from the arcades of the Palais Royal who convened in the courtyard and garden throughout the night, singing and chanting, so as to deprive me of my slumber. Louis, on the other hand, told me he slept through the cacophony. I do not believe he has passed a fitful night in our nineteen years of marriage. The entry in his hunting journal for the frightful day of October 5 when our life was forever disturbed by the arrival of the market women was a mere three words: *Interrupted by events.* Yet in the two decades I have known him I have learned that much lies beneath his laconic prose.

The market women ask how the king spent the night and his sister replies that he slept very well, *merci.* At this they seem pleased, but not fully satisfied. They demand to see the dauphin. Élisabeth and I exchange glances. Will these harridans terrify my son? He is frightened of loud noises.

Madame Élisabeth steps inside and returns with the dauphin, to the sound of exultant cheers from the women. How ironic, I think, that they wish to tear apart the monarchy and strip away the sovereign's powers and yet they are genuinely ecstatic at the sight of his heir, the future king of France. I do not understand their fickleness other than to hazard a guess that many of them are mothers, too, and are moved by the sight of such innocence. Under my watchful gaze, Louis Charles explores his new surroundings within the limited confines of the iron railings as the crowd beneath us begins to pepper me with questions and demands. At first they desire me to comprehend that they were not—do I believe them?—among the harpies (my word, not theirs) who marched in the rain to Versailles two days ago and tried to murder me in my bed. The real perpetrators, they say, wish you to believe the *poissardes* from Les Halles were the instigators, but that is a calumny. The true culprits disguised themselves inside the striped skirts and stained aprons of the Paris fishmongers. We are good and honest women, but make no mistake, *Majesté,* we are not without our grievances against you.

They demand that I listen to them, demand—no, *command*— that I send away all the courtiers who "ruin kings." If they refer obliquely to the propaganda disseminated about the duchesse de Polignac and her family, they are three months too late. *Mon cher coeur* Gabrielle was banished after the Bastille was stormed in July.

"Love the inhabitants of your good towns instead of the corrupt courtiers," cries one of the "honest" market women.

"I loved them at Versailles," I remind them courteously. Then, fearing this audience will grow more hostile, I hasten to assure them that "I shall love them just the same here in Paris."

This reply does not satisfy a red-faced *poissarde* whose teeth are as brown as her apron. "Ah, *oui,* but on the fourteenth of July you wanted to besiege the city and have it bombarded!"

Who has been stuffing these women's heads with lies? I must remain calm and dignified. I imagine how my mother might have handled this confrontation: with reason and a firm hand. "Someone told you this and you believed it, but it was not so. Someone deliberately intended to provoke you. *Et regardez!* Look at all the bloodshed and misery that followed. That is what leads to the misfortune of both the people and of the best of kings."

"Sind sie nicht ein Spion für Ihre Kaiserliche Majestät?" The woman speaks to me in my native language, accusing me of being a spy for my brother the Emperor of Austria, daring me to acknowledge my heritage by replying in the same fashion. But I do not rise to take the bait.

"Pardon, madame," I say, responding in French. "I left Austria when I was all of fourteen years old. That was nearly twenty years ago, and I have become so French that I have forgotten the language of my ancestors."

To my immense relief my reply is greeted with cheers and applause and shouts of *"Vive la reine,"* which I acknowledge with a deep curtsy and an expression of profound humility.

Now the market women decide to press their advantage. One of them compliments my bonnet, which is embellished with costly trimmings, and they all but demand them as souvenirs. It is impossible for me to refuse and so I pick it apart and distribute the ribbons and silk flowers, tossing them down from the balcony into the grasping hands below. The *poissardes* and other *vendeuses* are so delighted with their spoils that they remain in the gardens cheering *"Long Live Queen Marie Antoinette!"*

I would be amused, were I not so angry that they wish to emulate the Queen of France by bedecking themselves in her accoutrements, while in the same breath denigrating me for bankrupting the nation by purchasing such fripperies. I share this view later in the day when, as promised, I see the only face beside my children's that can coax a smile from my lips.

Time has been kinder to him than to me, although we are the same age. I will celebrate my thirty-fourth birthday in three weeks; Axel's natal day was in early September. Three years of war and an illness in the American colonies prematurely etched fine lines about his eyes and noble brow in the early 1780s, but since then he has not known the depth of sorrows that I have. When you have lost a child, the world ceases to spin. When you have lost two, you must remind yourself that the reason you rise every morning is for the love of the pair who remain alive.

Beneath the fine dusting of powder, Axel's hair remains a warm shade of brown, whereas mine, I noticed last night, has an uncommon number of silver threads among the apricot. "How can I make your life more bearable?" the count asks me. His eyes, today the blue-gray-green of the sea, convey volumes that can never be committed to paper.

I chuckle, wondering if such a thing is possible. Sighing heavily, I reply, "After the Parisians stormed the Bastille and the National Assembly demanded the king attend *them* in what I can only characterize as a command performance, the representatives of this new legislature hailed Louis as the 'liberator of his people.'" I swipe my hand over my brow. My temples are throbbing. I look Axel directly in the eye and lower my voice to a whisper. "But who will liberate *us*?"

He reaches for my hands to reassure me, but stops when I clear my throat to warn him that we are being observed. "I will," he says quietly and resolutely. "The king of Sweden is your greatest ally. Gustavus has commissioned me to be his eyes and ears in Paris and at the French court." He leans forward, so close that I can feel his breath upon my face. It smells of cinnamon and clove. "Tell me, *ma chère,* have you ever written in cipher?"

The following morning, the door to my bedchamber flies open unexpectedly. Madame Campan, who sleeps at the foot of my bed, and I clutch our nightgowns to our chests and expect the worst, but the breathless intruder is Madame Élisabeth. "There was just now a woman in my room," she pants. "A *poissarde*! I heard a stirring and I awoke to find her rummaging through my jewelry box. She was trying on an emerald bracelet."

"How did she get in?" asks Campan.

"They climb right over the iron railings. The gall!" Madame Elisabeth's face is flushed with fear. "I don't know if she only wanted to pilfer something or if she intended me some harm."

"We can't have market women—or any trespasser—entering our rooms at will," I insist. "Where are the guards?" They are ubiquitous, except when we are in peril.

Madame Élisabeth shrugs helplessly. She is so gentle, so pious, so self-sacrificing; no one is less deserving of any sort of injury. "They seem to believe, or perhaps they have been told, that their business is to prevent us from escaping, not to protect us from invaders."

During the next few days it becomes apparent that the royal family remains at the mercy of the people. From morn to nearly midnight they bring petitions and demand to be heard and we must present the appearance of the benevolent parents of France, ever willing to countenance the slightest whim of our children, no matter how rebellious. I would not do the same with my *chou d'amour* and Mousseline, no matter how much I adore them. Although I am a fond and doting mother, if my son or daughter misbehaved there would be consequences.

Determined to demonstrate to the market women of Paris who had once vowed to make cockades out of my entrails that I acknowledge their demands for reform, I request the royal dressmaker Madame Éloffe to construct 150 ribbon cockades in the revolutionaries' *tricolore* stripe of red, white, and blue. At one livre apiece they are larger and far more costly and elaborate than the *poissardes'* makeshift rosettes. It is such a simple thing, and it is the province of kings to show forgiveness. The *cocardes* are distributed and the women are delighted. But I know too well that their appreciation is as brief as the lifespan of a butterfly. I have not really purchased their loyalty. I have only bought 150 livres' worth of time.

FIVE

Red Heels and Red Bonnets

⚛ November 1789 ⚛

We are settling in and making the best of it. Madame Élisabeth has moved to an apartment on the first story of the palace, while I have vacated the first-floor suite adjacent to the king's. The children of France will occupy those rooms now so they can be close to their father. My new apartment is on the ground floor. Consisting of a boudoir, a dressing room, and a salon, it can hardly be called grand. Its very modesty and coziness somehow make me feel more secure. Louis's rooms lie directly above mine, although his library is adjacent to my suite. In the mornings, he comes downstairs with the children by a narrow private staircase that connects our apartments and we breakfast as a family. Only one attendant serves us our chocolate and toast, but we have not complained. Fewer servants mean fewer spies.

I have commissioned a number of new gowns from Madame

Éloffe that pay visual homage to the symbols of the Revolution. The *tricolore* cockade rather than the black rosette of the aristocracy is affixed upon my hats and pinned to my sashes. White, for "purity," is once again the fashion and I will wear a good deal of blue as well, ordering a few tailored redingotes to wear over a striped underskirt. Do the rebels recall how only two years ago my riding coats imported from England were mocked and derided as "mannish," and I was depicted as a harpy for wearing them? Yet now the same silhouette and even the identical hue are considered de rigueur for the modish revolutionary. It passes all bounds of reason that the garments now viewed as the height of "patriotism" to the new order were anathema when popularized by the queen of France.

Now that the tumult seems to have subsided, my children's education must recommence. Much has happened since their former *gouvernante,* the duchesse de Polignac, departed so hastily in July. The marquise de Tourzel is utterly devoted to Madame Royale and the dauphin. But there is much I would like to impart to Louise about my son's character in order to help him become a fine young prince.

After my *lever* one morning I speak to her with as much privacy as we are permitted while Madame Élisabeth makes sure the children do not get up to any mischief. I do not wish them to say anything in the presence of our guards, for I have cautioned them repeatedly that these men are not our friends. As his governess has surely seen by now, the four-year-old dauphin suffers no deficit of confidence. Rather, one of his deficiencies is the inability to apologize or to ask for forgiveness when he knows he has behaved badly. "He will only say 'I'm sorry' with tears of vexation in his eyes," I admit to Madame de Tourzel. "Like any little boy, Louis Charles can be thoughtless, impatient, and impetuous. His chief fault, madame, and above all, the one it is essential to correct, is his tendency toward indiscretion. Regrettably, he is all too ready to repeat whatever he has heard, be it a bawdy joke, a cruel taunt, or an outright lie. And often enough, without any intention to tell a falsehood, my son will embroider the truth. He has an active imagination." The marquise de Tourzel listens intently, nodding or smiling on occasion upon the recollection of certain events that match my description of the boy's less-than-perfect behavior.

"He is still too young to comprehend the exalted position he occupies," I add. "And yet his sister understands it all too well. Madame Royale knows her worth to the realm as a daughter of France is so little compared to that of the dauphin. I take great pains to show that Marie Thérèse is not loved the less for it, but I am never certain she believes me. Her brother adores her, and whenever anything brings him pleasure, his first instinct is to ask that Madame Royale be permitted the same indulgence." I reach for the governess's hand. "I should like this system of encouraging his instinctive benevolence to continue. And at all costs, I hope for as long as possible to shield them from whatever deprivations we adults may suffer here."

The king and I fight to retain as much of the status quo as we can. The princesse de Lamballe has returned to court, too distressed by our circumstances to consider remaining safely at the Château d'Eu with her father-in-law, the duc de Penthièvre. Upon her arrival at the Tuileries in October she resumed her post as superintendent of my household without missing a breath.

"How could I fail to be by your side, *Majesté?*" she had asked, her eyes brimming, as always, with sympathetic tears.

"It is more of a risk than you know," I'd told her. "Did you hear what happened to our dear baron de Besenval?" The princesse de Lamballe shook her head. "Imprisoned in the Châtelet—awaiting a trial that I fully expect to be another sham." I trembled with anger even as I spoke the words.

The princesse's cheeks grew pink with shock. "What did he do?"

"It's what the revolutionaries think he did *not* do. In July, he was in charge of commanding the Parisian garrison. He resisted those monsters who rioted at the Bastille, rather than allow them to continue their insurrection."

The princesse shivered. "What is happening nowadays?" she murmured, her hands clasped so tightly in her lap that her knuckles grew pale.

We no longer go to the Opéra or the Comédie-Française, where actors speaking lines that can be interpreted as "royalist" are drowned out by catcalls and forced to retreat from the stage, often under a hail of edible projectiles. But at the Tuileries we still cling to our routines: *Grand couverts*—public dinners—on Tuesdays and Thursdays, and cards on Sundays. I smile to think that I'd so detested dining in public when we began our reign fifteen years ago that I urged Louis to change the ancient etiquette and hold private *soupers* instead. And when I had yet to see my twentieth year I had derided the most popular pastime at court, a dreary lotto game called cavagnole, the delight of the prudish *collets-montés* who were north of the age of thirty. Nowadays, I am happy to reclaim these silly rituals, embracing them with a fervor equal to my prior disdain. Scorn has become the purview of the Revolution.

Louis has expected his ministers to remain in place as well, or at least to be part of the new government, and we have counted upon the support of the comte de Mirabeau in the National Assembly to assure this. Mirabeau proposed a number of names to us, illustrious men who were Assembly delegates, including Lafayette, Talleyrand, the duc de la Rochefoucauld-Liancourt, and Monsieur Target, the lawyer who so successfully defended the Cardinal de Rohan in the notorious *affaire du collier* three years ago, when His

Eminence had been swindled into purchasing a massive diamond necklace in my name. Jacques Necker, our popular Minister of Finance, has been suggested for Premier or Chief Minister, primarily, Louis believes, as a sop to everyone. Necker's liberal beliefs would please the Assembly and the people, yet he is a man who is already intimately familiar with my husband's government.

But on the seventh of November, Mirabeau's fragile house of cards collapses when Necker refuses to cooperate with him, and the National Assembly ultimately issues a decree that no member of the legislature may become a minister in His Majesty's government. I do not comprehend Necker's motives. From our thrones in the king's formal bedchamber, all hope of compromise, of working with the revolutionaries, of maintaining a powerful executive by virtue of gaining a more cooperative Assembly, crumble in a tense struggle for political dominance. Louis has already seen his powers reduced. In September, when we still resided at Versailles, he was permitted to retain only a suspensive veto. All French monarchs had always been given the authority to override the realm's judicial bodies, the Parlements, when they refused to ratify the king's edicts. My husband is gradually being reduced to a cipher.

The comte de Mercy-Argenteau, who has remained Imperial Austria's ambassador to the Bourbon court since my childhood, arrives at the Tuileries. He is doing his best, he assures me, to convince my brother Joseph to put the Hapsburg might behind us. Were Maman still alive I would feel more secure in Mercy's efforts. But Joseph has always been a reformer with progressive ideas. I recollect now the emperor's words after his visit to Versailles in 1777 when he urged me to curtail my frivolities and expenditures: *The revolution will be a cruel one, and perhaps of your own making.* Their sting is just as painful as it was a dozen years ago.

The sixty-two-year-old diplomat is finally beginning to wear his age. Beneath Mercy's wig his temples no longer require powder to make them silver-gray. Wrinkles fan out like spiders' legs from the corners of his eyes. I can see that events in Paris are making him nearly as anxious as I am. My papa, Francis of Lorraine, Holy Roman Emperor and Grand Duke of Tuscany, died of an apoplectic fit when I was nine years old. Since then, the suave and elegant comte is the closest I have known to a father. We have had our tussles, and over the years, particularly when I was dauphine, I teased him mercilessly for being such a scold.

How easy it is for a child to believe that the fun will last forever, I tell the comte now, when he asks how the king and I are faring. "As far as we are concerned personally, the notion of happiness belongs to the past—whatever the future may bring. We have seen too much horror and too much bloodshed ever to be happy again."

"Is there even some small thing that you take comfort in, nowadays?" Mercy asks.

"So that you can tell my brother that I am well and hale?" I reply, my words tinged with asperity. "You may inform Joseph that I am still permitted to enjoy long walks in the Tuileries Gardens, when I am not harangued by insults from the market women of Les Halles. That my greatest pleasure is my two children, from whom only God will induce me to separate. But we are far from well, though we do our best to conceal our opinions and our constraints and go on as before. I know that it is the duty for one king to suffer on behalf of all the others, and we are doing our duty well."

"From a gadabout, you have become a cynic," the comte observes.

"A mob that attempts to murder you in your bed will have that effect," I remind him quietly. And then, I dissolve into tears, missing my maman, her knowledge, her wisdom, her strength—for the comte is my final connection to her and to my vanished childhood, the youth I tried in vain to recapture with the building of the pastoral *hameau* in the gardens of le Petit Trianon. For that perceived extravagance, too, I am being made to suffer now.

I urge the comte de Mercy to extract a promise from my brother to come to our aid, whether it is in the form of money, mercenaries, or Austrian soldiers.

"You know His Imperial Majesty is not well," Mercy tells me.

"That is not an answer." At least, it is not the answer I seek. And all the more reason I need the ambassador's guarantee. Finally, the comte acquiesces to my request. But his eyes betray Joseph's lack of enthusiasm even as his lips agree.

∾ FEBRUARY 1790 ∾

Louison Chabry had laid aside her chisel and come to the Place de Grève because the ragged boys in Saint-Germain who cry the *nouvelles* and sell the latest broadsheets for a sou had announced that this execution across from the Hôtel de Ville will make history. So that afternoon she'd opened her reticule, fished for a coin, and purchased one of their newspapers.

She has never heard of Thomas de Mahy, the forty-four-year-old marquis de Favras, but the paper, published by one of the radicals from the Palais Royal coffeehouses, is written to inflame the heart of even the most phlegmatic citizen. For a start, Louison read, the accused was guilty of being a member of the nobility, not only by virtue of his title but because his wife was the daughter of some minor German prince. *This* detail the publisher connected, whether true or not, to *l'Autrichienne,* the German bitch who had stained the throne of France with her traitor's blood. The marquis had been the instigator of a counterrevolutionary plot to liberate the sovereigns from the Tuileries, where, according to the paper, they resided happily, grateful for the love and kindness of the good

Parisians. After carrying off the monarchs to the town of Péronne in Picardie, the marquis de Favras intended to have Général Lafayette and Monsieur Necker arrested. Thousands of mercenaries were alleged to have been at Monsieur de Favras's disposal—"twenty thousand Sardinians and twelve thousand Germans, and thousands of Swiss and Piedmontese!" Louison read, as well as twelve thousand cavalry in Paris alone. The sculptress had wondered how much of the report was true. It was clear, though, that it didn't matter. The people's thirst for revenge against the nobility had been denied when the baron de Besenval, one of the queen's old lovers, according to the broadsheet, was acquitted of any guilt in urging the regiment under his command to halt the insurrection of July 14.

Several hundred people have assembled on a frigid February night to see the marquis hanged, a most democratic form of execution, Louison's broadsheet proclaimed, as the rope is used to dispatch criminals of all classes. Before the Revolution, a nobleman would have gone to his reward with the swift stroke of an axe or the flash of a sword.

Below the gallows, which is illuminated on all sides with lanterns and torches, the people stamp their feet, less from impatience than to ward off the bitter cold. Those who have garnered the choicest views have been standing for hours on the hard ground, which since dawn has been covered with a layer of frost. The sight of so many people huddled in the shadow of the scaffold, their features lit now and again by the flickering flames, makes the night's proceedings appear even more macabre. Louison tugs her brown woolen cloak more tightly about her shoulders and blows upon her fingers. Her hands are her livelihood and she can't afford to freeze them off for the sake of an execution. And yet, her curiosity has drawn her to the Place de Grève precisely because she has never before seen one.

A shout goes up as the oxcart transporting the condemned man clatters into the square. He is impeccably dressed in a green silk coat. "The same color as the livery worn by the attendants of the comte d'Artois—another one of the queen's lovers," says the man standing next to Louison. His breath reeks of brandy. The man reminds her that the king's youngest brother was exiled in July, just days after the fall of the Bastille. "For treason," he adds.

Although the marquis de Favras has come directly from prison, he is clean shaven, having groomed himself for the occasion of his death as though he were going to church. In a way, thinks Louison, he is indeed about to have a conversation with his maker. On his black felt tricorn, the marquis wears without shame the ink-colored cockade of the aristocracy. His diamond shoe buckles wink in the torchlight as he climbs the wooden steps to the scaffold.

His judges hand him the writ of execution, smugly inviting the nobleman to peruse it. Below him, the crowd is in a holiday mood. Flasks pass from hand to hand, lip to lip. The noose has been illuminated with a hanging lantern, and the marquis de Favras steps toward it to read the writ. After a few moments of scanning the document, his brow furrows and his lips curl into a frown. He thrusts the paper at the judges. "I see that you made three spelling mistakes," he says. The crowd nods and murmurs among themselves. They have expected this sort of arrogance from a man of his lofty social stratum. Given the opportunity to offer his last words he avers his innocence, declaring, "Citizens, if the simple testimony of two men is enough to make you condemn a man to the gibbet, I pity you." He then turns to the hangman and says, "Do your duty, *mon ami!*"

The crowd responds with uproarious laughter and tremendous applause, but not because they are impressed by the aristocrat's bravado. Rather, they are cheering his imminent demise. "Skip, marquis!" they begin to chant, anxious to witness his silk stockinged legs writhing and wriggling above the scaffold's floorboards. *"Sautez, marquis, sautez!"*

The nobleman's wig is removed by the executioner, revealing a pale scalp that shines in the moonlight and resembles a plucked chicken. *Not so aristocratic now,* Louison thinks. The noose is placed about the marquis de Favras's neck and the *bourreau* adjusts the knot. Offered a blindfold, the marquis refuses it. His audience is all the more delighted by this, eager to watch the condemned man's eyes pop in his moment of extremis. The young sculptress considers raising her arm to shield her face. It suddenly seems so indecent, all of them standing for hours in the frosty air to watch a fellow citizen die. Louison had seen enough of death during the riots of October 6 at Versailles. But something makes her leave her arms folded across her chest to watch the marquis's execution with dry eyes. Perhaps she has convinced herself that she will someday sculpt the head of a hanged man. Or maybe it is morbid curiosity. Everyone about her is so certain that the marquis de Favras is a traitor to the Revolution and deserves to hang. Louison doesn't know whether the broadsheet she had stuffed into her pocket told the truth about his crime, had embellished it, or had fabricated bold-faced lies. It is clear that the accused has his own opinion.

"I die innocent. I pray God for me," he cries, just as the trap drops open beneath his feet. The last two words die on his lips as his neck snaps. The rabble roars their approval. And as the fresh corpse does indeed skip, Mademoiselle Chabry is shocked to discover that the mob's thirst for vengeance is not slaked. "Encore!" they cry, as if to demand another execution. Illuminated by their lanterns, their faces, contorted by a sick mixture of anger and glee, resemble the gargoyles of Notre-Dame. Louison shivers. If justice has been served this night and a guilty counterrevolutionary punished, that was one thing. But to bay for more blood as if the nobleman's execution had been a sporting event, no different from a stag hunt or a boxing match—this was a fever the sculptress feared.

She forces herself to look upon the hanging man. Her eyes travel the length of his trim and elegant form as it twists in the dark and frosty night, noting the pallor of his skin, the blood already draining from his body, down to his—the sculptress claps an icy hand to her mouth. It has never occurred to her what happens to a man's nether anatomy after he is hanged. But there it is, bulging against his satin breeches. Louison blushes, embarrassed for the corpse. If the marquis de Favras had not secured her sympathy in life, this ignominious and unfortunate occurrence of nature has made her a momentary royalist.

It has been a devastating month, for the monarchy and for our family. On February 20, 1790, the day after the marquis de Favras—a man I had never met, nor did I know of his plot to spirit the royal family out of Paris—is hanged in the Place de Grève, my eldest brother, Joseph II, Holy Roman Emperor and Emperor of Austria, takes *his* final breath. No well is deep enough to contain my sorrow.

And So We Must Dissemble

My brother and I often had a contentious relationship after I became queen, but I knew that I was his favorite sister and as a sibling, though he enjoyed the elder brother's prerogative to scold, being fifteen years my senior, he had also been very indulgent and fond of me, even across the great distance between Vienna and Versailles. I go into mourning, ordering a wardrobe of black garments, and grieve deeply for Joseph but life at the Tuileries goes on. A few days later an agitated Madame Campan finds me in my sitting room with Madame Élisabeth; I am writing a letter to my brother Leopold, the new Emperor of Austria. When I was nine, he became Grand Duke of Tuscany upon our father's death. I did not know Leopold the way I had known Joseph, who had been Maman's co-ruler since Papa's demise. Leopold no longer resided in Vienna during the remainder of my childhood, before I left Austria for France. "He only remembers a little girl," I fret, "holding a wooden doll, immortalized in a painting made by our sister Marianne. I fear that he will not help us purely on the basis of ties of blood." And yet I would willingly and immediately aid any of my siblings in a time of crisis, especially if their thrones were in danger.

Should we wait for Leopold to ask me if there is anything he can do? Or do I throw myself like a beggar at his feet?

Madame Campan offers no solution. Instead, she looks to me to resolve a difficult issue of etiquette. "Monsieur le marquis de la Villeurnoy wishes to invite the widow and son of the marquis de Favras to the *grand couvert* on Thursday."

"You must permit it, sister," Élisabeth pleads, her eyes suddenly brimming with tears. I have never seen her more incensed about something than the execution of the marquis, killed, she believes, solely because he was a monarchist, dying, Christlike, for our perceived sins.

I agree to host the family but the dinner is a frightening test. Behind my chair for the entire duration of the meal stands Antoine Joseph Santerre, the commander of a battalion of the Garde Nationale and a demagogue of the worst order. I hear him wheezing through his broken nose, making his presence felt so strongly that although I wish to express my heartfelt condolences, I dare not utter a single word to the widowed marquise and her little boy, who arrive halfway through the meal. I am afraid even to meet her gaze and I am certain she expects some show of sympathy from me. Instead, I fiddle with my fork, too troubled to eat a morsel. At the end of the meal, the grieving Madame de Favras and her son, garbed from head to toe in black mourning, are escorted from the royal antechamber with an utter absence of fanfare. I cannot wait to leave the table and find myself gazing at the clock on the mantel at the far end of the salon, desperate to be liberated from Santerre's hawkeyed surveillance.

After the *grand couvert* is over, I retreat to the solace of Madame Campan's room. I fling myself, sobbing, into an armchair. "We have come to weep with you," I say. "If I had been free to do as I truly wished, I would have accorded the son of this martyred marquis a place of honor at the right hand of the king. The son of a man who had sacrificed his life for us would have dined beside his sovereigns. And yet—surrounded by the executioners who condemned and murdered his papa, I could not even bring myself to look him in the eye!"

I fumble for my handkerchief. Madame Élisabeth gives me hers, embroidered with her cipher. "No matter what I do, I will be censured for it," I say, unable to control my tears. "The royalists will blame me for not recognizing the presence of the marquise and her little son. And the revolutionaries will vilify me for entertaining them in the first place."

My *belle-soeur* sits slumped over Madame Campan's worktable, her head in her hands. "Is this what will happen to anyone who tries to aid my brother?" Élisabeth murmurs.

At least I can help the *veuve* de Favras and her son. They will need money. "I am too carefully watched," I say to Campan, "but tomorrow you will see that the marquise receives this." I write a number on a slip of paper that corresponds to a certain amount of money—several rolls of fifty-louis coins that I keep locked in a chest beneath my bed. I desire the marquise to know that her sovereigns are sorry, that we are grateful, that I wish to have been able to give her a kind word, to hug her fatherless boy. But she may now be as closely observed as we. And so my gift must be given anonymously.

It pains me to be false, to sham my own moods and feelings. Confiding about this *grand couvert*, I write with a heavy heart to Mercy that as a rule I consider myself too wellborn to stoop to deception, yet "my current position is so delicate and so unique that for everyone's sake, especially that of my children, I have to change my frank and independent nature—the very character that was once so harshly criticized for being too 'Austrian'—and learn how to dissimulate."

It pains me to live a lie, but I also tell myself every day at Mass when I seek forgiveness for my transgressions that at least we live. We play our enemies' game, but do so in our own way, so that we don't seem transparently false by appearing overzealous to adopt an ideology we cannot possibly accept or believe in. Instead, measure by small measure, we do what we can to show that we are listening. My tricolored wardrobe, constructed from the same fabrics in the same hues as the garments worn by the highborn women who espouse the tenets of the Revolution, displays the patriotism of the Queen of France. Young as he is, the dauphin has learned to drill like a soldier. It gives me chills every time I watch my child crisscross the Tuileries gardens imitating the guardsmen's march, but whenever the people see my son, whether he is in my arms, or taking a stroll in the gardens with his *gouvernante* or hand in hand with his papa, a smile broadens their mouths. The people detest me. They are still willing to believe the king is a good man who has been misled. But the next king of France is an innocent little boy, so guileless that the heart of even the most hardened revolutionary is thawed by the mere sight of him.

Louis Charles cannot wait for the spring because I have promised him his own little plot in the corner of the gardens where he can plant and cultivate whatever he wishes. It has become the popular thing, to return to tilling the soil, especially for the intelligentsia, the citizens of the cities who are more accustomed to soiling their hands exchanging money at the *bourse* or turning the cheaply inked pages of the latest broadsheet at a nearby coffeehouse.

The dauphin will now be raised with a greater awareness of the needs of his people. His father has promised the Assembly to work more closely and directly with them. With Louis's characteristic dread of conflict and bloodshed, he has pledged to work for the good of all of his people. He speaks of the common need to establish the new social and governmental order calmly and with cool heads. And he has pledged, too, to defend his subjects' freedom, announcing, "I will do more than that, messieurs: in agreement with Her Majesty the Queen, who shares my sentiments, I will educate my son in the new principles of constitutional monarchy and freedom with justice."

His speech was met with cheers on one side and skepticism on the other. No matter what my husband says, he cannot please everyone. I am convinced that if the Assembly were to demand that the king concede the sky is green instead of blue, a cadre of hotheads would spring to their feet and throw their tricorns in the air denouncing him for a liar, insisting instead that the firmament is fiery orange—or red—or violet—any color other than what the king declares it to be.

What, I muse, does the notion of *Liberté* mean? Who will be free? The royal family is certainly not free to be as we were. The revolutionaries have three broad concepts they wish to foist upon their new vision of France. And *Égalité*? I do not believe that even a man such as the duc d'Orléans believes that he, with his breeding, wealth, and education, is equal to the laborer who digs ditches or the man who shovels away the manure after the carriages have passed in front of the Palais Royal. The same argument can be made for *Fraternité*. To hear Lafayette speak of the daily squabbles among the representatives in the National Assembly, they are not even willing to call *one another* "brother," let alone demonstrate that fellow feeling for every man within the new nation they envision. They are however, one step closer. On the thirteenth of February, the Assembly suppresses all religious orders. Monastic vows now carry the same credibility as fairy tales. Church properties are to be confiscated and appropriated by the nation as *biens nationaux,* national goods. The bankrupt government is printing paper money called *assignats* that are intended to represent the value of these confiscated church properties and is using them as currency, to finance the overwhelming national debt. How could a responsible man like Necker, who made his fortune and his reputation as a banker, see this as anything but fiscal and moral chaos? My husband has lost the courage and the will to stand up to the Assembly. Every day seems to bring a new capitulation. I am sick over it. I have never seen Louis more despondent.

And yet whatever he concedes is still not enough. Twenty-four hours in a day, sixty minutes in an hour, is insufficient for the new breed of revolutionaries. They have already ousted their predecessors for moving too slowly toward a constitutional monarchy, or perhaps no monarchy at all. In my view, what they desire will only lead to utter anarchy. Men whom my husband had finally convinced himself he might have been able to work with toward an acceptable compromise are gone, replaced with hardheaded ideologues, unwilling to budge from their own vision of France's future. The Assembly is literally divided, according to where the delegates sit inside the Salle du Manège, on the left or the right sides of the Great Hall.

The men of moderate revolutionary ideals who just a few months ago were planting trees of liberty in the public *places,* and encouraging every "citizen," as our subjects are now to be called, to demonstrate his or her patriotism to the Nation, the Law, and then the King, have been replaced by more radical thinkers who do not want Louis's words of compromise. Even his conciliation to their proposals is not enough. This second iteration of firebrands who call themselves lawmakers will stop at nothing short of complete capitulation by the sovereign of the realm—a man whose powers are God-given—to their atheistic new world order.

I pray daily for deliverance. The Almighty was surely in France when He took my two babies before they had the chance to grow old. He witnessed our eviction at the point of pickaxes, pitchforks, and bayonets from our beautiful home, the residence of the Bourbons since 1682. But where is He now, when His faithful and devoted acolyte is in such desperate need of His love?

SEVEN

Saint-Cloud

⁂ SPRING 1790 ⁂

Axel makes certain to carry his diplomatic pouch whenever he visits me at the Tuileries. Inside the portfolio are official papers embossed with the seal of the King of Sweden requesting Count von Fersen's regular reports to His Majesty on the state of affairs at the French court. The count has called on me several times a week since the royal family's mandatory *déménagement* last October. What I cannot tell him openly, and what he is unable to observe on his own, he gleans from my tears and my sighs.

We are often shadowed as we walk through the huge wings of the palace, from the Royal Court to the Court of Princes and the residential Pavillon de Flore, but we are never disturbed. Even the revolutionaries are cautious about the way they treat those with the credentials of an ambassador. The members of the National Assembly do not wish to have it bruited about in foreign courts that they are less than civilized or that their goals for the Nation are anything but lofty.

Axel and I often have our conversations in the chapel. The guards assigned to watch me have little use for the Almighty. They have now been indoctrinated to worship the Nation above all, followed by the Law, a deity that appears to change its shape by the week. I am convinced that the very fact that they are no longer supposed to fear God frightens them, and so they avoid the chapel, which makes it the safest haven in the palace for a royalist.

The count and I mount the sweeping staircase in the Central Pavilion. We stop on the first landing and enter the chapel. Sunlight streams in from the clerestory windows in visible rays, the way the divinity's presence is announced in a seventeenth-century allegorical painting.

The chapel in the Tuileries Palace has nothing of the grandeur and opulence of its counterpart at Versailles. And yet I find comfort in the relative simplicity of its décor. The panels of the vaulted ceiling depict Biblical and mythological tales. The eye of the worshipper is drawn upwards by trompe l'oeil pilasters painted to resemble pink-veined marble. Inside the hushed sanctity of the chapel there are plenty of places for me to converse quietly with Axel. Rather than remain in the open, seated in one of the pews, we step into the sacristy, just behind the altar. No one else is there. Even the court's confessors are making themselves scarce these days.

I motion toward a small table covered by a white cloth trimmed with lace, and we sit upon hard wooden chairs. Axel opens his leather portfolio and withdraws a smaller pouch that is secured with an intricate mechanism. He opens it and lays several documents on the table. I am about to peruse one when he places his hand over mine.

"You are looking exceptionally sad today," Axel murmurs.

"I am thinking about my mother. Today would have been her

seventy-third birthday. Every May thirteenth I light two candles: one for the Virgin Mother and one for Saint Theresa. I have not yet done so today." A tear escapes the corner of my eye and I catch it with my fingertip. "This November she will have been in the Kaisergruft for ten years. Where has the time gone?" I sigh.

I clear my throat and return to the paper. It is a table, filled with combinations of letters. "Polyalphabetic substitution ciphers," Axel says, "now that you have become proficient with monoalphabetic ones."

Yes—after more than half a year of practice, meeting several times a week with my charming and handsome tutor. I unsuccessfully suppress a chuckle, wondering what my mother might have thought about my mastery of these essential elements of espionage. "Do you know that when I was a child, I was such an appalling student that my governess used to write out my lessons herself and allow me to trace over her words?" The laugh now bubbles over my lips. "Maman was so preoccupied with the affairs of the empire that I don't think she ever noticed what remarkably adult penmanship I had for a ten-year-old!"

Axel squeezes my hand sympathetically. His palm is warm. I look into his eyes. This afternoon they are the color of a peacock feather's eye. "Louis does not know I am learning to write in cipher," I whisper. "There is much I no longer trouble him with. He has so many burdens . . ." My words trail off and I find myself looking at the windows, towards the darkening sky. The sacristy feels very gloomy when there is no sunlight to illuminate it. "I decided in October to assume as many of the responsibilities as I can. I never asked his permission. I think"—I begin to weep—"that he would refuse my aid on principle. He believes that by allowing the revolutionaries to triumph in any way, he has failed his people and he must be the one to remedy things. But I"—I lay my head upon my hands, as my striped silk sleeves muffle my sobs—"I am the reason the people are so unhappy, the reason they wish to destroy the monarchy. And I must be the one to do whatever it takes to save us."

I hear the scrape of Axel's chair as he pushes himself away from the table and stands behind me. And I turn into his embrace, throwing my arms about his waist and burying my face in his torso, staining his embroidered yellow *gilet* with salty tears. He holds me until my sobs subside, until my resolve to confront our adversaries returns. God is watching us, but He is wise enough to understand our interaction, Axel's and mine. He does not bear witness to a lover's illicit passion, but to the expression of comfort that one friend provides to another in deepest distress.

"We will have much more time to practice the cryptography this summer," I tell Count von Fersen. "The Assembly is permitting us to go to Saint-Cloud. We leave in less than two weeks." Axel can discern the relief in my face at the knowledge that we will be able to leave Paris and escape, if only for a few months, the crucible of revolution. "The air will be more healthful for the children," I say.

"And the climate more so for you," he adds meaningfully, referring to the ugliness of the current political debate here in the capital.

"We will not be so closely watched there," I say, absentmindedly playing with one of the silver buttons on Axel's vest. There are moments when I still regard him as a lover and wish for the touch of his lips against my skin. But more and more I think of him, yes, as a friend, *bien sûr,* but more than that, as a kind of savior. He is providing me with the tools and the knowledge to triumph over our enemies.

"Come. Explain to me how the polyalphabetic ciphers work," I say, settling down to the task at hand as I pick up the chart.

Axel sits beside me again and points out how each letter in the alphabet will be replaced or substituted with one of two letters in its partner pairing. "This is just an example of the enciphering. We'll practice by writing to each other. After you master this code, we will move on. Once it becomes necessary to correspond in cipher we will have to change the codes every week. Your memory will be taxed as it never has been before."

"And I thought learning the plays of Molière and Beaumarchais was difficult," I jest.

I want to write Axel a letter to express how grateful I am to him for teaching me this skill. It will take me hours before I am competent enough with the polyalphabetic system to write even the simplest encrypted sentence. It is nearly dusk when I finally manage to write two words on a scrap of paper. *Je t'aime.*

I am exhausted from the mental exertion. My head throbs. Axel strokes my hair, letting me weep in his arms for as long as the tears will flow.

We are only a little more than six miles outside Paris but the Château de Saint-Cloud is an oasis of calm compared to the seething cauldron of hatred in the capital. "Listen!" I say to Louis.

He cups his hand to his ear. Then he shakes his head. "I don't hear anything."

"Exactly!" I clap my hands with girlish glee. Gone is the constant cacophony of the rabble outside our windows, their promenading in the gardens at all hours, their insults shouted across the courtyard, cruel syllables that echo and bounce off the Tuileries' stone façades, and the distant rumble of drums and artillery.

It has been some time since we have visited Saint-Cloud. The king purchased the palace in my name three years ago when we sought a more salubrious climate for the first dauphin. Louis Joseph was never well; the poor child's spine was deformed and his lungs required all the healthful air we could provide. Even when the breezes were charming, the Château de Versailles smelled rank, the result of more than a century of hygienic neglect. The sewers never properly drained. The chimneys perpetually smoked. Countless cats and dogs marked their territory at will. In the absence of pisspots in every room, the thousand courtiers who resided under our sloping roofs, our visiting ministers, and any tourist eager to see how and where the king and queen of France lived, relieved themselves in the corners and stairwells, behind tapestries and draperies, in vases and urns. I could return to Versailles blindfolded and still know it by the smell.

The renovations I had commissioned at Saint-Cloud in 1787 from Monsieur Mique, who had designed le Petit Trianon's pastoral *hameau,* will seem unfamiliar now. We could not even afford to complete them. But whatever has been done will be preferable to the Tuileries where, like the animals in the royal menagerie at Versailles, we are permitted only the illusion of freedom.

Rushing into the palace ahead of their governess, our children immediately make a game out of traversing the black and white tiled entrance hall, hopping from one black square to the next and imposing a penalty—two squares backwards, on the diagonal—for accidentally stepping out of bounds and landing upon a white tile instead.

After only one day, the entire royal family is in a buoyant, festive mood. Even Monsieur and Madame are filled with uncharacteristic pleasantries and compliments, although they refuse Louis's offer to remain with us at Saint-Cloud, preferring to take up residence in a villa nearby.

Our sojourn at the château is most delightful. June brings a riot of color to the formal gardens, where every day the dauphin romps, growing more accustomed to the company of exuberant hounds. To my immense joy, after a few weeks, he no longer fears them. As a family, we walk all the way to the park at Meudon in the evening, although the air there hangs about my shoulders like a shawl woven of sorrows. For it was at Meudon that my firstborn son, only eight years old, drew his last breaths. I did not believe it a year ago when the abbé Vermond, in his endeavors to console me, assured me that the first dauphin had departed this life for a better one. After everything we have seen since last July, I am now certain my old friend was right.

"Louise, can you play billiards?" the king inquires one evening. The table, covered in green baize, is set up in the Salon d'Aurore. Above the heads of the players, which include Madame Campan, the princesse de Lamballe, and my husband, half-clad nymphs cavort with winged putti in a permanent depiction of daybreak, the painted sky tinged with soft yellows and pinks. The gilded walls of the gaming room are a riot of reds and vermilions, one of the only salons to incorporate my scheme for a Chinoiserie décor. The atmosphere deliberately invokes my childhood and the round Chinese Room at Schönbrunn, one of my favorite salons in the Hapsburgs' summer palace.

Madame de Tourzel shakes her head, too awed to try her hand with the cue in the presence of the king. "Nonsense," Louis insists. "Billiards are a fundamental part of anyone's lexicon of pastimes. I will personally take charge of your lessons!" And as soon as the game in progress is completed, the king keeps his word and gives the royal *gouvernante* her first tutorial at the billiards table. The children are frightfully amused for it seems their governess has dreadful aim and the balls do not roll toward the pockets but skip and jump all over the baize as if she were skimming pebbles over a lake. We have not laughed so much in months. I wish I could bottle this moment in one of Monsieur Fargeon's flacons and daub it on my wrists and behind my ears whenever I find myself once again in need of mirth and merriment.

EIGHT

The Lion Lies Down with the Lambs

~ JULY 1790 ~

A visit from the comte de Mercy at the end of June brings surprising news. He is accompanied by an old friend from the Bourbon court, the thirty-six-year-old comte de la Marck whose family has always served with distinction either in the Austrian army or in mercenary regiments fighting for France.

The two men ask to walk with me alone through the gardens. As we stroll past symmetrical rows of conical topiaries, the ambassador tells me that we may have an ally within the National Assembly. Fixing me with his bulging eyes, de la Marck concurs. "A mutual friend, *Majesté*, may be ready to put his talents at our disposal."

The color rises into my cheeks, enhancing the two-inch circles of rouge that I have not forsworn although our court at Saint-Cloud is far less formal than ever it was at Versailles. For example, where it had once been a perquisite of princes of the blood, here, anyone may dine at the king's table.

Mercy strolls with his hands clasped behind his back. "I believe the final straw occurred on May 19, when the National Assembly abolished the nobility. The comte de Mirabeau has always been extremely sensitive about his title."

The Assembly has suppressed all titles and coats-of-arms. Now, with the stroke of a pen, every man and woman in France is considered of equal birth and stature. All are addressed as "Citizen" or "Citizeness," followed by their surname.

"He is now called 'Riqueti Senior,' and it rankles," says la Marck. He pauses to admire a plot of purple tulips the exact hue of his coat.

"And what has this to do with His Majesty and me?" I ask him. "Why do you bring us news that this silver-tongued demagogue is displeased with the new laws? Perhaps he should have realized that the Revolution's hungry maw is always salivating for fresh meat. They have scarcely been sated by yesterday's supper than they crave a larger meal."

The men exchange glances. Mercy removes his spectacles and wipes them clean with a pristine handkerchief. He has always been a genius at playing for time, rolling out the ball of string just far enough to tantalize the cat. "Mirabeau is in financial straits," he says.

Diplomats are masters at approaching an issue from an oblique angle rather than coming right to the point. "Are you saying he can be bought?"

The comte de la Marck smiles, revealing blackened stubs of teeth. Only the very wealthy suffer such damage from an excess of sugar, a costly commodity. "Mirabeau owes money to the Jews, the stock jobbers, and the court of Spain. For all his radical posturing—

and I do think he genuinely believes that the people deserve a voice in their governance—*au fond, Majesté, le comte de Mirabeau est un royaliste.*"

A meeting is arranged. No one is to know about it except for the parties directly involved. I consider dressing in white, nowadays the color of patriotism. Instead I choose to wear blue. On the field of battle, white is the color of surrender.

The summer air is fragrant and still on the third of July when the comte de Mirabeau arrives at Saint-Cloud. Yet the hour is so early that the dew still sparkles on the grass. At eight in the morning I await him in a gated private garden at the farthest end of the palace grounds. Unaccompanied by any guards, the princesse de Lamballe escorts him to me. Before she leaves us she whispers in my ear, "His nephew drove him here in a two-horse chaise. He was dressed as a postilion and asked to change his clothes inside the château before he was introduced to you."

Everything about Mirabeau is large, from his head to his hands to his belly. I have been told to expect a misshapen, ugly man—"like a lion with smallpox," the comte de la Marck had warned me. And I am not disappointed, although I am surprised by his sense of fashion. The man I had so feared and hated is dressed not like a revolutionary, but like a courtier. No Phrygian cap or *sans-culottes* with shredded hems. Instead, his breeches are of black silk ottoman, his striped vest is embroidered with tiny pink rosettes, and his gray faille coat trimmed with silver buttons is embellished with sheaves of wheat sewn from golden threads on the cuffs and pockets. Tied impeccably, the stock about his thick neck is blindingly white, and his powdered wig is styled in a series of sausage-shaped rolls on either side of his head.

I expect an opening salvo from this notorious demagogue in the form of a fiery diatribe, and so I mean to disarm him before he can unleash a word. As my mother always liked to remind me, my only asset is charm, although I would prefer to think that I have matured a great deal since the days of my carefree youth. Smiling, I offer him my hand. "In the case of an ordinary enemy I should be making a great mistake at this moment, in welcoming the wolf into the sheepfold, but when speaking to a Mirabeau, in the case of a man of such renown, I find myself more awed by your presence than frightened by it."

He confides that he has been endeavoring for several months to arrange a tête-à-tête with either Louis or me. "The comte de Provence—Monsieur—has been ingratiating himself with the National Assembly and we have, I believe, established a rapport. But when I proposed a meeting with the king, I must tell you, *Majesté,* that his brother informed me quite succinctly that 'His Majesty's weakness and indecision are beyond words.' As Monsieur put it, 'Imagine trying to keep a rack of oiled billiard balls together.'"

I seethe at this insult to my husband. But I cannot reveal my discomfort, or my anger at my *beau-frère's* unforgivable attempt to postpone Mirabeau's effort to broker some sort of entente between the monarchy and the legislature.

"And so, through the good offices of our friend the comte de la Marck, I decided perhaps that the right person to speak to instead would be Your Majesty."

I wonder what Mirabeau wants, but I will let him tell me in his own time. After all, I am still queen. I will not be seen to beg. If it is true that the comte is short of funds, I will wait for him to broach the subject. I have been terrified to meet him face-to-face, this monster who has made his political reputation by denouncing the monarchy and traducing *me* as the genesis of France's ills. I sit beside him now, no winged harpy, but a flesh-and-blood woman, a mother and wife. And it is this all-too-human face that he continues to gaze upon with a mixture of awe and confusion.

"I am profoundly moved by His Majesty's present anguish," says the comte. "And by your own," he adds hastily. "The Revolution is moving more swiftly than anyone could have predicted. And in these past few months it has become clear to me that something must be done to create a healthy, workable system of government, because at present we are rapidly headed for anarchy, sinking more deeply into it day by day. When the hottest heads are permitted to prevail, we will no longer be able to recognize France as a civilized nation." The more he witnesses this descent into radicalism, the more he acknowledges the importance of preserving and protecting the throne.

I am both amazed and angry, but I bite my tongue. "I could have told you that anything other than monarchy would lead to chaos. And I read the newspapers. And I have heard more than an earful from the boys in the courtyard of the Tuileries who cry the *nouvelles*. What is it, then, that you have really come here to say to me, monsieur le comte?"

Mirabeau asserts his support for a constitutional monarchy along the lines of England's parliamentary model and assures me that he intends to use his oratorical powers to persuade the members of the National Assembly to adopt it. For himself, the comte proposes a unique role. He would still appear to be the outspoken lion of the Revolution, the firebrand of the Salle du Manège, but in truth he would be a clandestine agent for the crown, a secret monarchist, working behind the scenes with the king and me to maintain as many of the sovereign's powers as possible.

Mirabeau has his price, however. In fact he has prepared the particulars on a scrap of paper inscribed in his own bold hand, as neatly as a ledger sheet. A retainer of six thousand livres a month plus the payment of his debts, which amount to a staggering 208,000 livres. I do not ask whether he is fond of gaming or the turf or has mistresses, or if his estate is in disrepair. I do guess, however that the afternoon's sartorial splendor is unusual for the comte, who is not given to caring overmuch about his wardrobe.

We walk back through the gardens to the château. The king must be informed of the outcome of our tête-à-tête. I find my husband standing on the balcony of the Salon de la Verité peering through his telescope. He has never met the formidable Mirabeau, and I catch the surprise in Louis's eyes to see a man who is even larger than he. I believe, too, that he is astonished to discover that the rumors of the comte's ugliness were not exaggerated, for Mirabeau's face is heavily pitted and scarred and his features resemble something one might find in a vegetable garden. I am glad the dauphin is not present, for our son has the unfortunate tendency to blurt indiscreet remarks, or to repeat whatever rude comments he has overheard from an adult.

Louis is prepared not only to meet Mirabeau's terms but to offer a million-livre gratuity if the comte fulfills his promises by the end of the sitting of the National Assembly. As part of the agreement, Mirabeau will continue to meet with us in secret as an informer. Inside the Salon de la Verité the gratitude in three pairs of eyes is reflected in the enormous gilt-edged mirror. The Assembly may have declared the nobility abolished, but here at Saint-Cloud, we do not acknowledge the decree. The comte de Mirabeau, hat— though embellished with the *tricolore* cockade—in hand, bows deeply to the king and lowers his lips to my outstretched hand. He need never worry about his finances again.

I catch my husband's eye in the glass. Louis's mouth softens into a wan smile. We are placing our faith in a man for whom, until this afternoon, we had nothing but hatred and contempt. And now he has become our ally. For the nonce, the monarchy is saved. Even if he is not to be an autocrat, our son will someday sit on the throne of France.

NINE

La Fête de la Fédération

It seems as though every soul in Paris, although Louison Chabry overhears a soldier of the Garde Nationale say there are only three or four hundred thousand, is trying to crowd into the Champ de Mars. But why do the heavens always seem to part, dispensing near-biblical rain whenever she embarks upon a lengthy, patriotic trek?

The occasion is a birthday party of sorts, the first anniversary of the people's storming of the Bastille. But, fearful of the rumors that an insurrection would erupt during the Fête de la Fédération, a civil war that would lead to the massacre of many of the nobility, the deposing of the king, and the installation of the duc d'Orléans on the throne of France, Louison nearly stayed at home. She had seen enough of that sort of violence at Versailles. Another rumor had been circulating regarding today's events: that the revolutionaries would be the ones to have their throats slit by the royalists, that the most popular members of the National Assembly, including the venerated Lafayette, would be the targets of assassins' bullets, the faubourgs would be torched, burning the homes of innocent citizens to cinders, and that the king would reassert his autocracy.

Every day there is so much propaganda disseminated that Louison hardly knows what to believe. But she has two reasons to attend the fête, even though they appear to conflict. She wants to participate in the national celebration because she is excited to see what her brother Marcel has been volunteering to construct. Fearing they would not complete their work in time for the anniversary, the laborers called for all good citizens to come to the Champ de Mars and shoulder a shovel or pickaxe. But Louison also desires to see the monarchs again. Although *tout le monde* despises them, Their Majesties will host the festivities. Having met the king the previous October—the memory of that day's carnage makes Louison shudder—she feels as though she knows him. Recalling the kindness in his eyes as her delegation demanded bread, and his solicitousness after she fainted in his presence—oh, the humiliation—she feels disloyal and ashamed. Fervent patriots do not feel the least bit conflicted. Their hatred for both the monarchy and the sovereigns is visceral. And why not, when the National Assembly has revealed the outrageous expenditures during the fifteen years that their two well-upholstered derrières warmed the thrones of France?

Nearly thirty million livres were paid to the king's brothers, the wily, gargantuan Monsieur and the queen's whoring lover the comte d'Artois, to subsidize their lavish households. And an astounding 227,983,716 livres was spent by the crown on buildings, gardens, jewelry, pensions to the royal favorites, and lavish entertainments—although (to be fair to the sovereigns, thought Louison, when she'd read the broadsheets) half of that sum had

financed the royal army and navy, which had been at war for a
number of years. Yet twelve million had been spent personally by
the monarchs, most of it to purchase the Austrian bitch's diamonds,
it was said. How does a rumbling belly dismiss that with a shrug or
a flick of the wrist?

During her long walk to the Champ de Mars from her home in
the *quartier* Saint-Germain, Louison encounters hundreds of citizens with the same destination. They share umbrellas to shelter
from the downpour. Louison congratulates herself for planning
ahead and bringing her own. One or two people in front of her
begin to sing the *Ça Ira,* the Revolution's new anthem, lustily and
full throated, and within moments as though they had all caught
the same fever, the tune is taken up by everyone. The sculptress
already knows the melody, a popular *contredanse* tune, the *Carillon
National,* having kicked up her heels to it many times. But it has
been given a lyric by Ladré, a street singer who sells his ballads in
the shadow of the cathedral of Notre-Dame.

As they sing, their feet beat time to the melody and their stroll
becomes more of a march.

Ah! Ça ira, ça ira, ça ira, it'll be fine, it'll be fine, it'll be fine
The people on this day repeat and repeat
The one who is elevated shall be brought down
The one who is brought down shall be elevated.
Ah! Ça ira, ça ira, ça ira;
Let us rejoice, good times will come!
The French people used to have nothing to say
The aristocrats say Mea culpa!
The clergy regrets its wealth
The Nation will have justice
Thanks to the prudent Lafayette.
Ah! Ça ira, ça ira, ça ira!

There are many verses to the *Ça Ira*. The marchers sing them out of order. As soon as someone remembers a stanza, he or she begins and the others follow. By the time they reach the Champ de Mars, the citizens, though soaked to the bone, have convinced themselves that all will indeed be fine and they are prepared to celebrate their first year of triumph over their aristocratic oppressors.

The sodden field has been transformed into an arena of concentric terraces, stretching from the blindingly white stones of the triumphal arch three vaults wide built especially for the Fête de la Fédération to the École Militaire at the far end of the grounds. In the center is a podium atop a dais upon a platform, each level reached from a set of stairs.

After all that fearsome propaganda, Louison is much relieved to discover that there is not a hint of violence in the atmosphere. Instead, the air is filled with music. Military bands strike up martial tunes with fife and drum. Singers serenade the vast crowd with popular melodies, and a new song written expressly for the fête, *Le Chant du 14 juillet.* Eighty-three enormous banners striped with the red, blue, and white of the Revolution are unfurled about the field, denoting the place where each group of the nation's provincial Federates, comprising 14,000 individual *fédérés,* will convene. Outside the arena, blue-striped tents capped with red pennants convey the atmosphere of a country fair.

Although her feet ache, Louison does not wish to take a seat just yet. Marcel helped build the triumphal arch, so for that reason alone it merits a closer look. She walks through each of the three barrel vaults, playfully making her voice echo off the coffered walls. She admires the allegorical friezes, wishing that someone had offered her the commission. *The king of a free people is the only powerful king,* she reads. On every side of the arch is a quotation. *We fear you no longer, petty tyrants, you who oppressed us under a hundred different names.* A third quote exhorts, *You cherish this liberty, you possess it now; show yourselves worthy to preserve it.* And on the fourth side of the arch, *The rights of man have been disregarded for centuries; they have been re-established for all humanity.* Her eye is drawn from the etched letters to another tricolored flag, this one representing the infant nation whose freedom French soldiers gave their blood to defend and whose victory over a tyrannical king planted the seeds of liberty here at home. A delegation from the United States of America has come all the way from the other side of the Atlantic Sea just to partake in the events of the Fête de la Fédération as a way of expressing their appreciation.

By the time Louison decides to find a place to sit in the stands, it is raining so hard that the benches are dotted with thousands of colorful, opened umbrellas, like a field of huge silk flowers.

She is eager to see the monarchs, but perhaps they have no intention of appearing so early in the morning. In the meantime the crowd is entertained by folk dancers from Provence, oblivious to the weather. But within minutes they are joined by hundreds of citizens who descend from the stands onto the field and soon the entire arena is filled with whirling dancers, laughing, clapping, and holding hands. Louison hastens to join them. As she passes a German visitor on her way down the steps of the terrace she overhears the man remark, "Look at these French devils who dance *in Strömen regnen*—while it is raining cats and dogs!"

The sculptress can't resist a retort. "Who cares for bad weather when the sun is shining in our hearts?" she shouts as she scampers down the stairs to join the dancers.

Mock battles erupt spontaneously between the various Federates, turning the Champ de Mars into a muddy tourney. Lorrainers unsheathe their rapiers and challenge the Bretons. The Flemings face off against the Provençaux. Their *petites batailles* end in fraternal embraces and the dances recommence, despite the rain which offers no surcease.

The merriment is interrupted by a thundering rumble of drumbeats and a fanfare of trumpets. All eyes are drawn to the pavilion at the end of the arena dominated by the École Militaire. Louison feels her breath catch in her throat. Everyone who is anyone is about to emerge from behind those blue and gold striped hangings.

One has to participate, but oh, how I dread it, I wrote to the comte de Mercy, confiding my trepidation about this entire Fête de la Fédération. My mouth may smile before the hundreds of thousands of our "good people," as my husband still insists upon calling these rebellious "citizens," but my eyes are wary of them. They are not here in the pouring rain to celebrate *us,* but to congratulate Lafayette, and even themselves, on triumphing over everything we represent. As we rode to the Champ de Mars this morning, we passed a number of tents constructed especially for this event—and they call me wasteful!—their red pennants flapping like so many rude tongues. The area resembles a general's encampment. Even on this day of purported celebration I feel like a prisoner.

A pavilion has been erected for the notables at one end of the arena, opulently hung with fabric of royal blue and gold. I enter the private box tucked behind it, grasping my children's hands. Madame Royale and the dauphin don't seem to know what to make of this occasion. My son is too little to understand what it is all about. I have told him it is a big costume party. "Is that why I'm dressed like a soldier, Maman?" he asked. He is wearing the red, white, and blue uniform of the Garde Nationale.

"You must be in costume, too, like the other ladies, Maman," he observes of my simple white gown and tricolored sash. Feathers, instead of jewels, adorn my hair. "But why isn't Papa wearing one?" Ironically, for a man who has always been more at ease dressed like a commoner, today the king is garbed in pale blue satin, his coat and breeches encrusted with embroidery and gemstones. He wears no cockade on his plumed hat.

Beyond the private box, inside the pavilion two thrones, upholstered in azure velvet embroidered with golden fleur-de-lis, are placed three feet apart. When Louis and I enter, followed by our children and Madame Élisabeth, I assume the second throne is for me and begin to walk toward it. But no—the other chair is reserved for the *général,* Lafayette, the people's saint. Arrayed on either side of the pavilion are the government ministers and the members of the National Assembly.

"No umbrellas!" the people cry, angry that their view of us is thwarted. They have waited for several hours in the rain and if *they* can be soaked to the bone, their garments destroyed, so can we. We must satisfy their desire for a spectacle.

My gaze is directed toward the center of the arena, where an altar rises into the air, approached by four sets of staircases. At its pinnacle stands the statue of a woman representing Liberty. She holds aloft a banner bearing a single word: CONSTITUTION. At the base of the altar, enormous urns burn incense that settles like fragrant clouds of myrrh in the moist air.

Three hundred priests descend upon the field, robed in white albs. Instead of stoles, they wear tricolored scarves. The ecclesiastics fill the steps of the altar and as the bishop is about to say the Mass, the rain ceases and the sun emerges through the gaps between the dark clouds scudding across the sky as if some celestial properties manager is changing the scenery. Nonetheless, the shift in weather sends a shiver up my spine, for the storm is headed across the Seine toward the Tuileries.

The words of the bishop of Autun are accompanied by a military salute—artillery fire and a burst of martial music. At the elevation of the Host, the drums crescendo, the trumpets blare, and the entire crowd of nearly half a million souls are on their knees.

Once the Mass has been said, in rides the former marquis—now *Citizen* Lafayette—on a white horse with *tricolore* caparisons, including the dancing plumes atop its head. He dismounts and climbs the steps to our pavilion. Louis rises and hands his former *général* a slip of paper on which are written the words of the oath to the Nation. Lafayette returns to the high altar at the center of the field. With great pageantry, he lays his naked sword upon it, mounts the steps to the topmost point, and shoulders the mighty flagpole, brandishing it with a flourish that can be seen throughout the entire arena as a cue that the oath is about to be pronounced.

A religious hush descends. In a strong, clear, almost defiant voice, Lafayette pledges to always be faithful to the Nation, the Law, and the King—in that order. I steal a glance at Louis. How does he feel to be named third?

"At least they still mention me," he murmurs.

Lafayette is vowing to protect the person and property of every Frenchman, all of whom are united "by the indissoluble ties of fraternity." When he stops speaking, the crowd thrusts their arms in the air. Those who carry swords brandish them with gusto. Nearly half a million voices cry en masse, "I swear it!"

And then it is the king's turn.

Louis rises from the throne. Taking a few steps forward he declaims, "I, King of the French, swear to employ the power delegated to me by the constitutional act of the State, in maintaining the Constitution decreed by the National Assembly, and by me accepted." I watch his face. Such a slight distinction to some—from King of France to King of the French, but the nomenclature is separated by a chasm, this Constitution. Louis is no more pleased than I am to be standing on this dais praying to the nation as if it were a deity, more powerful than the king who rules by divine right. My husband has been a charitable, just, and tolerant sovereign. A devout Catholic, his policies have nonetheless been favorable to believers of other religions. But the new laws that strip the clergy of their property, turning them into salaried servants of the State, have shocked and appalled him.

I must be the one to remind our subjects of their future. And so I lift the dauphin into my arms and hoist him as high as I can manage. "Don't be afraid, *mon petit*," I whisper; and then to put him at ease, I lie, "They are all your friends." With the greatest humility, I tell the crowd, "My good people, I present to you my son. He joins, as I do, in the same sentiments uttered by his father, and by the great Citoyen Lafayette. I will teach him to uphold those laws of which I trust he may one day be the stay and shield."

I clutch the dauphin to my chest and hold my breath, and in those moments I can feel his little heart beating against mine. As the people erupt into cheers, my smile finally becomes genuine. *"Vive le roi! Vive la reine! Vive Monseigneur le dauphin!"* The day has become as optimistic as sunshine.

The coda of this grand spectacle is a Te Deum that commences at five in the afternoon. The strains of a full orchestra fill the arena. At night the obelisk on the Champ de Mars is illuminated and people dance about its base as if the stone needle is a gigantic maypole. On either side, acrobats daringly scamper up swaying, reed-thin shafts several stories high. Descending from the summit of these circus poles, strings of lanterns create the impression of a single, enormous lampshade.

Despite the recurring rain, there is a banquet for twenty thousand guests at la Muette, one of the royal châteaux. For a people who have built the foundation of their Revolution on the purported excesses of a tone-deaf monarchy, they show no interest in stinting on their *fête de l'anniversaire*. The Fédération's festivities are intended to last for four days with celebrations held throughout Paris. Lanterns are strung from tree to tree in the Champs-Élysées, illuminating the entire boulevard with twinkling fairy lights.

"Tell me why this is so different from Trianon or Versailles?" I murmur to Louis as we stroll amid so many other women clad in gossamer white.

"*Regardez, ma chère,*" he replies, remarking upon their smiles and shining eyes. "Because they are all so filled with hope and happiness."

All I see is hypocrisy.

TEN

Safety Is Merely an Illusion

Back in my bedchamber at Saint-Cloud, my slumber is interrupted one August morning when a movement at my window sash causes me to bolt upright. "Campan!" I shriek. In an instant Henriette, who sleeps in a cot beside my bed, is wide awake.

"Run!" she shouts. But where does one run when a man, his features concealed by a thick scarf, is leaping toward you wielding an unsheathed knife, and your door is locked to prevent intruders from the corridors?

My fingers fumble with the bolt. I pound upon the thick panels of the door, crying *"Au secours!"* shouting for help and praying that the guard outside my chamber has not deserted his post. I jump back as I hear a thud on the opposite side of the room and the sound of shattering porcelain. In an effort to disarm him, Madame Campan has hurled a vase at our intruder.

My bodyguard, with another at his side, sabers aloft, crashes through the door to find the queen and her lady-in-waiting at either end of the counterpane using it the way a swordsman might wield his cape to parry the advancing blows of his attacker. Within moments my assailant is lying facedown on the carpet, his arms pinned behind him, the guard's boot heel placed squarely in the small of his back. Wordlessly the man is whisked out of my bed-chamber, his cries for mercy muffled by his disguise.

My heart is beating so rapidly that I cannot catch my breath. The princesse de Lamballe comes running with a glass of orange flower water sweetened with sugar, which she knows will soothe my nerves. My first thoughts are for the king and our children. Has anyone tried to harm them, too? But when an interrogation reveals that I was the sole target of the assassin's blade, I ask that the entire event be concealed from Madame Royale and the dauphin so as not to alarm them. The danger has passed. I have no wish to cause them nightmares. And when I remember that the dauphin has on occasion asked permission to pass the night with his maman—like his late grand-aunt Sophie, he is terrified of thunderstorms—I am gladder than ever that I refused his request.

When Louis learns that the attacker came in from the gardens, he convenes a committee to discuss how to best ensure the security of the royal family without, if possible, altering the public's privi-lege of promenading about the palace grounds. Axel—who visits the château only after dark—is present, as are Lafayette and Mira-beau. More guards? But an increased presence of armed men is no guarantee of their loyalty to the crown, Count von Fersen argues.

Axel is, unfortunately, prescient. A few weeks after the appre-hension in my bedchamber of the would-be murderer, an Italian named Rotondo who was a known Orléaniste, I begin to share a few morsels of my supper with Odin, the Swedish elkhound who was the count's gift to me six summers earlier, feeding the dog bits of roasted chicken from my plate before I partake of the meal. Mo-ments later, Odin begins to whine and chase his tail in circles. He tosses his head back spasmodically as if to bite something on the back of his own neck. Something is very wrong. I push my plate away and try to comfort my pet. The count, who is dining with us, also rushes to Odin's aid. The dog emits sounds I have never before heard and slinks off to his bed in the corner of the salon, placing his muzzle between his paws. His eyes are glassy and his expression is the most woeful thing I have ever seen. I try to hold him and stroke his thick neck, but he jumps, panicking at my touch. "Is there some sort of emetic we can give him?" I ask. What does one feed a sick dog? Then the drooling begins, and soon Odin's legs can no longer hold him. The seizures are violent.

"Come away, *ma chère,*" Louis gently urges. But I will not leave. Trembling, I remain on the floor, my ivory striped skirts puddled about me, embracing my dog, my lover's gift to me, my tears bathing Odin's gray and white coat until his strange whimpering and erratic breathing cease.

Hours later, when it is over, Axel helps me to my feet. My face is puffy and my eyes are swollen from weeping. I, too, am now a murderer.

"You couldn't have known," he soothes, stroking my hair and dabbing my tears with his handkerchief.

By midnight, a cook's apprentice has been arrested for poisoning the queen's supper. Everything on my plate, including the *petits-pois,* was deadly, liberally laced with strychnine.

From now on, the preparation of my food is carefully overseen by one of my own trusted attendants. Insisting that one can never be too careful, Madame Campan herself changes the contents of the powdered sugar in the bowl that is maintained in my room for *eau sucrée;* these days I am more often in need of the sweetened orange flower water than ever. Still, I think she is being overly cautious, if not wasteful, and heaven knows I have been criticized enough for profligacy. The scare is over, the culprit caught and imprisoned. "Henriette, they will not employ poison against me again.

They will use calumny," I say bitterly, "which is much more effective for killing people, and it is by that they will make me die."

Never was there a viler creature, a more venomous serpent than the one within the bosom of the Bourbons, that prince of the blood the duc d'Orléans. He is Grand Master of the Freemasons, an arcane society that my favorite sister Charlotte, Queen Maria Carolina of Naples has cautioned me about. The Freemasons seem to be hand-in-glove with the Illuminati, a breeding ground for revolutionary intelligentsia who intend to overthrow monarchies and create God-knows-what. Charlotte has pledged to destroy their vipers' nests wherever she can find them in her own kingdom. "Sister, they are lodged within your own realm as well. Beat them now, with a mighty stick, before it is too late," she warns.

We depart Saint-Cloud in October and move back to the Tuileries. In November, during one of his clandestine visits to the palace, the comte de Mirabeau brings more bad news concerning the duc d'Orléans and a nemesis from my past. The comtesse de Lamotte-Valois had returned from London. She'd been hiding in the English capital ever since someone had aided her escape from the Salpêtrière prison, where she'd been incarcerated for masterminding the plot to convince the former Grand Almoner of France, Cardinal de Rohan, to purchase a diamond necklace worth nearly two million livres. The comtesse had won the cardinal's trust by assuring him that not only was she an intimate of mine, but that I secretly coveted the extravagant bauble.

"Upon her arrival in Paris she was immediately offered sanctuary by Orléans," Mirabeau informs us. "The duc has established her in a magnificently appointed home on the Place Vendôme."

"He intends the insult to be known!" I exclaimed. "The more this malevolent woman, this criminal, is cosseted, the more I am made to appear the fool!"

"No one is more indignant than I at this news," Mirabeau assures me. "They mean to demand a new trial for Madame de Lamotte-Valois, in which, you can be certain, every slander she leveled against Your Majesty more than four years ago, and some new ones besides, will be spewed like invectives before a tribunal of magistrates who, this time will not even make a *pretense* of impartiality."

How well I recall the lies this horrid woman has told about me. Not only did she manage to convince *tout le monde* that I was both covetous and covert, when in fact I knew nothing about the entire transaction, but that she and I were lovers. A new edition of her memoirs has just been published across the Channel, in which the erstwhile comtesse has the gall to write, *The Queen turned her eyes on what she called my "outstanding attractions," then her soft lips, her kisses following her greedy, hungry glances over my quivering body— what a welcome substitute I made, she laughed, for the lumpish repulsive body of the "Prime Minister,"—her mocking name for the King.* A copy of this repugnant screed had been sent to me anonymously, wrapped in brown paper and tied with twine. I opened it in error, mistaking it for a gift from my dear duchesse de Polignac.

I had never met the comtesse de Lamotte-Valois and still have not done so to this day, nor would I ever wish to set eyes upon her. *"Calumny,"* I remind Madame Campan. "They will murder me with calumny."

"Never! I will tear you from your executioners or die in the attempt!" Mirabeau vows, his pockmarked face growing red with vitriol.

Yet every week seems to bring a fresh danger. Like a giant bellows, the Fête de la Fédération fanned the flames of Revolution into a bonfire. No sooner had they been uttered, than the cheers for the royal family that rainy day in mid-July died on our subjects' lips. A new world order is beginning to replace everything we have

known and revered, instigated by the increasingly radical demagogues of the National Assembly. The State is rife with anti-
clericalism. The clergy are painted as greedy, superstitious, and
corrupted representatives of an ancient system of order, bent on
suffocating rationality and reform.

With the heaviest heart, Louis has been compelled to sign a
decree that forces all priests to swear an oath to the new Constitution. If they do not do so, they will face certain prosecution, and be
forbidden to exercise their clerical functions. Rome of course disapproves of the Constitution, but the Pope's opinion has no impact on
the deputies of the Assembly. My husband is torn apart. In his
heart he naturally concurs with His Holiness. Yet Louis cannot
afford to stand by his scruples. It is just too dangerous.

The king's maiden aunts, Mesdames Adélaïde and Victoire,
horrified by the new decree, inform him that they no longer wish
to remain in a country where they cannot practice their religion
with complete freedom. On the 19th of February, 1791, the two
surviving daughters of Louis XV steal away from their residence,
the Château de Bellevue, in the unmarked carriage of a visiting
friend. When their departure is discovered, there is an outcry in the
National Assembly. Insidious propaganda published in the Revolutionary journals announces that the king's aunts left with a large
entourage and an even larger cache of money and gemstones, intending to use them as bribes for counterrevolutionary activities.

It is Mirabeau who comes to the Tuileries to tell us that the
princesses have been arrested in Burgundy by a local unit of the
Garde Nationale who at the behest of the Assembly intend to force
their return to Paris.

I tremble at the comte's account of the event. What must these
two intrepid women have thought when the traces of their carriage
were slashed by a mob, preventing them from traveling farther?

Surrounded by angry faces, and angrier fists pounding upon the doors of their coach, crying, "To the lamppost!" How they must have feared for their lives!

"You must help them," Louis pleads. In his watery blue gaze is the reminder of the monthly retainer he pays Mirabeau for his loyalty. "What quarrel could the nation have with two aging women, who have lived retired from court life for years?" True, they were quite the *intrigantes* in their day, especially Madame Adélaïde, who had taken me under her wing when I was dauphine, a naïve fourteen-year-old who knew so little of the Bourbon ways, and had used me as the unwitting weapon to destroy her own enemies at court, including her father's mistress, the comtesse du Barry. But the claws of these cats have been dulled by disuse. And with far greater enemies baying for our blood, I have long since forgiven Mesdames *tantes'* trespasses against me.

Louis pens a letter to the Assembly. He expresses his regret at the separation from his beloved aunts after enjoying the pleasure of their company for so many decades, but acknowledges that he has no right to deprive his relations of the same privilege afforded to even the humblest of France's citizens—the freedom to travel.

The issue is hotly debated in the Salle du Manège, but Mirabeau finally prevails, appealing to the Assembly's aspiration to be viewed as a wise and authoritative governmental body, rather than a convention of hotheads. "The rest of Europe will undoubtedly be greatly astonished on hearing that France's National Assembly spent four hours deliberating the departure of two old ladies who preferred to hear Mass at Rome rather than at Paris," he thunders. "Their promenading about the ruins of a former civilization does nothing to prevent our attaining the new civilization to which we aspire."

After this display of convincing eloquence the Assembly believes it has won, when in fact the victory has gone to the monarchy. Other royalists are beginning to quietly cross the borders, discreetly taking whatever they can carry. It is becoming popular to convert one's wealth into jewels as well as currency. It would be rather indiscreet to transport such items as paintings, tapestries, and fine furniture into Italy, the Netherlands, and Austria. Some believe the émigrés are craven; others, wise. I must occupy myself with the tribulations of my own family. No sooner do we exhale with relief at the safe passage arranged for Mesdames *tantes* than a package arrives at the Tuileries, a gift for the dauphin. Not yet five years old and still learning to read, he hands me the box and asks me to tell him what is engraved on the lid.

"Dominoes," I say curiously, and as I read the inscription aloud, my stomach turns. *"These stones, from the walls which enclosed the innocent victims of an arbitrary power, have been converted into a toy, to be presented to you, Monseigneur, as an homage of the people's love, and to teach you the extent of their power."*

"What does that mean, Maman?" My son reaches for the box with eager, chubby hands.

Liars and propagandists! There were only seven prisoners in the Bastille when it was stormed, each one a genuine convict. "It means, *mon chou d'amour,* that this is not a toy at all, but an insult. And we have better things to play with." I suggest to Madame de Tourzel that we make a game instead out of one of the fables of Monsieur de La Fontaine. "We can each take a part and act out the story."

Madame Royale takes the box from me and peruses its inscription for herself. Moments later, with all the force she can muster, she hurls it across the room. The box hits the opposite wall of the salon, nicking the ivory paint, and clatters open, spilling its macabre contents about the room like dozens of tiny bones. Then, one by one, and without a word, my daughter angrily tosses each domino into the fire.

On the last day of February we receive word of another insurrection. Rioting has begun in the Faubourg Saint-Antoine, incited by Monsieur Santerre, the same commander of the National Guard battalion who had hovered ominously behind my chair when the widow and son of the executed marquis de Favras attended our *grand couvert*. The rebels attack the castle of Vincennes, demolishing a parapet and dismantling parts of the dungeon. Perhaps it is just a rumor that we are in danger, but several noblemen, their weapons concealed beneath their cloaks, hasten to the Tuileries to defend the royal family. When Axel arrives for his daily visit, he insists that I barricade myself in my apartment. The mood, both on the streets of the capital and in the corridors of the château, is ugly. Rumors have been flying that the aristocrats intend to assassinate the National Guards who are on duty.

"Preposterous!" I exclaim. "Absurd."

"*C'est vrai,*" he agrees. "But the people believe it, nonetheless."

Madame de Tourzel brings the children to me. Campan and Lamballe follow, sailing down the long hallway in a rustle of taffeta. We listen through the bolted doors, hearts thumping beneath our stays. The sounds of brawling echo through the high ceilings and hard surfaces of the palace, raised voices, cries of pain, the sickening thud of musket butts connecting with human heads and limbs. When the tumult dies down, Madame Campan opens the doors cautiously and, turtlelike, peers about. All is well for the nonce. But the following day, the event is inflated out of all proportion, reported in the newspapers as *la Journée des Poignards*—the Day of Daggers—an attempt by *hundreds* of nobles, *armed to the teeth,* to perpetrate a massacre.

We are no longer safe in this palace. Nor, in the rebels' eyes, is the royal family their only enemy. The aristocracy of France—nay, anyone who expresses loyalist sympathies for us—is now marked as a traitor to their cause.

ELEVEN

Go?

⫷ SPRING 1791 ⫸

Our last chance has been taken from us.

"They say the comte de Mirabeau saw his parish priest for an hour, so his arrival in the other world must have been extremely painful," remarks Madame Élisabeth piously as she turns her embroidery hoop in her hands in order to catch a shaft of sunlight.

I do not know whether to credit illness, the melancholy to which he had lately succumbed, or his dissolute manner of living for Mirabeau's demise. They say the comte attended an orgy at the house of an opera dancer on March 28, the night he fell ill, and four days later he was dead. But what does it matter, really? He is gone all the same, only forty-two, just seven years my senior. I weep for the lion of the Revolution, whose candle was snuffed out too soon. And yet the last time we had seen him, Mirabeau had confided in the king his fears that he had already done his best for us. "There are no more moderates in the Salle du Manège," he had intoned, shaking his huge head. "The deputies no longer wish to listen to me, or even to Lafayette. The *Journée des Poignards* in February was not the culmination of their fervor. It was the beginning."

The comte de Mirabeau is to be interred with great pomp within the new Pantheon. Louis is despondent, believing the statesman's passing signals the monarchy's mournful coda.

It is becoming clear that flight may be our best option. Paris is too hot, as Mirabeau might have said. Perhaps it is merely my imagination, but in the wake of his death the streets seem flooded with a new inundation of scurrilous pamphlets. Most denounce me in the same vein as the *libelles* have done in the past. But now I am presumed to have a different panoply of lovers, as so many of the nobles I was once accused of bedding have long since been banished or fled. Now they claim I have slept with at least two-thirds of the soldiers in the National Guard.

Louis takes to his bed with a fever. My husband, whose health has always been hale, is coughing blood. His body drips with perspiration. His hair, beginning to gray with woe, is damply plastered to his forehead. "I made the wrong decision," he repeats, referring to his Christmastime capitulation to the revolutionaries, his signing of the decree forcing France's priests to swear fealty to an entity and a document that is beneath divine law. The Pope is dismayed, if not angry with his action, insisting that even if the sovereign had to abdicate the rights inherent in the royal prerogative, he has no right to alienate and abandon what belongs to God, and as King of France, Louis is His eldest son.

"I did it for the public safety," Louis mutters, his voice choked with emotion. "If I had refused, it would have been a certainty that priests and nobles alike would be massacred by our enemies. If His Holiness could but see what is happening here . . . the awful choices that faced me . . ." My husband sobs like an infant. His conscience rent, he pens a pledge to build a church in honor of the Sacred

Heart. "O, God, You see all the wounds that tear my heart and the depths of the abyss into which I have fallen." I visit Louis's bedside several times a day, in between my secret sessions with Count von Fersen, wherein I am becoming a skilled mistress at the art of cryptography.

What will become of his family if Louis dies? Will I be sent back to Austria? Dispatched to a convent for the remainder of my days? Imprisoned for life? After all, I remain the revolutionaries' raison d'être for all the nation's ills. In October 1789, soon after we first arrived at the Tuileries, I became aware of a plan to effect my escape. Without my permission my private secretary, Jacques-Mathieu Augeard, a former tax collector, developed an entire plot where I would quit the Tuileries alone under cloak of secrecy and seek sanctuary with my brother the emperor in Vienna, leaving an apologetic note to my husband and children. Augeard was convinced that France might be saved from descending into the abyss of Revolution were I to martyr myself by sacrificing my family and my crown so that my husband might retain his, and the dauphin would have one to inherit.

"Unthinkable!" I'd exclaimed, when Monsieur Augeard revealed his idea to me. "I would never leave my children! Nor could I allow the king to remain in the bosom of his enemies. I have pledged, to myself, to His Majesty, and to God, that our family shall never be separated. And if need be, I will uphold my promise with my dying breath."

Yet—though we must stay together, we cannot stay here. The notion of emigrating to an area with strong monarchist sympathies, whether in France or across her borders, holds an increasing allure for me. Louis is still reluctant to leave his kingdom, but remaining in Paris is a dangerous prospect.

At least, after the Day of Daggers, we both agree that we cannot stay in the Tuileries. Most of our servants are spies. The new bodyguards, Lafayette's own troops, are our enemies. On Palm Sunday, just two weeks after the comte de Mirabeau drew his last breath, the king insists on hearing Mass said by the Cardinal de Montmorency, one of the brave nonjuring priests who continues to push back with all the might of his faith against the tidal force of the Revolution's new zealots. Upon Louis's return from the chapel, the grenadiers of the Garde Nationale refuse to line the route of his carriage, exposing him to attack.

This in itself is an act of defiance, yet that is how the Assembly views my husband's refusal to hear Mass from a cleric who has sworn the oath to uphold the Constitution. The following day I am awakened by Hanet Cléry, the king's loyal valet, with the news that His Majesty has decided to remove the royal family to Saint-Cloud so that he may convalesce in peace. We communicate in hushed voices only amongst ourselves and our most trusted attendants. The princesse de Lamballe and Madame Campan know our plans, although they will remain at the Tuileries. Ably assisted by Madame Élisabeth, the marquise de Tourzel prepares the children of France for the short journey, dressing them in their best clothes.

But word of our sojourn has somehow spread like a spark in dry straw. A crowd—no, a mob—is gathered in the vast cobbled courtyard, spreading into the Place du Carrousel, cawing and baying like animals, and as our family is assisted into our carriage they accuse the king of quitting the capital in order to *unconstitutionally* complete his Easter Week worship! "You saw me; I did not receive communion from the cardinal this morning," Louis mutters to me behind his handkerchief. Never in our lifetimes has the Catholic Church been under such an assault. There are nearly as many *libelles* denouncing nuns and priests for fornication and corruption as there are scurrilous pamphlets proclaiming me a harpy and a whore. Demagogues with loud voices and an aura of authority feed the poison to the illiterate, or those too lazy or too poor to read the lies for themselves. In January, Mirabeau had foretold that the resignation of 20,000 priests who preferred to leave their parish rather than swear the Constitutional oath would produce an anti-Revolutionary reaction within the kingdom that would cripple the National Assembly's authority. What would he say today if he knew that things had only become worse?

The jeering throng refuses to countenance our departure. The horses barely leave the confines of the Tuileries when their bridles are seized by a number of men and our coach is brought to a jolting halt.

"What is happening, Maman?" asks Madame Royale, and I unlatch the window and peer outside. The members of the Garde Nationale are making no effort to disengage the ruffians from the harnesses. I worry about the beasts, who are frightened by the commotion. They aren't war horses, which are trained not to shy from mayhem and artillery fire. I crane my neck and look to the rear of the carriage. Having deserted their perch, our bewigged postilions are racing to the front of the conveyance to offer their assistance to the coachman, yet as soon as they attempt to free the bridles, the grenadiers raise their sabers, threatening our royal servants with bodily harm if they dare to continue.

Our carriage is rocked from side to side like a child's toy. The dauphin begins to cry and I pull him onto my lap and gather him into my arms, covering his ears with my hands. Madame Royale's face is pale as hair powder. I shut the window when I hear a volley of muskets and a clatter of hoofbeats. The crowd suddenly moves away from the coach. Soon the faces of Lafayette and Monsieur Bailly peer into our windows. Then they step back and order the guards to do their duty and clear a passage for our departure.

But the general and the mayor face a surprising rebellion from their own troops. "We do not wish the king to leave!" shouts one of the grenadiers. Placing his hand upon his heart he adds, "We swear that they shall never leave!" This soon becomes a sickening chant.

Louis has had enough. He opens the window and calls for silence. When his command proves ineffective, he sticks his arm outside the window and frantically waves his handkerchief. I bury my face in my hands. Of all the things: a surrender.

But my husband's words are just the opposite of capitulation. "My good people," he begins, "it would be extraordinary if, having given the Nation its liberty, I should not be free myself!"

Reason and logic, alas, mean nothing to a mob nourished by the poison of their demagogues. "Fat pig!" *"Cochon!"* "Damn aristo!" The insults and epithets fly, accompanied by deliberately aimed spittle. Louis quickly ducks inside the window. With tremendous dignity, he takes the handkerchief and wipes away the gobbet of mucus that rests upon his cheek like a malevolent tear.

Agonizing minutes pass as we remain the people's captives. Finally, unable to subdue his own adherents, Lafayette taps upon the window with the handle of his riding crop. Louis unlatches it and receives his former general's suggestion to proclaim martial law. "Force is the only effective remedy, Sire."

"I do not wish blood to be shed for me," the king succinctly replies.

And so we sit. And bide the time. I steal glances at my father's gold watch. At length, the little dial with its white porcelain face and two black hands, like tiny arrows piercing Time and Memory, tell me that two hours have passed since we first started for Saint-Cloud.

"Papa, je dois faire pipi—" says the dauphin plaintively.

"Can you hold it in," I ask, "like a brave little boy?"

His eyes are moist, his mouth a fearful pout. *"Sais pas.* I don't know," he says apologetically.

Finally, the menacing mood outside the carriage begins to lift, and when he senses it is safe enough to do so, Louis opens the door and descends the folding steps. "So, you do not wish me to depart?" he asks, addressing the mob with his customary sangfroid. He waits for a response but not a single voice replies. "It is not possible, then, for me to leave?" Again, no one dares to speak. "Very well then, I shall stay," he says. His voice betrays no hint of disappointment or dismay as he starts to walk back toward the palace, his ambling, rolling gait evincing no sense of urgency, nor conveying any impression that the hundreds, if not thousands, of hellions who had prevented our departure had in any way disrupted his day.

I am less successful at containing my emotions. As we mount the steps of the Tuileries I slip my arm through the king's, drawing us closer. My tone is sharp even if my words are not. "You must admit now that we are no longer free."

TWELVE

An Old Friend Returns

Mademoiselle Rose Bertin stands before me majestically. I have not seen the influential modiste since 1787 when I severed our thirteen-year relationship during a time of considerable economic uncertainty and fiscal restraint. The intervening time has been kind to her. Beneath her high black hat crowned with red, white, and blue plumes, her brown hair is unpowdered although I detect some silver threads amid the sausage-thick curls that cascade past her shoulders. Powder, regardless of its origin, has fallen out of fashion. Only the nobility still favors it. The "people" deride us for being out of touch with their sympathies, recalling the Flour Wars of the mid-1770s; but I believe our tonsorial preferences remain in deliberate defiance of the current mode. What marquise or vicomte these days would not *desire* to set themselves apart from, and above, the filthy, clamorous rabble?

Where do Mademoiselle Bertin's sympathies lie? I must know this before I tell her why I have summoned her—invited, she would say—to my *lever*.

She looks about her, her sharp eyes undoubtedly remarking that no one else in the salon is paying homage to the mania for tricolored accoutrements. Hers is the only hat embellished with the striped ribbon cockade. She wears a simple royal blue redingote over a striped underskirt, the ruffle at the hem her only nod to a past enamored of the most feminine furbelows. The simplicity of the new fashion suits her height and broad shoulders, which are draped with a fichu of white organza—the same style favored by the women of means who fancy themselves enlightened, who have turned their backs on the monarchy and their duplicitous faces toward the forces of insurrection and instability.

Rose does not curtsy to me. But then, she never did, even in 1774 when I had just ascended the throne and she wished to secure the custom of the new Queen of France. I wait a few more moments to see if she will find her manners. At least she does not sit in my presence without being asked by me to do so. "I understand you are selling your designs to my enemies these days: the revolutionaries." I tilt my chin at her and smile.

"They call themselves republicans now," Rose replies with a soupçon of asperity. In spite of the wealth and notoriety she established from catering to the nobility, she is *au fond* a policeman's daughter. Now that the social battle lines have been drawn with even bolder strokes her tents, no matter how opulent, are pitched closer to Them than to Us.

"And I am a merchant, *Majesté*. A woman of business. Politics must remain *hors de marché* if any of us is to survive and thrive. If I were to shun a particular clientele, whether aristo or *sans-culotte*, I should soon be shuttering my shop."

Once the rituals of my *lever* are over I dismiss my entourage, except for Madame Campan, inviting Rose to remain. I motion to a chair closer to me, upholstered in aqua and green striped silk. "Are you not tired of creating so many tricolored ensembles, mademoiselle? All those virginal white gowns. True, the sleeves are no longer puffed, but straight, yet I would imagine that it must exact a toll upon one's imagination to create so many barely adorned ensembles, nearly every one identical to the last." I favor her with another smile. "One might as well go into the business of sewing uniforms."

Rose's upper lip quivers and I see I have struck a resonant chord. But she quickly regains her equanimity. "I sew what people wish to buy, *Majesté*."

"Ah! But what if one wishes to buy something else?" Folding my hands in my lap, I say, "I am tired of mumming, mademoiselle. I have spent nearly two years adorning myself like a 'patriot' as a way of demonstrating my comprehension of some of their demands, to show that I respect their desire for more equality and control. But the people continue to despise me nonetheless. They spread the vilest calumnies about me. So from now on I have decided to please myself. Madame Éloffe lacks your gifts of embellishment and she certainly has not your eye for proportion, color, and harmony." I wait for a reaction, but it seems that Rose is doing the same, biding her time to see what sort of proposition I will make.

"I would like to commission a number of new garments." Rose's eyes widen. Then she breaks into a laugh. She could have been a spider regarding a fly who had foolishly returned to her web.

I catch Madame Campan's eye and let it pass, for the *marchande*'s reaction is painfully close to the mark. "I would like you to make up gowns in shades of lavender and violet," I continue. "One or two in green, as well," I say, fully aware that this is the color of the banished comte d'Artois's liveries. I am feeling defiant. "And some yellow—perhaps a subtle damask, or a stripe resembling alternating butter and cream—with black trimmings." I wave my hand, a gesture that dismisses my efforts to design the entire wardrobe myself. "Well, I leave it to your impeccable artistry. And at least two black dresses: They call me *l'Autrichienne* with venom in their voices, but I am proud of my Hapsburg forebears and will wear my family's colors. Not only that, I would like some black cockades for my hats." I am changing my appearance yet again, perhaps for the fifth time during my sixteen-year reign; still, I can feel the tension dissipating within my breast as I voice the decision not to act a role anymore, at least not to play a part other than the one I was wedded to forever: that of Queen of France.

I do not yet know if I can trust Mademoiselle Bertin entirely as I once did. We used to spend several hours a week alone together and she knew nearly as much about me and almost as many of my secrets as Mesdames de Lamballe and Polignac, my closest confidantes. But would Rose now be willing to betray me for some revolutionary ideal? The gowns and accoutrements I am commissioning from her will be packed up and taken with us on our flight from the Tuileries. When we arrive at our ultimate destination, requesting sanctuary from our persecutors, I cannot resemble some apologetic, craven refugee. I must appear every inch the Queen of France.

I explain that the garments will need to be finished as soon as possible. "You will have to visit the palace several times a week for our discussions and fittings." I sink my chin and cheek into my hand, resting my elbow on the arm of my chair. "It will be like the old days." Rose thinks about my proposal in the way she always has, stringing me along, acting as though it is she who is doing me the favor. "There will undoubtedly be a great deal of comment," I add, wanting to make sure that she will accept the commission because she desires to renew her relationship with the monarchy. "Your republican clients may no longer wish to maintain their custom with Le Grand Mogol," I say, referring to her shop, "after they hear you are regularly visiting the queen."

Her cheeks flush. "No one has ever told me how to manage my

business! There is more than one reason I remain unwed." A slight smile plays across her lips. "If you think I am to be cowed by one patron for the sake of another, no matter who she is, you forget who sits beside you."

Mademoiselle Rose Bertin may be the one woman in France who is more imperious than her queen. I have summoned my former *marchande de modes* because I believe her to be one of the only citizens, and certainly the only Parisian modiste of her caliber, whom I can trust. But I do not divulge the purpose of her assignment. Not yet. After all, we are surrounded by spies. How can I be certain that she will not become another one, her proximity rendering it all the easier to study my daily habits and movements and discover our plans?

I turn to Madame Campan after Rose departs. Her gray eyes are filled with trepidation. She looks displeased. I splay my hands, emphasizing my incomprehension of her frown. "*Quoi?* What troubles you?"

She shakes her head, unwilling at first to reply, because I see that she wishes to challenge my judgment. When I remind her that she will not be punished for speaking her mind to me, she says, with increasing distress, "Where are you going to fit all that clothing?"

"Most of the trunks will follow behind us—in the coach with my two ladies-in-waiting." I can see that this is the first time Campan has realized that we do not intend to flee alone, but there is to be something of a caravan. Yet, how else could it be? Once we reach our destination, who would see to our needs? How could we resume our lives as if nothing had happened?

I have never seen Henriette so agitated. "With the greatest respect, *Majesté*, you will be able to purchase everything you require wherever you may find yourself. By acquiring an entire wardrobe in advance of your journey, with Mademoiselle Bertin coming and going at all hours—which will be known to every guard in the palace—not to mention the difficulty of packing so many items, when you may need to flee with haste and subtlety, and travel as light as possible the better to speed your journey to safety . . ." Her words trail off as her eyes fill with tears.

On the fifth of June the monarchy is dealt another buffet by the National Assembly when they deny the king his prerogative of the pardon. "What more can these monsters do to diminish your power?" I lament to Louis.

"I dare not imagine." He shudders. "As things stand now, I would rather be king of Metz than king of France."

After days of lengthy discussion, acknowledging that we have no alternative but escape, Louis has settled on Montmédy, a frontier town, from which we can seek sanctuary in the nearby fortress of Luxembourg. My brother, Emperor Leopold of Austria, already has 10,000 troops garrisoned there, kept at the ready on the border, should we require their aid. In Paris, the troops are becoming more republican by the day. Nobles are quietly emigrating. Few souls remain who can guarantee our security. There are more royalists in the countryside than in the city and one of them, an ardent loyalist, the Lieutenant-Général marquis de Bouillé, is in command of the town.

Although by now Louis is exhausted from all the pretense, past caring, I believe, about demonstrating any sympathy toward the Revolution, it is no reason to become careless. Every aspect of our flight must be meticulously planned. Count von Fersen has agreed to coordinate the details. He will secure passports for us and negotiate the purchase of a private, unmarked coach that is large enough to carry the entire royal family.

"But our funds are quite compromised at present," Louis informs Axel. "And this plan will be costly. We may even have to purchase the silence and cooperation of some of our guards and attendants."

Surely not the armed men who sleep on mattresses outside our doors so that we cannot escape, I think ruefully.

"I will handle all of the financial arrangements," Axel assures my husband. "*I* have funds. As well as a cadre of loyalist friends." I regard Count von Fersen, with his military background and bearing, and know there is no one else we can trust to save us. Axel has pledged his heart and soul to me and to my safety and he is the one man in the world I have never doubted. Unlike the king, his resolve does not waver. And heaven help us, we are in desperate need of a man such as he to carry out the plot unfailingly!

"About the escape route out of Paris," the king says to Axel. "We appear to have three options, none of them ideal. Bouillé suggests the road to Flanders as the shortest and safest, but that means quitting France, however temporarily, and entering Montmédy from a foreign realm. I refuse to leave my kingdom's borders for any reason."

Axel arches an eyebrow. "Not even to save your life and that of your family?" He glances at me, but intends the king to assume he is referring to the dauphin, the future of the Bourbon dynasty.

"During the Glorious Revolution of 1688, James the Second of England left his throne and sailed to safety in France. When he wanted his kingdom back, it was too late. In the eyes of most of his subjects, save the staunch Jacobeans, he had already forfeited it."

I argue that what happened to another king of another land in another time is irrelevant, but Louis scolds me and insists that history inculcates us with lessons that we are doomed to repeat unless we learn from our predecessors' mistakes. When he does not mention another king of Britain who lost both his crown and his head after his subjects erupted into civil war, I hold my tongue, for I know full well that the fate of James II's father Charles I is in the forefront of his mind. Still, Louis has always been stubborn. He has rejected, though rightly, Bouillé's alternate proposal to pass through Rheims. True, there are fewer towns and cities along the route, but the king's face is too easily recognized, as he was crowned there.

Axel and Louis discuss the third possible route of escape. This would take us through a number of small towns and villages, including Bondy, Châlons-sur-Marne, Clermont, and Varennes. "After the royal family reaches Châlons-sur-Marne, Sire, may I suggest that the coordination of the journey's details be consigned to the marquis de Bouillé, or at the very least, that he remain fully informed of the plans, for his knowledge of the area is far greater than ours."

Everything must be organized, not only with stealth, but with swiftness. Louis elects to leave the Tuileries just days from now, on June 19, between midnight and one A.M., after the last shift of guards has exchanged their posts with those who keep watch through the night.

Axel visits the Tuileries each day to keep us apprised of developments. I still cannot imagine how we will sneak past the six hundred armed men who are constantly on guard throughout the palace. "Two-thirds of them will not be on duty when you depart. You only have to evade two hundred," he reminds me with a grin.

But how to deceive *them*? I am followed nearly everywhere I go within the confines of the Tuileries. Members of Lafayette's bodyguard remain stationed as sentries outside the doors to each of the royal apartments.

"You escaped the mob of murderers at Versailles by ducking through a hidden door and down an internal corridor," Axel ruminates, as he runs a hand through his thick brown hair. He no longer powders it, his sole concession to Revolutionary tastes. He paces my salon, tentatively patting the walls and examining every seam in the hand-painted paper for a clue. At length, he stands before an ornate chest of drawers inlaid with Sèvres tiles and striated mala-chite. "Why would someone place this here?" he murmurs to himself. Axel taps the wall above the chest and turns back to face me with a dazzling smile. He extends his arm, motioning for me to join him, and I take his hand as he sweeps me into an embrace. "It's hollow behind there," he whispers triumphantly. I feel his heart beating wildly against mine and quickly bring my lips to his before we both turn to regard the wall.

Axel strips off his silk coat, tossing it on a chair. "We must move the chest aside," he announces, still whispering. "On the parquet it will make a noise unless I place something soft beneath each of the legs."

I have just the thing. I unlock a cabinet and bring him a stack of bound pamphlets. *Libelles.*

"You save these?" he asks incredulously. "If I were you, I would burn every single scurrilous, lying diatribe."

"Such a conflagration would engulf all of Paris," I sigh.

After moving the chest, Axel discovers a circular latch hidden inside the wall behind it. "Where does this lead?" he asks.

I shrug. "I'm not sure." Nor am I certain whether it is wise to explore, for the pair of us could walk right into the bayonets of the Garde Nationale. But Axel is all for taking the risk. He lifts the latch and turns it as silently as possible, then pushes the door open ever so slightly. At the sound of a creak my heart skips two beats and I nearly jump out of my gown. "Oil?" he whispers.

All I have is lamp oil, spermaceti imported from America. But it will do. Axel oils the hinges with the frothy cuff of his sleeve and peers cautiously into the darkness. The hidden door opens onto a narrow internal corridor. We tiptoe along the hall and encounter another door. "What is behind here?" the count asks.

"It must be Madame de Ronchreuil's room," I reply, closing my eyes and picturing the layout of the palace from the opposite side of this corridor.

"Is she to be trusted?"

"She is one of the few attendants the Assembly has permitted me to retain. But I think it is because she is not well known to the Revolution as one of my confidantes. Her mother was a friend of mine. When she grew ill, she asked me to take Anne-Sophie into my service so that the girl would have a future." I scratch the door with the nail of my little finger. Moments later, a pretty blond woman opens the door and peers at us.

She drops into a curtsy and, on rising, beckons us into the room. There are vases of fresh flowers on every surface. Madame de Ronchreuil spends quite a bit of time in the Tuileries Gardens. "Come in, *Majesté*. Monsieur le comte," she whispers, her expression confused. "What are you doing in there?"

"Following the trail of a mouse that skirted the edges of Her Majesty's floorboards and dashed beneath a chest when we tried to trap him," Axel lies. Anne-Sophie, given to giggles, and somewhat smitten, I have become aware, by what my childhood writing tutor Herr Mesmer would have called the comte's *magnétisme animal,* forgets her curiosity in favor of hospitality.

While I engage my attendant in a discussion of the various blooms that freshen the aroma of her small chamber, Axel is glancing about the room. A large framed mirror hangs over a door. "What does that portal lead to?" he asks mildly.

"Oh, that goes to the *appartement* of the duc de Villequier," Anne-Sophie replies. "But it is not occupied anymore. Monsieur le duc emigrated at the beginning of June."

I would have to procure the key to it. No sentries were ever stationed at the front door to the duc's rooms. If the royal family were to trace the steps Axel and I had just taken, we could manage to descend a flight of stairs that would lead us to the courtyard at an hour of the night when, just according to our plan, many people would be coming and going from the palace.

"Must find that mouse!" Axel finally says, giving us a reason to quit Madame de Ronchreuil's room. "You must be doubly certain of her loyalty," he warns me, once we have returned safely to my salon. "And then, either she must be taken into your confidence or you should find a pretext to send her elsewhere on the night of the nineteenth."

I agree to undertake the coordination of our escape within the palace. For some reason, my mind is filled with reminiscences of happier days spent in my little theater at the Petit Trianon. Madame Campan's father had been our prompter. Yet he also made sure that everyone was in the proper costume, holding the requisite stage properties, and standing in the wings on the appropriate side of the stage, ready to make their entrances at the proper moment. Could his loyal daughter ably assist me in this most perilous of productions? Perhaps if I focus my mind upon the specific movements of all the players, I will not be too overcome by fear or timidity to accomplish what we must at all costs.

Axel favors me with a look of pure admiration. "Do you know what Mirabeau once said to me? About you?"

I cross the salon and take his hand, turning it over and pressing my lips to his palm. "*Non.* I cannot imagine. What did he say? And why to you?"

"To whom else could he confide that 'The king has only one man with him—his wife!'"

THIRTEEN

Delay

Two boxes and two men are before me, cast in shadow by the candle glow flickering in my salon. I rest my fingers lightly upon the case covered in green cardan leather tooled with my cipher in gold and instruct the comte de Mercy to see that it is conveyed to my favorite sister, the Queen of Naples. "These are Hapsburg jewels," I explain to the ambassador. "If anything should happen to me, Charlotte should have them." I wear a brave mask, but the act of divesting myself of such treasures is overwhelming because I do so in anticipation of some mishap. A lump rises in my throat. I wonder, too, after we depart, whether I will ever see Mercy again. All these years I have accepted his presence in my life, both politically and personally, as something permanent. Now I feel what it must be like to stand barefooted upon the sand.

My *friseur* Léonard Hautier looks at me expectantly. "You know I will rely upon your services after we reach Montmédy," I remind him. Léonard has been dressing my hair since 1774, a month after my ascension. Pointing to the red leather box: "This is the jewelry that I will require once we reach our destination. I am entrusting you to ride on ahead of our carriage, taking it with you." Swallowing hard, I add, "As we intend to travel incognito, we cannot be observed at any of the checkpoints with such valuables in our possession. It would arouse suspicion."

Léonard begins to sob, clearly overcome by the responsibility. He whips a handkerchief out of the turned-back cuff of his yellow moiré coat before he stains the silk with his tears. Sinking to his knees, he clasps my hands in his, kissing my knuckles. "I am beholden to you, *Majesté*. I cannot find the words to express my gratitude for the honor you are bestowing upon me." His hands flutter nervously about his breast and I must convince myself that I have made the right decision.

"Well, you are the only one who knows how to do most of the clasps," I feebly jest.

I hear a scratching at the door leading to the inside staircase that links my husband's apartment with mine. Madame Campan opens it to admit the king, followed by Count von Fersen.

"The comte has purchased a carriage," Louis announces, "in his own name, of course," then regales me with the details of the heavy traveling berline, the sort of conveyance designed to comfortably transport a large party for a great distance. "This could take us all the way to Saint Petersburg, if need be!" my husband exclaims. "And with not one, but two iron cooking stoves, one of which will heat meat, and a canteen that will hold a greater number of bottles and a cupboard to store food, it will eliminate the necessity of our disembarking at every coaching station when the horses are changed." Axel mentions the luxuries that he knows are certain to delight me: the clothes press and the silver dinner service, and—for the dauphin, especially, who always needs to "*faire pipi,*" or more, the minute we embark anywhere, a close-stool. Then Louis rhap-

CONFESSIONS OF MARIE ANTOINETTE

sodizes about the elements that have always intrigued *him*: the method in which the carriage has been constructed, with additional features to strengthen it for the rigors of our flight—washers, bolts, rivets, buckles, and axle-nuts, clamps for something called swingle bars, and iron-fitted forks designed to steady the berline on vertiginous mountain roads.

I ask if there will be room to transport my collapsible breakfast table, a marvel of cabinetry, which, as various sprung wings open or fold inwards, functions as a work table and storage unit for my embroidery, as well as a *secrétaire* for my correspondence. And I have no intention of traveling without my walnut picnic basket that also functions as a dressing case, with its own silver basin, mirror, and miniature candlesticks to illuminate it. How else can I make my toilette each morning?

Axel assures me in the affirmative—although I may have to rest the basket upon my lap—but cautions that the more laden the berline, the slower it will move, and time will of course be of the essence, as will darkness, for we have chosen to travel on the second-shortest night of the year and we cannot depart until midnight.

"Do not forget your other news!" Louis reminds him. My husband is in higher spirits today than I have seen him in months. Perhaps it is the idea that safety lies but days away; the securing of the means of arriving at our sanctuary is now a reality.

Axel opens his diplomatic pouch and breaks the seal on an inner envelope. "A fellow countrywoman of mine, baronne de Korff, the widow of a Russian officer, has agreed to provide her own passports for your journey. One passport covers a family of four: herself, her husband, and two daughters; the other is for the servants."

"But won't she have need of them if she plans to emigrate?" I ask Axel. "Things are growing worse for our sympathizers by the day."

"After you have safely reached Montmédy, she intends to report her passports stolen. The Assembly will replace them."

I glance at Louis. "We should meet her to thank her for her generosity."

Axel shakes his head. "I do not advise it. The less she is implicated in the plan of escape, the better it will be for all concerned. We must protect the baronne's safety at all costs. In this way, if she is ever interrogated she can truthfully say that she has never met the royal family, nor had any contact with them whatsoever."

I sense that there is more, for Count von Fersen averts his gaze from mine. Is this widow something special to him? I know that he has taken a house in Paris but I do not know what Axel does with his time when he is not here, although he visits me daily. I do not like to dwell on the possibility that there could be other women in his life. After all, I once described Axel to Monsieur Fargeon, my parfumier, as the most virile man I knew, and despite my feelings I have no right to expect that sort of fidelity from him when it cannot be mutual. If I permit my imagination to run away with itself, I will make myself ill. And I must not allow my energy to be distracted from the matter of our escape.

"If I divulge this secret, you must promise to let it die on your ears the moment you receive it," Axel whispers.

My belly does a little flutter, as if a butterfly took wing from a blossom. But then, why would the count say such a thing in the presence of my husband?

"The baronne de Korff is one of the angels who is helping to financially subsidize your flight," he informs us.

I exhale and feel the natural color return to my cheeks.

"You must convey our immense gratitude to the baronne," Louis tells him, "as well as to our other saviors who wish to remain nameless for their own protection." He leaves us to discuss further particulars of our departure, having abrogated the lion's share of the planning to me.

In truth, it is Axel whose efforts on our behalf have been extraordinary. He remains in constant contact with the marquis de Bouillé, to be certain that the route we intend to take will remain open, checking with each communication to ensure that there is still not a hair's breadth of suspicion. And it is Axel who has secretly determined that three soldiers of the royal bodyguard, messieurs Monstrei, Valorg, and de Malden, remain totally loyal to the monarchy and are willing to aid in our flight, dressed as servants. He has also identified the nobles who will accompany us disguised as *estafettes,* mounted couriers. Louis is aware that Axel has received his sovereign's commission to be his eyes and ears here in France, but Gustavus of Sweden, while our sworn ally, is not funding our escape. I doubt Louis realizes that Axel has personally mortgaged his own estates there, and has even borrowed money from his steward to finance our journey. How can I not take him at his word, when, with a gaze that would melt the snows of the Grossglockner, he assures me, "I live only to serve you"?

A knock at the door of my salon indicates someone unfamiliar with court etiquette. It is Claudette Junot, the new assistant to Madame Éloffe, assigned to the daily care of my wardrobe. The National Assembly placed her in my retinue. The Assembly does not want the servants assigned to the royal household to stay too long in our employment, for fear that they will become too attached to us. As if Louis, Madame Élisabeth, and I possessed the magical powers of transforming them from revolutionaries into royalists!

Claudette ushers Mademoiselle Bertin into the room, never taking her eyes off the *marchande de modes.* Quietly she closes the doors and remains within the room, watching Rose's back as the modiste opens a satchel and removes a large parcel wrapped in butcher's paper and sealed with twine. The package contains some of the disguises the royal family will wear when we sneak out of the Tuileries.

Rose takes a handkerchief from her cuff and brings it to her mouth to cover a cough I know she does not have. Her eyes tell me to dismiss the girl from the room immediately.

"*C'est tout, Claudette. Vous pouvez allez maintenant.* You may go," I tell her. I can see that she is suppressing her disappointment, but when has she ever been admitted to a confidential tête-à-tête with Mademoiselle Bertin? Claudette backs out of the room, and when she closes the doors in front of her, she does so with deliberate *longueur*, as if she expects me to commence my conversation with Rose while the portals remain partially ajar.

We wait for an audible click, and then Madame Campan rises and bolts the door. The *modiste* cocks her head toward it, indicating her suspicion that Claudette is listening at the keyhole. We take chairs on the farthest side of the room, and Rose murmurs, "I don't like that girl. When I arrived today I saw her kissing one of the bodyguards. She has a sweetheart among Lafayette's men and doesn't seem to mind who knows it."

We have no time to waste wondering what Claudette may suspect, or if she has conveyed anything to her lover. At best, she is an ardent revolutionary with no respect for the monarchy. At worst, she was planted among my women as a spy.

"How much longer will she be at her post?" Rose inquires.

"Through the nineteenth of June."

"Impossible! You cannot take such risks. What would happen if you delayed your departure for twenty-four hours?"

A shudder undulates through my spine, zigzagging through every eyelet of my stays. *What would happen if we didn't?*

FOURTEEN

Flight

JUNE 20, 1791

Although I fight to conceal any outward show of anxiety, my nerves have been frayed ever since the break of day. Louis spends the morning alone in his study while I attend my children's lessons. The king had desired one of the courtiers to accompany the royal family inside the berline this evening—and he had named a few noblemen who were excellent shots with a pistol, should it be necessary to defend us—a prospect that nearly sent me into a panic. But Madame de Tourzel had tearfully insisted that whatever the dangers, she would never abandon her charges; and so she will join us tonight, along with Madame Élisabeth.

I do not yet tell my children about this evening's excursion. The dauphin is a garrulous little boy and is too young to entrust with such a big secret for so many hours. Madame Royale can hold her tongue, but she is an inquisitive child and I have no intention of holding a discourse on "why" and "because" with her now.

At noon, the entire royal family attends Mass in the chapel. I pray for our safety as well as that of Monsieur and Madame, who will also depart clandestinely tonight, taking the road for Brussels.

I take the children for our usual walk in the gardens at four. While Madame de Tourzel looks after the dauphin, I divulge our plans to Madame Royale in order to prepare my daughter's mind for the journey ahead. I realize my error in doing so immediately when she begins to color and grow anxious. Heads are turning. I take her by the shoulders and remind her to be strong. "You are a daughter of France, Mousseline."

"But what shall I say when everyone asks me why I appear so agitated?"

She is so serious that I forget sometimes she is only thirteen years old. I clasp her wrist and give her a cross look as I bend down and get so close to her that our noses are nearly touching. Then I wink so that she sees I am not in earnest. "Tell them you are upset because I scolded you."

Louis and I know that our entire day must have a semblance of normalcy. But even the king's phlegmatic temperament is ruffled when Axel is announced during our afternoon game of billiards. The count has come to discuss the final arrangements for our departure: confirming our various disguises, the order in which we will leave the Tuileries, and the plans for changing carriages, as the traveling berline cannot be left near the palace.

Louis studies the map, on which the several coaching stations have been marked. The final location where we change horses appears to be Varennes, 180 miles from Paris. After that we cross the river Meuse and head north to Montmédy. He looks up at Axel, then straight at me with a strange, sad look in his eyes, and, returning his gaze to the count, informs him, "You will relinquish the coachman's box to another at Bondy. From there, saddle a horse and ride to Brussels, where, God willing, you will safely meet up with my brother."

This is a change in plans. I feel as though I have been shot in the belly with an entire round of musket fire. Axel endeavors to mask his shock and dismay. He gives me a quick glance, and seeing the tears welling in my eyes, swallows hard and turns back to the king. "Whatever Your Majesty requires of me, I will humbly discharge."

Louis embraces the count like a brother. "Whatever happens, I will never forget what you did for me," he says, choking back his emotion. "And now," he adds, clearing his throat, "I must leave you." He points toward the open door of his study where a sheet of paper lies on his desk. A sharpened quill rests beside the inkstand. "I need to finish my manifesto on why it is incumbent upon us to flee the capital."

Axel and I wait until the door closes and then we descend the stairs to my apartment, where, locked safely inside, I fall into his arms. "How could he do this?" I sob. "Do you think he knows?" This is not all that agitates me. Axel is the only one who is conversant with every detail of our plans. If there is even the slightest snarl, he would know what to do. I have often wondered whether Louis has ever suspected my love for Axel. He is not the sort of man to make scenes or engage in confrontations. Once he said something odd on a staircase at Versailles after Axel and I had spent an entire afternoon together at le Petit Trianon, but he has never made a similar remark again. I do not know what I should have read in his look of a few moments ago. But instead of elation over the prospect of a safe escape, I now feel as though a leaden cape has been draped about my shoulders, one I must wear for the remainder of my days.

Axel smooths away an errant lock of my hair and lowers his lips to mine, crushing me to him, because we know we cannot bid farewell this way at Bondy. I taste his lips and tongue hungrily, fearing it will be for the last time. It is a lovers' frenzied adieu, for there is still much to accomplish before tonight's departure and our senses must be at their sharpest. Our passion is not the most important thing in the world—far from it. That, alas, is a beautiful fairy tale from another, earlier age. What matters most is the future, the safe passage to Montmédy of the king and the dauphin.

When we finally need breath again, Axel murmurs into my hair, "I live every day of my life for you, Antoinette. And no matter where I am, I will always do so." He kisses my cheeks, drinking my tears. I clasp his hands and press them to my breast. "Feel my heart," I whisper between sobs. "And know that it is yours."

The next time I see him, we should not be able to recognize each other, else our plot might fail.

The clock strikes nine. Léonard is in a panic. "What do I do with this letter?" he asks me for the third time this evening.

"There is a carriage waiting for you downstairs that will convey you to the duc de Choiseul." The thirty-one-year-old nephew of my dear old family friend and mentor has been enlisted, along with his royalist regiment, to participate in our flight by keeping the marquis de Bouillé and his troops apprised of our progress throughout the night, so that Bouillé's men will be stationed at Varennes, ready to meet our carriage and provide an armed escort for the final leg of our journey to Montmédy.

But the letter is sealed and Léonard remains unaware of its contents. I have deliberately kept him in the dark precisely because of his tendency to become indiscreet when he gets flustered. "You are to deliver the note—and my box of diamonds—to Choiseul. He will carry them to our destination—and yours."

"But this coat! And this hat!" he exclaims, indicating his disguise, a nondescript ensemble that is the antithesis of fashion. "I borrowed them from my brother—he is a lawyer—without his knowledge; and he will be very angry with me for taking them without permission. At least he must know when I intend to return them to him." My *friseur* throws his hands in the air helplessly.

"I cannot give you an answer, Monsieur Hautier. But I gave you this important commission because you have my trust. Am I right to believe that you still merit it, or should I relieve you of your obligation?"

"Oh, *non*," Léonard gasps. He sinks to his knees and kisses my hand with a flurry of emotion. "Please, *Majesté,* have faith in me to do this little thing for you, who have done so much for me!"

After he departs I find myself holding my breath for what seems like several minutes, though of course it cannot be so. I only hope he has been able to exit the palace undetected.

I join my husband in his salon where he is playing backgammon with Monsieur and Madame and the princesse Élisabeth as if it is any other evening. A few courtiers mingle about the gaming table, offering advice on their play and making small talk. They politely engage me in conversation, but my thoughts are elsewhere. The children need to be made ready.

At the stroke of ten, I begin to excuse myself. I have forgotten something in my apartment, I say, and slip away to the children's rooms—first to Madame Royale's chamber. I scratch on the door with my fingernail and moments later my daughter opens it herself, rubbing the sleep from her eyes. "You must get dressed, Mousseline," I whisper urgently. We open the trunk at the foot of her bed and remove a parcel containing an unadorned blue dress and bonnet, white cotton stockings, and black leather shoes with grosgrain ribbons, instead of buckles, to fasten the latchets.

"This is what the bourgeoisie wear, Maman," she observes. She summons Madame Brunier, her assistant governess, and asks to be dressed while I go to wake the dauphin. Madame Brunier and my son's *sous-gouvernante* Madame de Neuville are the two women who will follow us in the light carriage bearing much of my wardrobe.

I open his door with my own key because I know he will not awaken when I knock or scratch. Pulling aside the damask bed curtains, I take my son into my arms and murmur, "Come, *mon chou d'amour,* you must get up. We are going on an adventure!"

His soft warm arms about my neck, he asks groggily, "Where?"

"To a fortress where there are lots of soldiers."

"Oh, then I need my uniform and sword!" He is suddenly awake and ready to do fearsome battle as he slips from my grasp. But he grows confused when Madame de Tourzel, her daughter Pauline, and I rush to dress him in a frock of brown striped calico, slide his little feet into a pair of leather slippers, and tuck his curls beneath a cap.

"Why are you dressing me as a girl, Maman?"

I look to Pauline de Tourzel, who has a wonderful way with the dauphin. Not as old as Madame Royale, she plays games with my son when his sister disdains to do so, and he adores her. "Because first we are going to attend a masquerade!" Pauline answers encouragingly.

My son giggles. "What fun!"

I mouth my thanks to his little friend, then tell my son, "But we must hurry, *mon chou d'amour,* or we will be late. And we must be as quiet as mice—"

"But mice go *'eep, eep'*!"

"Quieter, then! We mustn't make a single sound because it's a surprise."

We fetch Madame Royale and creep down the staircase to my apartment. Tracing the path that Axel and I had previously discovered, we leave my salon through the secret door hidden within the wall, scuttle down the interior corridor, and dash through Madame de Ronchreuil's chamber into the adjacent apartment, the former residence of the duc de Villequier. Waiting for us—hidden inside a cupboard, for we are taking no precautions—is a gentleman sporting a dark blue greatcoat and one of the high-crowned round hats worn nowadays by men of fashion. I have met him just once before. He is a connection of Axel's, presented to me only as Monsieur de Malden, who will act as one of our bodyguards this night. Axel has somehow smuggled him into the Tuileries.

I tremble at the prospect of entrusting the safety of my children to a stranger. It is sobering to think that I have no choice but to rely upon him. Malden's knowledge of the palace's configuration cannot be as thorough as Axel's for, as far as I know, he has been inside the Tuileries only once. If he is discovered and questioned, what would he say? What would my children tell their interrogators? "I am so grateful for your assistance, Monsieur," I say to Malden, unable to still the quavering in my voice.

Monsieur de Malden bows and kisses my hand. "The pleasure is mine, Your Majesty."

From his accent, I realize that he is an Englishman, and I wonder how he has managed to infiltrate the guard, for clearly he is no soldier. Several brave British aristocrats are secretly helping our noblemen and women escape the Revolution and emigrate across the Channel, to the Low Countries, or to Brussels. I wonder, too, as we stand in this vacant room, if Monsieur de Malden had also aided the duc de Villequier in his departure. Sinking to my knees I embrace each of my children as if we might never meet again, bathing them with a mother's tears. "My darlings, you must go now with this kind gentleman. Promise to do everything he asks of you without making a sound. And Maman will see you very soon."

The dauphin smothers my cheeks with moist kisses while my daughter clings to me more tightly than she ever has before, betraying her frequent claims to independence and maturity. It cracks my heart to leave them, but every moment is accounted for this night and I must return to the salon where the king is playing backgammon with the rest of the royal family; then we must go through the mummery of our respective *couchers* as if nothing untoward is about to transpire. We bid good night to Monsieur and Madame, who, as usual, will quit the Tuileries and return to their residence in the Palais du Luxembourg. From there they will depart in a light post-chaise for Bruxelles. Our plan is to meet up with them two days hence at the Château de Thonnelle near Montmédy, which the marquis de Bouillé has already prepared for our arrival.

Cocooned within the damask bedcurtains I lie abed in my nightgown and cap staring at the underside of the tester, impatiently waiting for the clock to strike the quarter hour. The single chime will tell me that it is eleven fifteen. Enough time will have elapsed to permit my maidservants to return to their duties and allow me to don my disguise.

My traveling garments are more befitting Madame de Tourzel, for I am playing the role of my own children's governess. Madame Campan helps me dress in the plain gray-brown silk gown of a *gouvernante*, a short black coat, and a black hat with a heavy veil in a sepia-toned violet hue that obscures my face enough to render it unrecognizable. "Godspeed, *Majesté*," murmurs Campan, sinking into a deep curtsy.

I raise her to her feet and embrace her, kissing her on both cheeks. She is weeping. "Thank you for your devotion, *mon amie,* for indeed you are one of the few friends I have ever had. I will write as soon as we reach Montmédy."

"Go!" she whispers, practically spinning me toward the door.

I creep down the stairs leading to a side door that will open onto the covered arcade where Monsieur de Malden should be waiting to escort me to the fiacre that will then take us to the berline. Just outside I spy his coat, silhouetted against the palace's gray façade. "The children—?" I ask, grabbing his sleeve.

"Safe inside the hackney," Malden replies. "Fersen is on the box." He chuckles. "You'll never recognize him."

I exhale with relief. The seconds cannot tick by swiftly enough until we are reunited. Monsieur de Malden clasps my elbow and steers me along the arcade as we make our way along the Place du Carrousel toward the rue des Echelles where the first fiacre awaits to transport us to the traveling berline.

Without torchlight, though, we soon become disoriented. Monsieur de Malden seems unfamiliar with the grounds outside the Tuileries and the adjacent *rues,* and I never walk the streets of Paris alone, nor at night. I ride everywhere. How should I know where to go on my own? My fear and anxiety create an additional distraction, and before I know it we have somehow gotten ourselves turned around and have traversed the Pont Royal, ending up on the opposite bank of the Seine. I look up at the side of the building, trying to see the street name written on the façade. We are in the rue de Bac. Now we have to sneak back across the river to locate Axel and the carriage.

I hitch up my skirts and make a dash for it, with Monsieur de Malden right behind me, as we keep to the shadows the way children play at jumping from one mud puddle to the next. As we near the rue de l'Échelle, suddenly, the Petit Carrousel is illuminated with torchlight and I hear a clatter of hoofbeats. A coach appears to be bearing down upon us—is it because the driver spots our shadows? My heart pounds wildly. The flickering carriage lights on either side of the conveyance reveal the crest on the door as well as the illustrious passenger—none other than Lafayette, speeding away from the Tuileries, having completed his nightly inspection. Malden and I leap back into the shadows, cowering in a niche until the carriage passes.

The danger was so imminent, so tangible, I find it hard to catch my breath. "Steady on, now," Malden says reassuringly, and it is all I can do to put one foot in front of the other as we continue to make our way to the rue de l'Échelle. We scurry along the cobbles of the Petit Carrousel like a pair of rats; finally I spy the coach.

A plump man wearing an ill-fitting coat and a battered, over-sized tricorn pushed down over his straw-colored hair sits atop the coachman's box. He grins when he sees us, revealing blackened teeth, and spits a fat wad of tobacco. It sails an impressive distance, all the way across the *rue,* landing in the opposite gutter. He winks at me as Monsieur de Malden is about to hand me inside the car-riage and I realize that of course this bumpkin, only slightly better dressed than a *sans-culotte,* is Axel, enjoying his role immensely.

"And how is Madame Rochet this evening?" he asks.

"Tr—très bien, merci, monsieur," I stammer.

"La baronne de Korff et Mamselles Amélie et Agläe sont dedans." He nods and informs me that Madame de Tourzel and my chil-dren, who will be passed off as *her* daughters, are already inside the carriage.

I glance at my father's gold watch and realize the king is late. Louis should be right on my heels, disguised as the baronne's stew-ard. *"Où est Monsieur Durand?"* I ask Axel anxiously. He shakes his head. What if something happened to Louis? *What if he doesn't come?* How will we explain our costumes? I peer through the win-dow, my gaze fixed on the palace.

After an eternity, a stout man in a gray coat that all but obscures his satin waistcoat and gray breeches, an outrageous black curled wig, and an enormous lackey's hat comes huffing and puffing along the Petit Carrousel, escorted by Monsieur de Malden. When they reach us, Malden unfolds the steps and Louis all but tumbles into the coach with relief. "How glad I am to see you here, *ma chère*!" he exclaims, reaching over to embrace me with uncharacteristic ardor. He kisses each of the children as well, and then, at a sign from Monsieur de Malden, Louis raps upon the roof of the coach to signal Axel to depart.

Dressed as footmen and other menials, our attendants and outriders are in fact noblemen, but to appease their sensibilities, for they had balked so much at the nature of their disguises, I had commissioned brand-new liveries for them with frothy gold lace at the cuffs.

"He would not leave," Louis says breathlessly.

"Who, my sweet?"

"Lafayette! He attended my *coucher* and then lingered afterwards for a full forty-five minutes, discussing banalities. I might have sworn he knew something. I thought he would never quit the room."

I tell him of my own narrow escape. "As he left the palace, his carriage drove past, so close to where I stood that I could have touched the wheels."

The king nearly laughs to speak of it now as he tells us how he slipped between the drawn bed hangings while his valet was placing his clothes in the wardrobe; and, wearing nothing but his nightgown, crept barefoot into his study, where his wig and bourgeois garments had been concealed.

For the benefit of the children I propose that we play a game, and instruct the dauphin to curl up on the floor of the coach, hiding beneath Madame de Tourzel's full skirts. The little angel does so obligingly, as Axel deliberately takes us on a circuitous route through the narrow streets toward the rue de Clichy where the traveling berline awaits. Yet he seems to spend so much time driving up and down the same side streets searching for the coach that I am not entirely certain he has not become lost as well.

The king and I hold our breath as we approach the heavily guarded Porte Saint-Martin. Even at this impossibly late hour,

torches illuminate this fortified entrance to the city. A cluster of
soldiers and customs clerks crowd around two or three bonfires,
carousing and gobbling undoubtedly confiscated food and spirits.
Mercifully for us, the men show no interest in interrupting their
revelry to bother with an unmarked carriage clattering through
the gates.

With the city at our backs and only the dim coachlights to mark
our way, we continue to search for the unpaved *rue* where the traveling berline awaits. At this hour, everything looks the same and
every sound appears magnified. The hoot of an owl pierces the
night, startling me so that I nearly jump off the seat of the hackney.

The carriage halts and I hear Axel descending from the box.
He raps upon the window, informing us that he is going in search
of the berline. Minutes tick by; my father's watch, clutched in my
palm, turns warm. Finally, Louis, sighing heavily, announces, "I
will help him look." He reaches for the door handle.

"Mon Dieu, non!" The last thing we need is for the king of
France to be discovered wandering about the outskirts of his capital in disguise. But my husband will hear no remonstrance. He
descends from the hackney and disappears into the darkness. I
clutch Madame Élisabeth's hand as the dauphin asks, "What is
happening, Maman? Where are we?" I don't know what to answer, so I hug him to my chest instead and stroke his hair, hoping
he cannot tell how rapidly my heart is beating.

Madame de Tourzel, my *belle-soeur,* and I sit in anxious silence
as the exhausted children fall asleep once more. The two most important men in my world have been wandering about the countryside for what seems like an eternity. Finally, Axel returns, having
spotted the berline; the bottle-green and black conveyance was so
well concealed that the carriage lights had been veiled. In a matter
of minutes the hackney approaches it. Four horses are already in
the traces. Axel skillfully maneuvers the fiacre so that we can step

from one coach to the other without having to descend from the hackney into the muddy *rue*. Once we are safely inside the capacious coach, nestled upon its seats of green Moroccan leather, I worry whether the white velvet and silk interior is not too indiscreet, for the light color is so easily illuminated. I glance at my father's watch. It is just past two in the morning. According to our carefully laid plans, we should have transferred carriages at around midnight. Two precious hours have been irretrievably lost! How will we ever make up the time? Our schedule of arrivals in the various towns along our route has been meticulously plotted. The young duc de Choiseul is in charge of ensuring that the marquis de Bouillé's troops are prepared to meet and escort us at the previously agreed-upon locales. Léonard's rendezvous has been timed as well. If we are not where we must be at the right time, our fragile plans could collapse.

Another half hour ticks by as the additional horses from the first fiacre are finally harnessed. With all eight mounts in the traces, Axel cracks the whip and we are off at last for Montmédy, the heavy berline clattering along the rutted *rues* as fast as the count can drive the teams, our bodyguards disguised as footmen undoubtedly clinging to the box as the coach sways from side to side.

"I haven't felt so free in weeks," Louis remarks, stretching his legs. I draw open the green taffeta curtains. With each passing minute, as we speed toward freedom and the fetid winds of revolution grow fainter, the mood within the berline becomes almost jolly. Although the children are asleep, the adults begin to explore the coach's numerous concealed luxuries. My husband, hungry, wishes to break out the picnic hamper, but I suggest that we wait until Bondy, our first stop, only a half hour's ride from the gates of the capital. And yet, there is a tiny chamber of my heart that wishes it would take an eternity to reach this sleepy town, for it is here that Axel and I must bid farewell.

At Bondy, both the king and I descend from the berline to say good-bye to Count von Fersen. The barest sliver of moonlight illuminates the road. Axel's handsome face is obscured beneath his broad-brimmed coachman's hat. The two men embrace fraternally. I hear a catch in Louis's throat when he thanks Axel for his service to us, not only on this night of all nights, but in the entire planning and execution of our flight. "You have been a great friend to me . . . and . . . to my family," my husband murmurs. He turns away, as if to reboard the berline, affording me the opportunity to speak to the count privately.

I offer my hand to Axel and he takes it in his, subtly drawing me toward him. "I still don't understand it," I whisper. "Why must you leave us now?" I glance at the coachman who is to replace him, a French nobleman, also in disguise. "You are the only one who has been involved in every aspect of the planning."

He tightens his grip on my hand. "Perhaps His Majesty felt it would be more appropriate to arrive at Montmédy with an entourage comprised entirely of your own countrymen and -women." I fret about their lack of expertise. "Or he may not have wished to jeopardize my role in your escape, as I am in France as an agent of Sweden's sovereign." I sigh heavily, searching his expression, aware that I must not shed a single tear, nor display the slightest emotion at our parting. And yet my heart is so full.

"The king did not give me a reason. 'Il n'a pas voulu,' was all he said," Axel whispers.

It was not desired. At those words the sour feeling in my stomach rises and I taste it in my mouth. The very vagueness of the command makes it seem unfair; it sounds so arbitrary but as I seek the truth behind it, I imagine layers of meaning even as I remind myself that Louis is not a particularly inscrutable man.

"Thank you. And God save you," I say. "And may you reach

Brussels safely. I will send you word when we, too, have arrived at our destination."

"*Merci, Majesté.*" He raises my hand to his lips and kisses it and in this briefest of innocuous touches are numberless memories of myriad encounters. Our eyes meet, expressing the words that our lips must not convey. "Godspeed, Antoinette," he says softly. And for the benefit of the ostlers who are changing the horses, as he strides toward his own waiting mount, Axel tips his hat and waves at the carriage. "*Bonne nuit, Madame de Korff!*"

I return to the berline, aware that I must conceal the ache in my heart at parting from Axel. I must smile and face the road ahead, reserving my tears for the joy I will feel when we arrive safely at the frontier. With fresh horses and a new driver on the box, we continue to press on toward Châlons-sur-Marne, our party in a merry mood, now that we have put Paris well behind us. Every fifteen miles or so we must stop at the posting station in some remote town to change horses, but will not descend from the carriage. The postilions and grooms at these *relais de postes* are not known to us; and, with little to do in the dead of night it will surely engender gossip when a handsome equipage comes rumbling through at breakneck speed. We hope they will assume ours is a banking carriage transporting funds across the kingdom; and as our needs are well accommodated, we do not intend to call attention to ourselves by showing our faces.

"Who is hungry?" I ask, knowing the answer already. Louis is always famished, and the dauphin, his eyes sandy with sleep, mumbles "*Moi.*" Madame de Tourzel offers to open the picnic hamper and unlatch the doors that conceal the chests of silver, china, and drinking goblets, but I remind her, "You are a baroness tonight. You must accustom yourself to being waited on, just as Madame Élisabeth," who is garbed as one of her attendants, "and I must

grow practiced with such simple tasks as serving a meal and pouring beverages. Otherwise, we will give ourselves away, should we
be called to account."

As we rumble through the little town of Meaux after an un-
eventful change of horses, munching on a paillard of cold veal,
Louis's anxiety lifts.

"Believe me, *ma chère,*" he says, jovially taking my hand with
his greasy fingers, "once my backside is back in the saddle, I will be
quite a different person from the one I have been until now." So
much of his testiness of late he attributes to his inability to hunt
daily as he used to. It had been his sole source of exercise and he
had adored the untrammeled freedom of giving chase, in hot pursuit of whatever woodland creature was in season.

It is six A.M. and the sun has risen, casting a lemon-yellow glow
on the countryside. I peer between the curtains at the day, my heart
light, for no one had thought to ask the baronne de Korff and her
traveling companions for their papers at Meaux.

His breakfast finished—why did I not think to try one of the
two cookstoves; I could have fried him an egg!—Louis spreads a
map across his knees and invites the children to follow it with him,
although they must read it upside down because they are seated
upon the opposite banquette.

"See, *mes enfants:* we were just here—and we have this much
farther to go. Our next stop"—he places a thick finger over a dot
on the map—"should be La Ferté-sous-Jouarre. That's quite a
mouthful." He grins. "Can you say that?" he asks our little son.

The greater the distance between our party and Paris, the more
we can relax, even jest, although I cannot help but notice that my
husband's mood brightened considerably as soon as Count von Fersen left us. "What must Lafayette be thinking now?" Louis wonders aloud. No one is following us, and so we cannot even be certain
we are yet missed. As we clatter through the tiniest rural towns and

villages, we indulge ourselves by taking the opportunity to stretch our legs and enjoy the *plein aire* of the countryside. Louis, his round hat pushed down well over his eyes, even converses with a farmer about his crops while Madame Royale and her brother chase butterflies along the roadside on this first, most promising day of summer. I peer out the window of the berline and call to our bodyguards, offering them something to eat. "Perhaps our old friend Lafayette's head has been separated from his shoulders by now," I say jocularly to Monsieur de Malden as he accepts a helping of *boeuf à la mode,* served upon a Sèvres plate rimmed in gold.

"When we have passed Châlons we shall have nothing to fear," Louis says, once we are back on the road, clip-clopping over a narrow bridge bounded on either side by a stone wall. Yet hardly are the words past his lips when the berline suddenly lurches to a stop and we are all jolted sideways, tumbling upon each other. The horses whinny in fright, a terrifying sound that freezes my blood and mortifies the children, who begin to cry. I peer outside and from the precarious tilt of the heavy carriage, I fear we will topple into the river below. Monsieur de Malden raps upon the window. "I am terribly sorry, Your Majesty—I mean Madame Rochet, Monsieur Durand. The hub of the wheel scraped the wall. And when the coach pitched, the harness broke and the momentum caused the horses to fall."

Madame Élisabeth gasps. "Are the poor beasts all right?"

Malden nods. "But terrified, Madame Rosalie," he replies, remembering her nom de voyage. "And needless to say, we cannot travel any further until we repair the carriage."

"How long will that take?" the king queries anxiously. His hopeful countenance is but a memory now. "We are to meet up at Pont-Sommevel with the young duc de Choiseul and his hussars and if we are late for the appointed rendezvous, Choiseul may think we have elected to take another route, or have already passed him, and then our armed escort may be dismissed. How long will he be able to convince the citizens that the battalion is merely waiting to accompany a shipment of specie?"

I feel the skin on my arms begin to pebble beneath my sleeves. Choiseul has detachments waiting for us, not merely at Pont-Sommevel, but at three other towns along the route. If we miss the first connection, will the soldiers still be stationed at Orbeval, Sainte-Menehould, and Clermont-en-Argonne? I glance at the broken wheel, at the horses being soothed, at Madame Élisabeth murmuring her prayers and Madame de Tourzel endeavoring to engage my children in a game. "How long must we stay here?" I ask. In answer, Malden shrugs. We are in the middle of nowhere and our outriders are noblemen, not ostlers and wheelwrights. Among the lot of them, it is the king of France who has the most knowledge of mechanics and engineering, and he is the one who divests himself of his coat and pushes the sleeves of his chemise up to the elbow as he tackles the business of repairing the coach and harness.

Nearly two hours later, the traces are mended and the berline limps back onto the rutted highway. Off we rattle, as fast as the horses will carry us. Five leagues from Châlons-sur-Marne, at the relay station in the tiny village of Chaintrix, when we step outside to stretch our legs, we are immediately recognized by the son-in-law of the postmaster, a handsome young man with a cleft chin. "Welcome, You"—and I can see that he is about to say "Your Majesties," so I touch my finger to my lips and the youth quickly says, "*You* must be weary from your journey. The afternoon heat is oppressive in this part of the country. Please come inside and take some refreshment."

We accept his kind offer of lemonade and biscuits, but the murmurs begin and the words "*roi*" and "*reine*" are bandied about. Within moments, the hired postilions realize they are escorting their sovereigns across the realm. Someone saddles a horse and, with a spray of gravel, spurs his mount onto the road leading out of town.

We do not reach Châlons-sur-Marne, a distance of 106 miles from Paris, until five in the afternoon. It is the first location at which we draw a crowd—the arrival of a grand coach, although coated with a fine layer of dust from the road, reason enough to attract a gathering of curious onlookers. I think it best if we remain inside the carriage; as it is, our footmen with their gold-embellished liveries are gaining notice, for they are strutting about as if they are preening in the State Rooms at Versailles, rather than portraying lackeys in a remote town square. But before I can close the curtains, the town postmaster, a short, bespectacled man, approaches the coach and peers inside. He sees Louis and blinks in disbelief, then removes his eyeglasses, leaning toward us for a closer look. The postmaster removes a chamois cloth from the pocket of his coat and fastidiously wipes the spectacles, then gazes at my husband's face with even greater scrutiny. I find myself holding my breath.

"Why is that man looking at Papa so?" asks the dauphin, tugging at his gown in a most unladylike fashion.

"*Shh, Agläe,*" I caution him. "Say nothing," I mutter to everyone in the coach. "Face forward and pretend nothing is amiss." Finally, the postmaster's mouth curves into a faint smile of recognition and I can read the emotion in his gray eyes. He knows who we are. But he presses his lips together as if to tell us that they are sealed and raises his hat in a gesture of respect.

"How soon before we can depart?" I ask Louis, not wishing to remain in this town another moment. But when we reach the next relay station, Pont-de-Somme-Vesle, no one is there to meet us, according to plan. My heart plummets.

"There should have been a detachment of troops here," I whisper anxiously to Louis, squeezing his arm.

"Perhaps they have marched on ahead," he says, but his reply lacks much reassurance. Madame Élisabeth, sweetly hopeful as ever, has, at every posting station, been sticking her head out of the carriage window in search of Choiseul's hussars. The outriders, too, at any moment, have expected to spy the curved scabbards of their flashing sabers.

Finally, as the sun begins to set on June 21, we spot a lone horseman on the road outside Sainte-Menehould. Louis raps on the berline's roof to halt the carriage so he can speak to the cavalryman. From his uniform, the man appears to be an officer of the guard.

"Where is Choiseul?" the king inquires.

"Gone," comes the terse reply.

"What about the rest of the hussars?"

The officer shrugs as if to say, *Do you see them?* He clearly does not know he addresses his sovereign. "Not a one of them here."

My *friseur,* Monsieur Léonard, was to have met up with Choiseul. He has my jewels. My husband and I exchange glances. There is just one road and one way to go: East. We must press on. Something is amiss, but perhaps it will all be revealed when we reach Sainte-Menehould. Yet, upon our arrival in the town square, there is only a small parade of dragoons standing about listlessly while the ostlers change the horses. They recognize me and raise their swords in salute and I give them a subtle nod of the head in appreciation. But where are their mounts, I ask Louis. Shouldn't the dragoons be in the saddle, ready to escort us toward Montmédy?

In this town, too, we meet the suspicious gaze of the postmaster, an unshaven man with small dark eyes who does not touch his fingers to his hat. His act of disrespect tells me he is no royalist, but then I notice that he holds a fistful of *assignats* as payment for the exchange of horses. The fifty-franc treasury notes bear the king's likeness imprinted upon them. I want to retch.

FIFTEEN

Caught

✦ JUNE 21, 1791 ✦

If we must perish, let us do so gloriously.

I cannot even tell Louis to tug the brim of his hat down any farther, or turn his face away, for nothing we say or do will be subtle enough. In this opulent berline, however unmarked, I fear my precious family are but flies trapped in amber.

An anxious hour passes at Sainte-Menehould and we are not on the road again until well after eight P.M. Only three more relay stations remain until we reach the house that has been prepared for us at Montmédy! As we clatter through Clermont-en-Argonne, we are surprised to see so many villagers awake and about, and determine that it would be wise to remain inside the coach. In fact, it would be best if we stay put until we reach the frontier. We have everything we need inside the berline, including chamber pots. Soon we will reach Varennes. And after that, only the little village of Stenay will stand between us and freedom.

As we rumble along the road toward Varennes, two riders gallop past, riding hell for leather as if in hot pursuit of a highwayman. They fly by too quickly for me to discern their attire, but they do not appear to be in uniform.

Where, oh where, are our hussars?

I open the window to an indigo sky, the time of day we call "between dog and wolf." The late evening air is warm and dusky, almost soporific. Madame Élisabeth, saying her rosary, is certain the dragoons are following us, just a little way behind, although the only hoofbeats I hear belong to the lightly sprung carriage conveying my ladies-in-waiting and my wardrobe trunks. My *belle-soeur* closes her eyes and drifts off to sleep.

At half past ten we reach the deserted, unpaved *rues* of the upper town of Varennes. The houses are dark, every window shuttered. Monsieur de Malden takes one of the other outriders and, lantern in hand, goes in search of Bouillé, Choiseul, Léonard, and the detachment of dragoons who are scheduled to meet us here. As we wait silently inside the berline, the same pair of horsemen clatters past us, thundering across the little bridge that leads over the Aire into the lower town. I wonder why we have seen them twice. Where did they come from? And where are they going at this hour?

Malden finally returns to the coach. He looks grim. "We found no one," he informs us. "And it was not prudent to ask too many questions. The townspeople are wary. I rapped on one shutter and was rudely told to go away. Best to continue into the lower town, change horses as swiftly and discreetly as possible, and press on. We have less than forty miles to Montmédy. Varennes is so small there is no posting station, but Bouillé's son was instructed to wait with a fresh team at the Bras d'Or, one of the two inns in the village."

We have eight exhausted horses hitched to our coach. What

will changing only two of them avail? And what about the other carriage in our party?

We rumble over the little bridge, only to come to an abrupt halt when our coachman discovers that the road is blocked on the other side. Monsieur de Malden rides back to tell us that a cart laden with furniture impedes the way, leaving us with only one direction to go, which is through a vaulted passage surmounted by an old stone tower, a relic of the *Moyen Âge*. The berline is so wide that its sides scrape the mossy stone walls of the passageway, and I am certain the driver must duck as we canter through it.

Suddenly, the urgent clanging of bells echoes through the night. At this hour it can only be an alarm. I clutch Louis's wrist. "The tocsin," he says hoarsely. Madame Élisabeth jolts awake. Madame de Tourzel looks pale as moonlight.

The berline reaches the far end of the passage, where we are met by a detachment of armed soldiers. But they are not our hussars. They are members of the Garde Nationale. Some of the men shoulder their muskets; others seize our horses' bridles as we are brusquely ordered to halt, although the command is moot, as they have already stopped the carriage. From out of the darkness a number of men appear. They unhorse the berline and harness themselves to the coach.

We are at their mercy.

By the time we are escorted into the town square, the Place de Latry, a crowd has gathered in front of the Bras d'Or. On the steps of the adjacent building stands the man with the cruel eyes, the postmaster from Sainte-Menehould, and beside him, another, kinder-looking gentleman, with a medal pinned to his chest.

The berline door flies open, startling the children. At the sight of so many armed men and angry faces, the dauphin flies into my arms and Madame Royale flings herself at her father's knees.

"You will kindly step outside," orders one of the officers, his manner brusque. As we descend from the carriage, the two civilians come forward to greet us.

"I am Monsieur Drouet," says the postmaster from Sainte-Menehould. A badge stitched to the lapel of his jacket bears the insignia of the Jacobin Club. Drouet introduces his companion as the procurator, for all intents and purposes the mayor of Varennes, Monsieur Sauce.

Monsieur Sauce draws himself up like a bantam rooster. "Your passports, please."

My stomach lurches. Madame de Tourzel finds her voice. "Good monsieur," she begins haughtily, "I am the baronne de Korff and you have cut short our journey to Frankfurt. This is my lady's maid Rosalie," she adds, indicating Madame Élisabeth, "my steward, Monsieur Durand, my daughters Amélie and Agläe, and their governess, Madame Rochet." I bob my head at the mention of my false name.

"If you are making your way to Frankfurt, madame, you are on the wrong road," says Monsieur Sauce warily. He raises his lantern, illuminating our faces, one by one. As he reaches Monsieur Durand, he stops and holds the light very still. The candle flickers over Louis's face.

Addressing Louise de Tourzel, he says, "I do regret, madame, that it is too late to visa your passports at this time of night. It is my duty to forbid you to continue on your journey."

My breath catches in my throat. "Why is that, monsieur?"

"It is too dangerous," he replies, then adds, "because of the rumors."

"What rumors are those, sir?"

"People are talking of the flight of the king and the royal family."

"I do not see what that has to do with us," I insist haughtily.

"Roads may be blocked from now on; there will be soldiers, madame." He turns back to Madame de Tourzel. "Baronne, I must ask for your passports."

Madame de Tourzel hands the mayor the passports provided to Axel by the genuine baronne de Korff and he lowers his spectacles, the better to scrutinize them. I hear him muttering to Drouet as he shows them to the suspicious postmaster.

"They bear the king's signature," Monsieur Sauce argues, impressed.

"But not that of the president of the National Assembly. To be valid, they must be countersigned by him," Drouet insists.

My jaw begins to twitch. I clutch Madame de Tourzel's arm. "Messieurs, I have had these passports for years—the Assembly did not exist when they were issued to me," she says boldly. I have to admire the arrogance of her tone, the blue-blooded hauteur of her mien, the way she lifts her chin while peering down her nose at these inferiors. Louise is quite the actress. But will the men believe her?

The men thumb through the passports again. Drouet grumbles and mutters something into Monsieur Sauce's ear. He seems to be refusing to permit us to continue on our journey until he has verified our identities. "It is the king and his family, I tell you." His tone becomes menacing. "And if you let him escape to a foreign land, monsieur, you will be guilty of high treason."

The tocsin continues to sound, bringing more townspeople into the square, gathering like moths around the torches and lanterns. I approach the men, clutching my children's hands. "Messieurs, everything is surely in order. Let us be on our way. The little ones are tired from traveling all day and the sooner we reach our destination, the sooner I can put them to bed."

The postmaster ignores me. Instead he walks up to my husband and addresses him, his face so close to Louis's that I am certain the king can smell his breath. "You—what did you say your name was?" he demands.

"I didn't say, but it is Émil Durand. I am steward to the baronne," Louis replies stiffly.

"You don't say," Drouet drawls, drawing out the vowels.

"I do say," Louis insists hotly.

Drouet crouches a bit so that he is considerably shorter than Louis and peers up at him, narrowing his ugly eyes. Then he straightens and steps back, commanding, "Remove your hat, lackey." Louis complies, as Monsieur Drouet adds, "And *I* say that you are Louis Seize, King of France." He peels a fifty-franc *assignat* from the wad of notes and waves it beneath Louis's nose. "*I* say that this is quite a good portrait—*Majesté*!"

Louis holds his ground and refuses to concede the truth. Finally, Monsieur Sauce exclaims, "There is a barber here in the village who used to work for many years at Versailles and Fontainebleau. Bring him forward! We shall see if he recognizes this Monsieur Durand."

We wait in tense silence. Dozens of tiny midges swarm about the carriage lights. Across the Place de Latry stands Varennes's other inn, the Grand Monarque. The sign above its door bears the silhouetted likeness of the Sun King. I wish Louis would step away from the pendant, as it calls undue attention to his own features. The Place de Latry bustles with confusion as curious souls continue to converge upon the center of the town, chattering, gossiping, asking dozens of questions no one can or will answer.

An elderly man is escorted into the square. He wears a powdered perruque in the *catogan* style popular during the reign of Louis XV, given the barber's advanced age, undoubtedly the first monarch of that name to employ him. Dispensing with the formalities of introduction, Drouet, who behaves as though he and not the apologetic Monsieur Sauce is the authority here, asks the barber curtly, "Have you ever seen this man before?"

The old man's rheumy blue eyes become even more watery as countless memories appear to flash across his countenance. He whips his battered black tricorn from his head and falls to his knees before Louis.

"Sire!"

We are lost.

Utterly lost. And all because in this upside-down world an old man still respects his sovereign. Poor Monsieur Sauce, whom I now suspect is a secret royalist, looks beleaguered. The postmaster, however, is triumphant.

"Madame *Rochet*," Drouet snarls, then spits at my feet. "I am certain, *Your Majesty,* that *monsieur le maire* will make your little brats quite comfortable in the back of his establishment while we await the arrival of the warrant."

"You mean the arrival of Général Bouillé and his dragoons," I retort, too tired to suffer the arrogance of this wretched little man. "The duc de Choiseul and his hussars, too, should be here at any moment."

As the barber is led away by two members of the Garde Nationale, Drouet emits a braying laugh, displaying imperfect teeth stained with tobacco. I worry about the fate of the old retainer, now that he has revealed himself as a loyalist.

Monsieur Sauce offers us the hospitality of the mayor's residence. We have no other option but to follow him inside the unremarkable wooden house, its windows shuttered with weathered pairs of blue louvered panels. Two villagers volunteer to serve as guards and take up arms—pitchforks—on either side of the door. They are not there to protect us, but to prevent us from considering any thoughts of escape.

The Hôtel de Ville de Varennes is a grocer's emporium! And the overawed mayor, Monsieur Sauce, nothing more than a humble merchant. The residence is upstairs and it is there that he permits us the use of a little trundle bed where the dauphin, ignorant of the commotion about him, curls up and falls asleep under a counterpane loaned by Madame Sauce.

As there are not enough chairs to accommodate all of us, a few bales of goods are scattered about the cozy room to be used as makeshift *tabourets* by Madame Élisabeth, Madame de Tourzel, and mesdames Neuville and Brunier, my two attendants, whose carriage has caught up with ours. Louis insists on standing. He takes the mayor's hand as if the man is a brother and admits, "It is true, I am your king, *monsieur le maire,* and in your hands I place my destiny along with that of my beloved wife and sister, and my precious children. Our lives—indeed the fate of France—depend upon you." Monsieur Sauce's eyes widen; the furrows in his brow become more pronounced as Louis assures him he has no designs of leaving the country. "But," my husband adds, *"permettez-nous* to continue our journey. We are going only as far as the frontier, to a garrison town where I intend to regain the liberty that the *factieux* of Paris deny me." Sauce's eyes are sympathetic. "From there, I wish to make common cause with the National Assembly. Cowed by fear, they, too, are subjugated by the most radical factions. I have no intentions of destroying the Constitution, but *saving* it, and you may say as much to your watchdog, Monsieur Drouet. If you detain me, not only I, and my family with me, but all of France is lost."

Louis speaks urgently, but with simple eloquence. He is always at his best when he has the opportunity to convince one man at a time that he cares deeply for his individual welfare and for that of the kingdom. "As a citizen, as a man, and as a father, I urge you to clear the road and let us continue to Montmédy. Once that is done, in less than an hour we and France herself will be saved from the clutches of those who truly wish to harm every loyalist in the realm." Looking directly into the mayor's surprised eyes, Louis pleads, "Monsieur, if you genuinely respect the man you regard as your sovereign, you will obey my command to allow us to depart."

The corners of his mouth twitching involuntarily, Monsieur Sauce looks as if he is about to weep. "I cannot, Sire," he replies hoarsely. "Believe me, I would like to, but"—he looks across the humble room at his spouse, who is serving bowls of her warmed-over soup of vegetables and spring lamb to Madame Élisabeth and my attendants, reserving some for the children when they awaken—"I have a wife. And little ones of my own. I am not a brave man, *Majesté*. I am afraid of what will happen to them if I disobey men like Citoyen Drouet. The Jacobin Club . . . The soldiers . . ." The mayor's eyes droop like those of a beleaguered hound.

Louis sighs heavily, so quickly resigned. I despair. How can the passion he displayed only moments ago, bolstered by the soundness of his argument, have evanesced so quickly? Louis purses his lips. "Then we stay. Bouillé and Choiseul and their regiments will be here at any moment, anyway. In the meantime, my good monsieur, would you rustle up some bread and cheese to fortify my respite?"

I don't think my husband is hungry now. As he has always done, he overeats to assuage his anxieties. With so many woes it is little wonder he has grown so stout. I am the opposite. Sick at heart, I cannot eat a morsel.

Monsieur Sauce bows obsequiously, clearly relieved to have been excused of any further political obligation. Food, the grocer can easily manage. "A bottle or two of wine, as well, *Votre Majesté*? Or perhaps some brandy?"

My husband declines the spirits. He rarely imbibes. In the past, he has been accused of being a drunkard, when it was his short-sightedness and exhaustion that were to blame for his shambling gait.

The night drags on. I sit ignominiously on a lumpy bale of goods in a grocer's home, so close to the frontier and yet so far from freedom that I fear now we may never obtain it. Although the tocsin finally ceased its fearful alarm, the clamor below the first-story window has scarcely abated. Outside, the sky has changed from ink blue to raven black. The pastel light of dawn has yet to break when we hear a pounding at the door. I reach into the pocket beneath my gown and glance at my father's watch. Five in the morning.

The door to the chamber bursts open and there stands Monsieur de Romeuf, Lafayette's deputy. He has a formal document in his hand and regret in his eyes. Acknowledging his companion, he announces, "*Vos Majestés,* Citoyen Bayon and I are here to carry out this order to all functionaries. By this decree, every member of the royal family of France is under arrest."

Madame Élisabeth gasps and nearly swoons. Madame de Tourzel begins to weep.

I rise from the ridiculous bale, trembling with shock. "You of all people, Monsieur Romeuf?! I would never have expected it. I had always believed you were a friend." I am embarrassed that I cannot control the tremolo in my voice. It makes me sound weak. But I have seen Lafayette's aide-de-camp every day at the Tuileries and he has never had anything less than a smile for me. He is a handsome man, too. In another, brighter world, I might have marked him as a husband for one of my attendants.

With tears in his eyes, Romeuf hands the writ to Louis, who gives it a brief glance, then drops it onto the bed where his children sleep. "There is no longer a king in France," he says, his voice hollow. He has given up.

As if in a dream I watch the paper float like a giant snowflake onto the coverlet, but suddenly I am jarred awake. I snatch it up from where it lies as if it has changed its composition and will set the downy blanket aflame, immolating our son and daughter. "I will not have this—this *thing*—contaminate—my children!" I exclaim, tossing the writ of arrest to the floor.

"I will take that," says a gentleman, and I spin around to see— *finalement*—the young duc de Choiseul standing in the doorway; behind him, on the stairs descending to the main floor of Monsieur Sauce's emporium, are a number of his hussars. *Where have they been all this time?* Instead, I demand, "Where are Général Bouillé and his men?"

The young duc pales. "They have just awakened, Your Majesty. Your *friseur,* Monsieur Hautier, told them that you were not coming, and so they eventually departed to their billets in Stenay. It is only the next town, *Majesté.* But they are remustering as I speak and are on their way as fast as their horses will carry them."

I cannot comprehend a word of what I have just heard and so I demand an explanation. Choiseul stammers something about Léonard informing him that at some point during the night we had decided to take an alternate route, or some such nonsense. I cannot imagine what possessed my *friseur* to presume to speak for us when he had not seen me since our adieux or to assume the power to dismiss the regiment of soldiers that was prepared to escort us to safety and freedom. Every limb of my body trembles with fury. Léonard Hautier is no traitor; he is a royalist with every fiber of his being. But in a flash of clarity I see that he is also a scatterbrain and a coward, too easily spooked if things do not go exactly according to plan.

"There is still a way, *Majestés,*" Choiseul insists. He is but a pup himself, hardly possessing the gravitas or experience of his sainted uncle. I can hear Maman's voice inside my head invoking the adage about never trusting a boy to do the work of a man. "I have forty hussars with me. I can unseat seven of them, providing a horse for each of the adults and one for Madame Royale; the queen can ride with the dauphin in her arms. That leaves thirty-three to surround you as you make your escape."

A cry goes up from the street. I tiptoe to the window and open the shutter just far enough to steal a glimpse at the square. There must be ten thousand people gathered outside, being whipped into a lather of hatred and fear by the postmaster Drouet and his confederate, Citoyen Bayon. Where did all these villagers come from, for surely so many do not live in Varennes?

"If Général Bouillé arrives now, he will raze your homes, every one of you! He will destroy your fields and burn your crops. He will call you traitors. But you are not traitors! You will stand your ground and show that you are patriots and that the king and his family must be brought back to Paris as criminals."

I shutter the window again as "To Paris!" becomes an ominous chant. As daylight dawns, I hear a lone voice pierce the litany, "To Paris or I will shoot them all!"

Silence descends upon our little chamber. Monsieur Sauce shudders and his face turns ashen.

"What are our options?" Louis says methodically. He begins to weigh every word, stalling for time. "We could wait for the arrival of Général Bouillé and fight our way out."

"Can't you let the children sleep a while longer?" pleads Madame de Tourzel. "What harm would it do? You see how exhausted they are. They are only innocents."

In the street below, the crowd is baying for our removal to the capital. Suddenly, my lady-in-waiting Madame de Neuville shrieks like a madwoman and flings herself to the floor. Her body, seized with convulsions, spasms uncontrollably.

Louis clasps my wrist and draws me close. "You never told me madame la marquise was an epileptic," he whispers with great concern.

"She is not," I murmur. "But I daresay she is an actress worthy of the Comédie-Française."

We call for water, air, whatever one gives a woman in such a condition. We ask to summon a doctor but our request is denied. Then my husband announces that he is famished. Surely there is more bread and cheese. And where is that vegetable soup he has heard so much about? It is all I can do, even in my agitated state, to suppress a chuckle, for the king of France has always inhaled his food like a man half starved. I have never seen him eat a meal more slowly. He chews every crust with precision, allowing the seconds to tick by, hoping that any one of them will herald our rescue.

Yet after much deliberation, Louis decides not to attempt an escape. Among the thousands of people in the square below and in the surrounding streets, several must surely be armed, he says. They would have sickles and pikes; some undoubtedly will have muskets. He will not risk the life of a single one of us, nor will he endanger any of his subjects should the hussars fire into the crowd in retaliation. "There are innocent women and children among them," he insists. Woefully he regards the writ still crumpled on the floor. "Someone must see to their welfare."

By six A.M. Bouillé and his men have not yet arrived. Every minute I imagine that I hear distant hoofbeats, only to be disappointed.

"*Majesté,* what is your opinion?" Choiseul asks me. "My men are at your disposal."

I glance at my husband. Louis's tendency to indecision has always maddened me, and when the needle of his compass finally settles upon a course, it may be the right one, but he always seems to be setting it too late. Still, I am merely his consort, despite what the people believe. "Monsieur le duc, it is up to His Majesty to give the orders; my duty is to follow them. Besides," I add, thrusting my nose in the air for the benefit of the repugnant Citoyen Drouet, who has just entered the room, "Général Bouillé will not be long in arriving now."

Drouet flings open the shutters and the tiny bedchamber fills with noise. "Do you think they will dare to pass through *that*?" he exclaims, pointing down the stairs. "The loyal men and women of Varennes will cut them down as if they are mowing wheat."

We are lambs trapped in a pen.

At six-thirty our horses are in harness and the berline, as well as the carriage that conveyed my two attendants, is in the Place de Latry. Led by Drouet and Bayon, our party is escorted down the narrow flight of stairs and onto the steps of Monsieur Sauce's residence, where the postmaster announces that the "good citizens have won the day and will bring the king back to the National Assembly." Excited shouts fill the air, including a few of *"Vive le roi!"* although there are many more of *"Vive la Nation!"* I suddenly spy several heads sporting the ridiculous red "liberty bonnets."

The duc de Choiseul and his hussars part the crowd so that we may reach the coaches. As he hands me into the berline, I clasp the young duc's arm and look directly into his eyes. "Do you think Count von Fersen is safe?" I murmur.

"I am sure of it," he replies tersely, clearly having no idea of the truth.

"Don't leave us," I plead, an urgent whisper.

A moment later, a member of the Garde Nationale strikes him in the back, and the duc falls to the ground. He reaches for his saber but the guardsman steps on his hand. The sound of crunching bone, accompanied by a piercing howl, sends shivers through me. I turn back to aid our fallen champion, but I am rudely bundled into the berline by another armed guard. The coachman cracks his whip and as the horses begin to clip-clop out of the square I hear the chilling order to "Arrest Citoyen Choiseul!"

SIXTEEN

The Long Ride Home

⤞ JUNE 22, 1791 ⤝

We have not bathed in three days. No perfume can mask the odors of anxiety and fear. The interior of the berline is stiflingly hot and it is not yet mid-morning. There are so many jeering voices and leering faces crowding the carriage, it seems like an eternity before we can get out of the Place de Latry. I recall with perfect clarity that awful day in October two years ago when we were forced to depart Versailles. The taunts, too, are nearly the same, accompanied by revolutionary songs, including the vicious verses of the *Ça Ira*. The madmen are in control of the asylum.

Although we had galloped with all due speed toward the frontier, we return to the capital with the protracted pace of a funeral cortege, retracing the route we had taken on our eastward journey. When we stop to change horses and I wonder aloud why we are taking the same roads, one of our outriders, a soldier of the National Guard, tells me that because there are fewer houses along this route the chances are more slender that the royal family will be assassinated. My skin pebbles with fear and my mouth goes dry. "I understand," I reply, barely able to voice the words.

As the sun beats down upon the berline the family quarrels about whether it is better to open the windows. We are moving so slowly that to do so will only invite flies and bees into the carriage, making it all the more unpleasant.

At length we reach Châlons-sur-Marne. There a great crowd has gathered to witness our disgrace. Yet a single, brave soul, the old comte de Dampierre, doffs his hat and salutes our carriage as it enters the center of town. What follows is a tremendous uproar. The berline is halted by the mob, forbidden to pass any farther. I open the window and lean my head out to see what is causing such a clamor. "Nothing to trouble yourself with, *Majesté,*" comes the reply from one of our escort. "A madman has been killed for daring to approach your carriage."

The truth of the matter in this world gone wrong is illuminated moments later when the decapitated head of the poor comte de Dampierre, the stump of his neck still dripping with blood, is shoved at our window. Madame Royale shrieks. Madame Élisabeth begins to gasp in ragged breaths. She clutches the delicate golden crucifix she wears about her neck and begins to murmur a prayer for the soul of the unfortunate comte—cut down by the mob simply for displaying his respect for the crown.

My head swims; my mouth fills with the taste of vomit. Louis's expression is inscrutable. His jowls quiver as if he is about to weep and is straining to contain his tears. He stares straight ahead, willingly blotting out the spectacle before us, if only for the nonce, because he cannot be observed by his subjects displaying the violence of his emotions.

Departing the carnage of Châlons we divert from our planned route. We stop at the *relais de poste* in Épernay and while the ostlers are changing the horses, we decide to step inside the coaching inn to stretch our legs and avail ourselves of a light repast. As I am about to enter the hostelry, we are surrounded by another mob that flings mud and hurls obscenities at us. The men who had ridden as our outriders en route to the frontier, now handcuffed and huddled shoulder to epauleted shoulder on the coachman's box, have become sitting targets for their vitriol. Now they must be protected at swordpoint by the very guards who have restrained them.

Suddenly, the crowd begins to press closer, reaching, clawing for us, and the Garde Nationale whose job it is to escort us back to Paris find themselves defending the family they so despise. In the scuffle, the hem of my gown is torn. At length, when we safely reach the inn, the tavern keeper's daughter kindly repairs the gash and I give her a louis d'or for her pains.

Yet as Louis exits the inn, grimacing and sweating, his plain gray suit clinging to him like the skin of a shallot, a woman has the audacity to spit directly in his face. A glob of white spittle trickles down one cheek as a salty tear snakes its way down the other. It is all too much, and finally he has broken under the strain. This, people of France, is your king. As I hasten to my husband's side with the dauphin in my arms, a horrid man shouts, "Don't show us the brat. Everyone knows that fat pig is not his father!"

The villagers continue to pelt us with curses as we pick our way toward the berline. At least they do not throw stones, but one harridan mockingly taunts, as I mount the traveling steps, "Take care, *ma petite*! you will soon look upon other steps than those!"

"What did she mean by that, Maman?" inquires Madame Royale.

"*Ce n'est rien.* It's nothing. Bend your mind from it, Mousseline," I soothe, stroking her dark curls as I endeavor to push away my own images of the hapless marquis de Favras mounting the scaffold for the crime of being a royalist. He was hanged for his loyalty less than a year and a half ago. Scarcely could I have imagined then how much more dire things would grow in the ensuing months.

Glaring at the crowd I beg the soldiers of the Garde Nationale to ensure the safety of our own protective guard. I despair for Monsieur de Malden and his brave confederates. They must be parched as well, so I insist they be given some cool water to drink.

That afternoon, as we enter a tiny village not far from Dormans, three deputies from the National Assembly meet our carriage. *"Bon après-midi, Votre Majesté*. My colleagues and I have been enjoined to escort you the rest of the way to the capital." The speaker is Antoine Barnave, a staunch member of the first Jacobin Club, although I have heard that he, like Mirabeau in his day, espouses less radical beliefs than some of his confederates. Barnave introduces me to Jérôme Pétion de Villeneuve, an ardent revolutionary, who will also ride in the berline with the royal family, and to the comte de La Tour-Maubourg, who will accompany my ladies-in-waiting in their carriage. I recognize Pétion's name with a shiver. Just a few days before our ill-starred flight he had been elected president of the criminal tribunal of Paris. Does Pétion's presence here mean that we are to be tried as felons upon our return to the capital? It is unthinkable. I cannot fathom the attendance of the comte de La Tour-Maubourg, a member of the nobility. Only two years my junior, whatever is he thinking to gain by casting his lot with the revolutionaries? As he ascends the steps to board my ladies' carriage I meet his gaze unflinchingly. I hope that the sorrow and betrayal in my eyes burn him with shame.

While the interior of our berline is capacious enough to comfortably accommodate four adults and two children, the addition of two grown men makes the remainder of our journey all the more uncomfortable—particularly in the uncommonly sultry heat, where our silks cling to our skin as if we have bathed in them and the air is so humid it gums together the pages of Madame Élisabeth's missal. Citoyen Pétion, who has denounced me before the National Assembly numerous times, is now compelled to sit beside me, so close that I can feel the heat of his thigh against my skirts. Perspiration trickles along his cheek from hairline to chin and I am certain that as much of it is due to the awkwardness of the situation as to the stifling conditions inside the coach.

But my family is determined to behave as we might on any other day and we will treat the pair of deputies like honored guests, rather than the adversaries they are. Let the men discover for themselves that I am not the harpy depicted in the pamphlets hawked in the streets, the caricature that portrays me with the body of a winged monster. I offer them roasted quail and ducks' eggs, cold asparagus with sauce Mornaise, and the pick of the vintage bottles we carry in the berline's purpose-built wine coolers.

Citoyen Pétion, however, seems disinclined to make small talk. With all the social graces of a policeman, he questions me closely about the details of our departure.

"What was the name of the coachman who drove you as far as Bondy?" My stomach flutters.

"I believe it was driven by a Swede," Barnave persists.

Fixing our minders with a gaze so cold it momentarily changes the temperature of the berline's cabin, I reply mildly, "Messieurs, would I be likely to know the name of a hackney driver?"

We spend the first night in the town of Dormans at a humble wayside inn. Our room is guarded by sentries, lest we take a notion to flee in nothing but our night rails and slippers. The iron bedstead is so rusted that Louis prefers to sleep in a chair, although none of our family is able to catch a wink of repose.

"Maman, do you think they will ever stop singing?" Mousseline laments, rubbing her eyes. Directly below us, in the tavern, the members of the Garde Nationale have been carousing through the night. The thick soles of their boots resound on the floorboards to the accompaniment of an accordion and they sing lewd songs whose verses are unfit for my children's ears. The dauphin has curled up like a scallop in his shell with a counterpane tugged over his head. He whimpers fretfully. Heaven knows what nightmares invade his feeble slumber.

After a *petit déjeuner* of dry toast and weak coffee, we resume our progress on yet another impossibly hot day. Clearly it has not rained for days. The roads are so dry that the coach becomes covered with dust, cocooned in clouds of it as we rumble toward Paris like a traveling show of garish freaks.

An hour after imbibing a bottle of lemonade, the six-year-old dauphin wriggles in my lap and announces, *"Papa, je dois faire pipi."* It is all the Assembly delegates can do not to chuckle at the little boy's bluntness and his utter lack of embarrassment in front of a pair of strangers. But their cynical hearts soften when the king reveals himself to be no tyrant but a concerned father, raising the skirts of the dauphin's costume to unbutton the breeches the boy wears beneath them. And then, as the carriage lurches to and fro, the king of France reaches under the seat for the silver chamber pot and holds it steady while his little son and heir relieves himself.

To make the time pass, we play games with the children such as counting the number of white horses they spy—Madame Royale believes it will bring good luck to make a wish every time we see one. The dauphin wants to show the gentlemen how much he has improved at reading and asks to look at his papa's map. With a tiny fingertip he points to various little dots and sounds out the words. Fidgeting in my lap, he expresses the desire to sit upon that of Monsieur Barnave because he has such nice shiny buttons on his coat. That a son of France should be dandled upon the knee of a man who seeks the destruction of the monarchy chills my blood. But I permit it because this humiliating journey will be less intolerable if everyone's spirits can be maintained.

The deputies think they already know everything about the royal family because we live so much in the public eye, although they are growing to realize during this unfortunate journey that in so many ways we do not resemble the unflattering portraits that have been painted for years by the caricaturists and pamphleteers. I laugh and ask, "Oh, come, now, did you really think I had talons and scales, messieurs?"

But I wish to draw them out as well, and of the two, Monsieur Barnave, the younger, is the more voluble. "Being an attorney's son, I was raised with an unswerving devotion to the word and principles of the law," the deputy admits, then concedes that there was an occasion when he defied the authorities. "It was . . . an extenuating circumstance," he says, not daring to look any of us in the eye. "I was only sixteen. And my younger brother was thirteen. He was large for his age—prodigiously round—and his face was covered with spots and pustules, the ravages of early adolescence and over-indulgence. Damas was mercilessly bullied by the other boys where we lived in Grenoble. They called him *un crapaud*—a toad—and they would follow him home from his lessons, taunting *'crapaud, crapaud!'* One afternoon, they instigated an argument with him and shoved him into a ditch, breaking his arm. I was so angry when I discovered what had happened that I challenged the ringleader of the bullies to a duel, even though I knew that dueling was illegal."

"And did you fight?" I ask.

Barnave nods. "The insult and injustice perpetrated upon my brother was a greater crime to me than breaking the law for dueling."

All these years later, his eyes still darken with passion as he relates the tale. They still burn with empathy for his bullied brother. It does not take me long to recognize that Antoine Barnave is loyal to a fault and wears his heart on his sleeve. And he seems surprised to find me a doting mother and a loving wife, as well as a compassionate queen. And I am astonished to meet a revolutionary with a tender heart.

Inside the closed conveyance the acrid stench of perspiration has become overwhelming. I reach beneath my feet for my toiletry case and remove my atomizer, liberally spraying a fine mist of fragrance about the interior of the berline. Citoyen Barnave wrinkles his nose at the heady aroma as the dauphin plays with the brass buttons on the deputy's blue coat. "Maman, they say things!" he exclaims, running his finger along the raised lettering. Slowly he sounds out the words engraved on the buttons: *Vivre Libre ou Mourir.* "I know *'vivre'* means 'live,' but I don't understand the rest of it."

"It means 'live free or die,'" I murmur, meeting Barnave's blushing gaze. To cover my amazement at finding his face filled with sympathy, I give him one of my famous smiles. Despite what I am discovering about the man, I am doubly surprised to receive one in return.

On the opposite seat, Citoyen Pétion watches Madame Élisabeth crushed up against the door of the coach, reading her prayer book. He seems entranced by the way her lips move as she reads silently to herself.

It is mid-afternoon on June 23 when we reach La Ferté-sous-Jouarre. The berline is halted in front of the mayor's home, where I am touched to see a cluster of smiling children waiting to present me with bunches of flowers, and the deputies permit the royal family to walk about. It is mercifully quiet here; I cannot recall when the industrious hum of a honeybee has been so pleasing to my ear. Although the air remains thick and sultry, we enjoy a drink on their charming terrace overlooking the Marne; and the mayor,

Monsieur Regnard, invites us to stroll through his gardens. His wife is very proud of her roses. "I am glad that you could see them when they are in full bloom, *Votre Majesté*," Madame Regnard tells me, somewhat awed that the queen of France should visit her humble residence. Perhaps she has not heard why we are passing through her town. Perhaps there are still men and women in this country who love their sovereigns. Perhaps she has not heard about the poor comte de Dampierre, whose only crime was to show his respect for us.

I avail myself of the opportunity to converse with the two deputies. It is the first time I have become privy to the internecine workings of the National Assembly, and I am surprised to hear how much the delegates are not necessarily of the same mind. "I have been under the impression that they all desire a republic," I say to Monsieur Barnave, only to be corrected by Monsieur de Pétion.

"Kings and princes have always brought nothing but misery to their subjects," he tells me, "but the only people in France who favor the concept of a republic are those who have no interest in a constitutional monarchy and who wish to form a third political party—they are nonconstitutional royalists, who, once they obtain power, would then seek to overthrow the new Constitution." He casts a meaningful glance at Barnave.

Citoyen Pétion's explanation makes no sense to me. The interpretation I take away is that each of these rival factions craves power and none of them wishes to see the return of an absolute monarchy. The best that Louis and I can hope for, at least for the nonce, is to win as many adherents as possible who will support him as a constitutional monarch. With his rights of office increasingly stripped from him, it will not be easy to convince the majority of the Assembly that we can make common cause with them. We need another Mirabeau. I ask Antoine Barnave his age.

"Twenty-nine," he tells me. "But this afternoon I feel much older. I have grown up quickly in these past few days."

He is young. But he is smart. And he is ambitious.

That evening our party beds down at an inn in Meaux, but now the deputies will not permit my family to open our trunks so that we may change clothes. The king of France is compelled to borrow a night shirt from Citoyen Pétion, the larger and stouter of the two delegates who accompany us. Louis looks absurd, his girth straining the seams. I lie awake wondering what awaits us in Paris upon our arrival tomorrow.

Yet we may be lucky to make it that far. At Bondy, when we stop to change horses, a mob assaults our carriage, pounding on the exterior, clinging to the wheels, and endeavoring to open the doors. Only through the intervention of a regiment of grenadiers—who are waiting there to escort us into the capital, not to protect us from harm—are we not torn limb from limb. To thank him, and because I thought he might be hungry and ill-provisioned, I had offered one of the soldiers a piece of meat from one of our hampers. "Don't touch it! The whore has probably poisoned it!" a woman screeches.

The grenadier, who was about to accept the beef, rejects it and turns on his heel. In full view of our tormentors I give the morsel to the dauphin, who eats it happily and without intestinal incident.

But the crowd's appetite for violence has not been sated. Drunk on bravado and revolutionary ideals, a vicious throng assaults a *curé* who is merely making his way toward our carriage to offer us a blessing.

Horrified, Citoyen Barnave unlatches the window and shouts, "Frenchmen! You who consider yourselves so brave, do you wish to degenerate into a nation of assassins?"

At his words, the clamor miraculously dulls to a hush and the *curé* is able to approach us without further violence. He hands Madame Élisabeth a rosary, which she accepts and clutches to her breast. There are tears on the old priest's cheeks. I pray the mob permits him to depart in peace. I begin to regard young Citizen Barnave with fresh eyes. There is more mettle—and more good—in him than I had taken him for.

"I fear there is an even greater risk of assassination," he murmurs, as the coachman attempts to extricate us from the mob. For the next eight miles, all the way into Paris, the grenadiers will ride on either side of the berline.

We have been instructed to keep the curtains open so that the royal family may be on display, every expression on our exhausted, beleaguered, unwashed faces read and discussed by a disgruntled populace that detests us.

We do not take the most direct route into the capital, but circle the northern outskirts, finally entering Paris via the Champs-Élysées. Here, the crowd that lines the *rue* is frighteningly silent. Every man keeps his hat most insolently planted on his head. "They have been instructed not to remove them, on pain of punishment," Barnave whispers to me.

Soldiers from the National Guard flank the route, their muskets upturned, in the manner of funeral processions. The berline lumbers along the street at such a protracted pace that I can easily read the placards and handbills plastered to the walls. WHOEVER APPLAUDS THE KING WILL BE BEATEN. WHOEVER INSULTS HIM WILL BE HANGED.

But is not this dreadful silence insult enough? As we near the Tuileries Palace, the only cries we hear are *Vive la Nation!* Frightened by the spectacle, the dauphin, nestled in my lap, begins to cry. I bury my face in his hair so that I do not have to meet our subjects' angry, mocking faces.

It is eight in the evening by the time we arrive at the palace. As we approach the gates I spy a familiar silhouette: His expression radiant as a conqueror, Lafayette awaits us, accompanied by two noblemen who are now adherents to his democratic ideals, his brother-in-law the vicomte de Noailles, and the son of the toadlike duc d'Aiguillon, one of my old enemies during my days as dauphine. I shudder to think of their fathers' mortification—two courtiers who lived and breathed for every nuance of the Bourbons' rigidly prescribed etiquette.

The courtyard is thronged with citizens. Our family must run the gauntlet past them into the palace. But I fear they wish us all ill. Those who have accompanied us back to Paris may be misperceived by the rabble as royalist collaborators. "Save our bodyguard before everything, Monsieur de Lafayette," I urge the *général.* "They have done nothing but obey your orders."

We are surrounded on all sides and the grenadiers use their sabers to ward off the crowd so that we may quit our carriage. The folding steps are unfurled and Louis descends first. He is exhausted, his face and clothes streaked with perspiration and grit, but otherwise, he manages to assume the air of a man who has just returned from a particularly grueling hunt.

That is what makes a king, I think, just as a deputy from the National Assembly is shouted down by the crowd for daring to insult the sovereign. What a mad world we live in when I cannot be sure what anyone's opinion is from one moment to the next!

To my immense relief, the children are welcomed with good cheer and hastily ushered inside the palace. It is a long walk for the dauphin, however, and when one of the deputies scoops my son into his arms, I panic that he is being abducted and rush after them.

But a mob follows me through the courtyard, raining curses upon my head, blaming *me* for our ill-starred flight. The public warnings to neither cheer nor denigrate the monarch applied to the king, not to *me*. One woman manages to seize my shawl, pulling me up short. A band of men, every face menacing, surrounds me. Suddenly, out of the corner of my eye I spy a flash of steel. The duc d'Aiguillon's son has drawn his sword. With a *swish* of his blade he draws a wide swath across his body which frightens the rabble enough to keep them at bay. Satisfied they will no longer try to harm me, like a cavalier of old he sweeps me into his arms and carries me across the entire breadth of the courtyard and up the steps into the palace.

I thank him for his chivalry, then make my way to my apartments, where my first desire is to take a bath. On the Great Staircase I encounter Barnave speaking to Louis, and manage a feeble jest from ultimate royalist to confirmed revolutionary. "I confess, monsieur, I had never expected to spend three days confined in a carriage with you." The smile I give him is the last one that may ever cross my lips.

I ask Madame Campan to see that a tub is prepared, filled with lavender and bergamot, and for the next half hour I cleanse myself of the filth and sweat of four days on the road. It took three times as long to return to our gilded prison as it did to flee it.

Now, what? I wonder, as I stare at my reflection in a glass for the first time since our departure. I tug the dirty cotton cap off my head and my mouth gapes in horror at the sight. A loose curl tumbles over my shoulder. Shocked, I slowly raise my hand to touch it. Then, pin by pin, I dismantle my coiffure until I am crowned by a mane of white hair.

I remove a pair of golden shears from my toiletry case and snip off a single lock. That evening before retiring, I enclose the curl inside a letter to my beloved princesse de Lamballe. *"Blanchis par malheur,"* I tell her. "Turned white from misfortune."

SEVENTEEN

Entrances and Exits

⇜ SUMMER 1791 ⇝

Mon coeur,

I exist. How frightfully anxious I have been about you and how I pity you, knowing how much you must suffer, not having heard a word from me until now. Since our return our every move is watched and noted. Sentries are posted in every corridor, inside every room, and at every door. They even enter my bedchamber once a night to make sure I have not fled again. My privacy is a thing of the past; the door must remain open.

Four officers follow me from room to room and announce "the Queen" at each door, even when I go to visit my son. The dauphin had *un cauchemar* on our first night back from Varennes. He dreamt that he was surrounded by tigers and wolves and other wild beasts who threatened to devour him.

Our minders have even pitched tents in the courtyard. But
you must not write to me, for that would only endanger us,
and above all do not try to visit because the National Assembly
has us guarded day and night. They know that it was you who
spirited us out of here and you would be utterly lost if you were
to appear; the Assembly has already recast our flight as an "ab-
duction," absolving the king of any culpatory conduct.

I beg of you not to worry about me; the Assembly wishes
to treat us leniently. Louis has promised not only to remain in
Paris, but to countenance the Constitution. I shall not be able
to write to you again.

Will Heaven permit this letter to reach you?

~Antoinette

I hold the spoon of red wax over the flame and seal the letter to
Axel. Madame de Campan will see that it is posted to the Swedish
embassy in Brussels.

But I cannot keep my own word and the following day I risk
sending another missive to Count von Fersen.

Tell me you are safe. I cannot sleep at night without the
answer I crave. Write to me in cipher with your address, for I
cannot live without writing to you and I despair over who
might open our correspondence at the embassy. I can only tell
you that I love you, though really I have not even time for that.
I am well. Do not be uneasy about me.

Adieu, most loved and loving of men. All my heart goes
out to you.

Antoine Barnave has become my secret tutor in revolutionary
matters. I had been genuinely impressed by the intelligence of this
handsome young man as we grew to know each other during the

hot and dusty ride home from Varennes. And I discovered, too, that a few well-chosen words of flattery could turn the head of a committed revolutionary idealist as much as that of any other man, when my pious *belle-soeur* Madame Élisabeth, offered a spirited defense of her brother even as she endeavored to bend the deputy's mind to royalist ways. "You are too wise, Monsieur Barnave, not to appreciate the love the king has for his people and his genuine desire to make them happy. He has always felt this way. And as for the 'liberty' which you profess to love to such an extreme, you have not taken into account the disorder that comes in its wake. I was just a child when the queen of Denmark and her lover seized the reins of power from King Christian. They instituted all manner of freedoms. However, Monsieur Barnave, Caroline Mathilde and Herr Struensee could not control the demons they unleashed when a free society was at liberty to roundly criticize the architects of their newfound liberty."

Barnave had been listening to the princesse Élisabeth, but he had been watching me. He saw that I was no monster. And I saw that he was no zealot.

I had no idea how many revolutionary factions there are; when Barnave visits me at the Tuileries a few days after the royal family's return he explains the distinctions between them, and, like the dear abbé Vermond of my youth, catechizes me on the names and affinities of each of the deputies and their adherents so that I learn whose views are moderate, who may secretly be royalists, and who are so radical that none of their colleagues is a fervent enough anti-monarchist. Those who are members of the two prominent political clubs: the Jacobins, that includes Pétion de Villeneuve's protégé Maximilien Robespierre; and the Cordeliers, such as the scientist Jean-Paul Marat, the stammering journalist Camille Desmoulins, and the lawyer Georges Danton—who in innocent, happier days *walked* across the kingdom to attend my husband's coronation—

are calling for the king to be deposed or tried like a criminal. Robespierre has declared himself to be neither monarchist nor republican, and Pétion himself had told me that the notion of a republic was largely unpopular; but many others, Barnave informs me, are indeed calling for a republic, modeled on the democracy of the infant United States. I cannot hear America mentioned without recalling that the former English colonists would not have gained their political freedom without French soldiers, sailors, and sous.

Yet even those who hate us cannot agree on what is best for the nation. "Things cannot be left as they are," I tell Barnave when we meet. "Something must be done. But what? I do not know and I turn to you in the hope of finding a solution. I believe you have good intentions—and so do we, my husband and I. Whatever people may say, we have always had them." He asks me what I propose. "Let me work hand in hand with you," I reply. "If you discover a means by which we may exchange ideas I shall always answer you candidly and let you know if such a thing is within my power. Where the welfare of our people is concerned, I will shrink from no sacrifice."

In my view, the best thing would be a return to absolute monarchy: We are not a nation of shopkeepers like the English. The delegates of the National Assembly know nothing about governance; they are merely angry little men who don't know how to wield the authority they have wrested from us. Even as we pretend, Louis and I, to bow to the idea of a constitutional monarchy, I spend the greater part of every day with quill in hand, corresponding with my brother in Austria, with Axel, and with his king, Gustavus, who thus far has been the only sovereign brother to offer both his allegiance and his assistance to our cause. From the safety of Brussels, I fear that Louis's brothers plot against us. Monsieur, the comte de Provence, has already declared himself regent of

France as long as his brother and *belle-soeur* are being held captive in Paris. The revolutionaries wish there to be no kings whatsoever, while Monsieur at the very least, believes there are two kings. I desire only to see my husband reign. But Louis has become even more disconsolate since the debacle of Varennes, particularly when we receive word from Axel, who writes from Brussels that *the most unseemly joy has manifested itself here because the King has been taken prisoner. The comte d'Artois is positively radiant.* I despise myself now for ever having befriended the little viper.

Yet there are those far closer to home who wish us ill. *We are surrounded by spies,* I write to Leopold. I am not as close to him as I was to Joseph when he was emperor, and I am certain that Leopold cannot fathom how desperate our situation is becoming. *The possibility of poisoning is on our minds constantly. The pastry cook is a furious Jacobin. None of us will eat anything that comes from the kitchen that is breaded: no cutlets, no meat pies, no sweets. We will only touch plain roasted meats. I no longer have toast for breakfast unless the bread has been purchased by a trusted servant. One of the bed-chamber women goes to the market daily to buy bread, pastries, and pounded sugar, always disguising the purpose of her errand and always patronizing different merchants.*

On July 17, the Champ de Mars once again becomes the site of a national celebration when the National Assembly announces before an enormous crowd that Louis XVI will remain king under a constitutional monarchy, although the republican faction disapproves of this decision. We feign acceptance as I convince Barnave that we share his views, when in truth we are stalling for time, desperately waiting for Leopold's army and his mercenary forces to rescue us.

Yet instead of general rejoicing on the Champ de Mars, there is discontent. The journalist Jacques Pierre Brissot arrives with a manifesto demanding that Louis be deposed for his desertion of the throne, his intention to thwart the Constitution, and other, unspecified criminal acts, and amasses a crowd of people with counterrevolutionary ideals eager to sign the heinous document. Lafayette and the Garde Nationale manage to maintain order; but later that afternoon, the radical ringleaders Danton and Desmoulins inspire greater numbers to flood the Champs de Mars and a riot erupts. Martial law is declared on the spot. When Lafayette endeavors to disperse them, the petitioners fling stones at the National Guard. The soldiers' warning shots are unheeded; whether out of panic or anger they fire directly into the crowd. The reports we read disagree as to the number of people killed or wounded. Some say as few as a dozen or two; some as many as fifty. Two scoundrels who had hidden themselves under the platform simply to peer up ladies' skirts were mistaken for spies. The voyeurs were summarily executed on orders of the National Assembly, and their decapitated heads are displayed on pikes as a lesson to any potential counterrevolutionaries. It appears to be a matter of no importance that the beheaded men were put to death for the wrong reasons.

"What does this mean for us?" I ask Louis, Barnave, the comte de Mercy, and Axel, changing the keyword that day in our polyalphabetic cipher. Each man has a different vantage of the situation.

It is to the aging ambassador and political mentor of my youth that I confide most candidly:

My dear Mercy:

I correspond with the Triumvirs of the National Assembly only in order to temporize. Tell Leopold that we have not the slightest intention of following their exaggerated ideas. It appears likely that the king will be compelled to sign the Constitution, but we cannot be seen to fight it, even though he has no plans to honor his pledge. This fraud would be humiliating to me were it not absolutely necessary for us to perpetrate it. The leaders of the Assembly must remain duped until the allies can quite literally ride to our rescue, yet I remain hopeful my brother will recognize that in my present position I can do little but acquiesce to the Assembly's demands. Barnave tells me "The Revolution must be ended," and insists that it is not too late for me to win back the esteem of our people. Although I do not deny that these men, the Triumvirs of the Assembly, are strong-willed and hold very fast to their opinions, they are also quite open and motivated by a fierce desire to restore order.

Everyone (unsurprisingly) accuses me of dissimulation, and no one can believe that the emperor takes so little interest in his own sister's frightful position. By saying nothing Leopold exposes me to greater danger than he would were he to take decisive action. I can expect no aid from within France. Hatred and mistrust abound. A Fourth Estate is emerging, comprised of the rabble, their collective voice becoming as loud as that of the bourgeois who make up the Third Estate. They are not only reactionary but dangerous, and have no interest in any compromise that would still afford Louis an active role in the new form of government. Instead, insolence is king, given free rein because the people remain in a state of perpetual terror; yet at the same time, they do not believe that an attack will dare to come from across the frontier.

You will find my whole soul in this letter. Perhaps I am wrong, but it seems to me that the only means of retaining what little power and authority are left to us is to listen to what both sides have to say. I have formed my own opinion by studying that of my adversaries. Yet too often I feel as though I alone row the boat. You know the person with whom I have to deal. No sooner does one believe that he has been persuaded to accept a certain course of action, than a single word from someone else, the most trifling argument, can convince him to change tack without warning. This is why a thousand things I should like to achieve can never even be undertaken.

The scheme that I have adopted is the least unpalatable of several options. Whatever happens, I beg of you—never desert me as a friend; never withdraw your affection. And, after all the years you have known me, I must ask you to believe that whatever you hear, whatever misfortunes I may be plunged into, although I yield to circumstances, or appear to, I will never do anything that would dishonor me as a daughter of Austria and a wife and mother of France.

Tribulation first makes one realize what one is. My proud Hapsburg blood courses through my son's veins. I hope that the day will come when the dauphin shows his mettle and proves himself the worthy grandson of Maria Theresa.

The worst that could possibly happen would be for us to stay as we are, because we remain sitting targets for our enemies—those who, like a cancer, wish to destroy France, her monarchy, and our family, from within. However things turn out, only the foreign powers can save us. We have lost the army; we have no more money. There exists within this realm no power to restrain the armed populace.

> Yours in sorrow,
> ~Antoinette

I have received only one letter from Axel since our return from Varennes. Among the many reasons I sleep so fitfully is that I despair for his safety. The agents of the Assembly cannot touch him while he is in the Austrian Netherlands, but should he quit Brussels and attempt to enter France, who knows what orders have been issued to detain him—or worse? My thoughts are consumed with anxiety for him, with memories of our sunlit afternoons at le Petit

Trianon, of stolen glances in the dim illumination of my box at the Paris Opéra, or through our glittering masks at the balls that followed the Saturday performances. I wish to send him a token of my affection, to tell him he is always in my thoughts no matter how many miles separate us, regardless of the terrible risk I take in communicating with him.

In the open square outside Notre-Dame de Paris, where all manner of vendors retail their wares, there is currently a brisk trade in the latest fashion: inexpensive rings that, for a modest fee, sweethearts may customize for each other by having them engraved with a few sentimental words or a meaningful image. Although I am followed everywhere I go, when I mingle among the people, browsing the stalls, I make sure to linger for so long that I weary the guardsmen, literally boring them to distraction while I take care to examine every bouquet of flowers, all the shawls and fans, each piece of jewelry. Several items seem familiar; I am certain I have seen some of the pins or rings before, and then I realize that many of the aristocrats who have emigrated sold their gems for whatever they could get in order to begin a new life with money in hand, whether it is for rent, for food, or to bribe government officials.

By the time I have visited the sixth or seventh merchant and discussed at some length the number of threads in the weave of his cambric handkerchiefs or the beadwork on her silk purses, my bodyguards are shifting on their boot heels and their eyes are wandering in the direction of any pretty girl that passes or stray dog nosing about for a bone or a stranger's caress.

The uniforms no longer hover about me when I complete my purchase of a pair of rings, which I have engraved with a trio of fleurs-de-lis, although the rings themselves are not identical. I enclose them in a letter to a trusted intermediary, Count Valentin Esterházy, who has been one of my dearest friends since I was the dauphine. I rely upon him to comprehend my letter without the necessity of specifying the person I refer to by name.

Should you write HIM tell him that many miles and many countries can never separate hearts. I feel this truth more strongly every day. I am delighted to find this opportunity to send you a little ring which I am sure will give you pleasure. In the past few days they've been selling like hotcakes here and they are very hard to come by. The one that is wrapped in paper is for HIM. Send it to HIM for me. It is exactly his size. I wore it for two days before wrapping it. Tell him it comes from me. I don't know where he is. It is dreadful to have no news of those one loves and not even to know where they are living. I have requested an address but have received no word.

The inside of the ring I purchased for Axel bears the inscription: *Lâche qui les abandonne*—"faint heart he who forsakes them." Count Esterházy's ring, while it is also engraved with the three fleurs-de-lis, has no message. In truth, the reason I send him one of the popular keepsakes is to provide a cover for the gift to my beloved Axel.

When I finally hear from Count von Fersen, he makes no mention of the ring. Has he received it? Instead, I am treated to a completely unwarranted scolding that wounds me to the core.

Do you really want to identify yourself with the Revolution, or do you still want help from outside? Do you have a fixed plan as to what you intend to do? I can only hope that you haven't been taken in by those scoundrels. You say you must cozen the enemy and countenance the unthinkable as an unpleasant means to an end. But tell me that the rumors I hear are untrue—that you have not taken the deputy of the National Assembly, Antoine Barnave, into your bed as well as into your bosom and your confidences? I do not wish to believe my own ears, to credit the stories, but when you write to me yourself and cryptically allude to an unpalatable violation of all you hold dear, what am I supposed to think?

How dare he? Can he be insane? Has the whole world gone mad? Are people seriously bruiting it about Brussels and beyond that Barnave has become my lover? *Mon Dieu, non!* How absurd! It is the lying that I find intolerable; the notion that I am playing an honest and kind man false is despicable to me. Barnave is not a bloodthirsty radical. He truly believes that there is a role for the king in the new political order, and that most of Louis's subjects are fond of him as a benevolent father and do not want to see him deposed—if only his colleagues can be persuaded to see it. And Barnave genuinely thinks I share his view that a government can be created in which power is exercised by an executive as well as a legislature when in truth my goal is to restore my husband's autocracy.

It is poor Barnave I am guiltily deceiving, not my beloved Axel.

When, I wonder, will we receive a glimmer of good news? I cannot remember the last time any of us has smiled. Within the royal family itself, tensions abound. Louis is morose and indecisive. Madame Élisabeth refuses to believe that her brothers across the frontier are not loyal to Louis and have their own ulterior motives. "Monsieur and the comte d'Artois may pledge their allegiance to us," I tell her, "but what action have they taken to come to our aid?" I challenge her to name a single thing my *beaux-frères* have done to support the royalist cause. "They are raising neither armies nor funds!" I am finding it increasingly impossible to speak with her nowadays because every conversation disintegrates into a quarrel.

Our family life is a hell, even though the three of us have the best intentions in the world, I confide in a letter to my dear old comte de Mercy.

My beloved princesse de Lamballe wishes to return from exile in order to console me, but I refuse to jeopardize her safety.

Ma très chère amie,

I beg of you, stay in the country with your father-in-law. You would weep too much over our misfortunes were you to come back to Paris. The tigers who abound here now would cruelly rejoice in our suffering. At least the acceptance of the Constitution will allow us a few moments of respite from the gathering storm.

It has been a most horrific summer. At the end of August, we receive word from London that finally teases a smile from my lips. On the twenty-third of the month, the so-called comtesse Jeanne de Lamotte-Valois, the villainess who had plotted to steal the ostentatious diamond necklace from the court jewelers and then implicated me in the scheme by claiming I had commissioned its purchase, fell to her death from her third-story hotel room in the city. The newspapers disagree about the details of her demise. Some claim she had been pushed, while others assert that she had accidentally fallen out of the window as she was endeavoring to evade a visiting creditor. Then another tale emerges, averring that the comtesse had been poisoned.

Regardless of the circumstances, one of my greatest nemeses is now gone forever. Gone, too, I hope, are the insidious editions of her outrageous "memoirs" that she continued to revise and peddle until her death, which depicted me not only as greedy and conniving and impervious to the plight of those less fortunate, but as her Sapphic lover.

I dream that night that she is in the pit of hell, flames licking at her limbs while Lucifer laughs. When day breaks, I am not at all shaken by my vision. *Au contraire.* For the first time in six years, ever since the scandal of *"l'affaire du collier"* caused my name and character to be dragged through the mud by nearly everyone in France, from the judges of the Paris Parlement to the demimondaines outside the Palais Royal, and a mockery was made of justice—now, finally, God has had the last word. Justice has been served. And I feel cleansed.

EIGHTEEN

Tribulation First Makes
One Realize What One Is

⤳ SEPTEMBER 1791 ⤝

In a masterstroke of understatement, Louis's journal entry referring to the monstrous debacle surrounding our flight to Montmédy
and our ignominious return to the capital had been a terse *Five
nights spent outside Paris*. I wonder how he will describe the events
of the fourteenth of September, when once again the world as we
have always known it—as France has always known it, is upended?

Eleven days earlier we had been presented with the Constitution for him to review, although it would have mattered little to the
Assembly delegates if he had asked for any alterations. The following day, the king's acquiescence having been obtained, our restric-
tions at the Tuileries were lifted and the gardens were reopened to
the public. Monsieur Barnave delivered a stirring speech in the

chamber of the Salle du Manège, convincing his fellow deputies to vote for the restoration of a measure of royal authority.

The citizens erupted into a holiday mood. Madame de Lamballe returned to the Tuileries to be my solace in this time of great upheaval, taking up residence in the Pavillon de Flore. Louis was permitted to go hunting for the first time in months, and I was cheered in the streets when, on the advice of Barnave, who urged me to show myself to the public, I took a carriage ride one evening with my children. The *rues* were illuminated with lanterns. Citizens strolled arm in arm along the avenues. Turning to Madame de Tourzel, I said, "It's all so beautiful—but so sad, when one realizes that on the slightest provocation, they would all recommence the same atrocities."

Perhaps it is fitting that, in the words of the Assembly, my husband is being forced "according to the wish of the great majority of the nation" to become a constitutional monarch in a former riding stable. Of course there is no throne in the Salle du Manège. Instead, Louis is presented with the Constitution while he sits in an armchair with a fleur-de-lis painted on the back of the seat. There is no chair for me; as he affixes his signature to the heinous document, I am relegated to the role of spectator, just as I had been at Louis's coronation sixteen years ago.

Nor is there is a role for me in the Constitution. I am not even mentioned in it. Although the king's actions are protected by immunity, this is not so for any other member of his family, even the dauphin, who the Triumvirs wish to retitle the "Prince Royal." I am officially owed no respect as the king's wife. And as Louis signed his name with a heavy hand and a mournful heart, the boisterous sound of carousing wafted through the windows from the direction of the Tuileries Palace gardens. Soldiers were singing vulgar songs about me. When we passed another detachment on our way to the Salle du Manège, they did not even doff their hats. And to a man, the deputies of the Assemblée Nationale remained defiantly seated while Louis delivered his speech.

The Constitution, which also bears the heading "Declaration of the rights of man and of the citizen," permits the king to choose his own ministers; and while it strips him of the authority to declare war, the Assembly will now have that right, but only after the monarch has requested them to make such a declaration. Most important, the king retains the power of the veto, a measure passed by a majority of three hundred of the one thousand deputies to the National Assembly. But the very fact that we must consider ourselves fortunate to cling to the slenderest threads of power and privilege galls beyond measure. After the deed had been done and the deputies filed out of the chamber, Louis, who had been standing while they departed, sank into an armchair, disconsolate with humiliation. What would his ancestor, who, legend says, declared, *"L'État, c'est moi,"* think to see Louis reduced to "Representative of the Nation"?

I descended from the box where I had witnessed this public disgrace, of which I, too, have been a victim. Louis's eyes met mine with a watery gaze. "Ah, madame, why were you there?" he gulped wetly. "You came into France only to have to see—" He broke off, sobbing.

I draped my arms about his neck and chest, gently kissing the top of his head. A tear fell into his wig. When I looked up, I spied Madame Campan standing several feet away as if a sorcerer had turned her to stone. This whole time she has borne witness to our private mortification. "Go—for God's sake, go!" I cried, and suddenly, as if she had been struck with an electric current, she fled, as ashamed as we to have participated in such a sorrowful disgrace.

* * *

The young sculptress Louison Chabry finds herself among the thousands of patriots who have turned out to hear the proclamation of the new Constitution in front of the Hôtel de Ville. Tricolor buntings hang in triumphant swags from every window and wine flows freely from casks set up in the streets. Anyone with a goblet, tankard, or tin cup may fill it to the rim as often as they wish. Louison has a lover now, a handsome revolutionary who tells her that the Constitution is only the first step in ridding France of a despot.

Already drunk on Burgundy, and lustily bellowing snatches of Revolutionary songs—although he gets the words all wrong—as they pass a group of soldiers carousing around one of the overflowing spigots of wine, Armand assures her, "The tyrant will be brought low. This is the new world, now." Louison shudders.

One of the grenadiers tries to shock her by telling a popular vulgar joke. "What is the difference between the queen's vagina and the Jardin du Luxembourg?" Louison shakes her head, unable to think of a parallel between the vast public park and Her Majesty's genitalia. "Nothing!" the soldier exclaims, slapping his thigh. "They are both always open!"

Louison tugs Armand's sleeve. "Let's go." On their way to witness the fireworks celebration in the Place Louis XV, they pass a slogan crudely painted on the wall outside a cobbler's shop. LONG LIVE THE KING—IF HE IS HONEST! *"Je crois que oui,"* the sculptress whispers into her beau's ear. "That day at Versailles—when he promised us bread—I believed him."

Armand and Louison join the thousands of revelers in the Place Louis XV as the periwinkle dusk deepens into evening violet. Fairy lights have been strung about the square, twinkling the way Louison imagines the queen's private gardens at le Petit Trianon must have glittered when she fêted the young tsar of Russia and the handsome king of Sweden.

People are dancing in the street to cries of *"Vive la Nation!"* and several sympathetic shouts of *"Vive le roi!"* Louison even hears a few brave souls exclaim *"Vive la reine!"* and the revelers seem too happy to begin a brawl over it. "Does this means the Revolution is over?" Louison asks Armand, shouting into his ear to be heard above the cacophonous explosions of the fireworks. High above their heads the sky shimmers with cascading showers of red, white, and blue sparks.

Armand laughs. "Silly girl!" He pulls her into a delirious, drunken embrace and kisses her on the mouth, hard. "It is only the beginning of a new one!"

Throughout the autumn of 1791, the radicals shout the loudest. Their propaganda drowns out the voices of reason, intimidating a populace that had not personally despised their monarch into aping those who would mock him. The streets are paved with sedition. Revolutionary newspapers and broadsheets compete with each other for an audience. Camille Desmoulins prints *Les Révolutions de France et de Brabant.* Jean-Paul Marat churns out *l'Ami du Peuple.* Choderlos de Laclos, who nine years ago authored the provocative epistolary novel *Les Liaisons Dangereuses,* eviscerating the icy hedonism of the aristocracy, has turned his pen to politics as the editor of *Le Journal des Jacobins,* the most fanatical of the revolutionary factions. To keep abreast of the current events I force myself to read everything, no matter how unpleasant or vulgar. Louis is depicted by the caricaturists with the body of a hog and the head of a ram, an allusion to a pair of cuckold's horns. Desmoulins, who spares no praise for Lafayette, calls the latter the "Don Quixote of Capet"—never mind that we are the House of Bourbon and the Capetian dynasty ended four centuries ago—and Louis "our

crowned Sancho Panza." To the stammering zealot, they are figures of fun, straw men to be torn apart with the strokes of a pen.

I know we are despised, but have the citizens lost all reason?
The papers print nothing but lies and the people swallow them like
cool water on a sultry summer day. They say the king is planning
to place himself at the head of his army, intending to mow down
his enemies—his own subjects who dare to desire revolution. The
broadsheets publish false and malicious reports that Louis erupts
into frightful tantrums, smashing everything about him—crystal
goblets, and priceless porcelain vases—flinging three-legged stools
into mirrors, breaking them into shards. Laclos should return to
fiction.

Among the legislators, there is dissension and inconsistency.
The Assembly has renamed itself. As of October it is no longer the
National, but the Constituent Assembly. And that dreadful, super-
cilious little deputy from Arras, the lawyer Robespierre, appears to
be on the rise. He harbors an implacable and inexplicable abhor-
rence for my husband, which will make it all the more difficult for
us to persuade the moderate voices in the Assembly to seek common ground. I have never seen such a demagogue as Robespierre,
a horrid man who inveighs against the monarchy and the nobility
even as he still dresses like an aristocrat, in silk breeches, vest, and
coat—always ink-black—and blindingly white hose. Even the
comte d'Artois in his day was not nearly so vain in his tailoring.

Republicanism, of which Robespierre is a staunch proponent,
has become the watchword. But in their view France cannot
become a republic unless the monarchy is demolished, stone by
stone—which is how we live now from week to week—until it is
eventually abolished. And if that woeful day arrives—what will
become of the monarchs?

The few aristocrats who remain in the Assembly are no longer
our advocates. Now that their titles and feudal privileges have been

abolished, there is no reason for them to support the monarchy, for the king has no authority to grant them the offices and perquisites that for centuries were the nobility's bread and butter. They blame the Constitution for robbing them; and rather than sympathize with the moderates, those who have not abstained from voting altogether have, incomprehensibly, taken up the cudgels of the more radical elements of the Assembly, making common cause with the Jacobins. Their marriage of inconvenience has allowed another radical faction, the Girondins, who are fundamentally opposed to *any* form of monarchy, to gain ascendance in the Assembly, making it even more of a challenge for Barnave and his adherents to retain enough support for a constitutional monarchy.

Louis is more morose than ever. He spends hours in his library. His prayer book is never far from his hand and he is rereading the life of Charles I of England, a monarch whose unhappy fate he has always sought to avoid. It is why he is such a conciliator. He would rather cede a mile of ground or a measure of power than forfeit the love of his "good people" whom he genuinely cares about as if they were his children.

Since our ignominious return from Varennes we have not been permitted to say Mass in the palace chapel because it lies too far from our apartments. Does the Assembly think that one day on our way to prayer we will make a dash for it down the lengthy corridors that separate the vast wings of the Tuileries? Instead, a corner of the Gallery of Diana, decorated with a few vases of flowers, has been transformed into a makeshift place of worship, with a temporary wooden altar that bears an ebony crucifix. If God is everywhere then He will hear our prayers just as well here as He would have done a hundred yards away. But some nights I lie abed and wonder if He hears me at all through the thunder of revolutionary rhetoric that is transforming France into a nation of savages.

As we approach Christmas, the autumn air becomes more bracing. When we are permitted to open the windows an inch or two—never wide enough that we might consider flight—I welcome the chill. The stench of the palace is unbearable. No one cleans the floors or the carpets. Our minders have yet to discover the benefits of regular bathing. The soldiers never change their uniforms, which are rank with perspiration. Most of our chamber women and what pass for footmen stink, their breath as rotten as their teeth.

I cannot say whether Axel has recognized the folly of his accusations against me, if he continues to believe that Barnave is my lover and that I have bewitched him into becoming a secret royalist. Count von Fersen is jealous. I know that he alone wants to be my champion. I know, too, that he continues to work secretly with King Gustavus to liberate France's royal family and to restore the monarchy and that he desperately wishes to return to Paris to discuss matters of the utmost importance concerning their latest plan. But it is too dangerous now, even for such an intrepid soldier, for this most consummate of diplomats.

On December 7, I urge him not to try to visit me, reminding him of the bounty on his head should he be caught anywhere near the capital.

My longing to see you has never abated for an instant, but it is absolutely out of the question for you to attempt to see us. Your coming would risk our happiness, for I despair to think what may befall you, should there be the slightest mishap. Not only is the exterior of the palace heavily guarded and the Tuilieries Gardens turned into an armed camp, but we remain watched around the clock.

At least some of our sentries are more sympathetic than others. Saint-Prix, one of the old actors at the Comédie-

Française—remember him?—is the sentinel on duty in the corridor that divides the ground floor in two and which leads from my apartments to the king's, upstairs. He has facilitated many a meeting between Louis and me; and as he is fond of whistling to himself at all hours of the day, has devised a system of codes: certain melodies indicate who is coming along the passage and whether it is dangerous to enter it, as well as when it is safe once again. Monsieur Collot, the chief of the battalion of the Garde Nationale responsible for guarding my apartments, is also no ogre. But these are two men I name out of thousands who would cut you down with their bayonets, or worse, just as they did to poor Monsieur de Malden upon our return from Varennes. He lay near death for weeks, and it is one of God's miracles that he survived the horrific pummeling he received merely for being one of our *escorts* on that ill-starred journey. Can you imagine what your fate would be, were you to be found here?

Silhouetted in the amber glow of a guttering candle, I seal the envelope, as a breeze wafts across my shoulders, threatening to extinguish the flame. Even as my quill warns my beloved to stay away, my heart trembles with both fear and anticipation that he will nonetheless arrive unexpectedly.

Meanwhile, Louis has endeavored to effect a rapprochement with his cousin, the duc d'Orléans. Despite the latter's republican sensibilities, he *is* a prince of the blood. In September, the king extended an olive branch to the duc by appointing him a naval admiral. Philippe welcomed the assignment, informing the comte de Molleville, Minister of Marine, that it would provide him the opportunity to demonstrate to His Majesty how maligned he has been by accusations of disloyalty to the crown.

After decades of enmity, the cousins appeared, finally, to be reconciled. But at a banquet given in my apartments in January, several of the guests, unaware of the understanding that had at long last been effected, shout in horror when Orléans appears at the table, insinuating that he might have poisoned the food. The accusation is enough to shatter the fragile détente between the pair of noble kinsmen, and Philippe d'Orléans storms out of the Tuileries in a red-faced rage, insulted and infuriated.

Louis and I are incensed by the courtiers' ignorant outcry, and the troublemakers are given a dressing-down; but the damage is done. After such an attack upon his character, I worry we may have forfeited our last hope of obtaining the support of the most influential man in Paris.

My fears bear fruit even sooner than we could have anticipated; within days of the debacle at the palace the duc changes his name to Philippe Égalité—a chilling emphasis of his final breach with the crown and his support for the Revolution.

NINETEEN

Resté Là

I am seated at my escritoire scribbling a desperate letter to my brother Leopold as the sky behind me darkens. Owing to the vast amount of correspondence I engage in nowadays my handwriting has become so much worse. I hope he will be able to distinguish the words so that it may be deciphered. The clock on the black marble mantel chimes once to mark the quarter hour and I pause, mid-sentence, to glance at its golden hands. Five-fifteen.

I am nearly startled out of my chair by a key turning in the lock. My pulse races and I search for a place to hide the letter to the Austrian emperor, blowing on the ink and hastily sanding it, hoping that it will dry sufficiently enough not to smudge before I slide it beneath the blotting paper.

A hooded figure enters the room and my stomach seizes. A voice, muffled by the hood, says, "I have come to hear Your Majesty's confession."

Only priests who have sworn the oath to uphold the Constitution are permitted access to us now. If we do not wish to confess to these clerics who have become puppets of the Revolution, then we can choose to remain unabsolved of our sins. In any event, I would never tell my secrets to a tool of Robespierre.

"You may go the way you entered. I have nothing to say to you," I reply, endeavoring to remain calm. "And how did you come by a key to my chamber? Were you given it by one of the guards?"

The priest turns the lock. I am his prisoner now. "The watch has gone to supper, *Majesté*. And you gave me this key yourself. In happier times." He slides the hood away from his face and removes the cotton wadding from the hollows of his cheeks. The gray-blond wig that curls about the ears he leaves upon his head.

"Axel!" I breathe. And in the next moment, I gasp, "Don't look at me!" for he has not seen me since we parted at Bondy. Only eight months have passed, but in them I have become an old woman. I am thirty-six, although one who didn't know me might think the digits were reversed, for my eyes are hollow sockets, swollen from sleepless nights and red-rimmed from too many tears. My bosom, which measured forty-four inches after I had my children, has shrunk to almost nothing. And my hair is whiter than if I had powdered it for fashion's sake. I am no longer a beauty, if ever he thought me one. I long to rush into Axel's arms, to remain in his embrace, but I am rooted to the spot, terrified of stepping into the light of the candles that illuminate the chamber's perimeter, disbelieving that we are truly alone and undisturbed, and that it is really Count von Fersen who stands before me.

Finally, he strides across the room and clasps me to him. My senses, so dulled by heartbreak and melancholia, are instantly alive once more with recognition. The sensation of his body against mine, the once-familiar scent of his skin! I am dizzy with memories—*mon Dieu!* Axel wears the toilet water I had commissioned expressly for him so many years ago. Pressed against him, my cheek to his chest, I have never felt so petite. He tilts my chin with his fingers and our lips meet wetly, as hot tears bathe my face. "You shouldn't have come," I murmur, even though I am thinking *Thank God you are here!*

"I had to," Axel whispers. "For one thing, I could not bear the passing of another week without seeing you. For another, the plot I wish to discuss with you and the king is too sensitive to communicate by any means other than face-to-face."

I cannot fathom how he managed to cross the border into France without arousing suspicion: He tells me that he traveled under a false passport issued in the name of his orderly's servant, wearing a brown wig and several layers of clothing that made him appear shorter and stouter. "The lackey's disguise is safely hidden within the home of a friend," Axel assures me. And it was there that he was given a *curé*'s black soutane and skullcap. He perfectly resembles any one of the clerics who swore in 1790 to uphold the Constitution. "Should our meeting be interrupted, address me as abbé Benoit. I will immediately launch into a contentious political and theological discourse with you that will so bore and confound any guardsman, he will scarcely wish to remain."

I am amazed at the courage it took him to enter the kingdom, knowing that he might instantly be put to death, were his disguise detected. I cannot stop gazing at him with an expression as full of love as it is of sorrow. Suddenly, Axel, too, is overcome with emotion. "I reproach myself every day for bidding you farewell and leaving you to such a fate," he exclaims. I touch my finger to his lips to remind him to keep his voice low. Momentarily chastened, he begs me to relate every moment of the disastrous journey, sparing no detail. He is even interested in what repasts we enjoyed, and when we took them, especially because he was the one who provisioned the berline with my comfort in mind.

He chuckles at the irony that a grocer should be named Sauce and shudders at the malevolence of the postmaster Drouet.

But he bristles at my mention of all the missed communications and relays—so many things I learned after they had taken place, such as Léonard's inexplicable directive to Bouillé's men to quit their posts. And by the time Bouillé finally roused his troops from their barracks and made for Varennes, they crested the hilltop above the village only to see our berline on the road below, lumbering out of town, followed by the coach carrying my attendants.

The utter futility of the scenario continues to rankle. Had Bouillé arrived but fifteen minutes sooner, the monarchy—we—might have been saved.

My recounting of the insults and jeers, the humiliations to which we were subjected during our three-day journey back to the capital, stabs at Axel's heart and pricks at his conscience like an arsenal of bayonets.

"I should have been there," he says, choking back angry, guilty tears. "I should never have quit you at Bondy. Had I traveled with you for the entire journey, we would have been prepared for contingencies—and—and I believe you and the king would have safely reached the frontier." He glances at the door. "Does His Majesty visit you at night?"

I look at him, puzzled. "Most evenings he comes downstairs to my apartments to bid me *bonsoir*. If he finds the door locked, he will return to his own rooms; he is very solicitous of my feelings and doesn't wish to disturb me or trouble me in any way by his intrusion." Then I realize what Axel is really asking. "But to stay, you mean?" I shake my head. "We . . . we do not have regular relations anymore. My husband is not the sort of man to initiate romance; in nearly twenty-two years of marriage everything we have done between the bedclothes has been dictated by fidelity to our marital duty. He has never once come to my bedchamber to answer the call of *desire,* or even to comfort me when my soul, and not my body, is in need of succor or solace," I say wistfully. I glance away, at the shadows upon the blue velvet draperies made by the dancing candlelight. "We have never awakened beside each other, not even on the morning after our wedding night. He left the bed to go hunting," I add softly. How well I still recall the humiliation of *"rien"*!

"I would like to do that," Axel murmurs, enfolding me in his arms. "Tomorrow morning I would like to wake up beside you."

At his words, something far more powerful than a frisson—a tremor—courses through me from my scalp to my deepest and most private parts. I search his eyes, which appear lapis blue in this subtle amber light, and realize that he is in earnest. All I can think of is that we will be caught—the risk—the soldiers—they still come to check on me in the wee hours of the night.

"If they are only making certain that you are present, they will not think to search the room for someone who may be hiding."

I laugh for the first time in months. "You truly do not mean to jump into the wardrobe?" This is hardly the place to stage a scene from an *opéra buffa*!

"Then as soon as we hear footsteps outside your door, I will be sure to bolt from your narrow bed into that extremely uncomfortable-looking chair and chastise you at great length for all the sins you have committed against the kingdom and the people of France."

"And if they wonder why I am being scolded by a priest at three in the morning? Or six? And suddenly conclude that you have been in my rooms for hours?" I retort.

"I will tell them that you are being forced to confess the litany of your crimes to me and they will not for a moment doubt that it has taken this long. In fact, I will concede that I am as astonished as they, that after so many hours I am still worming out so many dastardly transgressions."

I rest my hand on his arm. "Perhaps you go too far," I say, gently. "You jest, but remember, these soldiers are not educated men. You tell them a falsehood built on hyperbole and they will simply swallow it the way a pike does a minnow."

We talk for hours, our voices never above a whisper. The new plan of escape that he and Gustavus are devising for us is a complicated one, relying on many factors. "But you must explain it all to Louis as well," I urge Axel. "Even if I endorse a scheme, only the king may decide on the course we may take. I have pledged to support whatever he chooses to do, and whither he goes, there go I."

I know that my husband will be unable to see the count this evening. Louis will hold his *lever* as usual, conversing with dignitaries and those members of the nobility in attendance. Then he will conduct his nightly meeting with Lafayette, who has a tendency to linger. Axel's arrival was an unannounced surprise; tomorrow I must alert the king to his presence so that Louis can do whatever is necessary to convince his guards that he requires solitude at a certain hour. Axel will have to remain here until he can share his plans with him. It is just as dangerous to attempt to leave the Tuileries Palace as it is to enter it.

Returning obliquely to the topic of unfulfilled marriages, we discuss his sister Sophie, who is unhappily wed. In Sweden, Axel shares a residence with Sophie and her lover, Baron von Taube. "I spare no confidence from them," he tells me. "Although my father may not be able to fathom why I am still a bachelor, my sister has known the reason for years." He places his hands on my shoulders and looks directly into my eyes. "She knows there is only one woman to whom I could completely dedicate my life. And since that woman cannot be mine, then I will have no wife at all."

His lips brush mine, ever so tenderly. When he touches my hair, so thin and white, I want to stop him, to tell him *no, I've somehow grown old, ugly, undesirable,* but he leads me into the adjoining room, guiding me to the bed. By now, the hour is late, the candles guttering stubs.

We sit beside each other. Axel pulls me into his embrace and softly, oh so softly kisses my brow, my eyelids, my cheeks, neck and throat. He teases away the fichu tied about my shoulders. I melt into his embrace, as our lips meet in a kiss born of desire, hunger, passion, and even despair. Axel begins to unlace the back of my gown and my body is acquiescent to his touch, until . . .

"I—" Suddenly I don't know what to say. And when I gather my thoughts I cannot express them. Instead, I shudder and Axel pauses.

"Is something the matter, *mon coeur?*"

The world has changed so much since I first gave myself to Count von Fersen. And it has changed me. I no longer recognize the carefree queen who gamboled in the fairy-lit gardens of Trianon. If I were to meet her today I do not know what we would converse about, except perhaps, having little in common with the husband that dynasty and destiny gave us. Yet I think about Louis now—

My muscles tense at the echo of footsteps in the corridor outside my apartments. In horror, I press my hand to Axel's mouth. All my fears of discovery are bearing fruit. I point to the next room and Count von Fersen tiptoes across the floor, leaving me on the bed. The only way for him to hide is behind his disguise. Several agonizing moments pass. Finally he moves his fingers as if to indicate claws, then wiggles his pinky—a scratching at the outer door. Only those conversant with the etiquette of Versailles would do such a thing.

My first instinct says it must be Louis. And it is vital for him to speak with Axel. But what if it is not? It might just as well be the princesse de Lamballe. Or Madame Élisabeth. The former would keep our secret, but with the latter, things are not so simple. For one thing, she has been too much in correspondence with her brothers in Belgium and they seem content to leave us to the blood-thirsty jaws of the revolutionaries. Nor would I wish to discuss with my pious *belle-soeur* the presence at this late hour of Count von Fersen in the guise of a juring priest and the reason that my gown is in disarray.

I know the door is locked. Privacy is such a rarity for the royal family at the Tuileries; thus we respect it so well that we do not intrude on one another without permission. If it is a friend, they will not try to open the door themselves.

If it is a foe, we are truly lost.

Finally, the footsteps retreat; I hold my breath until the sound recedes, leaving a tense silence in its wake.

"Do you think there will be any more intrusions?" Axel asks.

I shrug. Anything is possible. "Since you are already here, it is unsafe to leave the room. But neither of us should undress. If the guards enter when they change their shift we must be prepared to enact our little scenario with all the brimstone of Père Bourdaloue preaching to Madame de Montespan on the sins of pride and cor-ruption of the flesh."

He embraces me; and suddenly the tears begin to flow and all I want to do is burrow into his chest and remain there until life is once again sweet and pure and untrammeled.

"Je t'aime," I whisper into his open mouth. "I love you." And we kiss with the ardor of young lovers. "Hold me," I murmur. "I want to fall asleep in your arms. We have never spent the entire night together, greeting the dawn as lovers do." I return his caresses, stroking the fine planes of his cheeks and jaw, clasping a fistful of his hair, smoothing my palm along his torso and limbs, obscured

even as they are by the *curé*'s soutane. This will surely be our only night together and most assuredly our last chance to make love again.

Nevertheless, it is a different sort of intimacy I crave. I am seized with revulsion at the notion of Axel touching my bare flesh. I do not wish his final memory of our coupling to be marred by the recollection of my beauty's devastation, for him to leave me tomorrow, secretly thinking that he felt like he had pleasured his grandmother.

"*Non,* my love." Reclining, I clasp his hand to pull him down beside me, to do something with Axel that I have never experienced with my husband. "Just hold me close and do not let me go until morning." We nestle like spoons. His arm secures me, his hand strays to cup my breast as it swells above the top of my stays, his fingertips caress my flesh. My beloved's chest is warm against my back; I can feel the rise and fall of every breath, the warm exhalations blowing my hair off my neck, the pulse of the heart that beats for me, lulling me to slumber.

Awakening to Axel's hazel gaze—how long has he been watching me sleep?—reminds me that he must remain in hiding until I can arrange for him to discuss Gustavus's plan with Louis. Even a sympathetic guard like Saint-Paix cannot be permitted to discover Axel's presence, let alone his identity.

How sweetly fitting it is that today is Saint Valentine's Day. When it is safe to do so, Axel and I exchange loving glances and kisses, but from time to time as the hours pass and I await a message from Louis, sharing the food from my meal trays with the count, he does indeed sermonize, warning me to pray for my immortal soul, so that any passerby hearing voices in my rooms will not think anything is amiss.

At four o'clock, Saint-Paix slides a sealed note under my door. It is from the king, and advises me to expect his arrival in my rooms at six-thirty. Louis appears punctually and greets Axel with the warmth and effusiveness of a brother. For the next three hours we discuss the plot that Axel has devised with the Swedish sovereign.

Count von Fersen lays out the plan in detail. Monsieur de Malden will once again aid in our escape from the palace where we will be taken by light, swift carriage to Calais; and from there, across the English Channel to Dover. Meanwhile, the shores of Normandy will be invaded by the allied navies of Sweden and Russia.

Louis listens carefully, but I can tell from the troubled cast in his eye and the quivering in his cheeks that he is uncomfortable with the scheme. "I know my people accuse me of irresolution and weakness," he confesses, sounding as if he has given up all hope. "But name me another man who has found himself in such a difficult situation. I had one chance of escape and I missed it," he sighs, recounting for Axel's benefit the contentious debate over whether the royal family should flee or remain in France after the Bastille was taken. "Such a chance never came again." Louis swallows hard. "And now the whole world has abandoned me."

I glance at Axel. "We have not," I insist, placing my hand over my husband's.

"I have pledged my word and my honor to bring Your Majesties to safety," Count von Fersen avers.

Louis emits another ponderous sigh. The weight of France— her fate, too, it seems—rests so heavily on his broad shoulders. "And I have given my word to the Assembly that I will remain in Paris." For whatever my opinion is worth, because I have pledged to stay by Louis's side, no matter the course he chooses, I remind my husband that we cannot trust the Assembly as far as we can throw an orange. So why should His Majesty feel the necessity of upholding his promise when our lives are at stake and when the deputies will only betray us in the end?

Louis buries his head in his hands. In the candlelight the gem-stones on his rings spray the ivory-colored wall paneling with doz-ens of candy-colored sparkles. "Because, *ma chère femme,* a man is worth nothing if his word has no value."

I study Axel's face as Louis rejects the Swedish plot. Will the count be insulted that the immense amount of effort he has ex-pended to coordinate such an intricate plan will now be for naught? If so, he does not reveal his emotions. Axel says merely, "You are in truth, Sire, a man of honor."

The count stands, his errand accomplished. I begin to tremble, knowing that after he quits my rooms, it is doubtful we will see each other ever again. My lover may never give up trying to rescue us, even though my husband will never consent to his schemes. And I will never allow myself to be separated from Louis and our children.

The men embrace, regretful tears clouding their eyes. Louis glances at the clock. Taking my hands in his, he tells me sorrow-fully, "I bid you good night, *ma chère.*" Then, turning to Count von Fersen, he says, his voice and his words pregnant with import—or perhaps in my present state of mind I read too much into them—"You have always been the most stalwart champion of my wife and me, our Lancelot. But I fear that France will suffer the fate of Camelot nonetheless. Despite our best intentions, our genu-ine love for our subjects, and our desire to avoid bloodshed and keep the peace, the forces of rebellion foment confrontation. I fear they will ultimately destroy us. Please tender my profound thanks and esteem to your sovereign. Speaking for the two of us," he says, acknowledging me, "it has hardly escaped our attention that our sovereign brother Gustavus has been more of a sibling to us than the queen's blood brothers or my own. As for you: you have done everything you can, *mon ami,* well beyond the ordinary expecta-tions of your commission."

Louis's final words hang damply in the air. He departs through the door that opens onto the dark corridor and the narrow back staircase to his apartments, leaving me alone with Axel for a final farewell.

My tears flow unceasingly as though a dam has ruptured. For the sake of Louis's dignity, for all propriety, I had managed to contain them during the king's adieux, but there is nothing to conceal now. I all but fling myself into Axel's embrace, pressing him to me, caressing his strong back, wishing I could touch his soft brown hair beneath the ridiculous *curé*'s wig one more time. We cover each other's faces with kisses, careful not to neglect a single place; and as my lips linger on his neck I detect the bespoke cologne Fargeon concocted for him back in 1781, subtler now, but mingled with Axel's own scent, a complex aroma that will remain imprinted forever upon my memory, along with the sensation of his skin against my fingertips, the lilting baritone of his voice, the mutable color of his eyes, the way that he knows me as no one else in my life ever has. And when someone so cherishes you that he values your life above his own—that is a sacred gift that should never be squandered or belittled.

It is painful to accept that our parting now is not an "au revoir," because the chances are so slender that we will ever be able to meet again. It is an *adieu:* we each go with God.

And go he must, because the guards are about to change again. Axel must make his exit from the Tuileries as men and women hasten to enter and leave the palace, their nightly duties ending or about to commence.

A final kiss as our lips meet in ecstasy and sorrow. "I shall write about last night in my *dagbok*," Axel promises me. "With but two words: *Resté là.* And only you and I shall truly know what transpired between us."

One more embrace and he leaves my apartments from the entrance to the salon, slipping in amid the bustling commotion of dozens of uniformed guards, lackeys, and even a few other priests. As I lock the door once again, a tiny crescent of a smile emerges through my tears. Axel still has a key.

The following afternoon I receive a visit from Jean-Louis Fargeon, the *maître parfumeur* who has been creating fragrances for me and supplying perfumed candles, scented gloves, and aromatic pastilles since my verdant days at Trianon. The king and I have exhibited such exemplary behavior during the last few months, and Louis has indeed been true to his word not to quit the capital, that the deputies do not begrudge me such petty luxuries as bath crystals and body lotions. Besides, Citizen Fargeon, as he is addressed now, once the purveyor to the aristocracy, has become thick with some of the louder voices of the Revolution. No longer a friend of my friends, perhaps he has become an enemy. I do not know whether I can still trust him, even as I receive the items I recently commissioned.

Fargeon's mode of dress is not nearly as dapper as it used to be. He forswears hair powder now, and his pewter-colored locks are secured at the nape of his neck with a plain black ribbon. His "nose," however—by which I mean a perfumer's greatest asset, not the shape of his proboscis—remains as discerning as ever. Upon entering my salon, the expression on his face after a single inhalation is one of instant recognition. "Top notes of bergamot, oak moss, and jasmine. With a hint of leather in the bottom note," he murmurs, more to himself than for my benefit. His faint smile transmits a shared, distant memory. "You have recently had a very special visitor."

My breath catches in my throat. Citoyen Fargeon never knew precisely for whom he had created the gentleman's toilet water all those summers ago. But the world has since turned upside down.

Even what the perfumer does not know could be enough to condemn me.

How many purchases have I made from Fargeon's emporium throughout the duration of my reign? Surely the ability to name the Queen of France among his clientele has made him a wealthy man? But will my longstanding custom be sufficient to buy his silence?

TWENTY

Invasion

⤞ SPRING 1792 ⤝

From beginning to end, the month of March brings devastating news. Were I a superstitious woman I would be certain by now that we were cursed, like the characters in a tragedy of ancient Greece, punished by the gods for some grievous sins we had committed against man and nature.

My brother Leopold, emperor of Austria and Holy Roman Emperor, succumbs to a brief illness, dying on the first of March. His eldest son succeeds him, a twenty-four-year-old with no memory of his aunt Antonia. The new sovereign, Francis II, was all of two years old when I left Austria forever for France. He accorded a cool reception to the messengers we dispatched to congratulate him upon his accession, and thus far he has been markedly indifferent to my letters seeking his aid.

At the end of the month, a terrifying event compels us to fear not only for our safety but for our future. On the twenty-ninth, the greatest hope for our deliverance, King Gustavus III of Sweden, dies after being shot in the back thirteen days earlier during a masquerade ball. His murderer is a disaffected military officer who was aided by a pair of coconspirators. From Sweden, I now harbor even fainter hope of assistance. The new king, Gustavus's son, is only fourteen years old. Gustavus Adolph and his regent, his uncle Charles, are too busy courting an alliance with Russia to continue their support for the late king's foreign policy.

As the Girondins gain adherents to their antimonarchical views, Louis is compelled to accept a member of their faction, Général Dumouriez, as his chief minister. When the fifty-three-year-old Dumouriez requests an audience with me, I inform him that neither the king nor I can bear all these innovations in the Constitution.

I am surprised when Monsieur le Général falls to his knees and kisses my hand. "Madame, I have no interest in misleading you. Believe me. But as a military man with several decades of experience, I am in a better position than Your Majesty to judge events; and this is not, as you seem to believe, a passing popular movement where the winds will one day blow in another direction. It is the nearly unanimous insurrection against what the people perceive as long-standing and inveterate abuses of power. And yet some of us do have your best interests at heart," Dumouriez insists. "Allow yourself to be saved."

But his dark eyes are stern and it is hard to conceive that this face, which looks as if it has been carved of stone, is sympathetic. After all, the Girondins wish to do away with us altogether. "One cannot believe in the protestations of a traitor," I reply coolly. In my view, to a man, they are *all* traitors.

Louis, who has vowed to avoid shedding a single drop of his subjects' blood, now contemplates drastic measures. War is inevitable. The émigrés have been rattling their sabers for months.

Francis has permitted the prince de Condé, the only Bourbon with any military experience, to assemble an army of them in the Austrian Netherlands. I write to the comte de Mercy in cipher with details of France's intentions.

In order to prod the Austrians into military action on our behalf, and in the desperate hope that a foreign conflict will draw attention, resources, and troops away from the Revolution, on April 20, his eyes brimming with tears, my husband declares war against the king of Hungary and Bohemia.

My nephew Francis II, who is the Apostolic King of Hungary in addition to his other titles, is not the pacifist his father was and welcomes Louis's challenge. But I cannot endorse the scheme. It will lead to our ruin, I argue. We cannot be the aggressors. The monarchy will become more reviled than ever, I aver. But Louis refuses to look with my eyes.

My emotions are horribly torn by this turn of events. A part of me secretly hopes the countrymen of my homeland will prevail over those of my adopted nation who have never accepted me as their own. *Never have I been more proud than at this moment to have been born a German,* I write to Axel. But the better part of me despairs over our fate, keenly aware that Louis's declaration has only made things worse for us here at home. Vicious pamphlets bearing hideous caricatures of me are slipped surreptitiously beneath my doors or find their way into my embroidery workbox or my dinner napkin, accusing me, *l'Autrichienne,* of trafficking with France's enemies. Some propose my permanent removal to the convent of Val de Grâce; other less charitable souls demand my death. A new guardian watches over me when I sleep, a brown and white spaniel I name Thisbe, who makes her bed under my own and awakens me at the slightest disturbance.

The people sing a new song now, an anthem called the *Marche des Marsellois* and a deadly method of execution has been introduced by a man who had been a delegate from the Third Estate during the historic convening of the Estates General in 1789. Dr. Joseph Ignace Guillotin invented a method of dispatching a criminal that is rumored to be humane, permitting the malfeasor to meet his maker with dignity. This "blade of eternity" is a giant angular knife that plunges through a channel, decapitating the victim, who lies several feet below, at the foot of the channel, bound facedown to a board with his head secured in the manner of medieval wooden stocks.

I marvel at the notion that the words "execution" and "humane" should be uttered within the same breath, but the Revolutionary mind remains a mystery to me. Named for its creator, the "Guillotine" has been tested on sheep and goats, and even on corpses, but in April the machine is used for the first time to send a convicted highwayman and forger to his heavenly reward. On the twenty-fifth of the month, a tremendous crowd gathers in the Place de Grève to witness the blade's baptism in the first blood of the living. We hear that Charles Henri Sanson, France's public executioner, prefers the guillotine to decapitation by sword, because the latter, being the punishment accorded to the nobility, still bears aristocratic connotations, whereas the "national razor" knows no social distinction. Yet the mob that gathers for the spectacle of Monsieur Pelletier's bloody demise is almost disappointed with the effortlessness by which the hapless convict is swiftly despatched. The silver blade plunges so quickly and the severed head falls with a dull *thump* into the wicker basket beneath the neck cradle; the merest blink of an eye could cause an onlooker to miss the show.

Outside the city walls, the war does not go well for the French army. Secretly I rejoice that so many of them are inept, and countless others are cowardly. Two-thirds of the officers have emigrated; those who remain are deserting the army like rats at high tide. Even Axel's former superior, old Général Rochambeau, has re-

signed, unable to fulfill his commission at so great a disadvantage.
Three weeks after Louis's declaration of war, with the Austrian
troops advancing toward the frontier, Lafayette is desperately suing
for peace.

The propagandists take every advantage of the tension, playing
upon the people's greatest fears. Throughout the narrow *rues* comes
the hue and cry that not only are the Austrians coming to mow
down the capital's innocent citizens and destroy the liberty the
revolutionaries fought so valiantly to gain, but that the deserters
from the French army are about to descend upon the city en masse,
seizing what little food there is to be had and slaughtering anyone
who stands in their way. Red-bonneted rabble-rousers bearing
cudgels and pikes demand a call to arms. When they encounter a
man or woman who appears too well dressed, they attack the poor
soul, blaming the "royalist dog" for the astronomical price of firewood and beef, bread and wine, and leaving the battered body
lying in the gutter, to be pelted with refuse.

As the Assembly flexes its political muscle, passing the most
decisive antiroyalist measures to date, Louis pushes back. Yet he
has grown so melancholy that he appears somnambulant. A week
earlier, at the Mass in celebration of the Feast of Corpus Christi,
without even bothering to dress for the occasion, he'd moved so
sluggishly that palace lackeys spread gleeful rumors he was a
drunkard. June 16 brings a deluge of bad news. The king's constitutional guard, our only remaining source of protection, are to be
dismissed, replaced by members of the untrustworthy Garde Nationale. Nonjuring priests, the clerics who refused to take the oath
of fealty to the Constitution above the word of God, are to be de-
ported. And a camp—it might as well be an army—of twenty
thousand Federates is to be set up outside the walls of Paris, no
doubt as the capital's first line of defense against the anticipated
Austrian invasion.

The Assembly no longer feigns a pretense of giving a fig for our welfare. "They are a cancer, destroying us from within," I lament to Louis. He does more than agree. He dismisses every one of his Girondist ministers with the exception of Général Dumouriez. But on June 16, unable to convince my husband to accept the decrees—for our own safety—the *général* resigns his post. We are already unpopular, Louis concedes. But he will not allow the last shreds of power remaining to him to be stripped away. What good is a monarch if he cannot rule?

Three days after Dumouriez steps aside, the king continues to cross swords with the Assembly, formally banning their decrees. The Assembly's dismissal of our constitutional guard is a compromise, however dangerous, that Louis can abide if absolutely necessary. But the attack on the nonjuring priests and the amassing of twenty thousand National Guardsmen is both intolerable and unacceptable.

Louis's veto falls on a doubly inauspicious anniversary. It is June 19, the eve of the celebrations three years ago of the infamous oath taken by the delegates of the Estates General in the Jeu de Paume, the tennis court in Versailles. It is also nearly a year to the day of our disastrous flight to Montmédy. News of the king's veto spreads across Paris like sewage from a ruptured pipe. By nightfall, the streets fill with protestors angrily demanding the suppression of the vetoes. Fearing riots, assemblies are declared illegal, but no one seems to heed the authorities. Outside our windows, the mob in the Jardin des Tuileries has grown more restless than usual. Their collective, unwashed stench wafting through the night air is enough to make one retch.

Jerôme Pétion de Villeneuve, one of our enforced companions during the long hot ride from Varennes to Paris a year ago, is now the city's mayor. The crowds continue to gather through the night, growing ever more boisterous with the heavy consumption of wine and propaganda. I wonder aloud as I step away from the window—where, from the gardens below, the threatening verses of the *Ça Ira* send shivers along my spine—when Pétion will dare to show his face and convince the people, if not outright order them, to peaceably disperse.

Splaying his hands, Louis shrugs, his shoulders rising with resignation and falling with defeat. "Pétion may be more afeared of them than you and I, *mon amour*."

"Come—help me finish the lettering. Two artists can work faster than one." Armand beckons Louison to leave the window, where she has been intrigued by the tumult below.

"Where did you get the brushes and pigments?" she asks her lover. She picks her way through the tiny overcrowded room they share in the rue de l'Ancienne Comédie above Le Procope, a café renowned for its famous clientele. The delicious aromas emanating from the kitchen tauntingly wend their way up the narrow air shafts, reminding the couple how empty their bellies are and how much money they would have to scrape together to afford a single bowl of soup from a cauldron bubbling only twenty feet below.

"The master gave them to me."

"Monsieur David gave his own tools to an apprentice?" Louison picks up Armand's other shirt from the floor. "It will get even dirtier if you don't hang it on the hook," she scolds.

"David is one of us!" Armand exclaims. He holds up the partially lettered sign for Louison to read.

"'TREMBLE, TYRANTS, THE PEOPLE ARE ARMED! *À bas* . . .' *À bas quoi?*" she asks, trembling herself. "Down with *what?*"

"*À bas le veto!*" replies Armand, holding the wooden handle of a narrow paintbrush between his teeth. "You will come with me, won't you?"

Outside the small dormer window, stars are just becoming visible in the blue velvet sky. "Where?" asks Louison.

"To visit your friend," he answers with a hint of mockery, pushing an errant lock of dark hair off his brow with his forearm. At her look of incomprehension, Armand cheerfully expounds. "The *king*. Several thousand of us are going to pay him a call at the Tuileries." He brandishes the sign, missing only the word "veto" now. "Be a good girl and paint the final word." He reaches affectionately for Louison's thigh and brings her toppling to the floor beside him, her fall broken by a heap of dirty clothes and tattered rags spattered with paint and soaked with turpentine.

Louison crouches over the placard and dips the brush into the dollop of red paint that Armand had mixed on his wooden palette. As she begins to carefully draw each letter, her lover comes up behind her, slipping his arms about her waist and brushing aside her curls to nuzzle the nape of her neck. *"Ouf!"* Startled, she loses her balance, smearing the crossbar of the *t* in "veto," as the brush drags a jagged streak of carmine across the board. It looks like blood.

The clock in my bedchamber chimes eight times. It is unusual for people to bustle about the palace this early but I hear footsteps and voices outside my apartments. I tiptoe to the door of my salon and press my ear to the paneling. My husband is speaking to someone. I part the doors an inch to see that he is deep in conference with the Minister of the Interior, the marquis de Terrier de Montciel. "Do not be alarmed, *Majesté*," Terrier insists. "Yes, there were uprisings during the night in some of the faubourgs, but it was nothing that could not be contained."

"But are *we* safe here?" Louis asks. I know he must be thinking about what brought us to the Tuileries in the first place, the people's storming of Versailles less than three years ago.

"Absolutely," the minister assures my husband.

Yet only an hour later the minister sends a frantic message to the Assembly requesting a detachment of troops to defend the palace. Although the gates have been shut against their inevitable arrival, the rioters do not decide to go to bed after a night of unrest. They are on the march; their destination is the Tuileries Palace.

The narrow streets swarm with people; nearly everyone proudly wears a liberty cap. As the noisy crowd surges from one *rue* into another, Louison and Armand are swept along in a red tide of pulsing humanity, shouting, singing, waving their placards, and pumping the air with their fists, knives, pikes, cudgels, and hatchets. The weapons' handles are gaily decorated with tricolor ribbons. It all feels eerily familiar to the young sculptress, except that on this final day of spring the sun is shining and men and women march together with no attempt to disguise the purpose of their errand.

It is nearly two P.M. as they near the vast area encompassing the Tuileries Palace and gardens. A knot of dread lodges itself in Louison's bosom. The mood has changed; the taunts and jeers of the mob have grown more ominous, goaded by the rabble-rousing brewer Antoine Joseph Santerre. Blue-coated members of the National Guard, from the Faubourg Saint-Antoine regiment under Santerre's command and from other units as well, join the vociferous mob. At first Louison fears the soldiers are going to fire upon them, or at the very least order their dispersal at the point of their bayonets. Then she realizes they have joined the uprising.

We are on the razor's edge, she realizes. *Anything can happen.* Louison clasps Armand's arm and he places his hand over hers in a gesture of solidarity, the TREMBLE, TYRANTS placard briefly obscuring her view. She thinks, *He is too excited to notice my fear.*

Upon reaching the Tuileries the mob first tries to gain access to the Salle du Manège, to bring their grievances to the Assembly. Shouts of *"À bas le veto!"* fill the air. At four o'clock, having decided that *au fond,* the monarchs are to blame for all the ills of France, the collective anger of twenty thousand hungry souls, many of them red-faced with inebriation, is redirected at the gates of the palace.

"Vite! Hurry along—I don't want to lose you in the crowd." Armand grasps Louison's wrist and pulls her along like a toy on a string. Pressing forward as one, the mob moves so swiftly through the gardens, trampling the brightly colored blooms on the newly planted parterres, that she almost loses her footing, but David's ambitious apprentice wishes to be near the front of the pack when the wolves storm the gates.

The angry clang of steel against iron reverberates through the late afternoon air as the mob hacks at the high bars that separate them from their prey. Louison jumps at the sound of pistol fire, but Armand assures her that the report only announces to the thousands of people who remain too far from the gates to glimpse the action, that those in the vanguard have gained entry. Like a swarm of deadly flies, the rioters rush the battered and broken bars in their haste to reach the Place du Carrousel and the main doors of the palace.

Santerre stands on the shallow steps in front of the Tuileries Palace holding his unsheathed saber aloft as if to lead a brigade into battle. Suddenly, a thundering rumble rends the air and the ground trembles beneath Louison's feet. She glances about in a panic, fearful that the earth will open and swallow her where she stands; but no one else seems to be afraid. They are all rushing toward the palace doors, Armand among them, pressing his red Phrygian cap further down upon his head, so that it might not be knocked off and trampled in the mad crush to break down the portals.

"I must help them!" Armand shouts as he thrusts the placard into Louison's hands, briefly deserting his lover to assist a dozen or more men who are straining every muscle to push an ironclad cannon through the splintered doors. *What the devil do they mean to do with such a piece of artillery inside the palace?* Louison wonders. Armand is helping to heave the twelve-pounder, named not for its own weight but for that of the individual cannonballs, up the steps and onto the first floor of the palace. There it is left in an opulent antechamber with the gun barrel facing the door that, according to Santerre, leads to the throne room. The Garde Nationale makes no effort to halt the intrusion. Indeed, many of their number have already joined the uprising. And those charged with protecting the palace display their partisanship by shaking out the priming from their muskets, as if to alert the rioters that they need not fear reprisals or retaliation for their actions. In fact, the soldiers train their artillery *against* the palace, on anyone who would seek to halt the momentum of the protestors.

As one massive body teeming with myriad red-bonneted heads and limbs, the rioters surge up the stairs, demanding with a thousand voices to see the monarchs. But the vast marble halls are nearly empty. Everyone they spy, whether soldier or courtier, chambermaid or lackey, disappears behind closed doors, scurrying to escape the approaching onslaught. Louison is helplessly buoyed along by the mob like a cork bobbing in a raging stream, as dismayed as she was that awful October morning at the willful destruction of so much beauty and majesty. Oriental vases are removed from their pedestals and viciously dashed to the floor, shattering into hundreds of razor-sharp shards. Some of the fragments are scooped up by the rioters: you never know when you might need to slit an aristocrat's throat, and a fragment of Sèvres will do as well as a dagger. Portraits, still lifes, and dozens of scenic and allegorical tableaux are slashed; Louison feels heartbroken at the jagged sound of ripping canvas. She looks for Armand and wonders if he, a revolutionary to the core, would nonetheless endorse the destruction of an artist's handiwork, regardless of who may own it. And if the people believe *they* now own the palaces of France, isn't that all the more reason to cherish, rather than destroy, their priceless treasures—to save them for the Nation?

The men and women running alongside the young sculptress—*they aren't like me,* she thinks. Their armpits and breath are foul. They don't want to change things; they want to destroy them. Are they truly interested in voicing their complaints to the king? Or do they wish—she shudders—to assassinate him?

"Where is the fat pig!" shouts a man, no slenderer than the sovereign himself.

"To the Oeil de Boeuf!" cries Santerre, pointing with his naked saber to the room now housing the cannon. "We will draw him out of his comfortable sty!"

The halls resound with the tread of thousands of footsteps as the rioters hunt down their prey, pausing at every sealed chamber to batter down the doors, splintering them into sawdust with hatchet blows, the colored ribbons on the ax handles twirling and looping as if they danced around a hundred handheld maypoles. Locks are smashed apart. Golden hinges, hacked and pried from the doorposts, fly into the crowd; and a cry goes up each time someone is lucky enough to catch one of them—to be cherished as a souvenir of the day the rioter changed the course of history.

Ivory-colored paneling and gilded boiseries are reduced to rubble, priceless chandeliers dripping with thousands of crystal pendants are poked to pieces by pikestaffs; candles and any objets d'art small enough to fit in the palm of a man's hand are pocketed during the patriots' rage to seek and destroy.

As the leaders return to the Oeil de Boeuf in search of the king, they are nonetheless startled to find themselves confronting the tyrant himself. But for some, it is not enough. Cries of *"Où est l'Autrichienne?"* "Where is the bitch?" "Where is Madame Veto?"

pierce the air. An unshaven man taunts the sovereign with a grue-some prop: a stained rag doll suspended by her neck from a gibbet. A placard hangs about her throat like a macabre necklace, de-manding *"À la lanterne avec Marie Antoinette."*

"Louis—non!" I clutch my husband's sleeve to prevent him from confronting the rabble.

"Majesté, you must come with me now—do you not hear their cries?" The princesse de Lamballe slips her hand into mine. "Ma-dame Campan is right; we must retreat to the dauphin's rooms. The ruffians have not yet found their way there."

I hear their insolent cries. I hear them only too well. They de-mand my head. And I am as terrified of them as I have ever been. For my ladies' sakes I have endeavored to remain calm, but I have not been able to stop crying all afternoon. Poor Lamballe, always so skittish in the moment, and yet I have rarely known a woman as brave. She placed her own life at risk to join my family in our mis-fortune at the Tuileries and this is how the gentle soul's courage is repaid.

Louis and I had secluded ourselves when it became clear that the incursion would reach the palace and that the rioters would storm the gates. Now, he insists that we face a greater danger if he refuses to meet with the rebels. Somehow he has retained his sang-froid while I have grown more hysterical by the hour.

"You did so in October '89 and look where it got us," I'd ar-gued, throwing my hands in the air. *"Here.* Your honesty, your credulousness, your willingness to believe that the rioters' word was as trustworthy as that of a king—landed us *here,* in the Tuile-ries. And now, once again we are at the mercy of wild beasts."

"What will they think of me," I ask the princesse, "if they believe that I have run and hidden from them? What sort of reputation do you think I will gain from thàt?" I add rhetorically. "My place is beside the king."

Madame Campan argues that my presence will only endanger my husband further. "Should anyone try to harm you, and you hear them baying for your blood, it is his nature to leap to your defense; and in so doing, you may both be wounded—or worse." When she sees that even this argument will not dampen my resolve to remain by Louis's side, she begs, "Remember, Your Majesty, you are a mother as well as a wife."

I part from my husband with the greatest reluctance, ultimately swayed by her plea. But just as I have acquiesced, the Chevalier de Rougeville nearly skids to a halt before us, his powdered wig, a relic of the old days, askew. "Madame, do not go to the dauphin's rooms," he warns. "They have already broken down the door!" He frantically struggles to adjust his blue sash in my presence, making an absurd effort to appear more presentable before the Queen of France.

At his terrifying news my knees nearly buckle. "Where are—?" My mind floods with horrific images of what these monsters might have done to my son and daughter.

The chevalier divines my thought. "Madame Royale and monsieur le dauphin have been safely moved to the Council Chamber. They await you there, madame."

My precious children are in one room, my devoted husband in another. My body feels too weak to support my weight and suddenly it seems as though I am standing in a bucket of quicksand, unable to move in any direction. My attendants quickly usher me into the Council Chamber, siuated on the opposite side of the king's bedroom. There, *ma petite* Mousseline sits on a red brocade chair, staring into the middle distance and clutching the padded armrests with white knuckles. Although she is a princesse, Marie Thérèse

has witnessed much ugliness in her twelve years. The dauphin,
now seven and always more demonstrative than his sister, rushes
into my arms. I clutch Louis Charles to my bosom, embracing him
so tightly as I bathe his soft brown curls with my tears that he frets,
"Maman, you are *suffocating* me!"

"I'm sorry, *mon chou d'amour,*" I soothe, as the princesse de
Lamballe hands me a handkerchief. "Your maman is so very wor-
ried about your papa, right now." I sob anew at the thought of
Louis left to face the armed insurgents alone.

And then, with a jolt of horror I realize that his sister is with
him.

Amid the clamor a beautifully gowned woman enters the Oeil de
Boeuf. Upon seeing the king backed up against the wall with only
a table and an aged aristocrat wearing the medals and ribbons of
the Maréchal of France to protect him from their fury, her pale face
turns even whiter with distress and her light blue eyes dim with
tears. Arms outstretched, she attempts to make her way through
the throng in a desperate effort to reach the monarch.

"There she is! The queen!" some of the rioters cry. The men
and women closest to the rear of the room, where the king sits,
brandish their pikes and knives and try to reach her. Yet the woman
bravely presses through the throng. She clasps the monarch by his
coattails as if to attach herself there. Her soft features and despairing looks convey the warning that only violence could tear these
two persons asunder.

"It is not the queen!" Louison finds her voice. She recalls her
audience with the king that fateful October afternoon when she
stood as near to the royal family as if they were her own relations.
A sculptress remembers faces. Marie Antoinette has a haughty
physiognomy; many have called it insolent. Her receding chin and
protruding lower lip are legendary. This woman is clearly not the

consort. "It is Madame Élisabeth!" Louison cries. She is about to use the second-person plural but realizes that to say "you" might set her apart as a secret royalist. "*We* have no quarrel with the king's sister," Louison insists, hoping she will be heeded, for the eyes of all those who surround her with knives and cudgels have a wildness in them that terrifies her. She doesn't know what a revolution is supposed to be like, but surely assassination, even regicide, cannot be their goal.

Others do not agree. Far behind her, someone standing in the hallway shouts, "Have you killed them yet?" and another demands, "Throw us their heads!"

As if to answer the challenge, a drunken farrier, his face as red as the wine that inebriated him, thrusts his weapon, a sharp iron spike affixed to a long pole, at the king. But his progress is halted by another man who flings himself between the monarch and the would-be murderer. A melee ensues and the Samaritan is knocked to the ground, trampled underfoot by the mob as they try to reach the king.

A woman whose apron is smeared with gore lunges toward the sovereign with a pike in her hand, and then laughs like a lunatic when Madame Élisabeth gasps and jumps away, backing herself against the windows. Impaled upon the pike is a bloody bull's heart, with a placard dangling beneath it that reads HEART OF THE ARISTOCRACY.

A booming voice is heard over the cacophony. "Twenty grenadiers to protect His Majesty!" A man stands in the doorway of the Oeil de Boeuf. "The Finance Minister," Armand whispers in Louison's ear. He knows all the names and faces of the king's "evil ministers and minions" from reading the newspapers published by the great revolutionary leader Camille Desmoulins and the demagogue Jacques Hébert.

Moments later, the red-coated soldiers appear, forcibly entering the chamber as the rioters shout "Down with the veto!" and "Ratify the decrees!" Pushing back the crowd the grenadiers march to the rear of the room and form an armed guard about the monarch to a jeering chorus of *"Vive la Nation!"* Yet—astonishingly—although the grenadiers protectively stand their ground, the monarch appears to be waving them away.

As calm as if he were at a *grand couvert,* one of his famous public meals, the king says, "A man who has nothing with which he may reproach himself knows neither fear nor dread." The mob grows suddenly quiet, as if he has cast an enchantment over them. *"Et voilà!"* Louis says, seizing a nearby ruffian by the wrist and placing the man's filthy palm beneath the breast of his gold embroidered waistcoat. "See if my heart beats any faster, even in the face of my enemies."

But the answer is drowned out by another round of taunts and accusations. The mob begins to chant *"À bas le veto!"*

The king raises a little silver bell that had been resting on the table in front of him and rings it, in an effort to quiet the rabble. They do indeed pause at the delicate tinkling sound, its very incongruity in such a contentious atmosphere gaining their attention. A number of aristocrats wave their walking sticks in the air, urging the people, with all due *politesse,* to respect the law. Louison finds the scene rather comical until the angry protests are renewed and the monarch is accused of trying to deceive the people. Surely calling the king of France a liar to his face cannot be the way to win redress. He rings the silly little bell once more and assures the mob that he is no foe of the Constitution and that he will quietly listen to their grievances if they will present them in a reasonable manner. The sculptress knows from her own experience that in this, at any rate, he is a man of his word.

"Prove to us, then, that you support the Revolution!" The demand comes from a *sans-culotte* with brown teeth. He yanks the red liberty cap from his head and, sticking it on the end of a pike, thrusts it at the king. "Put it on, monsieur."

Louison grimaces. If she were made to wear the man's *bonnet rouge,* she would fear it was crawling with lice. What will the king do? Like a single organ, the mob holds its breath. But the sovereign claims the Phrygian cap from the menacing spike and without complaint or remonstrance places it gingerly upon his head. The room resounds with derisive laughter—cackles and guffaws, hollers and snickers—for the cap is far too small. It looks like a child's chapeau atop the monarch's enormous head. His Majesty raises his hands and tries to adjust the cap by tugging it over his brow. But it will never fit, which only emphasizes how ludicrously inappropriate it appears—at least to Louison.

But not everyone shares her secret opinion. Cries of *"Vive le roi!"* echo throughout the Oeil de Boeuf, and with so many people shouting at once she cannot tell whether they are cheers of mockery or approval. A wineskin is shoved into the king's hands and the owner demands that he drink a toast to the health of his people.

Then a man bearing a beribboned hatchet steps forward. "You believe that we are your enemies, Sire, but you are mistaken. Your adversaries are not in Paris, but amassing in Coblenz." Armand explains, whispering into Louison's ear, that the man in the gray blouson and striped *sans-culottes* refers to the Austrian forces. "The people, on the other hand, only desire to see you cheerfully abiding by the tenets of the Constitution." The *sans-culotte* looks about the room, and his words receive applause.

"I will lay odds that he is a lawyer," Armand murmurs. "No matter how meanly attired. Fishmongers don't speak like that."

"If you embrace the Constitution in good faith, *Majesté,* the people will love you all the more. Don't you see—they *want* to love you."

* * *

I do not know whether my husband is alive or dead. Frozen with
fear, my children, my attendants, and I sit like statues in the Council Chamber awaiting word of Louis's welfare, but we have heard
nothing.

Suddenly, we are startled by the sounds of a scuffle directly outside the room. "Where is the vile bitch? We have searched everywhere for her; she is not in her apartments—believe me, not a stick
of furniture remains intact!"

I discover who the madmen—*mon Dieu*, my rooms!—are ar-
guing with, when the heavy oaken doors to the Council Chamber
burst open and a half-dozen grenadiers rush inside, ahead of the
mob. "Get behind this table, madame, with the children of France!"
one of them orders me, as they drag a heavy table, gilded and
topped with marble, into place, forming a barricade against the
surging mob, positioning themselves in front of it like a row of
sentries.

The villainous Général Santerre is at the head of the pack.
"Stand aside, *citoyens!*" he snarls, nearly decapitating a woman
with his saber as he orders the grenadiers to divide and fall back,
"so the people can see for themselves the object of their hatred."
His voice drips with derision for the crown. But the people are just
as vicious.

"*À la lanterne!* String her up by the lamppost!"

"Put that long neck to good use!"

An old crone levels a bony accusatory finger at me. I believe that
if she had gotten close enough to poke me through the eye, she
would have done so without another thought. "You're a vile
woman!" she shrieks.

Fighting to keep my manner poised and regal and my voice
quiet and calm in the face of such scorn, I ask her: "Have I ever
done you any harm, madame?" To this she has no ready reply. But

her confederates remain undaunted in the presence of the queen. One manages to dash around the table just long enough to place one of the disgusting red liberty caps upon my head before the grenadiers apprehend him. I immediately snatch the offending bonnet from my person and am about to say something when an ominous glare from Santerre changes my mind. Instead, I diplomatically place the cap upon the dauphin's head, saying, "I am only a king's consort. But *he* is your future king." My seven-year-old son, terrified by this sea of angry people in front of him, is dwarfed by the *bonnet rouge*. The cap falls down over his forehead and eyes. He cannot see a thing, which is probably all for the best. At the sight of a little boy in a blue satin suit who better resembles a broomstick with a liberty cap for a head, the rabble hoots with laughter. It is at our expense, I know. It is embarrassing and ignominious. But at least we are alive. Beneath the cap, my son's shoulders are heaving involuntarily. My heart is breaking.

Like a master of ceremonies at a circus sideshow, Santerre invites the crowd, one by one, to get a closer look at our humiliation. Barricaded behind the vast table, we are the freaks on display. "See the Queen of France and the Prince Royal," the *général* booms, urging the invaders to queue up and walk by the table in an orderly fashion to feast their eyes upon "Madame Veto" and "the little bastard."

For at least two hours we sit behind the makeshift barricade as thousands of people file past, each with a vulgar insult on his or her lips. One woman, who had kept her head bowed so that no one could see her features clearly, approaches the table and when she believes no one can hear her, murmurs to me as she passes, "The king is safe." Her voice catches me by surprise. Madame Élisabeth has bravely quit her brother's side to join this macabre queue solely to bring me news of my husband. It is the first report I have had in hours.

* * *

Somewhere a clock strikes the hour of six. "Your Majesty, good citizens of France, I come to announce that all is well." The face is familiar, but Louison cannot place it. "It is the mayor, Monsieur Pétion," Armand informs her. Louison wonders why he has not arrived with another detachment of the National Guard. Isn't it the mayor's responsibility to quell any riots or disturbances in the capital?

Pétion approaches the king. "Your Majesty, I have only just learned of your situation."

"How astonishing," the king replies, his tone indignant, "for this has been going on for quite some time."

Hoisted upon the sturdy shoulders of four grenadiers, the mayor compliments the crowd on their behavior. "You have comported yourselves this day with the pride and dignity of free men," he declares, before ordering the mob to peaceably disperse.

Louison wonders by what portal the mayor entered the palace, for if he had come by way of the Place du Carrousel, he surely would have witnessed the destruction that the willful rabble had left in its wake.

Suddenly the king speaks. "Would the people of Paris like to see the State Apartments?"

Louison can hardly believe her ears. Is the king of France offering to usher thousands of unwashed citizens through the grand rooms of the palace? She tugs at Armand's sleeve and tells him she would like to follow the king. But her eagerness earns her a cross look from her lover. "It is only to see for ourselves what the Bourbons have stolen from the people," he says churlishly. On their way out of the Oeil de Boeuf, at the sight of a massive silver urn embellished with vine leaves and bunches of grapes, he spits. "If they sold that, they could feed the residents of the Faubourg Saint-Germain for a year."

The doors to the Council Chamber are thrown wide for this impromptu tour, and to the astonishment of all, particularly the king, there sits Madame Veto with their children. As the sovereign rushes to his wife's side, the queen flings herself into his arms. "Thank God you're safe!" She bursts into undignified tears, sobbing against his ample breast, and Louison feels a pang of guilt. The poor lady is vilified for behaving regally, yet derided when she acts like any other woman would do under such terrible circumstances.

"The duc de Mouchy will lead whoever wishes to remain through the rest of the State Rooms," says the monarch, blotting his tears with a handkerchief. He still wears the red liberty cap. The old courtier who had placed himself in harm's way by standing in front of the king when the mob surged into the Oeil de Boeuf beckons the intruders to join him. As Louison and Armand join the stragglers the sculptress casts a backward glance at the royal family. They are hugging and kissing one another as if they feared they would never reunite. The queen removes the *bonnet rouge* from her son's head and dashes it to the floor. A lump rises in Louison's throat. She is not supposed to pity them.

Realizing that he still wears the liberty cap, Louis yanks it from his head and tosses it on the floor where it joins the one I have just taken away from the dauphin. "Ah, madame, why did I take you away from your homeland, only to associate you with the ignominy of such a day as we have passed!"

It had not been my choice to quit Austria to wed a youth I had never met, and until recently, did not realize how deeply I loved. But now, more than twenty-two years after our wedding, I have no regrets.

I cry until there are no more salt tears to weep. I have never missed my husband as much as in these last three or four desperate hours. But our family is not yet permitted the luxury of rejoicing in privacy. Deputies from the Assembly have lingered, and as dusk descends outside our shattered windows, they display no haste to depart. If I cannot enjoy this time alone with my husband and children, I will make the most of the delegates' presence. As I escort them toward my apartments, which I heard have been reduced to rubble, I politely caution the men not to step on any of the broken glass that litters the halls. It is my first opportunity to assess the awful damage as well. "This is what your mayor calls 'pride and dignity'?" Entering the dauphin's rooms, "This is what your *dignified* citizens did to the chambers of an innocent little boy," I exclaim angrily, pointing out the smashed locks, the pastoral murals, now utterly demolished. The ruffians have even broken his toys. Our attendants approach with reports of the destruction done to the palace—on the staircases and in every salon the monsters entered. Hardly a door stands on its hinges. Even the roof has been damaged. "Who will pay for this?" I demand. "You call *us* spendthrifts, but *we* did not render these rooms uninhabitable! *Regardez,* messieurs, this wanton destruction of a palace and its treasures that has stood since the days of Catherine de Medici. You should be ashamed to call yourselves Frenchmen."

Even when the royal family is finally alone, we remain subjected to scowling guards and suspicious looks. The dauphin clings either to his father or to me. Ordinarily a voluble child, he does not utter a word. When he is addressed directly, he bursts into tears. His sister moves as if in a dream, the events of the twentieth of June so terrifying that it would seem she wishes never to see or hear again, for fear that the news will never be joyful.

The morning after the riot, awakening in my bedchamber because his own rooms were too damaged for him to return, my son finally speaks. In a plaintive query to Louis's valet, Monsieur Hüe, he asks, "Is it still yesterday?"

TWENTY-ONE

The Wolves Return

✦ SUMMER 1792 ✦

I still exist, but it is only by a miracle, I write to Axel in cipher, after the incident on June 20.

It was a dreadful day, not to be imagined. It has become clear that the people are no longer bitter toward me alone; nowadays their hatred is just as forcefully directed toward the king. They no longer trouble to conceal their scorn. Some have demanded his life. He demonstrated a dignity and strength yesterday that momentarily impressed the citizens, but the mood is ugly and we are keenly aware that their show of affection can change at any moment. As the band of assassins grows larger every day, I am endeavoring to persuade the king to wear a vest of mail beneath his waistcoat. Madame Campan has fashioned a bodice for me which she assures me will resist bullets and knives, but I refuse to don it. Nevertheless, I no longer walk in the gardens. Even if I were to enjoy the flowers, one of the few things that can still make me smile, the *citoyens* who are constantly encamped there sing the *Ça Ira* in a ceaseless refrain. This vicious anthem has numerous verses and it seems as though every week a new refrain has been added. My ears are assailed now with the incessant strain, "Madame Veto has promised to butcher all of Paris." I no longer ask myself, "How can anyone believe such absurd propaganda?" I still don't know the answer: all I know is that they *do*. Even the chapel orchestra plays the *Ça Ira* and we must sit through it when we attend Mass. The only comfort I derive from this madness is the knowledge that if God hears how we are being so falsely traduced, He will deliver us.

I remain unguarded at night. I am convinced this is not because the Assembly is graciously offering me this modicum of privacy, but as a means of permitting access to anyone who will murder me. Thisbe is not as much of a watchdog as I had anticipated. I woke the other night—and she did not—to see a shadowy figure tiptoeing about my bedchamber. I lay as still as I could, praying the assassin would not have the courage to fulfill his errand. Yet, in the morning, nothing had been moved or stolen and the windows and doors were as I had left them. I wonder now if I dreamed the whole incident.

There are days when I think if my life ended, it would solve everything and bring about the rapprochement between the people and the crown that France so desperately needs. If the insurgents assassinate me it will be a blessing, for it will deliver me from a miserable existence.

I hope you are receiving news of us. Farewell for now and for our sake, take care of yourself.

I know that Count von Fersen is secretly working on new plots to rescue us. In the wake of the invasion of the Tuileries, he is collaborating with the Duke of Brunswick, commander of the allied forces, on the drafting of a manifesto to present to the Assembly, which has declared that France is "in danger." The National Assembly believes that the king and I are clandestinely in league with the foreign powers; mercifully, they have no proof to substantiate their contentions.

On July 3, I inform the comte de Mercy, *Our condition is becoming ever more critical. On one side, we have only violence and fury. On the other, weakness and inertia,* I add, referring to Louis's reluctance to commit to any definite course of action.

We can no longer depend upon the Garde Nationale, or the army, to defend us. I am convinced that every one of them is a scoundrel. And so we do not know whether it is better to abandon the capital, despite Louis's promise to the Assembly, or to stay in Paris. There is no stability here; the ministries change every few weeks—sometimes as often as every few days.

I do see merit in your plan to decamp to Compiègne, and agree that it will be easier to flee from there, where fewer eyes are watching us. Insofar as where we might go from Compiègne, either Amiens or Abbéville, as you suggest, would be acceptable as long as the royalists there are prepared to aid us and will not panic and turn us away when they realize they have placed their own lives at peril to shelter us.

You may convey our thanks to the Landgravine of Hesse-Darmstadt for her generosity, but I must decline it. For one thing, I fear the efficacy of a plan to smuggle me out of Paris. Moreover, I have pledged never to leave the king and it is a

promise I will not retract. Nearly every other day we are secretly presented with alternate plans of escape. Another smug-
gling plot, one involving the king alone, was rejected for the
same reason I must decline the Landgravine's offer.

Lafayette has returned to the bosom of his sovereign after
serving him so faithfully during the American War of Independence. The violence of June 20 turned his appetite from
the madness of Revolution. The general has urged Louis to
remove himself from harm's way immediately, and no one
knows as well as Lafayette how perilous our situation is. I am
terrified that the radicals are planning to assassinate the king.
Lafayette has suggested a conspiracy by which he would take
over the government by force—removing those who only a
few months ago he dared to name his friends and colleagues.
But the king continues to vacillate. He believes that any decisive action would merely endanger us further. He insists that
the best course remains not to challenge the Assembly, but to
wait for the foreign powers to rescue us. Reassure me, please,
that we are not dreaming!

The same day, I pen another letter to Axel. We have decided
that it is best for me to invent a different identity, and so I write as
the paramour of a French émigré named Rignon whose affairs I
manage in his absence.

Our position is dreadful: Some days it seems impossible to
wait any longer, but I beg you, do not be too worried. I feel
courageous, and something deep within me tells me that we
will soon be happy. We will soon be saved. This idea alone is
enough to sustain me from day to day. You are always in my
thoughts. When, I wonder, will we be able to see each other
again?

On the fourteenth of July, the third anniversary of the storming of the Bastille, a celebration is held on the Champ de Mars. Louis is compelled to swear yet another meaningless oath to the Nation. It is the only occasion thus far when he has acceded to my pleas to wear the metal vest beneath his clothes.

Your friend is in the utmost danger, I write in cipher to Axel on July 23, referring obliquely to Louis. *His illness advances in a most alarming fashion. The doctors no longer know what to do. If you want to see him again, you must be quick about it. See that his relations are informed of his critical condition.*

If my letters cannot reach Mercy and the Austrians quickly enough, I hope that Axel can convey to them our increasingly perilous situation. It has taken its toll on the entire royal family. My hair is the color of fresh snow and I look old enough to be my own mother. Louis has become monstrously obese. Mousseline has grown shockingly withdrawn. And the dauphin, a malleable boy who is sensitive to any change in the winds and remolded by every event, weeps now at the slightest provocation.

Three days later, I write to Axel, *For the moment, our main thought must be to escape dagger thrusts and to defeat the plans of the conspirators who swarm about the throne. It is a long time since one of the factieux have taken the trouble to conceal their plans of annihilating the entire royal family. Only an immediate crisis can save your friend. Time is short.*

On August 3 the news reaches Paris that at Coblenz on July 25, the Duke of Brunswick announced his Manifesto, which I know has Axel's touch all over it. Immediately dubbed the Brunswick Manifesto, the document proclaims that if the citizens of Paris harm a hair of our heads, the allied armies will march in retaliation straight into the capital, sparing nothing and no one.

But it is not the miracle I have prayed for. In fact, it is a disaster. The wording of the manifesto contains every spark that will set the

Revolutionary tinderbox ablaze. Citizens will panic at the very possibility of a foreign invasion and arm themselves against it. They will grow angrier at our continued refusal to accept the crushing wheels of Revolution and our willingness to countenance an invasion of the country and the capital by allied armies of foreign powers. The people will charge us with collusion and they will exact their revenge.

Axel has baited the bear with a hunk of fresh red meat, and the bear has clenched it in its maw, ready to repay the gift with more blood. The Brunswick Manifesto is tantamount to an outright declaration of war on France.

When I visit Louis's rooms one morning soon after, I find him feeding countless papers into the fire. He escorts me into one of the narrow corridors behind his apartments and shows me a section of paneling concealing a cache of documents that he must retain, but which would surely incriminate him were they ever to be located. "If anything should happen to me, madame, please make sure that these papers remain undiscovered." He fears the worst, and yet he also fears taking a decisive action against the Girondins and their confederates.

To protect us, the sixty-one-year-old marquis de Mandat, commander of the National Guard since Lafayette's resignation, summons reinforcements: nine hundred Swiss Guards from Courbevoie and Rueil. He assures us that these elite troops have not been tainted by the antimonarchical fervor that has poisoned the Parisian regiments. Another nine hundred gendarmes, the royalist battalion of the Filles-Saint-Thomas and two thousand men from the Garde Nationale, now defend the Tuileries. I confess to the marquis that I have little faith in the local guardsmen. "They shouted 'No more king!' at Mass in the palace chapel this past Sunday."

"Another invasion is imminent," he confides anxiously. "You

will need all the men we can muster." Yet his face is gray with worry. Will fifteen hundred be enough?

The following morning, three hundred noblemen, armed with any and every weapon they own—swords, pistols, even shovels and fire tongs—present themselves at the palace to offer their protection. Their loyalty brings me nearly to tears, but I must appear courageous, if only for their sakes. They cannot be led to believe that I fear all may already be lost.

The family spends the day in Louis's apartments, as if to take shelter there from the gathering storm. Throughout the night of August 9, we are visited by representatives from the capital. Each bears news more dire than the last. Pierre Louis Roederer, the public prosecutor and prefect of the Paris Commune, informs us the entire city is in revolt.

Minutes later, Mayor Pétion appears, as if to send a message to the citizens that he intends, despite their plans, to guarantee the preservation of the royal family. I never know with him what side he is really on. He still speaks like a revolutionary, but now I begin to believe that even he does not countenance this impending uprising.

"Get some sleep, *ma chère*," Louis urges, but this is one command I cannot obey. At a quarter to one on the morning of August 10, we hear the faint knell of a distant tocsin. By half past two, the alarm has reached Paris. Every church bell peals, announcing the call to arms. With the princesse de Lamballe following me like a spaniel, I wander restlessly through the Tuileries, stopping at every balcony and window to try to detect signs of movement outside the palace. I enter my daughter's room and enfold her in my arms. Her skin still bears the fresh, natural fragrance of youth. Mousseline is trying to be brave, acting far older than her tender years, and even as I try to assure her that everything will be all right and she will be safe, I do not discourage her fearful tears.

At four o'clock Madame Élisabeth calls to me, "Sister, come and watch the day break." No sooner do I join her on the balcony but the tocsin ends. We slip our arms about each other in a relieved embrace. Perhaps the palace will be spared.

I gaze over the rooftops of Paris. On this morning, the dawn sky is not lemon yellow and robin's egg blue, but bloodred.

Surely this is an omen.

An hour later, dripping with unseemly perspiration, Lafayette arrives with terrifying news. "*Vos Majestés,* it is with extreme regret that I inform you of a most unfortunate incident." With every word, my stomach sickens as he announces that the marquis de Mandat has been shot to death on the steps of the Hôtel de Ville. "Even the soldiers under his command did not respect him at the last." Lafayette's face is as white as milk. "The poor marquis's corpse has just been fished out of the Seine."

TWENTY-TWO

The Second Revolution

≈ AUGUST 10, 1792 ≈

Clad in a suit of violet velvet, his hair still unpowdered and clinging damply to his forehead, Louis descends the stairs to offer a few words of encouragement to the detachments of palace guards, while I see that food and beverages are dispensed to these valiant men who have come to protect us. I fight back tears as I hand a goblet to one of the noblemen, painted and periwigged as the courtiers were in the days of Louis XV, and proud of his jewel-encrusted rapier. He is old enough to have been my father, as are most of the aristocrats who have voluntarily joined us. No matter their age, and despite the revolutionaries' abolition of France's ancient aristocracy, these men will remain loyal to the end. They represent only a fraction of the nobles who still remain in Paris; the rest have already fled the country in anticipation of the coming bloodshed.

I do not hear what Louis says, but it cannot be a stirring call to arms because the shouts of derision that greet his exhortation echo through the halls. *"À bas le veto!" "Vive la Nation!" "À bas le gros cochon!"*

"Mon Dieu, they are reviling the king himself!" Monsieur Duboucharge, the minister of the navy, exclaims in horror. What can I say to this? My eyes, red-rimmed and swollen with spent tears, are answer enough. I lower my head and turn away so the minister will not witness my despair.

"All is lost," I murmur to Madame Campan. "His Majesty's review of the troops has done more harm than good."

As the clock strikes six in the morning, the first wave of insurgents is seen marching on the palace. By now, Louis has rejoined us in his bedchamber. The comte de Roederer, who has been on his feet for hours, as etiquette requires that no one but duchesses and princes of the blood may sit in the presence of the sovereigns, urges the king to bring the entire royal family to the Salle du Manège, demanding that we be placed under the protection of the deputies of the National Assembly.

I refuse to countenance this suggestion. "It will be interpreted by the rebels as fleeing in the face of our enemies. To abandon the palace to them might as well be to abandon the crown. Monsieur, we have a strong enough force here," I add, the coldness of my tone an indication of my disagreement. "Now is the time to decide who has the upper hand: the king and the Constitution, or a ragtag army of rebellious citizens."

Having no luck with me, Roederer turns to the king. "Sire, the rebels have already entered the gardens. They have reached the gates, with cannon trained upon the palace. You have not five minutes to lose; any moment they will begin to fire upon us. The only place you will find safety is in the Assembly!"

My poor husband looks utterly beleaguered. "But—but I did not see very many people in the Place du Carrousel," he argues feebly. "And I have given orders that no one is to fire unless the assailants have fired first."

"Monsieur le comte—we have troops," I insist. "I would rather die nailed to the walls of the palace than desert those who have come to defend us."

"But madame—all Paris is marching," Roederer replies, refusing to be persuaded. "You are hopelessly outnumbered. My accounts estimate a force of twenty thousand citizens, armed not only with all manner of deadly weapons, but in possession of a dozen cannon. By counseling His Majesty to resist my advice, you will become responsible for the murders of the king and your children, as well as your loyal courtiers and ministers who will be compelled to remain here."

Louis regards Roederer intently for several seconds. Then, turning to me and placing his hand gently on my forearm, he says, "Come, *ma chère*. Let us go." His voice is heavy with regret and resignation.

I summon Madame de Tourzel and ask her to ready the children of France for our departure. A dozen members of the Garde Nationale surround us as the king leads the way toward the Salle du Manège. A few steps behind him, I cannot control my tears, even as I clasp the dauphin by the hand. Following me are Madame Royale and her aunt Élisabeth, Madame de Tourzel, the princesse de Lamballe, the ministers who have remained with us through the long night, and a few loyal courtiers. These are the only people the prefect permits to accompany us. Hundreds of attendants have been left to an uncertain fate—several of my waiting women, cooks and laundresses, footmen, and page boys scarcely older than my son.

"We shall be back soon," I call to the Chevalier de Jarjayes, one of the crown's most trusted emissaries. Do I believe my own words?

As he passes the maréchal de Mailly, Louis says, "You are now in charge, here. I will return the moment that order has been restored." The maréchal, a cousin of the infamous Mailly sisters who, one after another, were royal mistresses to Louis's grandfather, offers a courtly bow to his sovereign and vows to defend the palace to his last breath. The maréchal has enjoyed a long and distinguished military career. But what chance do we have, I wonder, with an eighty-four-year-old man leading the palace guards against the encroaching incursion? As we hurry through the Oeil de Boeuf, Louis informs the detachment of National Guards of his decision to retreat to the Assembly, and for some reason he exchanges hats with a nearby soldier. Does Louis wish to exit the Tuileries incognito? But the horrified guardsman snatches the king's chapeau from his head and hides it under his arm. The guard's eyes fill with panic, as if merely being seen with the king's hat is a death sentence.

By the marble colonnade at the foot of the grand staircase, Louis clutches the comte de Roederer's sleeve. "What will happen to those who have been left behind?" he asks urgently, his voice low.

The prefect presses his narrow lips together in an expression of grim acceptance. "*Mon Sire,* they are not in sufficient number to resist for very long."

"In that case, I should tell the Swiss Guards to lay down their arms. I have never countenanced the shedding of French blood and I will not start now." Louis may vacillate and equivocate, but he is nothing if not consistent. My husband still clings to the conviction that if he does the opposite of England's Charles I, he can heal our nation's wounds.

We can reach the Salle du Manège only by walking through the Tuileries Gardens. We are promenaded between two rows of soldiers as if we are making a funeral procession, enduring derisive jeers with every agonizing step. From the gardens we can hear the riotous *fédérés* roaring the *Marseillaise,* with intermittent exhortations of *"Aux armes, citoyens!"* It is a great distance for a small child to cover in haste, and I worry about the dauphin keeping up with us. Too young to comprehend the terrible gravity of our circumstances, he amuses himself by kicking at little piles of dead leaves along the path as we are ushered along the *allées* toward the Assembly. "They are falling early this year," Louis mutters to himself.

By the time we near the Salle du Manège, the crush of people around us is so terrifyingly close, despite our armed escorts, that a guardsman the size of a giant scoops my son into his arms and hoists him high above his shoulders. I shriek, fearing he is being abducted. But the giant turns to me and says thickly, "Do not be alarmed, madame, I have no intentions of harming him." My eyes become moist with tears when I realize that the guardsman means to protect the dauphin from the encroaching mob.

Behind us, the assault on the palace has clearly begun. The air resounds with the rumbling of artillery wheels, with musket and cannon fire, and the piercing, desperate shrieks of the wounded and dying. I turn back to press my hands over Madame Royale's ears.

The Assembly president, Pierre Victurnien Vergniaud, welcomes us with the assurance that Louis may rely upon the firmness of the National Assembly. My husband manages a weak smile, although I am certain he doubts Citoyen Vergniaud's sincerity. Nonetheless, peering at Vergniaud through his double lorgnette, Louis replies, "I have come here to avoid a great crime and trust that my family and I cannot be safer than in your midst."

But we are not permitted to remain in the vast barrel-vaulted hall because the Constitution prohibits the king's presence during legislative debate. Instead, we are escorted to a shabby room tucked behind the public gallery, a few steps below the deputies' banquettes. The chamber is usually reserved for journalists, who have the opportunity to observe the proceedings through an iron grille; the room is barely ten feet square and the ceiling so low that a grown man cannot stand fully upright in it.

Fearful that the mob might dare to invade the Salle du Manège and attack the royal family, and that the deputies would be unable to protect us, several members of the legislature break down the grille that separates the tiny recorders' box from the Assembly hall. Louis himself helps the men tear apart the bars. I tend to forget how strong he is. In happier days he would follow the stonemasons about Versailles, and after my desperate struggle to give birth to Madame Royale, I was told that when I lost consciousness he was the one who ripped the protective seals from my bedchamber windows and threw them open.

It is only seven thirty in the morning and already it is oppressively hot. With nowhere else to go until we are told it is safe to leave, we have no choice but to overhear the deputies above us—the republican Jacobins and the more moderate Girondins debating the future of the monarchy. Their first order of business is to dispatch a delegation to halt the progress of the insurgents, explaining that there is no reason for them to storm the palace because the king and queen have already left it and have been granted sanctuary in the Assembly.

But it is too late. The delegation is forced to retrace its steps, driven back by the forces that have already begun their attack. Moments later, a half-dozen wounded Swiss Guards, covered in gunpowder and gore, burst into the Assembly, chased like rabbits by a ravenous pack of *fédérés,* who dare to enter the Salle du Manège wielding pikes and muskets. Peering up through the now grille-less opening into the Great Hall, we can read the terror in the deputies' faces.

"They fired upon us first!" cry the rebels, continuing to threaten the Swiss with their weapons. Louis cannot believe it. The Swiss

Guards are loyal and true; they would never have countermanded his orders. Shouts of "treason!" *"Mort aux traîtres!"* and accusations of a royal counterrevolution fill the hall, as the *fédérés* insist that the Swiss Guards lured the citizens into the palace, only to ambush and massacre them. The petrified deputies, who only minutes ago were so willing to offer us sanctuary, are capitulating to the mob crying out for our blood.

"How many are dead?" president Vergniaud demands to know.

A guard shrugs helplessly, his battered face pale. "I dare not say. Could be hundreds by now. There were so many—thousands—we could not stop them. Butchered corpses litter the steps, both inside and outside the palace. The gravel of the Place du Carrousel and the grass in the Jardin des Tuileries are already dyed crimson with blood."

Louis stands and demands that another order be sent to the Tuileries, telling the Swiss to lay down their arms. "This senseless massacre must end now. I will never countenance bloodshed."

The frightened messenger is dispatched, while the Swiss Guards who were lucky to escape with their lives become immediate prisoners of the Nation, marched off to be incarcerated within l'Abbaye, one of the vilest penitentiaries in Paris. Meanwhile, as the morning drags on, and we remain inside the reporters' box, utterly powerless and drenched in sweat, the deputies debate the fate of the monarchy. The day belongs to the most vitriolic voices of Revolution—the burly Danton, the brutish Santerre, pugnacious Marat, who denounces the royal family as "enemies of the people," and the ascetic, raven-garbed Robespierre—demagogues all. They shout down and drown out the moderates' desperate calls for reason and order.

Shortly after ten A.M., as the echo of the guns grows fainter, the doors of the Assembly are thrown wide once more, and a surge of rioters spews like vomit into the Great Hall. "What are they carrying?" asks Madame Élisabeth, wondering why they come bearing heavy sacks.

The madmen's pockets are turned inside out and the canvas bags are tugged open, their contents dumped noisily upon tables set out hastily in front of the president's rostrum. My eyes water when I recognize these spoils of victory: priceless treasures looted from the palace—silver flatware and enamel snuffboxes set with precious gems, my own jewelry and fans, sheaves of *assignats*, and boxes of my personal correspondence. There are even letters that in our haste to quit the palace I had left upon my desk. A painted miniature clatters onto one of the tables and even from where we sit I can identify it. It is a portrait of my mother. Thank God she is no longer alive to learn of this day's carnage and willful destruction of royal property! Her greatest diplomatic triumph, of many, was my marriage to Louis. What would she think to see us now?

Thoughts of how I had failed Maman are nearly enough to drive me to tears again, but I will never let these ruffians see me cry. They shall not know how painfully they have wounded me; they have ransacked the Tuileries, slaughtered God knows whom, but my tears are a victory I will not concede them.

We are reduced to further punishment to hear the deputies of the Assembly, many of them educated men of the Enlightenment, praise the good work of the looters for collecting these treasures. It is merely a smirking license of theft.

"Maman, I wish to take a walk." The dauphin tugs at my sleeve. He has finally stopped crying. Madame Royale has kept her head lowered for hours, in a silent world of her own, as if to shut out the evil all around us.

"I'm sorry, *mon chou d'amour*. It is too dangerous right now," I murmur, taking him onto my lap.

"*J'ai faim,*" he complains.

"I'm sure your papa is hungry, too. I shall see if they will give us something to eat."

But we have been utterly neglected by the deputies. No one comes to offer food; it is all I can do to get a cup of cool water for my son. We are all thirsty and perspiring profusely. None of us had time to bathe and the stench of sweat, from fear and the stifling heat in the overcrowded chamber, makes the atmosphere even less tolerable.

"When can we go home, Maman?" the dauphin asks, hours later.

Each discharge of a cannon, every *rat-a-tat* of musket fire, makes him tremble. "I don't know, *mon petit*. Soon, I hope. Soon." I try to reassure the child, but from the debate raging in the Assembly, the deputies are not inclined to see us return to the Tuileries. For one thing, word has come that the residence is by now completely uninhabitable. The destruction is too massive. Every door and window has been shattered, every mirror smashed or thrown from the windows, along with our furnishings: chairs and tables, chests, bedposts and bibelots, irreplaceable paintings, and other works of art.

All through the sweltering afternoon we remain in the cramped reporters' box like penned sheep awaiting slaughter. In answer to the cynical leers of a few of the deputies, I plead, "*S'il vous plaît, messieurs,* at least provide the children with something to eat." After hours of neglect, an elderly doorkeeper takes pity upon us and brings us bottles of wine and a plate of dry biscuits. They are nearly inedible and I fear the children will crack their teeth upon them, but the dauphin is so famished that he scarcely minds. I counsel him to suck on the cookies as if they were sticks of arrowroot candy, for that will not only soften them but will make the meager repast last longer.

Yet the porter had risked his own life to purchase these goods on our account. I reach for my purse to repay him and realize, in a moment of panic, that I have lost it. Not only did I have coins inside it, but the reticule contained a locket with a miniature of my children. And still I cannot let them see me weep. I will my face to remain impassive, burying any sign of emotion. In some measure the revolutionaries have already assassinated me; I am dead inside.

Above us, as three banners are raised proclaiming the nation's new motto—PATRIE, LIBERTÉ, ÉGALITÉ—and the events of this "Second Revolution" are discussed, we remain powerless to refute the deputies' litany of distorted facts and scurrilous lies. The Swiss Guards no more instigated this revolt than I am Catherine de Medici. And suddenly, the *monarch*—the man who insisted, *in spite of* such carnage, that the blood of his subjects not be shed—has been transformed by the deputies into the aggressor of this second revolution, and his immediate deposition is demanded.

In the afternoon, the debate turns to the future of France's monarchy. Speaking from the rostrum, after sanctioning the enforced exile of some four thousand nonjuring priests, Vergniaud calls for the immediate adoption of two measures. "The head of the Executive Power is hereby provisionally suspended and deprived of his functions, including the power of the veto, which is to be permanently rescinded. From this moment on, the National Assembly is the sole and supreme legislative power." He goes on to request with the same eloquence that ensured his success as a lawyer that the royal family be placed *"sous la sauvegarde de la Nation,"* under the "protection" of the citizens of France. He speaks euphemistically. Even when he calls for our removal to the Palais du Luxembourg and, as a sop to any royalist in the hall, agrees that the Nation should provide the dauphin with a tutor, I know that we are not going to be "safeguarded." We must face the grim reality of our circumstances. From this day on, no matter where we are sent by the Assembly, we will be imprisoned.

By early evening, we are permitted to welcome a handful of survivors into the recorders' box, and the tiny room grows even more suffocating. The comte de la Rochefoucauld-Liancourt, son of Louis's master of the wardrobe, is still trembling with fright an hour after his arrival. Yet he gallantly offers me the loan of his handkerchief to mop the perspiration from my face and throat. I notice him rooting through the pockets of his embroidered coat for the square of linen. "Isn't that it?" I ask, seeing the corner of a handkerchief poking from his sleeve. The duc pulls it out, then hastily tries to hide it. It is caked with blood.

"Are you wounded, Alexandre?" I ask, blanching. He shakes his head. His eyes darken with tears. "Who, then?" I whisper.

"Monsieur le duc de Mailly," he murmurs. At my gasp of horror, he tells me that he believes the courageous duc still lives. "He may yet outlive us all, *Majesté,*" Alexandre adds, referring to Mailly's advanced age. "I stanched his wounds with this handkerchief. He begged me to leave him and escape with my life."

With a rustle of silk taffeta, and the sound of stifled sobs, Madame Campan is ushered into the chamber, followed by my attendant Madame Auguié. Henriette looks a fright; her gown is torn and smeared with blood. I cannot tell if she has been wounded. She requests a basin and when none is forthcoming, the detainees back away, clearing a space so Madame Campan can vomit in a corner. Afterwards, mopping her mouth with a rag, she begins to tremble. I am unable to calm her for several minutes; finally she confides what she has witnessed.

"They came in from every door, slicing and hacking at everything and anyone in their wake. They derived as much pleasure from slashing tapestries, bed hangings, and bolsters and smashing any piece of furniture they encountered as they did in murdering whoever they saw." She describes the halls, littered with corpses, heads, and limbs. The rioters did not pause to ask whether a man or woman—or even a child—was a royalist or a Jacobin, loyal to the monarchy, or a clandestine spy. All were massacred with equal ferocity; the ruffians were not interested in explanations.

"Some of the decapitated heads they stuck on pikes as trophies. As I had no desire to be one of them, I ran for sanctuary, slipping in puddles of blood; finally I came to a room where several of your ladies were huddled together on chairs merely waiting to die. A band of Parisians burst into the room, intending, I am certain, to butcher us all. They approached us with such menace and malice in their eyes; we clung together in fear, expecting our next breath to be our last. Suddenly a wild-looking man with a long beard shouted at the men to stop. 'We do not kill women!' he said. 'Spare them. Do not disgrace the nation.'

"To our surprise, the assassins heeded his words. I went off to find my sister, searching every room for her—*Majesté,* everywhere, there were bloody hand- and footprints, almost *proudly* smeared, all over the bedclothes and upholstery. Suddenly, I heard the sound of footsteps rushing toward me. I ducked into the very next chamber that I came to, where a dozen or more courtiers were hoping to wait out the invasion." Madame Campan finally pauses for breath although she still trembles with panic.

"The monsters charged into the room and began to slaughter everyone, one by one, stabbing and decapitating innocent men. The women threw themselves to the floor, begging for mercy. I ran toward the staircase and just as I reached it, I felt someone grab me. My assailant thrust his hand down the back of my gown and clutched at my chemise. I fell to my knees and could not move."

Madame Campan begins to cry anew. "All of a sudden, amid the mayhem, a voice from the foot of the stairs called up to my molester, 'What are you doing?' To this the man made little reply. 'We don't kill women,' the voice said. At this, my executioner released my chemise. He spat upon me and snarled, 'Get up, jade, and be off. The Nation pardons you.'

"He spared my life, but not my dignity, *Majesté*. They made me stand on a bench facing the window and shout as loudly as I could into the courtyard below, 'The Nation forever!'

"Hours later, my gown was torn and stained with blood, though not my own—these are the badges of numberless brave royalists." Her trembling hands try to smooth her rumpled skirts. "I tried to leave the Tuileries. But was mistaken for a young Swiss Guard disguised as a woman, and for the second time in a single day, I was nearly killed.

"Finally, I was able to quit the palace, picking my way over countless corpses, some of which had been viciously dismembered." Choking back sobs, Madame Campan lists the bodies she recalls seeing, so many of them innocent servants who took no part in the combat. "They said 'We do not kill women,' *Majesté,* but I saw many dead and dying. Their sex did not save them."

"They laid down their lives for the crown," I say bitterly. "We can never repay their debt."

As Henriette describes what she saw between the palace and the Salle du Manège—the bodies leeching blood into the verdant gardens, dismembered limbs and scraps of grenadier and Swiss Guard uniforms hanging from trees, and the hags from the marketplace picking over the corpses, stripping them naked, even disemboweling them with a bloodlust she had never thought possible for a female—I, too, feel the need to retch.

During the evening, the acrid smell of smoke wafts toward us. "The Tuileries is burning," observes the comte de la Rochefoucauld-Liancourt. But soon, an unfamiliar stench settles heavily in our already fetid chamber. The sickening smell awakens Madame

Royale, who, along with her brother, had finally dropped off to sleep. Louis's eyes droop heavily and his head lolls against his chest.

"What is that?" my daughter whispers, pinching her nose closed.

"Bonfires," the comte answers. "They are burning the bodies."

Madame Campan begins to weep afresh.

Near midnight, the deputies vote to convey us for the night to the Couvent des Feuillants, disused ever since the Assembly declared the suppression of the monasteries and convents.

But it is another hour or more before we are permitted to leave. When we finally quit the recorders' box, Monsieur Barnave crosses the hall to speak with me. "As I am very sure of paying one day with my head for the interest your misfortunes have inspired in me, *je vous prie,* madame, as my only recompense, the honor of kissing your hand," he murmurs.

I nod my head, almost imperceptibly, raise my hand, and Barnave bends over to claim his reward. Over his shoulder I spy Robespierre watching us. He has witnessed everything.

We do not depart the Salle du Manège until two A.M. on August 11, our party shuttled to the Feuillants inside two royal carriages. The convent is not far from the Assembly hall, but the coachmen have been instructed to take a deliberately circuitous route, driving as slowly as possible, and we have been ordered to keep the curtains parted so that the carousing mob, still celebrating their hideous victory with wine and song, can jeer at us as we pass. Henriette Campan had warned me that the gutters of Paris were running with blood. Until now I confess I had thought it hyperbole. But she had not lied.

Our carriage takes a detour through the Place Vendôme, separated from the Convent des Feuillants by the broad rue Saint-Honoré. Louis stares numbly in horror and disbelief. His statue has been toppled from its pedestal and desecrated, sawed off at the knees. Citizens dance joyfully about the rubble, lobbing insults at our coach as we rumble past, accusing me of being a whore, "the infamous Antoinette who wants to bathe the citizens of France in blood." They demand the entrails of the king and queen even as their garments are steeped in gore and they play macabre games of catch with gobbets of dead flesh. Every man sports the tricolor cockade on his hat, an accessory that was declared compulsory in July. In solidarity, many women and children wear the red, white, and blue cockade..

The interior of the convent smells of mold. The last time I spent the night in a nunnery, I was fourteen years old. Maman had insisted on a pilgrimage to Marizell to pay tribute to the Blessed Virgin, the patron saint of Austria, before I left my homeland forever to become a bride of France. But this is not the country I wed: the violence, the vitriol, the dolls like voodoo poppets from the Antilles that hang me in effigy. These people loved me once.

I am shown to a narrow cell boasting a truckle bed, a wooden stool, and a basin. The walls, like those of the other cells in which the royal family will lay their heads tonight, are covered with a dark green paper that only enhances the gloom. Our garments reek and we have no fresh clothes to don. Everything we owned was in the Tuileries. My purse is gone and I have nothing to offer as a *pourboire* for anyone who does us a favor.

Shortly after our arrival, we are given a parcel wrapped in a bedsheet. It bears a sympathetic note from Lady Sutherland, the wife of the British ambassador. She has sent clean linen for me and my children. The women's accoutrements will be too large for Madame Royale, but I accept the gift gratefully. For the dauphin, Lady Sutherland sent a suit that had belonged to her own son, a boy of the same age. Monsieur d'Aubier, a former minister as portly as the king, dispatched linen and a silk suit for Louis.

For the first time since our installation in the Salle du Manège,

I allow myself to weep. My handkerchief becomes so wet with tears that I am compelled to accept one from Monsieur d'Aubier. He presses the cloth into my hands along with a purse that contains twenty-five louis. When I have nothing to offer in return except a grateful smile, he turns away, as though his own heart is about to crack.

In the cell adjacent to mine, Madame Élisabeth is sobbing quietly over her rosary.

"Oh, God, they are going to kill me!" I exclaim, struck with the harsh reality of our straits.

I have the rest of the night to spend with my terror; as exhausted as I am, there is no hope of sleep. Outside the grilles that separate us from the street, the citizens gather, singing choruses of the *Marseillaise* and hurling a continuous stream of abusive language at the convent walls. I suppose I eventually drop off into a fitful sleep because in a few hours, when the morning light seeps through the grille, I awaken with a start. I bolt upright in the narrow bed and look about me, confused by my unfamiliar surroundings. Memories of yesterday's nightmare come flooding back. With a shudder, I murmur to myself, "I had hoped it was all a dream."

Madame Campan and the princesse de Lamballe enter my cell. At the sight of me, Lamballe bursts into tears and kneels at my feet. To soothe her, I stroke her hair with sisterly affection, but her sadness is infectious. "I weep for you more than I do for myself," I blubber unregally, "for it is I who have brought this misfortune upon you—upon everyone who comes near me. It is me they blame for every ill. I am the one they despise."

At seven o'clock the royal family and our attendants are led to the refectory, where we are served an inedible *petit déjeuner* of stale toast and weak coffee. Even Louis lacks the stomach for it. At ten, we are conveyed back to the cramped reporters' box in the Salle du Manège, sentenced for another suffocating day to witness the deputies argue over our fate. One by one they rise to pontificate, condemning the monarchy and praising the new republic and the courageous revolutionaries, congratulating them on murdering some six hundred of the 950 Swiss Guards who valiantly defended the Tuileries. Sixty more have been taken prisoner.

Above our heads a heated discussion rages regarding where the royal family will reside, the Couvent des Feuillants being only a temporary solution. Yesterday's proposal of the Luxembourg Palais is rejected today, for fear that we can escape from it too easily. Rejected, too, is the pledge to retain a tutor for my son. Instead, they vote to send us to the Temple, so named because it is the Parisian fortress that in medieval days was the headquarters of the Knights Templar. Only in the Temple, Santerre argues, will it be possible to ensure the safety of the *"détenus."* By referring to us as detainees, it is abundantly apparent that we are truly prisoners of the state, entrusted from now on to the deputies of the Paris Commune who promise to conduct the royal family to the Temple "with all the respect due their misfortune." If they gave a fig for our "misfortune," they would not treat us so ill.

As the Temple needs to be prepared against our arrival, we are returned to the Feuillants to endure for another night the taunts outside our windows. But at least we will eat well. Louis's *valet de chambre,* Monsieur Thiéri, arranges for meals cooked in his own kitchen to be brought in to the convent. The king tucks into his food even more voraciously than usual. He is so often derided for caring more about his stomach than his subjects, but his detractors do not know the man I married twenty-two years ago. Louis's ravenous appetite is the result of the stress and strains of kingship, just as I once danced and gambled into the wee hours of the morning to stave off my unhappiness at our childless, celibate state. He eats—*comme un grand cochon,* they grumble—because he cares so *much* for his people.

Late that night a man named Dufour begs admission to the Feuillants. He asks to see the queen. Every nerve stills; surely this is the moment the citizens of France have been howling for like wolves. He has come to murder me. It would be an absurdly simple thing to do: one well-placed thrust of a poignard and Louis becomes a widower. The princesse de Lamballe bravely pretends to be me and allows Monsieur Dufour to approach, but he tells her, "You are not the queen." At her protestations he insists, "I have seen Her Majesty. You are not her."

"Why are you so sure, monsieur?" la Lamballe asks him, feigning my natural hauteur.

"Because I have her picture," Dufour replies. He reaches for something within his dark brown coat and I gasp, imagining the knife he will withdraw from the pocket. The princess turns ashen.

Monsieur Dufour reveals his hand. He is clasping my purse.

I look inside and every sou is there. So, too, is the miniature of me with my children. The man refuses a reward. He begs just one favor: "Don't tell anyone else I was here," he says, and disappears into the inky night.

We spend another full day cooped up like hens in the cramped chamber within the Salle du Manège and a third night at the convent. Finally, at six in the evening on August 13, the royal family and our attendants begin a two-hour journey through the narrow streets of Paris. The coachmen take many detours, providing us with a good look at the wreckage of the Tuileries Palace. Every window has been shattered, and in several places the façade is charred around the gaping holes. Three nights after the carnage, the courtyard is still ablaze with bonfires, tended by drunken Reds, mercenaries from Marseille who have not tired of singing their anthem. Our nostrils are assailed by the pungent stench of decaying flesh. Outside the ruins of the palace, someone has posted an enormous, crudely lettered placard that reads HOUSE TO LET.

Turning into the Place du Carrousel, our humiliating carriage ride toward the Temple continues, rumbling along at a snail's pace so as not to deprive the citizenry of their opportunity to witness the ultimate degradation of the once omnipotent King and Queen of France.

That night, the nation's razor, Dr. Guillotin's hideous invention, is moved from the courtyard of the Conciergerie to the center of the Place du Carrousel, directly opposite the central portal of the still smoldering Tuileries Palace.

TWENTY-THREE

Hideous Adieux

The Temple, consisting of a walled fortress some sixty feet high to the parapets, built around a quadrangle, and a palace with a pyramid-shaped roof, had been the residence of the Grand Priors of the Knights Templar. The last of the Templars' Grand Priors was the comte d'Artois, and before him, Louis's cousin Conti, a prince of the blood. I have always harbored an absolute horror of this gloomy edifice: its pointed towers remind me of torture chambers. A thousand times I have urged Artois to tear it down.

I last visited the little palace fourteen years ago, a guest at a fête hosted by Artois. The air that wintry night was icy and I was driven by sledge over a cover of snow that blanketed the packed earth and froze the *rues*. Then, I was swathed in white marten and jewels; my red-gold hair, lightly powdered, had been teased three feet off my scalp and dressed with diamond aigrettes and egret plumes. Now I am grateful for a borrowed gown; and beneath my simple cap, my hair is the same color as that distant snowfall.

The Temple, too, has changed considerably. Ivy snakes up the base of the four towers. Weeds choke the gloomy inner courtyard and wayward tufts of grass sprout up from between broken cobbles. Louis and I alight from the coach to find every window in the palace illuminated in anticipation of our arrival, but even in the torch-lit quadrangle we can hear the wind whistling through the bars on many of them.

Mayor Pétion stands at the main portal of the palace to welcome us. He conducts our party upstairs to the mirrored Salle des Graces, where a sumptuous meal awaits, served on Sèvres from silver vessels. After the leisurely supper, which does not end till nearly midnight, Louis and I take a turn about the various salons, their furnishings still opulent after all these years of disuse. "These rooms would make a charming apartment for you, *ma chère*," he tells me, referring to a capacious suite on the main floor, furnished in some of my favorite colors. He then goes on to assign rooms to the children and Madame de Tourzel—"This is perfect, for she can sleep adjacent to her charges"—and selects a suite for himself with a salon, a bedchamber, and a library. "We will be quite comfortable here, Citoyen Pétion," says my husband, adding, "If one must be imprisoned, we could do considerably worse."

At this remark the mayor's face reddens. He clears his throat. "*Erhm*—I am afraid it is my duty to inform you, monsieur, that your family will be lodged within the fortress itself—inside the archivist's apartments at the Tour de César, the small tower. However, those accommodations are not yet available, as the gentleman has yet to vacate the premises; and until they are ready for you, your family and attendants will reside elsewhere within the tower."

They have lured the mice into a pretty trap, only to feed them poison. How cruel it was to dangle before us the prospect of comfort and elegance, first satiating us with a fine meal, only to trip the springs, catching us unaware and exacerbating our mortification!

Louis and I refuse to allow the mayor to gloat over our dismay, so we maintain a stoic and tranquil mien in his presence. Yet this news makes it clearer than ever that we are indeed prisoners of the state. A medieval edifice intended to repel invaders, the stone walls of the fortress are ten feet thick and permanently damp. The children risk catching the ague. I hope there will be sufficient tapestries to line the walls.

It is one in the morning by the time we are conveyed to the disused rooms in the tower. Slime drips from the vaulted stone ceilings. The chambers are impossibly tiny and cramped and smell of stale urine. Madame Royale shrieks at the sight of a monstrous rat scuttling along the floorboards. "I will not sleep in here!" she declares, clinging to her father. The beds are scarcely better than boards, barren of all linens. The mattresses are filthy and who knows what vermin they may house?

Pétion smirks that we will be well protected here, for no one can penetrate the fortress. In sober truth, we have been incarcerated here for precisely the opposite reason: the Commune fears our escape. If there was any question of our being rescued, the small tower's enormous oaken portal, strengthened with iron sheeting, answers it. So do the men assigned to watch us. Soldiers are stationed on every level and a detachment of eight municipal officers guards the ground floor. Louis and I have forfeited all rights of privacy; a representative from the Commune must remain in the room with us at all times.

Even behind the thick walls of the Tour de César, sleep is as much of a luxury as it was at les Feuillants. Far below us, the guards, underscoring their animosity, sing a taunting refrain throughout the endless night: *Madame mont à sa tour. Ne sait quand descendra*—"Madame climbs her tower, not knowing when she will descend."

The following morning, I suggest that we all take a stroll about the inner courtyard so that the children can enjoy some fresh air and a bit of exercise. But the sunlight does not penetrate into the quadrangle and they grow frightened by the high stone walls. "I don't want to play here, Maman," the dauphin complains. "It feels like a tomb."

We settle in as best we can, in the hope that the allied armies that are on the march will soon be at our door. In the meantime, we must endeavor to enjoy a normal family life. The king is a beast defanged; he has no more power. What else does the Nation want of us? But less than a week later, on August 19, I receive the reply: our friends. Outside the Temple the newsboys cry the latest *nouvelles*. We learn that Antoine Barnave has been arrested and imprisoned, charged with being a clandestine royalist.

Escorted by Pétion, two officers from the Paris Commune arrive at the Temple late that evening. The taller of the two bears writs of arrest for the princesse de Lamballe, Madame de Tourzel, and even for Louise de Tourzel's young daughter Pauline, who, having survived the horrific massacre at the Tuileries in August, has been living with us ever since. My six ladies-in-waiting are also under arrest, all in the name of the Commune.

"What have they done?" I demand, my heart pounding. "What possible harm could a young girl and a handful of women who sit about all day and do needlework cause the Nation?"

"They are enemies of the state," the officer replies curtly. "This writ remands them forthwith to the women's prison of La Force."

My knees tremble. I can barely remain steady on my feet. My head begins to spin. "I refuse to let them go, messieurs." Flinging open my arms to shield them I declare, "These women are under my protection."

"You have no power here, madame," Pétion replies coldly. "Their fate is not yours to decide."

Pauline, my daughter's companion, is just a child. They are all in tears. I cannot send them away. They will be worked to death in La Force. They will starve or succumb to disease there. Laying aside all dignity, I clasp the mayor's hand, imploring, "At least spare the princesse. Not only is she a kinswoman of mine, but she is unwell. She is too frail to endure the hardships of imprisonment."

Madame de Lamballe's eyes are huge with terror. With her flaxen curls framing a paper-white complexion, she looks as though she is already one of the angels. She flings her arms about my neck and the two of us burst into uncontrollable sobs. I feel as if I am saying farewell to another sister.

The officers of the Commune are deep in conversation, speaking too low for me to overhear. At length, the man with the writ announces, "The carriage awaits, mesdames."

None go quietly. Their weeping grows more hysterical with each passing moment. I break the embrace with the princesse in order to bid adieu to each of my other ladies, urging little Pauline to be brave. "*Sois courageuse, ma petite*. Mousseline and I will pray every day for your safety." But I fear she is doomed. The nation did not spare the children of the Tuileries on the tenth of August.

"*Ma chère* Louise, I can never thank you enough," I tell the royal governess. "But I must beg of you one final favor: Look after my dear Lamballe." As I kiss Madame de Tourzel good-bye, I whisper in her ear, "And try to prevent her from having to answer any awkward or embarrassing questions." Louise understands what I mean: Axel.

The princess once again embraces me and whispers an urgent plea to look after her Scottish terrier.

"I will cherish him as I will always cherish you," I promise her. The words choke in my throat.

My ladies are led away. Their shrieks of terror echo off the courtyard walls and rise into the moonless night. The people blame me for destroying the nation. I blame myself for destroying my women's lives.

Nearly three weeks after our transfer to the Temple, we are informed that the archivist's five rooms are ready for us. The small but well-appointed chambers are as pleasant as can be under the circumstances. The tenant we have displaced was evidently a man of discerning taste, and the chambers are filled with maps and books, enough to keep Louis occupied for months. He immediately places an order for 250 more volumes, a sop that the Commune readily grants. The Nation's insult is keenly felt, but we intend to maintain our composure in the presence of our jailers, particularly the vicious Jacques Hébert, who also publishes an incendiary newspaper called *Le Père Duchesne,* writing in the guise of a crusty and cantankerous old republican. Although Hébert is as fastidious about his wardrobe and toilette as any Versailles courtier, the fictional Père Duchesne is depicted in a red liberty cap, perpetually puffing upon his clay pipe. No sooner does Monsieur Hébert return from his weekly visits to the Temple, intended to represent a show of respect for the royal family, than he publishes another screed issuing from the lips of Père Duchesne, demanding that "the boozer and his whore be shaved with the national razor."

Yet even in the midst of our enemies we are gradually building a new household. Louis's faithful *valets de chambre,* Monsieur Hüe and Hanet Cléry, escaped the massacre at the Tuileries by flinging themselves out of the windows. Three of our former cooks have managed to sneak into the Temple by informing the guards, who had no idea who they were, that they had been sent by the Commune to work in the kitchens. One of them, Louis François Turgy, makes good use of his thrice-weekly excursions to shop for food and wine—as we eat even better here than we did at the Tuileries—passing messages to our friends, and acquiring news of them and of the Duke of Brunswick's armies.

But we have few friends to wait upon us nowadays. After the removal of my ladies to La Force, the Commune sent a married couple, the Tisons, and their daughter to serve us. Bearded and built like a bear, Monsieur Tison is surly and resents his assignment, while his wife is a vain and selfish woman who becomes incommoded at the slightest provocation. She refuses to dress either my hair or the king's, so the tasks of *friseur* have fallen to Louis's faithful Monsieur Cléry, whose father used to be a barber. He is even teaching Madame Royale to style her own tresses.

Proper newspapers are forbidden to us here, so we must devise alternate methods of learning about the world beyond our heavily guarded stone walls. To outwit our jailers, Monsieur Turgy fashions bottle stoppers made from pieces of paper bearing notes written in the "invisible ink" of lemon juice or with an extract of gall nuts that will dissolve once the message has been deciphered and read. Wrapping them in cotton wadding, Turgy conceals notes between the mattresses of Mousseline or Madame Élisabeth, whose personal effects are less likely to be searched. He also stuffs the notes inside of hollowed lead pellets which he then hides within bottles of almond milk.

Turgy and I develop a code consisting of subtle gestures, each pertaining to a specific troop movement. In this way, Louis and I are able to remain informed regarding the location of the individual detachments of allied forces that we pray will deliver us and whether—and where—they have gained a victory. When the Austrian and Prussian forces are only fifteen leagues from Paris, Turgy will bring his fingers to his lips.

Yet the cruelty and ignorance of our minders knows no bounds.

One morning Mousseline approaches me with a tearstained countenance. In her hands are scraps of paper.

"What is that, *ma petite*?"

"My drawings," she blubbers. "Madame Tison ripped them up because she says they are pictures of enemy generals. I told her that they are the heads of the Roman Caesars, emperors who died before the birth of Our Lord, but she did not believe me. She asked me how I would know what an Octavius or a Nero or a Caligula looked like. I *hate* her. She's fat and stupid and is missing half her teeth."

Madame Royale wishes me to confront Madame Tison and put her in her place. "You're the queen. She has to obey you," Marie Thérèse says angrily, stamping her foot.

Endeavoring not only to calm her but to school her, I try to make my daughter understand that her father and I are determined to appear unperturbed in the face of our servants' cruelty. "To scold them or behave haughtily in their presence will only reinforce their prejudices against us. But if they come to see that we are kind and compassionate and sensitive and our temperaments and manners no different from anyone else's, they will surely find their own hearts and become kinder and more compassionate to *us*." Taking her hands in mine I remind Mousseline, "We have been given the opportunity to demonstrate to some of our loudest detractors that we are not in fact the monsters they portray us to be."

It is a difficult lesson for a young girl whose world has been upended. Since the first assault upon the Tuileries, she has grown even more sullen and withdrawn.

The dauphin is too young to comprehend the gravity of our situation, and so he appears pleased when one of the municipal guards, Monsieur Goret, confiscates the multiplication tables that

Louis has instructed him to practice. *"Mais pourquoi, Papa?"* our son inquires, wanting to know the reason for it.

"Perhaps—perhaps Monsieur Tison desires to learn mathematics," Louis replies gently. "But he is too mortified to let anyone know it and so he borrowed yours." Turning to address me and Madame Élisabeth, the king shakes his head. "The imbecile thinks the tables contain some sort of secret formula for breaking ciphers," he murmurs.

In our dining room, a copy of the Declaration of the Rights of Man is tacked to the wall. Madame Tison makes a point of showing me that the stove's brass doors are embossed with the motto of the Republic: *Liberté, Égalité, Fraternité.* That afternoon, under orders from the Paris Commune, our bread rolls are once again served to us crumbled and torn to pieces. Our jailers suspect that messages have been baked into the bread by royalist sympathizers. The inspection of our food is but one example of the intimidation and insults perpetrated upon our family by the nation.

"It is for your own protection, Monsieur," Goret sneers, to Louis's demand whether such scrutiny is necessary. He removes his pipe from between his lips just long enough to reply. Well aware of the king's antipathy to pipe smoke, the officer deliberately exhales directly in his face, encircling Louis's head with an acrid wreath.

Because every stitch of clothing and stick of furnishings we had owned was ruined during the invasion of the Tuileries, the Commune grants us a surprisingly generous allowance with which to purchase new goods. Employing Rose Bertin is out of the question; her life and livelihood having been imperiled by our lengthy association, she emigrated to England a year ago. The thirty seamstresses kept fully occupied with creating petticoats and chemises, bodices, skirts, lawn cotton sashes and bonnets, coats of Florentine taffeta, lace caps, black beaver hats, and simple gowns of cotton dimity and toile de Jouy are—with the exception of the court dressmaker Madame Éloffe—staunch republicans. I order garments and accessories in my favorite muted tones: puce, dove gray, pale blue, and the cool brown color we call *"boue de Paris."* Sprigged cotton gowns are ordered for Madame Royale and sailor suits for the dauphin. Louis is content to alternate between his two nearly identical chestnut-colored coats with silver filigreed buttons, paired with waistcoats of white piqué. His sole extravagance is a silk riding coat in a shade that was once fashionable at Versailles, the peach-gold hue of my hair known as *cheveux de la reine.*

I look upon it as a measure of revenge on our jailers by being profligate with their *assignats,* commissioning shoes and gloves, fichus, fans, and lace-edged handkerchiefs. Yet the Commune has not complained about the expense. And since I cannot abide the stenches that permeate the walls of the Temple, I have ordered countless scented candles and pastilles, as well as numerous perfumes. What is 100,000 francs' worth of fragrances when the Duke of Brunswick is on the march? Soon the allies will be in Paris. I have taken to studying the maps in Louis's new library, comparing them to the itinerary for the allied invasion that the comte de Mercy's courier was able to smuggle into the Temple.

"They plan to cross the frontier and enter Verdun on the first of September," I confide to Madame Campan, showing her the itinerary. Then I tell her the date the forces will besiege the city of Lille. From there I begin to count the days until the soldiers will reach Paris. I live in hope of our rescue. When we are freed, we intend to journey to Strasbourg in order to preserve this most important frontier city for France. One day this madness will end—it must— and the monarchy will be restored. I came to France to bear the Bourbons a son. Louis Charles must have a legacy.

Meanwhile, they are enlarging our prison, demolishing homes adjacent to the Temple in order to expand the walls that enclose us. On the morning of September 2, Louis, fascinated as always by

masonry, stands at the window of his room overlooking the destruction. Beside him is Monsieur Daujon, the Commissioner of
the Commune. With every splintering crash of wood and falling
stone, my husband bursts into laughter, discoursing with Daujon
upon the masons' efforts, enjoying the spectacle the way I might
savor the performance of an opera.

Their conversation is interrupted abruptly by the rumble of
cannon fire, distant, but unmistakable. The king glances about
fearfully as a second report is heard, followed by a third terrifying
boom. Louis looks helplessly at Monsieur Daujon, who informs us
grimly, "Those are the warning guns."

"Warning of what?" Louis inquires warily.

Moments later, the church bells of Paris clang with the frightening alarm of the tocsin, calling the people to arms. Louis begins
to tremble, his sangfroid deserting him entirely. Soaked with fear,
he tries to mop his brow with a handkerchief, but can neither contain nor control his perspiration. Approaching the commissioner, I
implore, "Monsieur, you must save my husband!" Madame Élisabeth sinks to her knees and, clasping Daujon's hand, urges, "*S'il
vous plaît,* have pity on my brother!"

But it is not the commissioner we need to fear. After several
agonizing hours of pacing the carpets, unsure of what will befall
us, Monsieur Turgy bursts into the room, his mustard-brown jacket
and breeches spattered with blood.

"Have you been to the abbatoir?" I ask, aghast. And if so, why
has he intruded upon our private rooms still smeared with gore?

"All *Paris* has become an abbatoir," Turgy replies breathlessly.
"Notices are affixed to every lantern post calling upon the citizens
to take justice into their own hands." He thrusts a crumpled paper
at the king. I read it over Louis's shoulder. The broadsheet proclaims, BEFORE WE RACE TO THE FRONTIER TO MEET OUR FOR-

EIGN ENEMIES, WE MUST PUT THE BAD CITIZENS OF FRANCE TO
DEATH.

"Who are they calling 'bad citizens'?" I demand.

Louis squints as though he has the migraine. "I believe I can
answer that, madame—from the people's perspective. We must
protect the priests who refused to swear the oath to the Constitution, the near and dear of the émigrés who remained in France,
aristocrats and their servants who have been wrongfully imprisoned merely for being our friends—"

He breaks off. Surely he is thinking about the princesse de
Lamballe and Madame de Tourzel and her daughter. My God,
how can we protect them now?

"The nonjuring priests are already being massacred," Turgy
tells us, his face contorted with the horror he has witnessed.
"This—this blood is theirs," he says, pointing frantically to his coat
and breeches. "I—I lost my hat—no, I did not lose it—I covered
the eyes of one soldier of God who was in the throes of agony,
death so close and yet so painfully far away. He had been bayonet-
ted several times through the belly and then gutted like a fish. I
could not bear the thought that he would take his last breaths staring helplessly at his own entrails."

"*Sacré Dieu,*" Madame Élisabeth murmurs to herself. Clutching her rosary, she hastens from the room to find a basin in which
to vomit.

"The murderers were bare-armed, their complexions swarthy,
like Greeks or Corsicans. To a man, they wore the *bonnet rouge,*"
Turgy tells us after the princesse has quit the chamber. His description of the assassins sounds like the brutal Reds from Marseille.
Have the Parisians imported mercenaries to do their bloody work
for them?

News arrives late that evening that Verdun fell today to the

Austrians. A woman wearing the *tricolore* as a sash, secret royalist or rabid republican I know not, manages to get into the courtyard of the Temple, and holds a placard up to our windows. VERDUN IS TAKEN.

"Is that why this carnage has begun?" I ask the king softly.

"Who can say?" Louis replies. His pale blue eyes mist over. With so much mayhem in the streets we cannot even savor the allies' victory. "I don't know how the citizens could have gotten word so quickly."

Hours later, two commissioners from the Commune arrive with another writ of arrest. This one is for Louis's *premier valet de chambre,* Monsieur Hüe. The king immediately springs to his servant's aid. "He dresses me every morning, messieurs. He shines my shoe buckles. This man is no criminal."

"Is it not enough that we are, all of us, prisoners of the Nation, cooped up behind the thick walls of a castle keep?" Fuming and cursing with a fervor I have never before seen in her, Madame Élisabeth levels an accusatory finger at the officers. "What possible glory can you hope to win by depriving innocent men of their livelihood?"

"It is merely their latest and most cowardly method of torturing us," I interpose, fighting back bitter tears. "It is evident that the Commune's intention is to separate our family from the people who are most attached to us and in whom we continue to place our trust."

"Silence!" bellows Monsieur Mathieu, the taller of the two commissioners. His face has become the color of a ripe persimmon. "The alarm guns have been fired!" He points to the window. "Do you hear that? The tocsin is still ringing its call to arms. The enemy is at your doors, baying like wolves for blood—anyone's blood—and demanding heads. Will it be yours that they take first?"

Mathieu's words send chills along my spine. But they do not

lessen my desire to protect an innocent man, about to suffer for the sins of his sovereigns. "Monsieur Mathieu, if the situation is so dire that the prisons are being broken open and the inhabitants cut down like summer wheat, by arresting Monsieur Hüe tonight you sentence him to death."

By now the commissioners have each grasped one of the valet's arms to haul him away. "If you wish to demonstrate good faith, at least take him to the lockup of the Commune," Louis urges, in a final effort to preserve his lackey's life. "If I cannot stop you from imprisoning him, at the very least I beg of you to guarantee his life."

The men look to Monsieur Daujon. After a few moments he nods his head. "Take him to the Commune."

Monsieur Hüe clasps the king's hands and bends his head to kiss them. "Sire, is there anything more I can do for you?" he murmurs.

"*Oui,* monsieur. Stay alive."

"*Et vous aussi, Votre Majesté.*"

Beyond our walls, the carnage continues throughout the night. Word reaches us the following morning that the Bicêtre, Salpêtrière, and La Force prisons have been emptied, and the detainees slaughtered like livestock. Commissioner Manuel assures us that the princesse de Lamballe has survived. Under the pretext of visiting the green market, Monsieur Turgy is willing to risk his own life to deliver a message to her, if he can find her. His cousin, a Madame Bault, is employed at La Force.

A few hours later, he returns, his complexion a sickly shade of green.

"Did you find the princesse?" I ask, desperate for news. "And Madame de Tourzel—and Pauline?" If La Force has been emptied, what is their fate?

But he begins to speak of little boys instead, stories he has heard in the streets about urchins from the Bicêtre which, along with the Salpêtrière, incarcerates a disproportionate number of humanity's fallen souls: children, beggars, and prostitutes. Turgy is shaking, raging against the horrors he has witnessed today. As if yesterday's carnage had not been vicious enough, now the monsters—women as well as men—are butchering children.

"I saw a boy—perhaps he was the son of one of the whores; he could not have been older than monsieur le dauphin—being torn limb from limb. The swarthy men with no sleeves dragged him out of La Force by his legs, his little head bumping along the cobbles. He was battered and bruised but still he did not die. Then the little boy was set upon by the mob, stabbed from all sides, and still he clung to life. A woman offered me her knife and asked if I wanted to participate. I didn't know how to say no without imperiling myself so I told her that she was doing a fine job without me. At the sudden crack of a pistol I nearly jumped out of my skin and saw that someone had shot the child in the head. As the light went out of the beggar boy's eyes, he was surrounded by a halo of blood. 'At that age it is hard to let go of life,' said his executioner casually, as if to explain why he needed to discharge the fatal shot. When I left, they were pissing on his corpse."

We are being visited by the slaughter of the innocents. What has this to do with revolution? With the formation of a republic from the ashes of the monarchy?

I cannot express my shock, my anger, when Turgy remarks, shaking his head in disbelief, that the restaurants and theaters in le Marais remain open, as if nothing unusual is occurring. "Meanwhile the gutters overflow with the blood of your subjects, Your Majesty. Drunk on cheap wine, the rabble attacks almost everyone in sight, splitting heads as easily as hacking cabbages." The cook's mind is so disarranged by what he has witnessed that it takes me several attempts to elicit any information about my precious Lamballe and the Tourzel women.

"My cousin told me she saw the Tourzels with a man—an Englishman, she believed, from the sound of his voice. He told them to follow him out of the madness."

The only Englishman I can think of who continues to aid our cause is Monsieur de Malden. Could it be he?

As for those terrifying placards and notices demanding that the people bring to justice—in the words of Maximilien Robespierre—the "implacable enemies of the Nation," the rabble have declared themselves "people's courts" and have been staging mock trials and summary executions of the priests and aristocrats disgorged from the prisons. Many of the Swiss Guards who survived the debacle of August 10 only to be incarcerated afterward, have been gruesomely murdered. The lawyer from Arras has the gall to sanction these ad hoc tribunals and grisly verdicts by declaring that the "will of the people is being expressed." Although the news of every new death sickens us, it is no surprise when we learn that no one has been ajudged innocent.

Late in the afternoon on September 3, Monsieur Daujon arrives with the most devastating news of all. My first friend at Versailles, and one of my dearest, the sympathetic and sorrowful companion during all my tribulations, has not survived what the Assembly has dubbed "the September massacres."

Even a man such as Daujon, whose masters are the Commune and the Nation, looks shaken. He speaks haltingly, aware that every syllable stabs my heart, as if I, too, suffer every blow, every kick, every thrust of the bloodstained knives. "The rumors were false, madame. The princesse de Lamballe did not escape the terror." I begin to tremble, my lip quivering with the onset of tears. "Are you certain you want to hear everything?" he asks solicitously. I nod, but I want to shriek until the walls of the Temple vibrate with my anger. If such men have compassion somewhere within their hearts, how can they be such butchers?

"Madame de Lamballe was brought before one of the impromptu tribunals," Daujon begins. "Asked to denounce you and the king, she refused. It is said that she told them with tremendous dignity, 'I have nothing to reply to you. Dying a little earlier or a little bit later is of no consequence to me. If it is the price I must pay for my silence, I am prepared to sacrifice my life.' Her judges took her at her word. They conducted her to the exit at La Force for the Abbaye prison, the people's metaphor for summary execution. This portal is nothing but an entrance to hell. The princesse was forcibly dragged into the courtyard of La Force and set upon by her executioners. Like a pack of rabid dogs, they made quick work of her. She was clouted over the head with a hammer, knocking her to the paving stones. After that, she was stabbed repeatedly by numerous assailants with filthy knives and stolen swords—Are you sure you wish me to continue?"

I nod as if in a dream, as if someone is holding my head underwater and I am hearing the commissioner's words—slurred and distant—from the bottom of a bucket. Monsieur Daujon can no longer look me in the eye. "Her limbs—and her head, madame were hacked off as though she were a hog at the abbatoir. It has been said that she was violated as well. No one can say whether she lived to suffer this indignity, or if the attackers defiled her decapitated corpse. She was then disemboweled—one man boasts of having eaten her beating heart right there in the rue du Roi de Sicile. No one can vouch for his veracity. Some say that her breasts and genitals were sliced off. It is impossible to discern what is lies; but I can unhappily confirm that her head is being paraded about the city on the point of a blacksmith's pikestaff as a trophy of the Revolution. Other pikes display her entrails and pieces of her white gown, now stained with blood and excrement."

Daujon is startled by my anguished cry, the high keening wail of a broken heart. Minutes pass before I can summon my thoughts, let alone force any words past my lips. "Her blood might as well be on my own hands," I mutter. "The people murdered her because they hate *me*."

I want to take to my bedchamber and never emerge again, but my husband needs me, too. To help distract Louis's mind from the horrific carnage that we remain powerless to halt, I indulge him that afternoon in a game of backgammon. But the calm the king so sorely craves is broken by an ear-shattering shriek from Madame Tison. Beyond the Temple courtyard, there is mayhem in the streets. Louis's valet Monsieur Cléry, rushes upstairs and urges the officers of the Commune who are charged with watching our every movement to bar the shutters. "A mob is approaching from the rue du Temple. Keep Their Majesties from the windows," he cautions. He draws Monsieur Daujon aside and murmurs, "They have come with the head and viscera of the princesse. Because so many of the citizens rejoiced in the mistaken belief that it was the queen who was beheaded, the monsters even stopped to have Madame de Lamballe's hair coiffed in the manner of her golden days, to ensure that she—that her remains—are immediately recognizable."

Does their savagery know no bounds? Is it possible that even the republican-minded duc d'Orléans could not save his delicate sister-in-law? This is no ordinary civil war where opposing armies clash. Innocent Frenchmen, women, and children are being slaughtered by their own countrymen. At the battle cry of *"À la lanterne!"* the mob drags anyone who looks like an "aristo" to the nearest lamppost and hangs them upon these impromptu gallows, stringing up innocent people for the "crime" of dressing too well or neglecting to wear the *tricolore* cockade, offenses that trigger the immediate suspicion of clandestine loyalty to the crown.

Has any great civilization been as vicious to its own people? I

clutch the arm of the closest chair. Daujon orders his commissioners to hang a tricolor bunting upon the main portal of the Temple,
a device guaranteed to prevent the rabble from entering as sure as
the mark of lambs' blood on the lintels of the Israelites' doorposts
saved their firstborn sons from Egyptian slaughter.

Louis demands to know the reason for all the commotion.
And, "What are they trying to hide from us, messieurs?" I ask
anxiously. "From the sound of her screams, Madame Tison has
clearly seen it."

Below, the mob choruses for my appearance at the window, demanding that the shutters be opened. One of the members of the
Garde Nationale mounts the stairs to inform us that the rioters
have begun to scale the rubble of the recently destroyed houses in
an effort to reach the upper story of our residence with their grisly
trophies. They have not given up on their intention to force me to
witness the results of their barbarity. "The head of la Lamballe has
been brought here to show how the people avenge themselves
against tyrants," the soldier declares.

Cléry is too emotional to speak, but Daujon answers the king
tensely. "If you must know, monsieur, they are trying to show the
queen the head of her favorite. They are demanding that she kiss
the waxen lips of her lover."

A horrified gasp escapes my lips and the room begins to spin
with alarming velocity as I fall, fainting, to the floor.

TWENTY-FOUR

Citoyens Capet

When I regain consciousness I overhear Monsieur Daujon speaking to the rabble in the courtyard. In an effort to stave them off, he praises their courage and their exploits this day, but tells them that if they wish to enjoy the full effect of their revenge, they are in the wrong place. "The head of Marie Antoinette is not for you to claim. It is unwise to destroy such valuable hostages of the Nation, especially while our enemies are already crossing our frontiers." Referring to the remains of my dear Lamballe, Daujon demands, "By what right should those of you who brandish these relics of Revolution enjoy the fruits of your victory alone? Do they not belong to the entire citizenry of Paris? Dusk approaches and soon it will be too dark for your comrades to witness them. You should be displaying them in front of the Palais Royal or in the Jardin des Tuileries— for so long the bastions of the monarchy and the entitled nobility who have trodden the people underfoot with no more thought than they give to an insect. Plant your pikes in the gardens as an eternal memorial of your triumph."

To further appease the madmen, Commissioner Daujon permits them to parade about the Temple towers with their spoils before dispersing into the encroaching twilight. His quick wits have not only prevented them from tormenting me further, they have saved the royal family from certain violence.

All through the night the tocsin rings and I cannot sleep for weeping. Although I was shielded from witnessing the princesse's decapitated head, its gruesome image dances in my mind. Her wide blue eyes will never again look upon a sunset.

"I heard you crying, Maman." Madame Royale tiptoes into my bedchamber and slips under the coverlet beside me. My thirteen-year-old daughter wraps her arms about my neck, and burrows against me as if she wishes to crawl back inside my body where it is warm and innocent and safe. Her muffled sobs stain my night rail with tears. "*J'ai peur, Maman.* I'm afraid," she says softly, her voice as small as it was when she was a little girl.

Holding her tightly I murmur into her fragrant hair, "I am so sorry, *ma petite* Mousseline. I am so sorry you have had to grow up so fast."

The rioting continues until five the following morning. After the tocsin finally ceases, the authorities estimate the number of dead as a result of these September massacres at more than twelve hundred. Surely hundreds, if not thousands more, were injured. The citizens speak of a new dawn for France, baptized in blood. The deposed relic of a society they call the *Ancien Régime,* does not have a scintilla of authority. My husband no longer rules France. Instead, the reign of a many-headed monster has begun.

The Legislative Assembly is dissolved on September 19, replaced the following day by the establishment of the National Convention. On September 21, with a stroke of the pen this new legislative and administrative body abolishes the great and illustrious monarchy of France. All garments embroidered with the emblem of a crown are ordered destroyed. Madame Élisabeth will need to spend the next several days unpicking the stitching from her brother's linen while I do the same for the children's clothing as well as my own. Even our undergarments must be altered.

The king and queen are dead—and yet we live. In consequence, we must be rebaptized by the people. The members of the National Convention debate over what to call us. "Louis the Last" is one disrespectful suggestion. In the end, the sixteenth king to bear the Christian name of Louis, and the fifth sovereign born into the House of Bourbon, along with his consort, are to be known henceforth as Citizen and Citizeness Capet.

The same day, we receive news that the French troops have repelled the foreign allies at Valmy, halting their advance. Within the week the Revolutionary forces occupy Savoy and Nice, as well as three major cities along the Rhine. It is impossible not to despair.

We live a shadow existence now; and yet during the first few weeks after the formation of the National Convention, once Louis has been deposed, we are permitted more freedom. The Commune allows us to read newspapers again, perhaps because they contain so much discouraging news. The French armies are turning the tide, forcing the allies to retreat across the frontier. Despite these setbacks, Louis and I make a point of savoring the small pleasures offered by the puzzles and mind teasers in the *Mercure de France,* exchanging periodicals with each other every morning when the family convenes at nine for breakfast. After more than twenty-two years of marriage, relieved of the responsibilities of monarchy, we have grown closer. The irony does not escape me that only after the most horrific degradation and the ultimate deprivation of our crowns and titles have I obtained the warm, affectionate, simple family life I had dreamed about as a girl.

After breakfast it is time for our son's daily lessons. Louis is an exemplary tutor, kind and patient. Louis Charles, however, is not always a perfect pupil. True, he is only seven years old, but his penmanship is sorely wanting. With an indulgent grin I am reminded of my own childish hand when Louis encourages him to "Show Maman your efforts." The phrases Louis Charles has been told to commit to memory by the commissioners of the Paris Commune are horribly misspelled, even though Louis has asked him to copy them directly beneath his own example. When he continues to sign his lessons, "Louis Charles, Dauphin," his father swallows hard and forces himself to tear up the page. "You must sign only your Christian names from now on, *mon fils,*" my husband says gently, his voice colored with melancholy.

Although there is no longer a monarchy for our son to inherit, his father insists on preparing him to be the future Louis XVII, filling his head with geography and teaching him to memorize passages of Racine and Corneille, which the poor child can barely comprehend, though he gamely recites the verses from rote, eager to please his Papa and Maman. As Louis corrects the boy's diction and suggests that I might demonstrate how to declaim with passion, "because your lovely maman was a charming actress in her youth," a smile comes unbidden to my lips. A flood of distant memories surface—of rosy days with my little theater troupe at Trianon, and before that, of our clandestine performances in an entresol room at Versailles where we had to hide our stage from Louis's *grand-père* the king, and then reminiscences of abbé Vermond's battery of lessons to prepare me to become dauphine of France. The only subject in which I had excelled was the chronology and history of the queens of France. A little gasp escapes my lips. Will I be the last of that line?

Madame Élisabeth and I have undertaken the education of Madame Royale. Owing to her aunt's tutelage, Mousseline is already more proficient in mathematics than I ever was.

In the afternoons, even when the weather is inclement, we avail ourselves of the opportunity to stroll about the gardens *en famille*. One day, as a fine autumn mist falls, Louis Charles urges, "Give me a ride, Papa."

"What did you forget to say?" I prompt.

"S'il vous plaît," he replies docilely, a blush suffusing his pretty cheeks.

The king—for my husband will always be the king to me—hoists our son onto his shoulders and prances like a horse around the beds of greenery as the gentle rain soaks their hatless heads. I insist that the pair of them change into dry clothes before we head in to supper.

At least the Commune has never stinted on the quality as well as the quantity of our comestibles. Thirteen servants minister to our needs, both at the main meal and for the evening repast. Unfortunately, as Louis is deprived of the ability to hunt or ride, he is gaining more weight, drowning his sorrows every afternoon in the three soup courses, four entrées, six roast meat dishes, and the four or five desserts that are served, in addition to the stewed and fresh fruits that are provided afterwards to cleanse the palate. He eats almost as much in the evenings, when nearly the same number of courses are provided.

As we have done every night after supper since our incarceration, the family gathers in the salon for games of backgammon or piquet while the children amuse themselves. Madame Élisabeth often sits by the fire, immersed in her devotional. On other occasions my *belle-soeur,* Mousseline, and I quietly ply our needles, while Louis reads and the dauphin sits on the carpet, contentedly playing with his toys, although his tiny leaden soldiers have been confiscated by the commissioners of the Commune.

On September 26, after the main meal, while the king is preparing to descend into the courtyard, having promised our son for days that they would fly a kite together, a delegation from the National Convention arrives, led by the commissioners Daujon and Manuel, the Public Procurator. Their expressions are grim, although behind them I detect a note of triumph.

"I bear instructions to remove Citizen Capet to the Grosse Tour," Daujon announces.

I feel as if someone has struck me in the chest with an ax. *"Non!"* I cry. "But why?" Madame Élisabeth drops her prayer book; it lands on the nearby tabletop with a dull *thump*. The children begin to bawl hysterically. Madame Royale throws her arms about her father's neck and, turning back to the commissioners with a look of pure rage, screams, "Why must you take my papa? Why do you hate us so?" Clinging to his father's coat and staining it with his tears, the dauphin cannot even summon any words.

"What does this mean, messieurs?" I breathe, suddenly sick and dizzy. What earthly reason would they have to separate us?

Daujon shrugs, reiterating that his orders are to escort Citoyen Capet into an apartment on the second floor of the large tower. Monsieur Manuel approaches my husband and with a violent tug, rips the *cordon rouge* from his breast. He dashes the red sash and the cross of the Order of Saint Louis to the floor. The gold and enamel medal skitters under an armchair.

"Was that necessary?" I demand, fighting to contain my tears. "Have you not humiliated the poor man enough?" And then, the rationale for Louis's removal painfully dawning, "I know," I add, "why you wish to isolate him. But if these are truly to be his final months, what do you—what does the Nation—gain by depriving him of the comforts of his family? Why must you take him from us? Allow us, I beg of you, by all that is holy, let my husband remain among those who love him."

In that moment I am struck with the powerful realization that this may be only the second time in all our years of marriage that I have openly admitted my love for *mon mari*. By now my shoulders heave with sobs. I attempt reason with the commissioners. I beg. I will do anything to keep Louis with us. "Do not remove him from the sight of his children," I plead. "Do not deprive them of their final weeks with their papa."

Hearing a loud sniffle, I turn in the direction of the sound. Monsieur Goret, the municipal guard on duty today in our salon, is struggling to stifle his emotion. Goret has two children of his own whom he rarely sees; his duties at the Temple encompass the *plupart* of his days. I catch his eye and he averts his gaze. Perhaps a compassionate heart beats within his breast after all.

Will sympathy save us?

Goret approaches the commissioners, engaging them in a hushed and furtive conversation. Finally, Commissioner Daujon turns to us, saying abruptly, "Meals only. Louis Capet may join his family for breakfast, dinner, and supper—providing that everyone speaks only in French and in a clear, loud voice."

I curtsy to him—the Queen of France bending her knee to an officer of the Paris Commune!—and murmur my thanks, adding, "Please, messieurs, see that my husband is well looked after." I worry about the state of Louis's mind without the affection of his family about him. "Will he at least be permitted his books?" I ask.

Commissioner Manuel nods. "Citoyen Capet may read to his heart's content," Manuel replies. "But paper and writing implements are henceforth forbidden to him."

Louis and I exchange a forlorn look. I think about the hunting journals he has kept since I've known him, the sting of some of the notations he has made over the years—including the one word, *rien,* that he wrote with reference to our wedding day, when nothing indeed occurred in the matrimonial bed that night. Now he will not even be allowed to record the day's events—an endless string of "nothings" because the Commune has prohibited him, not only from riding, but from leaving the confines of the Temple.

Clasping my hands in his, Louis says, "Don't cry, madame. I will see you at supper tonight." He forces a feeble chuckle. "Think of it as if we were at Versailles, where I spent the day in my apartments tending to the business of the kingdom."

How foolish and young I was then, so eager to be rid of Louis, the bore who cared only about locks and masonry and history and hunting and had so little interest in my own pleasures! How I delighted in the time away from him! He has always been a good man, but once I thought it a chore to suffer his presence for several hours at a time. Now, I would give anything to remain in the same room.

"What is it like up there, Papa, all by yourself?" the dauphin asks his father that evening, as we linger over our meal. Every minute together has become a gift. Never have we chewed more slowly.

"I did not see them take our good Cléry away," Louis mutters, more to himself than to answer our son. He shakes his head. "The shutters are sealed closed. The only light I receive comes from the transom above the windows."

"Then you did not see Monsieur Cléry return, brother." It pleases Madame Élisabeth to give him the good news. "After questioning him for several hours, the Commune determined that he was ignorant of whatever they suspected him of doing—or knowing—and so they permitted him to rejoin our service."

Outside the Temple, although Louis is denied the view, the nights grow longer as the leaves turn. The season of dying approaches.

At the end of October Commissioner Daujon informs me that

we are to be reunited with Citizen Capet. My breath catches as I anticipate Louis's return to our cozy apartment in the small tower. But Daujon quickly disabuses me of this hope. The rest of the *famille* Capet is to join Louis in the large tower. What does it mean? To allow us to live as a family again, yet deprived of the opportunity to see the sun and the stars?

The dauphin is to sleep in his father's bedchamber from now on. Madame Royale and her aunt must share mine, a boudoir tastefully decorated with blue and green furnishings that are pleasing to the eye and soothing to the soul. My new rooms lie directly upstairs from Louis's quarters, four stories above the cobblestone courtyard. Wicket gates have been installed at a dozen intervals along the winding tower staircase, forcing me to stoop each time I pass through one of the barriers. And on every landing, sturdy oaken doors are reinforced with iron bars and bolts, and heavy chains must be unlocked, one by one, before we can progress to the next landing.

Immediately upon my arrival at the apartment in the large tower, I close the charming white cotton curtains; I do not wish to be reminded of the permanently shuttered windows.

Once again the disgraced royal family settles into a routine. Fastidious about punctuality even in our strained circumstances, Louis rises at seven every morning and prays for an hour before breakfast. Often he is joined by Madame Élisabeth, who has chosen since girlhood to dedicate her life to her brother. No husband could have been the recipient of so much fidelity and devotion.

At eight o'clock, Louis and the dauphin join the rest of us for breakfast in my apartments and then my husband returns downstairs with our son to resume the boy's tutelage. At least we are still permitted to stroll about the Temple gardens, which we do as a family at eleven every morning. It breaks my heart the first time Louis Charles asks his Papa if he will fly a kite with him as they used to do. I catch Louis's eye. How do you tell your little boy that there will be no more kites from now on because Maman and Papa have been deprived of paper and string?

We eat dinner every day at two o'clock and then sit down to cards and other pastimes. Louis is teaching the dauphin how to play chess. I overhear him explaining to our son that "when your opponent corners your king, placing him in an untenable position from which he has no legal move that will not result in his capture, the game is—" As he realizes what he has just said, he halts, midsentence. I turn away, overcome.

Madame Élisabeth gives a little gasp. She is mending a tear in her own gown, and bites off the thread with her teeth after securing it. Her shears were taken from her as were my embroidery scissors. We are to own nothing sharp anymore. Even our tables are set without knives. Forks are permitted only during the repast; they are spirited away by the servants before the compotes are served at the end of the meal.

Louis takes a two-hour nap precisely at four. We allow him his undisturbed slumber, but when he wakes, he insists that the dauphin return for his additional lessons. Father and son pore over books and maps and mathematical problems until supper. At nine P.M. Louis Charles is tucked into his bed with a glass of warm milk and many kisses, while his papa retires with a book.

One evening, with a look of suspicion in his small dark eyes, Monsieur Goret asks me what I am doing. "You are not supposed to have paper, Citoyenne Capet," he warns.

"I-I had this from before—when we were still in the Tour de César," I reply, folding the little packets closed. "I would never use this for any other purpose, monsieur—I give you my word. See?" I show him what the little papers contain. "This dark curl, this is my daughter's. And this one," I add, showing Goret the other packet, "this light brown lock is the dau—my son's." I bury my nose in each of the papers, inhaling the comforting scents. "I take them out of my jewelry case and look at them every day. I have so little nowadays in the way of comforts," I implore. "Please do not take them from me."

Reluctantly, he relents. "*Merci,* monsieur," I murmur gratefully. I mean it.

But the autumn days will only grow darker and more bleak. Even through the shuttered windows of the Grosse Tour we can hear the boys in the *rues* below crying the *nouvelles*. "Robespierre declares, 'The king must die so the Nation can live!'" they shout on the third of December.

In the past month the French forces have routed the allies; they have even entered Brussels, and the National Convention has announced its support for any nation wishing to regain its liberty. It is a war cry against monarchs across the continent. But they have already taken away my husband's throne. Why must they demand his life as well?

We hold our breath. Perhaps the lawyer from Arras is only posturing. But the insults and deprivations escalate. On December 7, Louis appears at breakfast with stubble on his cheeks and chin. He resembles a peasant. "They have taken away my razor—and even my shaving soap," he says incredulously. "They believe that it contains poison."

"In that case you would only be poisoning yourself," I reply. "Does the Commune think you will fling lather at our guards? Or wrestle them to the ground and play at being a barber?"

Later in the day, Monsieur Goret demands Louis's tinderbox. Surely he doesn't suspect the king will strike a flint and burn down the Temple? From now on, someone else will have to be summoned to relight his candles if they gutter and burn out. Goret extends his hand. "Your toothpick, too, Citoyen Capet." His cheeks are as red as his guardsman's *gilet*. From Goret's doleful expression, I sense that he would not make such a petty demand, were he not under strict orders from his superiors.

The Commune is intentionally stripping every vestige of dignity from the benevolent soul who was once the most powerful man in the land. Louis will no longer be able to groom his beard except in the unlikely event that some munificent lackey in the employ of the Commune assumes this tonsorial responsibility, nor can he keep his teeth adequately clean. The quickest way to debase a man is to deprive him of his ability to attend to his personal hygiene. Soon Louis will resemble the vagabonds who sleep beneath the bridges that span the Seine.

Four days later, escorted by armed and uniformed soldiers, to the accompaniment of ominous drumrolls, Mayor Pétion arrives with a delegation from the Commune. Without preamble, Commissioner Manuel states, "By order of the National Convention Louis Charles Capet, the *ci-devant* dauphin of France, is to be moved from the apartments of Citizen Capet to those of his mother." Louis, Madame Élisabeth, and I exchange anxious glances.

"What is this about?" I demand, my voice strained. I have a sudden, sick sensation in my belly, as if it is crawling with worms.

"Louis Capet is accused of treasonous crimes against the nation," Commissioner Daujon answers tersely.

"*Non*—it cannot be possible!" I cry, rushing to my husband's side and protectively slipping my arm through his. Madame Élisabeth turns white.

"The former king of France enjoyed clandestine correspondence with, among others, enemies of the Revolution." I feel like I am holding my breath, waiting for Daujon to elaborate. "He kept the papers locked in an *armoire de fer,* an iron chest, hidden within the Tuileries. The information was recently brought to the attention of Citizen Roland, Minister of the Interior."

"The Tuileries Palace was ransacked—everything we owned destroyed months ago," I insist, adding, "My husband is an honorable man." *But we have indeed corresponded with the enemies of the new French Republic.* Mon Dieu, *what have they found? What do they know?*

"There were no secret documents. This purported *armoire de fer.* is a fiction," Louis says evenly. He is perspiring heavily.

"We have evidence to the contrary, monsieur," Manuel replies. "A reliable informer, a friend of the Revolution, told Citoyen Roland exactly where to find it—concealed behind a false door within a section of wooden paneling."

We cannot imagine who the informer might be. Louis endeavors to maintain his composure as Manuel presses his case. "You made the lock for the iron chest yourself, Citoyen Capet. Now, how would I know this," he adds silkily, "unless a little bird told me?"

Since he was a youth, and for several years under the tutelage of a master locksmith, Louis has made many locks for many chests. "I wish to know the name of this purported informant," Louis says. "Every man in the republic, no matter how low or how high, deserves to know the name of his accuser."

Manuel's lips curve into a triumphant smile. "I think you already know his name, citoyen." After a tense, dramatic pause the commissioner says, "His name is François Gamain."

Louis and I exchange a horrified glance. Betrayed by the master who was his own mentor, a man whom he has known all his life, whom he trusted implicitly!

The subterfuge is over. We are lost.

Noticing our expressions, Commissioner Manuel twists the knife even deeper. "The iron chest has been located, exactly where

Gamain said it was. Inside it we found several incriminating documents, most intriguingly, His Former Majesty's correspondence with several royalist ministers, financiers, and advisors—including Général Lafayette and the late Citoyen Riqueti, the comte de Mirabeau, whose duplicity and betrayal of the principles of the Revolution were exposed quite clearly. In consequence, the remains of the traitor Mirabeau will be removed from the Pantheon. He is no hero to our cause."

It is a cruel game these men play, unspooling information bit by bit in an effort to trip us up, to compel Louis to reveal something to them. "We have come to believe, however, that Minister Roland, due to incompetence, or perhaps to secret royalist sympathies, has attempted to obstruct the motion of the wheels of justice," says Commissioner Daujon. At Louis's quizzical look, he elaborates. "The minister may have destroyed some of the contents of the *armoire de fer,* including correspondence with his fellow Girondist, Citoyen Danton. Moreover, after the chest was confiscated from the Tuileries, Citoyen Roland left it unsealed, either accidentally—or deliberately. Despite his efforts to suppress the documents, five days ago, by order of the National Convention, they were delivered to the National Printing Office to be published. These papers will reveal the widespread complicity of many prominent sympathizers of the Revolution with the former monarch himself. Citizen Capet has corrupted the morals of these officials."

Louis doesn't move; he seems to be holding his breath. Commissioner Manuel shifts his weight impatiently from foot to foot. "Therefore, in the name of the Commune, we have orders to remove Citoyen Capet from the Temple, pending a trial on charges of high treason."

Her face drained of color, Madame Élisabeth sinks into a chair. *"Non—c'est pas possible!"* I cry, flinging my arms about Louis's neck as if my weight, like a human millstone, would anchor him to the floor and prevent his removal.

Madame Royale begins to weep. "You cannot take my papa!" she shrieks angrily.

"Will you come back, Papa?" the dauphin asks naively.

Lifting our son into his arms as if he weighs no more than a sack of apples, Louis kisses his brow, and then, playfully, his nose and chin. "Of course I will come back, *mon petit*," he promises, casting me a heartbreaking look. "But in the meantime, you must be very brave for your maman, your sister, and your *tante* Élisabeth. You are the man of the house, now."

I sink to my knees to plead with Pétion, "Please, *monsieur le maire*—I beg you—by all that you hold sacred. Do not take my husband. He is an honorable man who has sought only to preserve the lives of his family and to lessen the burdens of our captivity."

It is Louis who raises me to my feet. "*Sois courageuse,* madame," he murmurs, taking me into his arms. "It is you who must be brave for the children."

"We will visit you every day," I insist tearfully. "Send word to us where we must go."

He shakes his head. "It will be too painful for us both, Toinette. And too difficult for them," he adds, nodding his chin at Madame Royale, who is comforting her brother.

"You will miss her fourteenth birthday, then. She will be brokenhearted not to share it with her papa." Mousseline has always been the light of her father's eyes. When I finally bore a daughter after so many years of celibacy, even though her birth meant that France remained without an heir, Louis assured me from the start that he would never love Marie Thérèse the less for her sex.

"It is better this way; trust me," Louis avers. "Absence, time, and distance render it more easy to forget."

"You are speaking as though we have already begun to mourn," I whisper. "I won't hear of it. It is not true. Cooler, more pragmatic heads will prevail. The Girondins will gain the upper hand over the radical Jacobins. You *will* return to us."

Louis makes no answer. He kisses me gently, then embraces his sister. Praising her impeccable dignity in the face of every adversity, he encourages her to maintain it even now. "Only Heaven knows when we will see each other again," he says, donning his hat. He will not leave the Temple bareheaded, like a penitent.

That night, with the dauphin in my arms, I cry myself to sleep.

TWENTY-FIVE

The Widow Capet

⁓ JANUARY 1793 ⁓

During the remaining weeks of December our kitchen attendant Monsieur Turgy and Louis's valet Hanet Cléry deliver whatever news they are able to glean in the streets of the capital. And, to my surprise, I discover a sympathetic friend in François Adrien Toulan, one of the Commune's commissioners. Although Citoyen Toulan, a former music seller, is a fervent republican, he has bribed a newsagent to cry the *nouvelles* within earshot of the Grosse Tour, so that I might learn about the latest troop movements, victories, and defeats between the French army and the allies, as well as any reports from the National Convention regarding Louis's trial.

Mais hélas, I have only a tenuous hope for an encouraging word about the king. On December 22, 1792, the venomous Jacques Hébert is appointed Deputy Public Prosecutor. Hébert has never desired anything less than our deaths.

From what we can surmise from the news criers of Louis's trial, the delegates to the National Convention cannot agree on his fate. Some propose exile; others imprisonment. Still others desire his execution. The balloting goes on for several days.

On the morning of Sunday, January 20, one of the republic's priests visits the large tower to conduct Mass although Madame Élisabeth remains in her room with her missal, refusing to accept the Host from a clergyman who swore an oath to the Constitution. Early that afternoon, when we seek a breath of fresh air upon the parapet below the tower's cap, the *nouvelles* announce the worst. The news crier, not much older than the dauphin, shouts for all and sundry to hear, "The National Convention has reached a verdict in the trial of Louis Capet! A single vote—cast by Philippe Égalité—has tipped the balance between life and death! The Convention decrees that Louis Capet shall suffer the death penalty. The execution will take place within twenty-four hours of notification to the prisoner!"

My head begins to swim and my eyes become blinded by sudden tears. Philippe Égalité—the *ci-devant* duc d'Orléans—Louis's own cousin—a prince of the blood, has murdered my husband just as surely as if he were Monsieur Sanson, the public executioner. Placing my hand upon a crenellation, I steady myself and vomit over the serrated parapet. My sobs are uncontrollable. A *poissarde* might just as well have gutted me with her knife and left me to bleed to death. Surely my weeping can be heard in the streets below the Temple.

I do not permit Madame Royale and the dauphin to leave my sight. We cling to each other in our despair. Our tears are interrupted by a visit from an officer of the National Convention. The blue trousers of his uniform and the red facings on his coat are stained with food. He hands me a paper folded in three. It reads, BY AN EXCEPTIONAL INDULGENCE ISSUED ON BEHALF OF THE CONVENTION THE *FAMILLE* CAPET IS PERMITTED TO VISIT THE

CONDEMNED IN HIS FORMER ROOMS WITHIN THE GROSSE TOUR
FOR THE PURPOSES OF SAYING FAREWELL.

At a few minutes before seven, we descend the stairs from my apartments so that the moment the clock strikes the hour, we will enter Louis's rooms. I want him to remember me in one of his favorite colors, a gown of gunmetal-gray silk with a delicate white fichu about my shoulders, secured by a sapphire brooch at my breast. The shawl's fullness masks the fact that I have lost so much weight, my once ample bosom has shrunk to nothing.

At the sight of my husband I stifle a sob with my fist, for he is much changed. Although he remains stout as ever, his skin has a greenish cast to it made more bilious by his sage-colored coat, and his hair has grown thin. In the six weeks that have passed since he was led away from the Temple, his teeth have become yellow and appear more prominent within his large head. His hands tremble as though he has a touch of the palsy. The stresses of his trial and, perhaps even more devastating, the absence from his adoring family, have turned him into an old man at the age of thirty-eight.

At the sight of us, tears begin to bathe his face, far too many to be successfully blotted away with a handkerchief. "I do not weep for myself," Louis says softly, meeting our own anguished faces, "but for you, for the grief you must endure on my behalf." We rush toward him eager to throw our arms about him, never wishing to release him from our collective embrace.

"You are so thin," my husband says. "I think I could wrap my arms about you twice."

"I cannot eat," I reply. "I have had no appetite since they took you away."

As the clock chimes half past eight, we are ushered into the dining room and I gently shut the glass doors that divide this chamber from the others. Our minders are able to witness every gesture we make, but they cannot hear our voices. Tonight, Louis seats himself at the center of the table. Madame Élisabeth and I flank him, on the right and to the left. The dauphin is perched upon Louis's lap and Madame Royale sits across from her papa. Only fourteen, *ma pauvre* Mousseline, the light of his eyes, will lose him at the same age I was when I wed him.

Every sentence the king utters triggers renewed embraces and fresh tears. "I could never have wished for a kinder and more devoted family," he says, kissing his sister's hands. "You are Papa's most beautiful jewel, and always will be," he assures our daughter. "Never permit your sadness to dull your beauty or cloud your self-worth." To the dauphin he says, "*Mon fils,* you must give me your solemn promise never to think of avenging my death. I have never condoned violence against another man and I will not begin to do so in my final hours. If you are ever so unfortunate to become king, you must dedicate your life instead to the happiness of your people, just as I have always endeavored to do." Louis Charles regards his papa solemnly then starts to bawl again. "Did you hear what I said?" Louis asks the boy. "Lift your hand and swear that you will fulfill your father's final request."

"*Je le jure,* Papa," the dauphin manages between sobs. "I swear."

"I asked the National Convention for three days' grace, so that I might have more time to prepare for the end—to say adieu," Louis confides, clasping my hand to his cheek. "But they refused my request."

At half past ten, he rises from the table and opens the doors. The royal family follows him, unable to check our weeping. "I will see you tomorrow morning at eight o'clock," Louis tells me.

My face drains of color. "Eight? Why so late? Why not seven?"

"Seven then it will be," he says, averting his gaze, so I know he is lying, in a hopeless effort to make the awful circumstances a tiny bit more bearable for me.

"I wish to accompany you, Papa."

Louis looks aghast. "To the scaffold, my son?" He shakes his head, but the dauphin explains, with all the desperate passion of naïvete and youth, "I will stand on the platform and speak to the people. I will order them to forgive you."

Louis lifts the boy into his arms, hoisting him so that they can see eye to eye. "My precious, precious son, *mon brave*—" He chokes up, unable to complete his thought.

Setting our son back down, Louis takes my hands in his and draws me into an embrace. "I have never been a man of words," he confesses. "And I have always become even more tongue-tied in your presence, Toinette. I have not shown you proofs of my honor and esteem, perhaps, as much as I should have. I can count on one hand the occasions I have told you I love you. Our union was not of our making, and it took me far too long to acknowledge and appreciate your beauty and your grace. I am sorry if I have never been the husband you might have dreamed of, if I have disappointed you all these years. I brought you from your homeland to"—he gestures helplessly—"to this." He kisses my brow, my cheeks, my lips. "Please, *mon amour,* forgive me for all the ills you have been made to suffer for my sake and for any grief I have caused you during the course of our marriage."

The pain of parting is unspeakable. "*Mon très cher mari,* you have nothing to reproach yourself for. It is *I* who has ever been the cause of *your* misery. I am the one whom the people have always despised and whom you have always defended. And now you are paying the ultimate price for my sins. I should be apologizing to you!"

Louis shakes his head. "I will never believe that," he murmurs through his tears.

Madame Royale craves one more farewell embrace from her father. But after launching herself into his arms she sinks to the floor in a swoon. Louis stoops, scooping her up and placing her gently onto the divan. He presses another kiss upon her brow.

Enfolding me in his arms once more, the king murmurs, "Don't think of this as au revoir, my sweet. Try to imagine that we are only bidding one another *bonsoir*." Our mouths meet for the last time, tasting of tears and bitter defeat.

I do not sleep this night. Nor do I undress. The fire has gone out and I lie shivering with cold upon my bed, drenched with an endless supply of tears. In the darkness I am visited by a parade of memories: the day I first met Louis in the forest of Compiègne, complete strangers to one another, yet by virtue of a proxy ceremony in Austria, already husband and wife. He was so shy and sullen I thought he despised me. His wincing when he saw me in my wedding dress; his palms always so moist. All those years when he could not bring himself to consummate our marriage—innumerable nights of *rien*—and then, when I was finally brought to childbed, it was he who saved my life when I was suffocating by ripping off the paper that sealed the windows shut and raising all the sashes; his perennial defense of my conduct, no matter the accusations against me; and his enduring patience and kindness.

At five I hear a rustling coming from the direction of Louis's rooms and bolt upright, listening to every sound. It is Cléry lighting the fire in the king's bedroom. An hour later, there is a knock on my door and, startled, I rush to open it, expecting to see my husband one last time. But is only an officer of the Garde Nationale.

"I have come to borrow the princesse's missal," he announces. "For Citoyen Capet's celebration of Mass."

Entering the chamber, Madame Élisabeth kisses her prayer book and crosses herself before handing it to the soldier. It will give her comfort to know that her brother will have something from his family when he receives his final Communion. The officiant, at Louis's side by his invitation, is Madame Élisabeth's confessor, l'abbé Edgeworth de Firmont.

The rumble of rolling drumbeats fills the air. At nine o'clock, I hear Santerre giving commands in Louis's rooms amid the tromping of boots. Although our shuttered windows prevent us from seeing anything, outside, the hubbub of hundreds of voices fills the Temple courtyard and beyond. Troops, I assume, assigned to line the route from the Temple to the Place de la Révolution and to escort the king to the scaffold

Minutes later, the footsteps descend the stairs, receding to the *rat-a-tat-tat* of drums and the blare of trumpets. I approach my window, imagining that as Louis crosses the courtyard and prepares to climb into the coach that will convey him to his final destination on this earth, he will pause mid-step and turn back, hoping that I stand at my window. I touch my fingers to my lips and press them to the shutter.

The clatter of carriage wheels informs me that the king is leaving the courtyard. I wonder what sort of day it is. Will Louis's last glimpse of the world be the glaring rays of sunshine? Will a fine mist settle upon his shoulders as he mounts the scaffold? Will fog obscure the view of his execution, depriving the crowd of the ending they have long lusted for?

Louison Chabry's back aches and her feet are tired. Armand has insisted that they arrive at the Place de la Révolution before dawn to secure an excellent vantage. Her lover was prescient, as it turns out, for at daybreak the perimeter is already secured by a regiment of soldiers from the Garde Nationale, as resplendent as the *tricolore* itself in their blue coats with red facings, white breeches and gaiters. Their white vests glint with brass buttons that look as though they might have been given a particularly vigorous polishing in honor of the tyrant's demise.

A damp January mist chills Louison to the bone. Her woolen cloak offers minimal protection and she gazes enviously at the soldiers' black bicorns, embellished with the revolutionary cockade. Their heads are doubtless warm and dry. A few hours more in this weather and she is certain her brown curls will drip with icicles.

"Follow me." Armand clasps Louison by the hand, threading his way through the excited mob, his destination the raised wooden platform upon which Madame Guillotine awaits her fatal appointment with the *"gros cochon,"* the fat pig of a former sovereign. But a military unit, bayonets pointing skyward, prevents onlookers from getting too near. *Is this to deter any clandestine royalist from rushing the scaffold?* Louison wonders. She is not entirely sure how close she wishes to be after all. If she and Armand were to stand right up front they would have to crane their necks to catch a glimpse of the blade when it falls, as the platform looms several feet off the ground. She would rather not be sprayed with blood, no matter whose it is.

"Regardez! Les tricoteuses!" Armand exclaims excitedly, drawing Louison's attention to the women who sit just below the platform, their wooden knitting needles clicking away ceaselessly during the entire spectacle. The *tricoteuses* attend every public execution, pausing only to shout *"À bas les aristos!"*—Down with the aristocrats!—after each severed head is displayed to onlookers thirsty for blood and hungry for revenge. The sculptress wonders if it's true what the people say—that the *tricoteuses* knit locks of victims' hair into the scarves that depict each aristocrat's coat of arms. What do they do with their grisly trophies?

As the morning progresses, Louison stamps her feet to keep

warm. To occupy her mind, she searches the throng for familiar faces and begins to tick off on her fingers the ones she recognizes from seeing their likenesses drawn in *Père Duchesne* and Jean-Paul Marat's radical newspaper, *L'Ami du Peuple*. Conversing with the executioner are Marat himself and Citoyen Robespierre. Near the foot of the stairs approaching the scaffold are Danton and Desmoulins, accepting the acclamation of the crowd. Standing aloof, although he is surrounded by people pressing for his attention, is the king's cousin, Philippe Égalité. *How he must hate his own kinsman to sentence him to death,* Louison muses. *Or is it because he is a Revolutionary partisan now and places the needs of the Nation above ties of blood?* Watching the former duc standing lost in thought holding a fresh white handkerchief to his very red nose, she wishes she could ask him.

Soon the drummers begin to tap out a tattoo. "The tyrant must be near," Armand exclaims, pulling Louison to him affectionately. He has never been so excited about anything, she thinks. Not even when the renowned David accepted him as an apprentice. As the unmarked black coach bearing the deposed monarch approaches, the jubilant mood in the Place de la Révolution becomes infectious, a rising soufflé of anticipation and glee.

Armand grumbles. "What is the matter?" Louison shouts, in an effort to be heard above the din. He draws her close so he can whisper in her ear, complaining about the *cochon* being driven in a closed carriage. "He does not merit such dignity. And they agree with me," he adds, gesturing as broadly as he can in the mad crush, referring to the jeers that greet the arrival of the Nation's nemesis. Someone lobs a cabbage head at the *ci-devant* sovereign as he descends the coach's folding steps. Absurdly, given the circumstances, a pair of soldiers whirl to face the crowd, lowering their bayonets menacingly.

There was a time, thinks Louison, when we did not despise

him so. Wasn't there? When Louis XVI was not a subject of scorn and ridicule? We were mere children then.

The National Guardsmen form two lines, flanking the former king. Are they preventing the mob from doing the executioner's job, or warning Citoyen Capet not to entertain any final thoughts of escape? He would never run, however. Louison knows this. When she joined the march on the Tuileries that rainy autumn day more than three years ago, the king bravely faced thousands of angry citizens, women—and men as well—who would willingly have assassinated him. But he listened attentively to her enumeration of the people's grievances. He was kind when she fainted. Armand would not have missed this day for all the world. He has talked of little else for months—how important it is to be standing in the Place de la Révolution when the oppressor is shaved by the national razor and history is made. "The tree of liberty must be watered by the blood of tyrants," he is fond of saying. But Louison has not risen before dawn to witness a macabre act of horticulture. And she isn't comfortable with the way her lover continually refers to the man who was King of France as a tyrant. Although she can never admit it to Armand, she has come to the Place this morning out of respect for the disgraced sovereign. Because for one tiny fragment of time, a king was kind to her. Louison has come to say good-bye.

Wearing a simple brown suit, his hair lightly powdered, the king mounts the wooden staircase that leads to the scaffold. The executioner permits him to say a few words, but the roar of the crowd and the thundering drums all but drown out his final remarks. Louison and Armand are close enough to hear him protest his innocence, which elicits howls of derision from the crowd. "Death to all tyrants!" Armand shouts.

Chevalier Charles Henri Sanson de Longval, the *bourreau,* asks Citizen Capet to remove his coat, vest, and neck stock. In his white chemise with its billowing sleeves, the accused looks even stouter. Then the executioner tugs the shirt away from the former king's neck so the guillotine blade will strike true and his death will be more humane. His strong hands, those of a workman, only much whiter, are bound behind his back; when he refuses a blindfold, Louison gasps. In his final moments Louis XVI desires to look upon his subjects.

The drummers are given a signal. The fusiliers shoulder their muskets. The king is guided to the horizontal plank and lowered onto his belly, earning hoots of laughter at the sight of his broad stomach balanced upon the narrow board. Armand's gaze remains riveted, but Louison wonders if, as a measure of respect for the sovereign, she should look away.

And then, in a blinding flash, the angular blade descends. A moment later, Sanson lifts the late king's head out of the basket beneath the plank and holds it aloft for the crowd to ogle. Louison covers her mouth, suppressing her urge to vomit. Louis Capet's eyes are wide open, as if he can still see her—see all of them—rejoicing at his death. His mouth is open, too, as if he has something else to say. The sculptress feels something warm on her face; when she reaches up to touch it, her fingers become smeared with blood. The blood of a tyrant. Of a king. Of a man.

After his head and body have been removed from the scaffold and the onlookers reluctantly disperse, Louison notices that some are rushing toward the platform instead. Eerily drawn to the grisly scene, she follows them. The king's blood puddles on the floor-boards, leeching into the wood. When she sees someone dip his handkerchief into the blood, Louison gasps. Some of these trophy hunters are zealots who seem to crave a souvenir of the greatest event of their lives. Others, judging from the reverential manner in which they stain their handkerchief, as if they are collecting the relic of a martyr, must be clandestine royalists.

Louison is neither. But she knows she has to dip her own square of linen in the pooling blood. Something to show to the children she will bear one day, to prove that she was there. To be able to tell them, "Your maman knew a king."

At about ten, I suggest to the children that they might like some breakfast, but they are too disconsolate to eat.

The drummers in the courtyard begin to beat a frenetic tattoo. I glance at my father's gold watch. It is 10:22. The cry of *"Vive la Nation!"* is nearly drowned out by the distant reports of muskets being fired in a salute. From the direction of the Place de la Révolution comes a thundering rumble of drums, the staccato snap of sticks against snares, rising to a terrifying crescendo.

The eerie silence that follows is pierced by my daughter's shriek.

"Monsters—now are you content?" Madame Élisabeth exclaims, raising her eyes heavenward.

I am rooted to the floor, cold and immobile, as if I'd been carved of marble. My mouth twists in a silent, agonizing scream and I double over in torment. When I finally lift my head, I meet my son's teary gaze, so fearful and inquiring, and I drop to my knees. "The king is dead, long live the king," I murmur, kissing his hand. *"Vive le roi Louis dix-sept."*

TWENTY-SIX

"Everything Leads Me to You"

≈ WINTER-SPRING 1793 ≈

On the afternoon of Louis's death, Monsieur Cléry scratches at my door. It is a measure of respect that he adheres to a custom that the Revolution, in its ruthless abolition of the monarchy, has relegated to the dustbin of time.

"From His Majesty," Cléry tells me. "The Commune confiscated these effects when he was detained." He empties the contents of a soft black velvet bag onto my dressing table.

I gasp at the sight of the wedding ring Louis had sent me to wear for our proxy marriage in Vienna. Here, too, are locks of each of the children's hair, as well as his own, and the royal seal with the arms of France embossed upon it. I caress the individual curls, memorizing their texture as I rub them between my fingers, wondering when Louis obtained them. No one would have imagined him such a sentimental man. "How were you able to secure these items?"

The valet touches his finger to his lips. "You have an advocate in Citizen Toulan. The Commune had locked them up. Monsieur Toulan stole them. But he made it look like an ordinary burglary, so no one will imagine he had anything to do with the theft."

I run my hands over these treasures, amazed at how Cléry came by them, moved by his dedication to our family and by the enormous risks Commissioner Toulan has taken on our behalf.

"The king wished you to have this, too," Cléry says, reaching into a pocket. He takes out Louis's wedding ring, engraved with the letters M.A.A.A. for Marie Antoinette Archduchess of Austria, and presses it into my palm. "His Majesty said, 'Tell my wife that I part with this ring only because I am parting with my life. I commend my children to her and I beg her to forgive me. Poor princesse; I promised her a crown,' he lamented. 'Please tell her that I leave her with sorrow.'" Choking with emotion, the valet buries his face in his hands.

Non! It is I *who should beg this fine and noble man's forgiveness for the suffering* I *surely caused* him! I know Louis believed he had failed me—as a king, as a husband, and as a man. I slip his wedding ring onto my finger and slide it toward my own band, watching the two gold circles kiss. "What did he say at the end?" I beseech Cléry. I want to drink in every word. I want to know each one Louis said after we bid adieu, to hear the ones he uttered before entering eternity. "On the scaffold? Did he address the people?"

Hanet Cléry turns back to me. His voice barely rises above a whisper. "His Majesty said, 'I die innocent of the crimes of which I am accused. Yet I forgive the authors of my death and pray God that the blood you are about to shed may never fall back upon the people of France.'"

Will the people of France be satisfied, now that they have murdered their king? Will their thirst for blood be quenched with Louis's death? All he ever wanted was for his people to be happy. I know that if the answer to these morbid questions is "yes," my husband would have believed that he had not died in vain.

I, however, am a skeptic.

Madame Éloffe comes to measure us for mourning clothes. My accessories are to be all black as well: fichus, underskirts, stockings, shoes, fans, and gloves. She clucks in disapproval as she wraps her tape about my *poitrine*. "You have lost ten inches," the dressmaker scolds. I confide a less apparent secret. The black petticoats will mask some of the accidents I have been having. Générale Krottendorf, as we Hapsburg ladies called our monthly courses, has never in my life been a punctual visitor. But for the past year at least, I have bled between my times and with little rhyme or reason.

In a final act of patronage—perhaps the Commune would see it as defiance for returning to my old ways—I spend a percentage of my wardrobe allowance for mourning garb with Mademoiselle Bertin, sending my commission to her in London, although I can afford a mere fraction of what the same coin will purchase from Madame Éloffe. Rose embellishes a petticoat and a few bonnets and fichus as well as a black gown with a sizable train and a high headdress of black silk bordered in white organza. She also provides me with two dozen black ribbons with which to dress my hair.

The wintry days are dark, and precious little light seeps in above the shutters. Were it not for my father's timepiece I would not know the time of day. Little do I care. Grief has cast its icy pall. The only sense of purpose I can summon in the early days after Louis's death is to continue the education of our son. To his family he is Louis XVII and it brings me a measure of hope that he must be prepared to assume the throne someday. Madame Élisabeth and I devote a few hours a day to the boy's studies of geography, mathematics, and the history of France. It is what his father would have wanted.

When the young king is not at his lessons, my *belle-soeur* and I sit before the fire knitting or reading our missals. Cards and backgammon in the evenings are a relic of happier days.

"You must take some air," insists Monsieur Goret at the end of January, noting that the royal family has remained indoors ever since the king's execution. "At least for the sake of your children." Despite his assignment to watch our every move, he remains secretly sympathetic to our circumstances.

"I cannot go into the courtyard or the garden," I reply. When Goret asks if the reason is because I do not have a warm cloak, I shake my head. "I have no desire to pass the door through which my husband left, only to die," I reply.

"Then if you will not descend the stairs, why not step out upon the parapet near the top of the keep? No one will see you from the courtyard. You can be alone there with your grief."

I accept Goret's suggestion, if only because it will provide me with the opportunity to discuss my future and that of my family with those who have pledged to aid, or even to rescue us. During the first week in February, Madame Royale and I are joined in our aerie by Claude Antoine Moëlle, one of the members of the Paris Commune assigned to oversee the towers of the Temple.

A bracing wind whips about the pointed turret like the veil of a medieval hennin. Moëlle clutches his ink-blue cloak about him, hunching his shoulders as if to retreat inside the woolen carapace. "What news from the National Convention?" I inquire anxiously. "What do they intend to do with me?"

"There is talk of banishment—exile," the commissioner confides.

"Do you mean that Francis the Second will reclaim me in the name of Austria?" I have never met the current emperor, the eldest son of my late brother Leopold. He is only in his twenties. But there is a grand tradition of queen consorts being returned to their families when, for any number of reasons, they prove unsatisfactory.

"You are shivering, madame." Commissioner Moëlle offers me his cloak.

Would it be such a terrible thing if I were carried off by a sudden chill? "You are too kind, monsieur. But I think you require it more than I do."

"*C'est possible.*" Moëlle chuckles and tugs the cloak more tightly about his throat. "The Convention believes that any new excess would be a gratuitous horror." He is speaking euphemistically of my own execution. I exhale with relief, a puff of warm breath that floats in the chilly air. "Moreover, it is contrary to policy. Justice has already been served."

Marie Thérèse grips my arm. "There is hope, Maman." It is the most she has said since her father met his death.

"Then let us pray that the National Convention has no further interest in a tired old woman from Austria." I smile at the commissioner. At least my teeth are still healthy.

Moëlle's cheeks turn rosy. "I cannot answer for the opinion of the Convention, but to me, you are still lovely, *citoyenne*. And hardly old," he hastens to add, extending the compliment. "For if *you* are old, so then am I!"

I may have a modicum of good fortune when it comes to charming my captors, but the rest of February brings discouraging news. The conflict between the new republic and the allies escalates and France declares war on England, Holland, and Spain. I pray that the recent allied victory will bode well for us, but the opposite appears to be true. The emperor of Austria takes the same neutral stance with regard to the politics of France as my favorite brother Joseph had done. My nephew will not lift so much as a finger to rescue me, let alone my children and my *belle-soeur*. Moreover, the various factions of the National Convention cannot agree on a course of action. The Jacobins continue to tar the Girondins as too moderate. The flames of Revolution, they say, must continually be fanned with propaganda so that the people will never lose their thirst for blood. "Little fish grow big," Jacques Hébert rages in *Père Duchesne*. "And liberty hangs by a thread. The people must not rest until the Widow Capet and her foul progeny have been destroyed."

Such poisonous diatribes have the intended effect but they inspire counterrevolutionary sympathies as well. In early March, I receive several visits from Commissioners Toulan and Lepître, who have formulated a plot to spirit the royal family out of the Temple. The scheme also involves the participation of the Chevalier de Jarjayes, a trusted emissary of the crown who has been working closely with Axel to devise plans for our escape.

Late one evening, Madame Élisabeth and I rendezvous with the commissioners in our salon. "I will provide the men's garments— as well as the *bonnets rouge*," Lepître says, approaching the fire. It is nearly banked, with little left but glowing embers, and he rubs his hands together to warm them. "You women will catch your death in here," he remarks. "Are the children warm enough?"

"Won't we be detected?" the princesse inquires anxiously.

Citoyen Toulan shakes his head. "Not with cotton batting. We will pad the coats to disguise the shape of your bodies."

"But what about the children? How is Madame Royale to be costumed?" Afraid they have made no contingencies for my children, I will never leave them.

"Your daughter will be provided with a suitable disguise," Monsieur Lepître assures me. "The lamplighter makes his rounds at five thirty every evening. She will leave the Temple with him, as if she is one of his children. The chevalier will see that she is delivered safely. He intends to disguise himself as one of the people. Toulan will tell the lamplighter that he has a friend who is curious to see the inside of the palace and wishes to follow him on his nightly tour. He is a gullible fellow and when I suggest that my friend wishes to look like another lamplighter, the man will be happy to lend him another set of clothes and let him carry his equipment."

"And His Majesty?"

The men exchange a brief, confused glance, until they realize I am speaking of Louis Charles. Toulan blows on his clenched hands. The chamber is frightfully cold. "We have two possibilities under discussion. Dressed little better than an urchin, he can join his sister as the lamplighter's son—"

"Or we can schedule the flight for the same night that the laundry is taken out of the Temple," Citoyen Lepître interrupts excitedly. "The ki—Louis Charles Capet—will be hidden inside the hamper beneath the soiled linens."

"How then will we get past the Tisons?" The couple charged with overseeing our welfare lacks the slightest vestige of sympathy or kindness.

"Their Spanish tobacco," Toulan says, referring to their penchant for snuff. "If we secretly drug it, Citoyen Tison and his wife will be unconscious for several hours. By the time they awaken, your family will be long gone, already en route to your rendezvous with the Chevalier de Jarjayes. He will safely conduct you to the Normandy coast and from there you will board a ship bound for England."

Commissioner Lepître has undertaken to secure false passports for us through Général Dumouriez. Although the general was responsible for defeating the Austrian army at Jemappes last November, after he publicly advocated against Louis's execution, he was accused by the National Convention of not being a true patriot—in my view, the finest compliment a man could receive in these dark times.

For the next several days my heart is lighter. With renewed

hope I continue my son's lessons. Although I was always an appalling student, as a teacher I strive to excel. I wish to make Louis
proud.

As we wait for news, at the end of March I entrust the Chevalier de Jarjayes with a painful task: to deliver Louis's wedding ring
and the royal seal into Monsieur's safekeeping. My brother-in-law
remains out of harm's way in Brussels. As my husband's senior surviving brother, the comte de Provence should possess these treasures, for they belong to the Bourbons. In the same letter I dispatch
the chevalier on an additional, and more cryptic, mission, writing,
"Toulan will give you the things that are to go to the princes. But
the wax impress on the sheet of paper that I include here, taken
from a little gold signet ring, is something else again. When you are
in a safe place, I would very much appreciate it if you brought it to
my great friend who came to see me last winter from Brussels, and
you are to tell him when you give it to him *that its motto has never
been more true.*"

The image is a device I had conceived in collaboration with
Count von Fersen and it is to Axel that I am sending it, as a way of
informing him that he remains in my thoughts. Now more than
ever I am convinced that only he can devise a successful plan to
liberate my family. The motto depicts what at first we had believed
to be a pigeon in flight with the·motto *Tutto a te mi guida*—All
things lead me to you. It was Axel's emblem, although we later
discovered that because the wax seal had partially melted, blurring
the image, we'd mistaken the flying fish for a bird. Each night as I
lie abed endeavoring to fall asleep, I see Axel's face before me.
When, I wonder, will we see each other again?

"What is the Committee of Public Safety?" I ask Commissioner
Toulan, after I hear the *nouvelles* from my window on the sixth of
April.

"It is Danton's latest office," he replies, "charged with organizing food supplies, raising new armies, if necessary, and"—he rakes his hand through his lank, unpowdered hair, the tonsorial style affected by the *sans-culottes*—"rooting out France's enemies from within and without her borders."

"What does this mean for the royal family?" I whisper.

"It means," the commissioner says sadly, "that it is time to formulate another plan for your rescue."

Within the week the news crier in the rue du Temple announces a shocking turn of events. Philippe Égalité, the *ci-devant* duc d'Orléans, a prince of the blood and the man who had evidently cast the vote that decided the difference between my husband's exile and his execution, has been arrested by the Committee of Public Safety. If such a prominent and outspoken friend of the Revolution, the most influential of the aristocrats who turned republican after the abolition of noble titles, has been placed under arrest, what does it bode for me?

And then on the morning of April 20, the crier declares, "Général Dumouriez turns his coat and defects to the allies!" According to the *nouvelles,* Dumouriez's desertion was precipitated by the publication of a letter revealing the former Minister of War's threat to march his army on Paris if the National Convention did not agree to his leadership.

What does *this* mean for our plans?

Butterflies dip and spiral in my belly. It is difficult to conceal from Madame Tison my anxiety about the next visit with Commissioner Lepître, for the jailer's wife regards my every move with undisguised suspicion. I cannot unfold a napkin or lift a spoon, or speak to my own children without sensing her malevolent stare. "All traitors to the republic will be rooted out and punished!" announces the news crier. They are waiting for us to make a misstep.

But it is Citoyen Toulan who arrives with the devastating news.

"Our friend is in a panic, madame. Dumouriez's open betrayal of
the republic means that my colleague will no longer be able to secure the passports from him." He twists his coat buttons anxiously.
"Fearful that something might go wrong, he regrettably hesitated
to request your *laissez-passers*. Now, of course, it is too late. Dumouriez can do nothing for you. And your family's safety is not a prior-
ity to the Austrians, I'm afraid."

The faithful Toulan suggests that it might still be possible to
attempt a much smaller plan that will smuggle me out of the Temple, but I would have to leave alone. If we cannot quit this prison as
a family, then we must all remain, I tell him.

I write to the Chevalier de Jarjayes, *we have dreamed a beautiful
dream—nothing more. However, my son's interests must be my sole
guide from now on, and however happy I may have been to escape
from this place, I could never agree to leave him. No matter where I
might be, nothing could bring me joy if I abandoned my children.*

That night we are already abed, the candles extinguished,
when the sound of someone pounding at the door fills me with
panic and dread. I hear voices on the narrow staircase, followed by
a jangling of keys and the scrape of a bolt as the door is unlocked
from the outside. Madame Élisabeth clutches her nightgown about
her and whimpers, too frightened to reach for her silk wrapper.

At the head of a formation of armed guards, the white X of
their bandoliers glowing in the torchlight, stands Jacques Hébert.
Perhaps it is only my imagination but his expression appears even
more diabolical when his face is cast in flickering shadows. Removing a piece of parchment from his coat, he announces coolly, as if
he has not invaded a residence and interrupted women and children in their slumber, that by this decree the Convention has ordered our premises to be searched.

"Searched? For what?" I breathe.

Madame Tison pushes through the cluster of soldiers and

catches me roughly by the arm, pulling me to my feet and subjecting me to the most indecent groping of my person. Whatever would I hide under my night rail? When she completes my humiliation she compels Madame Élisabeth to submit to an equal degradation. Supervised by the grim-lipped Hébert, the soldiers pull open every drawer, and rummage through all of our personal effects. When it is Madame Royale's turn to succumb to the probing and poking of Madame Tison, she stands still and stiff as an oaken plank, silent tears trickling along her pale cheeks.

"The mattresses, too," Hébert commands; and the blue-coated fusiliers begin to thrust at them with their bayonets. "That one, too." Hébert points to the truckle bed. A soldier raises his rifle and is about to stab at the coverlets when I shriek at him, throwing my body between the deadly blade of his bayonet and my slumbering son. "There is a child in there!" I scream. "Can you not tell?" For amid the commotion, the little king has somehow managed to remain fast asleep.

Hébert remains impassive. "Then I suggest you awaken him, Citoyenne Capet, if you wish him to live."

I rush to the bed and lift Louis Charles into my arms, struggling to balance his weight while keeping a blanket wrapped tightly about his shivering form. Now that he has been disturbed, he blinks open his eyes and at the sight of so many strangers with nasty faces ransacking the room, he begins to bawl hysterically.

The soldiers search for hours. Yet all they can find is a small wax cameo of the ancient princess Medea, given to me by an officer of the Temple—an odd reminiscence, (although Citoyen Jobert could never have known it), of a tapestry that hung upon one of the walls of the temporary pavilion on the Île des Epis when I was handed over by the Austrians to the French; a slip of paper with the address of a shop written upon it—a sentimental memento, but useless now that Rose Bertin has shuttered Le Grand Mogol and fled to England—a stick of red sealing wax belonging to Madame Élisabeth; and my daughter's Sacred Heart of Jesus. In these secular times, do they consider Marie Thérèse's small comfort a sacrilege?

"What is this?" Hébert demands, lifting a black bicorn from the seat of a chair with the tip of his walking stick.

"It belonged to the—my brother," Madame Élisabeth replies quietly, grasping for the hat. But Citoyen Hébert, taking pleasure in her distress, taunts her by moving it out of reach. He confers for a few tense moments with the guards and then announces that the hat is being removed from the premises because it is a suspicious object.

Her customary mildness forgotten, the princesse grows hysterical. "*S'il vous plaît, monsieur,* it is just an ordinary hat. Unimportant to you. But I beg you to let me keep it for the love of my brother." Choking on her sobs, she sinks to the floor and clasps the commissioner's wrist.

"Take away the hat," Hébert commands, ignoring her plaintive entreaties.

The clock chimes four as the soldiers file out of our rooms. Dawn will break soon, leaving us to salvage what we can out of the wreckage left in their wake. I believe they have done as much to destroy our dignity as they have to our precious few remaining possessions. No sooner has our door been locked against further intrusion, than gasping for air in short, convulsive breaths, I stagger and collapse.

Over the next several days it becomes clear that the events of April 20 have disordered our minds and taken a toll upon our bodies. During the first week of May, Doctor Brunier is summoned to minister to Madame Royale. In the throes of her first visit from Générale Krottendorf, she is bleeding more copiously than I believe is normal. My son has a high fever and ever since the soldiers frightened him in the dead of night, he has been suffering from headaches and convulsions. The poor boy's digestion has become terrible as well. Dr. Brunier fears an attack of worms. He is concerned about our diet, but Madame Tison insists, her hackles raised, that our soups are nutritious and that the meat and fowl roasted for our dinners and suppers is always of the first and freshest quality.

We must be saved or will surely perish during this incarceration. Doctor Brunier returns only a week after his first visit because the little king complains of excruciating pain around his privates. There appears to be a slight bulge down there, as well as in his lower abdomen. After securing permission from the Tisons for a new visitor to the *détenus*—by explaining that Louis Charles Capet is more valuable to the revolutionary cause alive than otherwise—Brunier sends for Hippoy Le Pipelet, a celebrated maker of trusses.

"But he's just a child—only seven," I protest to Monsieur Le Pipelet. "What has happened to him?"

"He has developed a hernia in the groin; that is the reason for the swelling in his scrotum and all the discomfort the boy is experiencing," Doctor Brunier explains. "Monsieur le Pipelet can build him a truss, which will alleviate the swelling."

"But he has a bruise as well," I add. "In the same place. I cannot imagine what has caused this."

The *médecin* kneels so that he meets my son at his eye level. "Tell me, *mon brave*, what sort of games do you play? Do you toss a ball about with your sister when you take your exercise in the courtyard? And did you perhaps get hit down there one day when the ball came at you?" Louis Charles shakes his head dolefully. "What then?" the doctor inquires gently. The boy shyly points to his hobbyhorse. "I suppose you place that stick between your legs and ride as strenuously as your papa used to do when he hunted."

Tears fill my son's eyes. "I never got to hunt with Papa. They wouldn't let him and when he did hunt I was too little to join him. I ride to the frontier as fast as my horse will run, *monsieur le médecin*. Because we didn't go fast enough before."

Something between a sob and a gasp escapes my throat. At his age, while he plays he should still be singing the nursery rhyme my friend the Duchess of Devonshire taught him: "Ride a cockhorse to Banbury Cross to see a fine lady upon a white horse . . ." Instead, he dreams of another desperate flight to safety.

Addressing me, Doctor Brunier explains, "I am afraid that such energetic exertion is the cause of the bruising about his testicles. His inguinal hernia may have its origins with the hobbyhorse as well. The condition is highly unusual in such a young child." At the doctor's suggestion that the hobbyhorse be consigned to the rubbish heap, Louis Charles becomes hysterical. Clutching the horse's head he begs the *medécin* not to take away his trusty mount. "Tonnerre is my friend," the boy bawls.

I manage to convince the doctor and Monsieur Le Pipelet to reconsider confiscating my son's favorite toy. But Louis Charles's fantasy of escape is never far from my own mind as well.

"You have sympathizers in surprising places," Baron de Batz informs us in June, as a new plot has been set in motion. The baron's experience as a financier enabled him to attain a prominent leadership position during the brief life of the Constituent Assembly. But he has always been a clandestine royalist, receiving payments from the crown for his efforts on our behalf since the Revolution began. I am forever indebted to the baron for his efforts to subvert Louis's execution on January 21 when he tried to incite the crowd gathered in the boulevard de Bonne Nouvelle to protest the regicide. Although he was unsuccessful, he has never abandoned his plans to liberate the royal family. "Citoyen Michonis," he tells me.

"The Temple administrator?" I confess I am shocked by this

revelation. Never would I have believed that the governor of our prison is anything but a staunch revolutionary. Like many of the men who have risen to positions of responsibility in this new republic, Michonis is a true son of the proletariat. In his former métier he sold lemonade on the streets of the capital.

Baron de Batz nods. "The administrator's well-being has been significantly augmented," he says, rubbing his fingers against his thumb to indicate a bribe.

"But how do you intend to effect our escape?" I inquire.

"Military uniforms," he replies succinctly. "And one by one the sentries will be replaced by men who are loyal to me—and to you, madame."

I study his face, the chiseled features of a hero from a novel. People used to say the same of Axel. "I rely upon you to be our champion now," I tell the baron. "Yet I don't see how this plan can work. We would hardly be mistaken for soldiers from the Garde Nationale."

"We will pad the uniforms so that your—your feminine silhouettes remain undetected." This solution has been proposed before. I confide my skepticism. "Madame Royale can also be outfitted with a military cap, cloak, and musket," the baron adds.

The notion of my slender young daughter managing a heavy, loaded gun terrifies me. Moreover, there remains another issue to be solved. "What about the king? The disguise will hardly suit him." Baron de Batz agrees that he must speak with his confederates regarding the most effective way to secure the liberation of my son. Then, with the greatest reluctance and delicacy he concedes that the plot has a greater chance of succeeding, the fewer of us there are to release. "If you are considering rescuing me alone, then I am sorry, *monsieur le baron,* but I will never consent to the arrangement. Madame Élisabeth and both my children will accompany me. We leave together or not at all."

The baron confides that certain members of the National Convention have been conducting secret negotiations with the emperor of Austria. Georges Danton has quietly proposed an exchange of prisoners. But my nephew continues to evince little interest. His priorities lie elsewhere. "Moreover," the baron informs me, "even if Francis were to entertain the idea, you would be the only one to be freed."

"What about my son? An impressionable and already terrified little boy who will say anything that pops into his head when he becomes frightened. Do you expect me to leave him to the mercy of these monsters?"

Baron de Batz clears his throat and smoothes his hands over his green wool breeches. *"Je regrette, madame."* He cannot meet my eyes. "But unless you *are* willing to do so, Danton believes that you intend to oppose the Convention. He does not interpret your insistence on remaining *en famille* as an expression of a mother's love, or even of her anxiety over the fate of her children. He believes that by refusing to leave your son, you are seeking ways to effect a restoration of the monarchy on your son's behalf."

As I will only leave the Temple with my children and *belle-soeur,* the baron's plan, set to be executed in the dead of night on June 21–22, the second anniversary of our ill-fated flight to the frontier, now requires alteration. My family waits in hope, anxiously counting down the days. Maybe this time, on our third organized attempt, we will finally succeed.

On the evening of June 21, swathed in blue military cloaks, we wait with anticipation and trepidation in our rooms, scarcely daring to breathe. This time, unlike Montmédy, we will travel light. What few possessions we intend to bring are already packed away, hidden under the beds and in the wardrobes behind the things we will leave in the Temple, Tonnerre among them, as the hobbyhorse is too large and oddly shaped to hide within a satchel.

The children take a nap while Madame Élisabeth and I play republican cards to pass the time. Even the most innocuous pastime has been corrupted by the Revolution. The face cards that once depicted images of kings, queens, and knaves or knights have been replaced in these decks by red-bonneted figures, some of them drawn in the classical robes worn during the Roman Republic and some in contemporary garb. The figures represent iconographic ideas, such as the Spirit of Peace and Prosperity, Genius of the Arts, and Equality in Marriage. In each of the four suits the kings have been replaced with figures of *Génie* or Spirit; the queens with the new republic's various iterations of *Liberté;* and the knaves have become numerous kinds of *Égalité.*

I glance at my father's gold pocket watch. The Baron de Batz should be waiting for us by now, stationed in the appointed place just beyond the rue du Temple. I wait breathlessly for a sign. Shortly before ten thirty there is a knock. Madame Élisabeth reaches across the card table and clasps my hand expectantly.

But when I unlatch the door, it is the commissioner Antoine Simon, a former shoemaker, who stands there, gray stubble stippling his cheeks and chin, his blouson half tucked into his striped trousers. He bursts into the room and thrusts a scrap of paper into my hands. I unfold the note to read, *Citoyen Michonis will betray you tonight.* The warning is unsigned. It could have been penned by anyone.

I shiver and say grimly, "*Merci,* Monsieur Simon." The *ci-devant* cobbler has never impressed me as knowing more than the rudiments of literacy. I wonder if he even knows what is written on the paper. I hand the note to Madame Élisabeth, conveying through my eyes that she should betray no emotion upon reading it.

Another plot has failed. It is impossible not to despair.

A few days later we learn that Michonis has managed to evade prosecution for his participation in the plan by convincing the

Commune that the entire incident was a grand joke he had played on Simon, who was a credulous fool to believe a few words scrawled on an anonymous letter. "There are two hundred and eighty guards at the Temple. How could an entire conspiracy organized by a half-dozen or more strangers hiding inside the fortress escape their detection?"

Like a whisper of vapor the Baron de Batz disappeared into the shadows on the night of our intended escape. At least he is safe and his complicity undetected. But the royal family remains at the mercy of the Nation and Madame Tison has denounced commissioners Toulan and Lepître to the Committee of Public Safety. In consequence, our allies have been dismissed. Their every movement will be observed; it may be impossible for them to ever aid us again.

Our hopes for a rescue grow dimmer by the day. I have not heard from Axel in weeks. And I do not know whether the baron will dare to devise a new scheme.

On the night of July 3, as I am preparing my son for bed, a delegation of commissioners from the Commune arrives. With them is the Commune's Procurator. Pierre Gaspard Chaumette is a man whose face looks as though someone wearing heavy boots has stepped on it. He glances about our rooms, frowning at what he sees. Madame Élisabeth, clutching her missal, receives a glare from this champion of the Cult of Reason who disdains all religions. I fear that he will confiscate her prayer book, the princesse's greatest comfort during our captivity.

But this is not an antireligious visit. Chaumette takes a scroll from inside his jacket, unties the ribbon with a tug, and unfurls the paper. His sunken eyes are cold, his manner frosty enough to chill the room. "Madame, by this order of the National Convention dated the second of July, 1793, your son Louis Charles Capet is to be remanded forthwith into the care of the Nation."

TWENTY-SEVEN

What More Can You
Do to Break My Heart?

~ JULY 1793 ~

My son shrieks in terror. Erupting into hysterical sobs, he flings himself into my arms. I hold him, barefoot and shivering in his nightshirt. "Don't let them take me, Maman! I don't want to go!" he bawls, gulping for air and choking on his words. "I don't want to go with those men. They will kill me as they killed Papa!"

I clutch him tightly, pressing his sweet head against my belly as his arms encircle my waist, holding on to me with every bit of his strength. I glare at the intruders with the ferocity of a tigress. "You will have to tear me to pieces before you harm a hair of my poor son's head!"

His sister and aunt begin to weep. Madame Royale sinks to her knees and regards Citoyen Chaumette imploringly. "Please, monsieur, I beg of you. Do not take my brother away." She glances desperately about the room as if she is looking for something. "Take me instead!" she blurts.

Chaumette laughs. Laughs at the girl's anguish. Laughs at Madame Élisabeth who rushes to her side to soothe her. Laughs at my hysteria, my fervent pleas.

"Please, Citoyenne Capet. Release the boy from your arms. We do not want to injure you."

"You have injured me already. Haven't you injured all of us enough, messieurs?" I look from one to the other in desperation. Citizen Simon, who seems immune to the benefits of a razor, has elbowed his way into the room. My nose is sniveling in an undignified manner from weeping and I grope for a handkerchief. "What greater torture can you do to me—to any mother—than to take her son from her?"

"Let the boy go, madame," says one of the soldiers, lifting his rifle off his shoulder.

Are they threatening to shoot me if I do not comply? "You will have to kill me before you rip my child from me." Incarceration has turned me into a feeble woman, but I will fight to retain my children with every ounce of strength. If I had ever been willing to abandon them, I might have been free by now, safe in Austria or Brussels, or Switzerland. I have even heard about some Americans who have prepared a home for me on their wild continent so that I might begin a new life among sympathetic strangers.

"Surely you have better things to do than to bully a grieving widow!" Madame Élisabeth exclaims. "Louis Charles is just a little boy. What harm has he ever committed? What harm will it do to allow the family to remain together?"

"Little boys grow up," Citoyen Chaumette retorts. "I understand he is proud. Too proud. From what I hear, he has not been learning his lessons properly. You, mesdames, are filling his head with the history of the royal families of France. Clearly he has not learned that the kingdom is a thing of the past and that all men are equal now in the new republic." He thrusts Simon into the center of the room. The man does not even have the good manners to remove his *bonnet rouge* when he confronts me. "From now on, Citoyen Simon will superintend the education of Louis Charles Capet. To help him lose the idea of his rank, he must be taken from his family."

"Tell me then what you wish *me* to teach my son from now on. I will fill his head with whatever you direct me to—only please leave him with me. He is only eight years old."

"With all due respect, citoyenne, the Nation finds it difficult to conceive that you would comply with such a directive, even of your own volition."

It is true; if I *were* compelled to fill my son's head with a lot of nonsense I do not agree with or believe in, even for the sake of keeping him by my side, my heart would not be in his tutelage. But I have only two treasures left in this world.

"We have never been separated," I inform Chaumette. "The boy has already lost his father. Do not cause him to lose his mother as well."

But the men are impervious to my entreaties. "You may still see your son," Citoyen Chaumette assures me, pointing skyward to the pinnacle of the tower where I will be able to peer through the iron bars that have been installed over the windows. "When he is permitted to play in the courtyard. He is being removed only to the apartments directly beneath yours: those that belonged to the late Citizen Capet."

"*Non*—Maman, there are ghosts in there!" wails Louis Charles. He has been hysterical ever since Chaumette's arrival.

"We are not here to negotiate with you," the Procurator says coolly. "The boy will be removed from your guardianship regardless of your opinions, pleas, and tears. If you do not wish him to be forcibly removed by my men, you will release him to me of your own accord. I have orders to kill you—and your son—all of you, in fact, if you continue to resist the order of the National Convention."

I remain rooted to the floor with my arms about the little king, his face, blotchy with weeping, pressed against my *lévite.* Finally, I kneel so that I am looking into his red-rimmed, swollen eyes. "I want you to understand, *mon chou d'amour,* that I would never let you go unless the bad men forced me to do so," I whisper into his ear. "I am counting upon you to be brave, just as your papa was. Oh, my darling—my sweet precious darling," I say, clasping the boy to my bosom. He is so slender. Will they feed him properly and see that he remains well? The air in the Temple is unhealthy: drafty and damp. "Promise your maman, who loves you more than she loves her own life, that you will never forget her. *Promets-le moi?*"

"Je te le promets," he replies, his lower lip moist and trembling, his high voice barely audible.

"At least allow me to dress my son," I urge Chaumette. "I will not send him out in his nightclothes." I linger over each article of clothing, inhaling the child's scent in his chemise and *gilet,* helping him to maintain his balance as he inserts his legs, one at a time, into his breeches, rolling his white hose over his pale feet and legs, putting on his leather shoes and fastening the latchets with silver buckles. I slip his arms into his black mourning coat and hand him his little black tricorn. "Don't forget your handkerchief," I sniffle, placing the folded square of linen into the pocket of his coat.

"May I take Tonnerre?" he asks tearfully, and without waiting for an acknowledgment from Chaumette and Simon, I fetch the hobbyhorse from its "stable" in the corner of the salon.

"Allow him just this one comfort," I urge the men. Louis Charles clasps the beloved toy horse's head in his arms as if to embrace a house pet.

Chaumette nods brusquely and Citoyen Simon steps forward, grabbing the boy roughly by the elbow.

"Do not presume to touch my nephew like that!" Madame Élisabeth cries, stepping between them.

"I urge you to back away, madame, unless it is your intention to get hurt," Chaumette orders. My *belle-soeur* shivers with fright, never doubting that his threat is genuine.

We are startled by a commotion outside on the stairway. Shrieking incoherently, Madame Tison pushes her way through the knot of soldiers and flings herself to the floor. Reaching for the hem of my silk wrapper, she presses it to her cheek, crying, "Forgive me, madame! Forgive me! I did not know it would turn out this way!"

"What is she raving about?" I ask Monsieur Chaumette. The poor woman is convulsing, her body wracked with spasms as she continues to implore my forgiveness for her past transgressions. Hers is the unseeing gaze of a madwoman. In her ranting, she stains my gown with flecks of spittle.

A pair of guards lifts Madame Tison by the armpits. Her anguished cries echo through the winding stairwell as she is dragged forcibly down the precipitous circular staircase.

"You have had sufficient time for your adieux, citoyenne," the Procurator warns.

"Give your aunt and sister a kiss," I instruct my son. He embraces them tearfully, for he has not stopped crying for a moment, and then turns back to me, throwing himself into my arms one more time. *"Donne-moi un bisou,"* I sob. "Give your maman one more kiss." He complies and I stipple his little face with moist kisses. He is led from the chamber still bawling.

My gaze is riveted on his retreating form. At the doorway he turns back to look at me. I touch my hands to my heart and mouth the words *Je t'aimerai toujours*—I will always love you—knowing, even if my son does not, that we will never see each other again.

The hollow tower is full of echoes. I hear the hideous scraping of the two massive doors leading to the apartment below—the rasp of the iron bolts and the rattling of the heavy padlocks that confirm all too well that my little boy has become an official prisoner of the Nation. I imagine him in the shuttered rooms, perched on the edge of his late father's bed, frightened and alone. For two straight days the excruciating sound of Louis Charles's incessant sobs penetrate the thick floorboards of my rooms. "What are they doing to him down there?" I ask, of no one in particular. Madame Royale steps around the back of my chair, entwining her arms about my neck. My *belle-soeur* looks for solace within her prayer book. "You must take comfort in your faith, sister, as I do," she exhorts me gently.

I glance down at my trembling hands. "God Himself has forsaken me," I murmur in reply. "I no longer dare to pray."

TWENTY-EIGHT

The Devil's Catechism

The day after Louis Charles was ripped from my arms, eight men convey Madame Tison out of the Temple, incarcerating her in the Hôtel-Dieu, where she is to remain hospitalized, away from public scrutiny. Even as the guards forcibly remove her, she is shrieking about being haunted by ghosts and shadows, blubbering incoherent fearful cries that those she had denounced would be put to death and return to remind her of the lives she had ruined. Later that day, I receive a visit from her husband. "I believed you to be a demon, a monster, madame. It was not until I came to know you— through spying upon you, I confess—that I came to see who you really are: a loving wife, a grieving widow, and a devoted mother, like any other woman who has been touched by sorrow, regardless of her rank."

I assure Monsieur Tison that I bear his family no malice and request that he keep me informed with regard to the health of his wife. Overcome with guilt, she has lost her mind. Perhaps it seems strange that I do not condemn a woman who persecuted my family, but I hate to see anyone in torment. This Revolution has claimed enough victims.

On the third day of my separation from Louis Charles his unceasing sobs are met with reproofs from Citoyen Simon. I hear their muffled voices through the floor, and I suspect that Simon shouts deliberately, knowing that he tortures me as well when he torments my child.

"I wish to know what law it is that says you can take me away from my mother," my son demands imperiously, finally remembering who and what he is, despite his tender years. "If there is such a law, then show it to me."

"Hold your tongue, you little imp, or I'll tear it from your head. And don't think I'm fooling." I can just imagine the evil man thrusting one of his filthy cobbler's tools in the boy's face, hinting at their use as instruments of torture. "We're going to have a music lesson today," Citoyen Simon tells him. He begins to whistle the *Ça Ira*.

"My maman will not let me sing that song," Louis Charles protests. "She says it has bad words."

"Your maman isn't your teacher anymore, boy. Your maman is a slut and a whore and not fit to live. Now, repeat what I said."

"Non!" the little king shouts.

"What was that?"

Louis Charles raises his voice. *"Non!* I will never say nasty things about my mother."

In reply to his feeble protest comes a frightening sound, like the staccato crack of a whip or a slap. Has that horrid cobbler struck my child? A sudden stabbing pain in my chest makes me double over. If these monsters want to kill me, all they have to do is touch my son. He begins to bawl again. The *crack-snap* is repeated, generating another round of hysterical tears. I rush to the door of our apartment and pummel it with my fists. All of us are now at the complete mercy of the Commune and the Committee of Public Safety. The only time Madame Élisabeth, my daughter, and I have contact with our jailers is when they ascend the winding staircase three times a day to bring our meals and to take Thisbe, my spaniel, and Madame de Lamballe's terrier for a walk in the courtyard. I am not even permitted to exercise the dogs myself anymore.

As the lonely days without my little boy drag on, the remorseful Monsieur Tison, who often carries the meal trays himself, manages to slip me brief notes, scribbled on scraps of paper in his uneducated hand. They indicate that Louis Charles is healthy and cared for, despite Citoyen Simon's campaign to poison his mind. But when I ascend the dank stone steps of the tower in order to glimpse my son through the narrowest of windows, my eyes inform me otherwise.

They have confiscated the black silk suit I had dressed him in, obliterated any visible trace of mourning for his father. He is outfitted now in filthy beige *sans-culottes* and a *carmagnole,* the short red jacket favored by the peasants and laborers in the Piedmont village of Carmagnola that the revolutionaries have adopted as an identifying garment. Beneath the *bonnet rouge* that Simon compels him to wear, my son's soft brown hair has become lank and greasy. If they do not regularly tend to the child's hygiene, in no time he will be crawling with lice. Is this how the revolutionaries intend to break his spirit?

Already Simon is poisoning the child's mind against everything he was raised to believe, beating time on a snare drum as Louis Charles marches in a circle about the courtyard with a miniature musket—which I sincerely hope is a toy— on his shoulder, singing the vicious verses of the *Ça Ira,* although I doubt he understands their meaning.

That night I hear my son crying again when Simon endeavors to teach him a new song. The lyrics of the *Carmagnole* are nothing more than hideous propaganda intended to incite even the most ignorant to violence. It has a simple, lively melody, much like a children's nursery rhyme, easily learned within five minutes as the tune is the same for every verse.

"Come now—loud and clear, so your mother the whore can hear you," Simon demands. After a few moments of tense silence, I hear the cracking sound again and I flinch. "Do it, you little brat," Simon shouts.

" '*Madame Veto threatened to cut everyone's throat in Paris; but her plot failed, thanks to our cannons,*' " Louis Charles sings.

"Louder."

I know that my son is being terrorized into complying, petrified that this big unshaven brute who stinks of onions and brandy will hurt him again. So he sings more lustily, but Simon remains unsatisfied.

"Sing it like you mean it, you little spawn of the devil."

" '*Monsieur Veto promised to be loyal to his country, but he failed, and gave the people no quarter.*' " My son fairly shouts the words. " '*Antoinette resolved to drop us all on our bums, but her plan failed and she got* her nose *broken instead.*' "

For the rest of the hour Simon drills the refrain into the boy's head. *"Long live the sound! Let us dance the Carmagnole. Long live the sound of our cannons!"*

And yet, I would give anything to see my son, even though he is being taught to despise his parents. How could I ever stop loving him, no matter what he sings? It is not his fault. As I climb the stairs and peer between the iron bars that cover the windows of the Grosse Tour, pressing my cheek against the cold metal in an effort to get as close as I can to my child, to bathe in the sight of his sweet, trusting face, I gasp at the telltale signs of his coercion. His right eye is swollen shut. Beneath it spreads an angry blue-black bruise, like an indigo crescent moon. There are cuts on his forehead, cheeks, and hands. He is a brave little boy, but how much torment is an eight-year-old expected to endure? I am sure he will say—or sing—anything to stop Citoyen Simon from striking him. I become physically ill when I consider what other abuse his new tutor has perpetrated upon his innocent body.

A few days later, I witness another effort to transform Louis XVII into a radical revolutionary, to fill his head with hatred for everything he used to know and love. Louis Charles is standing outdoors in the pouring rain without an oilcloth coat to protect him. Simon has even removed the child's liberty bonnet so that the raindrops pelt him like God's tears, weeping at such a travesty. "What is your name?" Simon demands.

"Louis Charles Capet." My son replies meekly.

"And your rank?"

"Royal brat."

What parody of a catechism is this?

"And your father?"

"Louis Capet," the boy replies dutifully.

"And *his* rank?"

"Tyrant and oppressor."

"And what happened to him?"

Louis Charles mumbles something and begins to cry. I wish I could pull apart the bars with my bare hands and fly to his rescue. I would hold him, comfort him, tell him that Maman will make everything all right again.

"Speak up, brat; your mother can't hear you," Simon cries derisively, tossing a glance toward the window where he knows I stand. "What was your father's fate?"

"He was executed by the will of the people," my son says.

"And what is your mother's name?"

"Marie Capet," he replies, without emotion. "Also known as Madame Veto. *Mais, je ne comprends pas,* Monsieur Simon. Why are we all named 'Capet' when we are Bourbons? The last of the Capetian kings was my ancestor Charles le Bel who died in 1328. Why are you my *gouverneur,*" he asks in utter innocence, "when you do not know about the history of France? Why isn't my maman teaching me anymore? Or my *tante* Élisabeth? *She* knows everything."

Simon cracks a horsewhip that lands within inches of my son. The little boy leaps back and I repress a cry. "Your mother is unfit. She is no teacher. What is her profession?"

Louis Charles buries his face in his hands. The whip cracks again. "I won't say it."

Crack. "The next time I release this whip, you brat, it will land on your back. What is your mother's métier?"

My son trembles. "Whore."

"Say it, brat. Loud enough for all Paris to hear."

"My mother is a whore."

"And your aunt?"

"My aunt Élisabeth is a whore too."

His aunt has never even known a man's caress. Silent tears trickle down my face, but I cannot tear myself away from the window.

"Good boy," Simon exclaims, giving my son such a hearty slap on his back that he loses his balance and stumbles.

Citoyen Simon reaches into his coat and removes a plain silver flask. He unscrews the cap and takes a swig, then thrusts it into the boy's hands. "Good work, today," he says, tossing an upwards glance at the tower. "Here's your reward." Simon forces the bottle to my son's lips and tilts it toward him.

Mon Dieu, he is making an eight-year-old child imbibe spirits!

Day after day I climb the interior steps of the tower, hoping to glimpse Louis Charles, even though it becomes ever more excruciating to witness what he is becoming. He now sings the Revolutionary anthems—carouses—with the members of the Garde Nationale, swearing and swilling alcohol alongside them like an old campaigner. Much to the amusement of our jailers, the compassionate child who used to play bilbo catch with his ball and cup is being taught to toss dice and indulge in other games of chance. It is impossible to control my tears.

When he is indoors, I take care to make as little noise as possible so that I might overhear him through the floor. But one day Madame Élisabeth fumbles with a wooden spool and it falls and rolls away. Unable to locate it, we begin to move the furniture, hunting for the spool under chairs, tables, and beds.

When we pause for a moment to wipe the dust from our brows, I hear Louis Charles below us shout impatiently, "Haven't those two whores been guillotined yet?"

My hand flies to my mouth in horror. Only a month ago, this solicitous little boy, so kind and compassionate that he would never have squashed an insect, wept for two straight days because he missed his maman.

TWENTY-NINE

Nothing Can Hurt Me Anymore

⟶ SUMMER 1793 ⟵

One day toward the end of July, Monsieur Tison manages to smuggle a newspaper to us. I gasp at the headline. "They have guillotined that young woman from Caen who stabbed Marat to death in his medicinal bath!"

"At least she died for something she believed in," remarks Madame Royale. "Instead of simply for existing. For having blue blood. And she rid France of an evil man. Charlotte Corday is a martyr, but you know they will turn Marat into the martyr instead." She reaches for the paper and begins to read about Mademoiselle Corday's trial. "*Et Voila!* It says here that when the prosecutors examined her in the witness box she told them, 'I killed one man to save a hundred thousand.'" My daughter sighs heavily. "I wish there were more like her. One to stab Robespierre and one to stab Danton and one for Desmoulins—for all of them, an army of women to take charge of what the men lack the courage to do."

It is a clever idea, although somewhat misguided. "Do not be so quick to enshrine Mademoiselle Corday, *ma chère,*" I tell Mousseline. "She was also a revolutionary—a Girondin who was angry with Marat because he attacked the more conservative leaders for not being as bloodthirsty as he. The Revolution has begun to eat its own, *ma petite.*"

Marie Thérèse continues to peruse the paper. *"Mon Dieu,"* she exclaims. "There will be no end in sight to the carnage, now. Maximilien Robespierre has been elected to the Committee of Public Safety." She looks up, meeting my gaze. "He scares me, Maman."

"Moi, aussi," I murmur.

"I think, perhaps, that Robespierre is the cruelest of all of them," muses Madame Élisabeth. "God forgot to give that man a heart. Is there anyone else so cold, so dispassionate?"

I take the broadsheet away from my daughter. She has read enough horrific news for one day. And there is even more that I did not permit her to see. Under Robespierre's directives, the Committee of Public Safety has ordered the desecration of the tombs and mausoleums of France's former kings. Afraid that the people have grown weary of all the violence, the Committee has fired up their blood by giving them a new purpose and a renewed hatred of the monarchy. I have heard the *nouvelles* cried in the streets; the people are now demanding that I be brought to justice for crimes against the Nation. "With counterrevolution sweeping the Vendée on the western coast south of the Loire, and the allies advancing on Paris, the revolutionaries fear their cause is threatened." I raise my eyes to the window, gazing dolefully into the middle distance. "They will demand a scapegoat."

They arrive in the predawn darkness of the second of August. I am convinced that the Commune enjoys inflicting additional terror by dispatching armed guards to surprise us in the dead of night, rousing us from our slumber. I bolt upright at the sound of someone pounding on the door and clutch the thin blanket about me. But I am rooted to my mattress, my breath caught in my throat. Madame Royale climbs into my bed, throwing her arms around me. "Don't let them take me away, Maman," she weeps, assuming they have come for her. A look from her aunt, and Mousseline realizes that the situation is even more dire than she'd feared. As the padlocks are opened from a ring of skeleton keys and the bolt scrapes across the door, my daughter clings to me as if her fierce embrace will protect me from harm.

The door to our apartments is kicked open, hitting the wall with a shudder. At the head of the intruders, holding aloft a lantern, is the Temple administrator, Citoyen Michonis. But this time, undoubtedly afraid for his own safety, his eyes convey no sympathy.

"You are to dress immediately, Citoyenne Capet," Michonis says without emotion. "By this decree, authorized by the National Convention, the Commune de Paris, and the Committee of Public Safety, you are to be conveyed without delay to the Conciergerie to await trial before the Revolutionary Tribunal." I listen, immobile as stone, while he reads the order. And then, as if I am in a dream, I gather fresh linen, a petticoat, and a black silk gown and walk toward the salon where I can dress in private.

"Halt." I turn at Michonis's command. "You are not permitted to leave our sight." The four soldiers from the Garde Nationale shoulder their rifles. The Temple administrator points to a chair where I may seat myself to roll my stockings on and don my shoes. Clearly I cannot make my toilette in the presence of these five men, nor dare I change my linen in front of them. With the emotionless precision of an automaton I remove my wrapper, exposing beneath the thin batiste of my nightgown the figure of a woman who has become old before her time. I slip my petticoat on over the nightgown and then wrap my stays about my torso. Madame Élisabeth's hands tremble so much that she fumbles with the laces. Then, biting back her tears, knowing that if she weeps I will break entirely, she helps me into the gown.

"Please, messieurs, let us go, too," Madame Royale entreats. Monsieur Michonis ignores her, his face impassive.

With the same dispassion I wrap up a parcel of clothes, then place a few prized possessions into a small drawstring bag: a handkerchief embroidered with my cipher, a tortoiseshell comb, my prayer book and my father's gold timepiece, a vinaigrette of smelling salts, my son's well-worn yellow leather glove, and the locks of hair of my husband and each of our children, including the first dauphin Louis Joseph and baby Sophie, who have departed this cruel world for an ethereal one.

Mousseline tearfully promises to look after the princesse de Lamballe's terrier. As she clutches the dog, finally, I lift our other pet, Thisbe, into my arms. Astonishingly, Citoyen Michonis raises no protest. Sensing danger, the spaniel begins to bark and I try to hush her before the Temple administrator changes his mind. *"Suis prête,"* I tell the guards. "I'm ready." I walk past my daughter and the woman who has been a sister to me for the past twenty-three years, knowing that if I look back, I will lose my resolve to remain strong. Yet more than anything, I long, like Orpheus, to turn, aware that this will be the last time we ever see each other.

Balancing Thisbe in one arm with my keepsake purse and parcel of clothing tucked beneath the other, I lift my head and exit the chamber with dignity. My jailers may no longer view me as the Queen of France, but I will always be a daughter of Maria Theresa of Austria.

I descend the tower's winding staircase, pausing at each gated landing for the soldiers to unlock the wickets. When I reach the second story I stop, hoping to hear my son's voice through the door one last time. Louis Charles is singing as someone—Citoyen Simon or his wife—accompanies him on a fife. He is being taught the words of the *Marche de Marsellois,* or the *Marseillaise* as the Parisians call it.

"*Allons, enfants de la patrie, le jour de gloire est arrivé.*"

His maman is being conveyed to the Conciergerie, the foyer to Madame Guillotine's salon, as the prison has become known: death's antechamber.

The day of glory has arrived.

I continue to descend the cold stone steps in a haze, my gaze fixed straight ahead although my mind is so clouded with sorrow that I see nothing. If only Mousseline could have known how much I wanted to rush back and embrace her before I left our chamber, how desperately I wished to hold for one final moment my first-born child, the girl it almost killed me to bring into the world. The girl with her father's eyes. Near the foot of the stairs, I forget to duck as I have done eleven times out of twelve in order to pass through each of the gates, and my forehead strikes the beam, enough to send me reeling.

"Did you hurt yourself?" Citoyen Michonis inquires, hearing the cracking sound of bone on wood. His tone indicates that he is afraid to sound too solicitous of France's most famous *détenue.*

They have already wounded me past all bounds of human understanding by murdering my husband and denying me my children. In a hollow voice I reply, "Nothing can hurt me anymore."

Guarded by armed outriders, the carriage, a plain black hackney, rumbles through the indigo night toward the center of Paris, over *rues* rutted and unpaved, and irregular cobbles that cause the axles to sway and jolt. If the Revolutionary Tribunal is so keen on prosecuting me for being the scourge of the nation, I would have expected them to parade me through the streets in broad daylight, drawing people out of their homes to witness my degradation.

The clatter of the wheels echoes off the stuccoed and brick façades of innumerable residences as we manuever through the narrow, dimly illuminated lanes. With tremendous solemnity we rattle past a lamppost just north of the Hôtel de Ville. The figure of a man, his hair barbered to a stubble, dangles from the lantern, a hempen noose about his throat. His shoes have been stolen and obscenities have been scrawled upon the dead man's stockings, but his cravat remains oddly pristine. The poor soul, an aristocrat by his wardrobe, is slack-jawed, as if he is shocked to have been strung up like a ham. I shudder and look away. The carriage crosses the Pont Notre-Dame over the Seine onto the Île de la Cité and turns into the courtyard of the Conciergerie, a turreted fortress on the left bank of the river that ensconces Sainte-Chapelle, the glorious thirteenth-century chapel built by Louis IX. A member of the Garde Nationale opens the door to the coach and begrudgingly unfolds the steps. He does not extend a hand to help me descend and I must manage on my own with my spaniel and my few belongings.

The prison is ominously dark. Not even a torch burns outside the gates. The guards who had escorted me out of the Temple pound on the bolted wooden door with their musket butts, an incessant thundering that reverberates throughout the courtyard.

A familiar face answers their call. "*Est-ce* Louis Larivière?" I ask. Once, he was a pastry cook's apprentice in the kitchen of le Petit Trianon. "Are you the turnkey?"

He nods, astonished to see the Queen of France standing before him, a frail, white-haired woman in black mourning clothes, her face as pale as moonlight, little resembling the curvaceous, bejeweled, exotically coiffed, and opulently gowned monarch for whom he had filled pastel-hued macarons with flavored cream. Does this mean I will have a friend here? Or has Larivière become like Gamain, Louis's former locksmithing tutor, who betrayed him to the Convention?

As I mount the stone steps of the prison, crossing the threshold from freedom to incarceration, from the possibility of life to the certainty of death, memory transports me into the past. A naïve archduchess of fourteen reaches the Île des Epis where she will forfeit everything she has heretofore known to become a Frenchwoman. With her are her two most prized possessions: the golden watch that once belonged to her father, Francis of Lorraine, and her beloved pug. Back then, she was permitted to retain the timepiece, but not her Mopshund, an *Austrian* dog.

The irony is not lost on me that when I was welcomed into the kingdom, my dog was taken away in those final moments before I stepped across the manufactured border between Austria and France; yet now that I am at the edge of another boundary, one that will undoubtedly lead to my ignominious exit from the country that welcomed me with open arms so long ago, they do not insist upon confiscating my four-legged companion.

I enter a vast medieval hall with rows of thick pillars and groin-vaulted ceilings of honey-colored stone, a cathedral of misery. The Hall of the Guards is populated with all manner of people awaiting admission, from street urchins to nonjuring nuns who managed to survive the September massacres only to find themselves in Heaven's antechamber. Also among them are the dregs of humanity; the Conciergerie is renowned for housing the worst criminals in France. Dozens of guards are stationed throughout the hall, some alert and at attention, others smoking, joking, spitting. The men who have conveyed me to the Conciergerie escort me up a flight of stairs to a desk in front of an iron grille where a grumpy man in a dirty *bonnet rouge* sits behind an enormous ledger. He raises an eyebrow when he sees me, exhaling a violet plume from his clay pipe. Although he knows it full well, the registrar demands my name.

"Look at me," I reply quietly. I will never say the words "Citoyenne Antoinette Capet." Who am I? Who do *I* believe myself to be? Marie Antoinette, the *ci-devant* queen of France? Maria Antonia of Austria and Lorraine?

I remove my handkerchief from my reticule and blot my brow. I am wet with anxiety and fear. It is hot in here despite the cool stone that surrounds me. The registrar inscribes my name in the next empty column of his ledger and neatly writes a number beside it: from this moment on, this Hapsburg daughter, this Bourbon wife and mother, will be known as Prisoner 280.

THIRTY

The Conciergerie

I am escorted to my cell by Madame Richard, the wife of the jailer, and Madame Larivière, the elderly mother of the prison's governor. "It is not what you are accustomed to, of course," says Madame Richard sympathetically, and I marvel that it might be possible to find friends in this horrid place. "But Rosalie and I have done our best to make your cell comfortable for you." She indicates the exceptionally lovely dark-haired young woman scurrying to keep up with us, whom she introduces as Mademoiselle Lamorlière, her own maid.

My new abode is minuscule, less than twelve feet square. "Who are those men?" I ask, upon seeing a pair of uniformed gendarmes seated in the cell playing backgammon. "Should you ask them to leave?"

Madame Richard emits a soft chuckle and fusses, embarrassed, with her white fichu. "Citoyen Gilbert and Citoyen Dufresne will remain here throughout the night. At daylight they will be relieved by another two National gendarmes."

"In this tiny cell with me? How—where am I to dress?" I ask, shocked.

Madame Larivière points to a folding screen. "And I will patch your gown for you," she whispers. "When you raised your arms I noticed how threadbare the fabric is beneath them. Your hem, too," she adds. "It is all worn out. If you don't mind it a little bit shorter, I can mend it."

My eyes dim with grateful tears. I cannot believe these women are so kind to me, so solicitous. I had expected monsters and instead I have found sisters. "But the screen?" I ask. It cannot be taller than four feet high; it would barely come up to my chest, affording little in the way of modesty. "Why must they see my face and my—my *poitrine* when I dress and undress? What do they think I am going to conceal from them?" Another thought occurs to me as I notice a bucket placed in the corner. My jaw quivers with humiliation as I realize that these men will be able to watch me relieve myself. At present, they are otherwise occupied. Thisbe is investigating her new surroundings, nosing about the meager pieces of furniture—the guards' table and chairs, a narrow camp bed, a three-legged stool with a splintered seat, a small rickety table beside the bed, and two empty chairs—and is attempting to convert the pair of gendarmes into friends by sheer dint of her engaging personality.

Glancing at the guards playing with the spaniel, "We will ask them not to peek," says Madame Richard pragmatically, tucking a wayward blond tendril beneath her mobcap.

"And Madame Richard has instructed me to help you dress and undress," Rosalie adds. "I will stand between the screen and the officers in order to protect your dignity."

What choice do I have? Things could, in truth, be considerably worse.

The kindly Madame Larivière asks me to hand her my black

silk gown for repair, explaining that they will send to the Temple for additional garments. In the meantime I can wear my other mourning dress. I look about the cell for places to store my few possessions. I am so exhausted, physically and emotionally, that I am nearly asleep on my feet, wobbling on the cold and uneven brick floor. The gendarmes, who have paused from their game to stare at me, do not move; it is Rosalie who clasps my elbow to steady me.

"I will ask my husband to locate a bit of carpet," Madame Larivière says. "At least it will make things warmer and a bit more comfortable. And first thing in the morning I will send him to buy an ell of black silk to mend your gown."

The amusing thought of the white-haired turnkey shopping for fabric brings the first smile to my lips in days.

"Perhaps I should dispatch *my* husband," suggests Madame Richard. Turning back to me she explains, "Before the Revolution, we were haberdashers."

I empty the contents of my reticule onto the little bed. Someone has endeavored to make the cot more welcoming by covering it with a pretty blue counterpane and a pillow edged in Battenburg lace. "Do you think it might be possible to hang this where I can see it?" I ask, separating my father's watch from the rest of my belongings. I scan the filthy walls for a hook. There is not even a mirror hanging in the cell. I don't know how I will be able to make my toilette every day.

"Citoyen Gilbert." At the sound of Madame Larivière's voice, one of the gendarmes looks up. "Would you kindly locate a carpenter's nail and hammer it into the wall"—she points to a perfect location and looks to me for confirmation—"here, by the bed?"

Gilbert immediately rises from his chair, as if he had been given an order he could not refuse by his own *grand-mère*. Within a half hour, Papa's watch is suspended from a nail by its golden chain.

Only a few hours remain until daybreak and the women, my

three graces, encourage me to sleep. The tiny cell is naturally gloomy, but the candles are continually replaced so that I am never permitted to enjoy the solace of complete darkness. Tonight, however, I am too exhausted to mention it. Although the bed is barely big enough to accommodate me, the prisoners' straw pallet has been improved with the addition of a pair of mattresses and a bolster. Rosalie unlaces me and helps me unpin my hair before I sink into a fitful slumber, my final thoughts, as ever, on my children.

I have always been a creature of routine; without it, I can't imagine how I will be able to endure the ignominy and deprivation of my new life. When I awaken, thanks to a wet-nosed nuzzle from Thisbe, and glance at Papa's watch, it is seven in the morning. I sit up against the bolster and blink the sleep from my eyes. Two different gendarmes are sitting at the same table where Citoyens Dufresne and Gilbert had been a few hours ago. But these officers are not occupied with a pastime. It is clear they have been staring at me as if I were an exotic creature in a menagerie, waiting for me to do something unusual. I am afraid to get out of bed, but I must avail myself of the bucket. To my horror, the gendarmes do not look away. They continue to watch me, as if they expect my body to release a family of toads when I raise my skirt to relieve myself. Giving birth to Mousseline in front of the highest-ranking members of the French aristocracy was not as degrading as this.

Rosalie Lamorlière arrives with a tray of food. "I did not know whether you would prefer coffee or chocolate, *Maj—madame,*" she says, correcting her urge to address me as the queen in the presence of the gendarmes. "So I brought you a cup of each. Madame Richard didn't think you would want to drink the same water that the other prisoners do—it comes from the Seine." She makes a face. "Madame Richard sent to the Temple for your Ville d'Avray water."

The breakfast tray also contains dry toast and a soft-boiled egg sitting in a china cup. "You need to keep up your strength, madame," Rosalie murmurs, leaning over me as she sets the tray upon the little table by the bed. "Madame Richard says you are as thin as a twig." I am so moved by these expressions of generosity that my nose stings with tears and a lump of emotion rises in my throat. She makes a kissing sound designed to get Thisbe's attention and scoops the spaniel into her arms. "While you eat your *petit déjeuner*, I will take her for a walk."

My dog grows so quickly accustomed to her new surroundings that perhaps I could learn something from her, although her ability to withstand the putrid odors that pervade every corner of the Conciergerie, the fetid stenches of urine and excrement and hundreds of unwashed, terrified prisoners, as well as the acrid smoke from the gendarmes' clay pipes, passes all comprehension. After Rosalie returns, I will ask her to mask the cell's nauseating aromas by burning some juniper in a cachepot.

I eat slowly, trying to savor my meal. If I devour only half of it now, the other piece of toast will satisfy my hunger later. Who knows how long this generosity will last?

When Rosalie returns with Thisbe, I decline her offer to help me dress. "I am not your mistress. In addition to Madame Richard, I expect that you have many other people to look after."

"But I wish to aid you, madame," she insists, taking a length of white ribbon from her pocket. "Here. At least allow me to dress your hair with this. If you look pretty, perhaps—perhaps—it will make things seem easier." Although I permit her to style my coiffure, I have no thoughts of vanity nowadays. Fear for my children occupies my mind instead. In mid-afternoon, when Madame Richard brings a tray for my dinner of bouillon, boiled vegetables, and roast duckling—did someone know that duck is my favorite dish?—as well as a pastry for dessert, I cannot be anything but truthful when she asks how I am faring.

"I miss my son and daughter," I confide. "I can live without lavish palaces, without fine clothes, and certainly without opulent jewels, but I cannot live without my children. They are the air I breathe," I add, looking about the dank cell. The only source of light filters in from the Cour des Femmes, the Women's Courtyard, just beyond my walls. Reaching beneath my fichu I retrieve a locket that dangles from a chain I wear about my neck. I keep it hidden under my gown because I am afraid the jailers will confiscate it. I open the locket to show Madame Richard. "This is a miniature of my son, painted when he was dauphin. And this is a lock of his hair."

Like any mother, she coos over the portrait, remarking what a handsome boy Louis Charles is. "One day I will introduce you to my son," she replies. "I think you and Fanfan would like each other very much." I nod appreciatively; I have never met a child I did not adore.

Citoyen Michonis arrives during my first afternoon in the Conciergerie; under his arm he carries a package wrapped in butcher's paper. "I was able to take some things from the Temple for you," he says. I unwrap the bundle to find a fresh petticoat, two pairs of black filoselle stockings, a clean change of linen, a few lace-trimmed chemises, three white lawn fichus, a cloak, and my other pair of *prunelle* shoes, plum-colored satin with a heel *à la Saint-Huberty*. These slippers I intend to save until the ones I am wearing have completely disintegrated. Owing to the dampness in the cell, it may not be very long indeed before I will need to discard them.

I take nothing for granted anymore. I eat only a quarter of my dinner, giving one quarter of the duck breast to Thisbe for her meal. The rest of the meat will feed us both again. I do the same when Rosalie brings my supper tray: *fricassée* of pigeon and slices of braised beef. All of my meals are prepared by Madame Richard herself, a mark of respect, or dare I imagine affection, that startles me, for I never expected to find such goodness here. The concierge's wife proudly informs me, and Rosalie confirms it, that when they go shopping for food and tell the vendors in the marketplace that it is "for the poor queen," they are given the choicest cuts of meat, the plumpest chickens, and the freshest fruits and vegetables.

Even the gendarmes who guard my cell in the evenings are not altogether cruel. Although the two men who have been assigned to watch me throughout the day are indifferent to my distress, talking loudly and filling the tiny space with smoke, those charged with watching over me at night fulfill the requirements of their job while endeavoring to afford me a modicum of privacy by averting their gazes and concentrating on their hands of cards or their back-gammon board. Of all of them, Citoyen Gilbert, younger than his compatriots, and with an open, trusting face, is the only man who seems genuinely kind and noble. The day after my incarceration began, he returned to take his place in my cell with a bouquet of late summer blooms. I am certain he must have purchased them with his own money. Brightening the prisoners' quarters with flowers is hardly customary at the Conciergerie.

For so long I have been terrorized by the people's hatred for me, told that there wasn't a soul among the bourgeoisie and the labor-ing classes who harbored a shred of sympathy for me. How ironic that in death's anteroom, of all places, I discover that I have been taught a lie. Although I insist on dressing myself, Rosalie nonethe-less comes to my cell every morning with a fresh length of white ribbon to adorn my hair. I suppress a sad smile: Our little ritual invokes memories of happier and oh-so-much grander days at Ver-sailles when my *dame d'atours* would deliver a pristine yard of rib-bon every day with which to tie my *robe à negligée* after I emerged from my bath.

On Sunday morning, August 4, after I have breakfasted and made my meager toilette: a few drops of scented water and a bit of face powder daubed on with a swansdown puff, viewing myself in a cheap hand mirror bordered in red with quaint Chinese characters on the back—an illicit purchase Rosalie had made on one of the quais, as inmates are not permitted to own a looking glass— Citoyen Michonis returns with a pair of visitors. He introduces me to a Mademoiselle Fouché, a pretty blond thing in a gown of printed muslin, and her uncle, Monsieur Charles.

When the guards are not looking, the young lady drops into a subtle curtsy. "You do not know me, madame, but I am a friend. There are still many of us here in Paris, more than you know. And I felt certain that in your season of peril you would wish to become acquainted with my 'uncle.'"

The soi-disant Monsieur Charles motions to the screen and the three of us step behind it, to shield our bodies from the guards' watchful gaze. He removes his black cloak to reveal a clergyman's white stock tied about his throat. A small box dangles from a silken cord around his neck.

"He is not really my uncle," Mademoiselle Fouché informs me as her companion takes off the necklace and opens the box to reveal the Host. The man holds a finger to his lips, then whispers, "I am abbé Magnin, madame, living in sanctuary with the Fouché family because I refused to swear the oath to uphold the Constitution."

My eyes well with tears of amazement. These two souls have risked their lives to enter a prison so that a nonjuring priest can hear my confession and I might receive Holy Communion. I don't know how to thank them, especially when the abbé promises to return.

Later that afternoon Rosalie brings me a paperboard box. "I thought you might like this for your linen. To keep it in a cleaner place, madame."

I want to hug her. Clasping her hands, instead, I express my gratitude with such effusion that one might have imagined she'd given me the key to my freedom.

Liberation, of course, is a dream. My jailers have been kind thus far, but I am not even permitted to walk in the courtyard just beyond my window, the only area of the prison where one can step outdoors and breathe fresh air. I hear that the male prisoners are envious because only women are permitted this luxury. When I am not eating, there is nothing to occupy my time. I have no playing cards or games. Denied my knitting, although I have a needle and some thread to mend any ripped garments, I have started picking the loose filaments from the fabric that has been nailed to wooden frames hanging on the stone walls to warm the cell, using straight pins to make a crude sort of lace with the threads, and employing my knee as a board. And with so much time for despairing thoughts, I have sought to escape in the only way I can for now— through adventure stories. Michonis has delivered some volumes from Louis's library and it brings me comfort to imagine my husband reading these same pages; *The Voyages of Captain Cook* and *Un Voyage à Venise,* which mentions people I knew when I was a child. *A History of Famous Shipwrecks* was a particular favorite of the late king's. Louis had a reverence for books; if he only knew that I, having never been a reader, was finally developing my own romance with them! Abbé Vermond, too, wherever he is, would undoubtedly be amused, for now I crave the sort of information he tried to cram into my girlish head.

The following day Madame Richard comes to my cell with a special companion and I scramble behind the screen to change my linen before I will let them see me. I have started bleeding quite profusely again, an ailment that continues to plague me. When the concierge's wife notices that I have left my dinner tray untouched, she inquires whether I am well. "You are dreadfully pale, madame," she remarks.

"It's nothing. A stomach complaint," I lie.

With maternal solicitousness, she promises to have Rosalie bring me a bowl of beef bouillon. "Madame Larivière makes it herself." And then she introduces me to the boy standing by her side. "This is my youngest. We call him Fanfan," she says, tousling his blond hair.

François Richard is an exceptionally beautiful child, the sort that Gainsborough is so fond of painting, with enormous china-blue eyes and soft curls. I sink to my knees and clasp him in my arms. "How old are you, *mon petit*?" I murmur.

Fanfan looks to his mother before replying. "Eight," he says proudly.

"You're the same age as *my* little boy!" I exclaim, clasping the surprised child to my breast. I smother Fanfan with kisses, caressing his hair, his cheeks. And then, the dam bursts and I find myself unable to control my tears. Hugging the concierge's son reminds me just how much I miss Louis Charles. Over my sobs I show them the lock of hair, and a little yellow glove I have preserved as mementoes, rhapsodizing about my own boy, his sweet, innocent, obedient nature, and my heartbreak over his reeducation. "He has such a tremendous desire to please his elders, to give them the answers they want whenever they ask him a question." Covering Fanfan's ears I tell Madame Richard, "Citoyen Simon and his wife are teaching him to say the most appalling things about his relations. Michonis brings me word of my family, although he is not supposed to divulge anything."

I embrace Fanfan tightly, as if my affection for him could somehow be transferred to *my* son, and the little king would once again feel his mother's embrace, know her undying love. But the poor child isn't sure how to react when this strange woman with the white hair fusses and fawns over him. When he looks to his mother again, I apologize profusely to Madame Richard. "I did not expect to become this sensitive. It is so very difficult for me to be separated from my children. Night and day, I think of them every moment."

They bid me adieu, and Fanfan even offers me a shallow bow. That evening, old Madame Larivière brings me a steaming bowl of bouillon and reminds me that I need my strength.

"For what?" I sigh. "Jacques Hébert wants to kill me." My hand trembles as I try to steady the silver spoon and fill it with broth. From my pocket I retrieve the latest delivery from Citoyen Michonis, an excerpt from a recent edition of *Père Duchesne* that he smuggled into my cell in his boot. In a low, hollow voice I read, " 'I have promised my adherents, as well as the National Convention, Antoinette's head. If there is any further delay in giving it to me, I will cut it off myself.' "

The soup spoon slips from my grasp and clatters to the floor.

On the fifth day after my arrival at the Conciergerie, Monsieur Richard visits my cell with Michonis. Their expressions are grim. "*Je regrette,* Citoyenne Capet," the jailer begins, visibly uncomfortable with his errand. "But the authorities have demanded the forfeit of your watch."

I spin about, and lift the chain from the nail on the wall, clasping the golden timepiece in my fist. "It belonged to my father, Francis of Lorraine. It is all I have left of him, messieurs, all I have left of my"—I am about to say "homeland," but think better of it. "My childhood."

"Do not humiliate yourself, madame, by forcing us to pry it from your fingers," Michonis says coolly, and I am reminded that even though he brings me word of my children's welfare, he is not my friend. I have no friends here. I cannot let them destroy this treasure by wresting it from me, and so I uncurl my fingers and hold out my hand, like a little girl showing her governess what she discovered while playing in the meadow. I kiss the watch as if it were a sacred relic. The metal lies heavily in my palm, but when

Citoyen Richard takes it my burden feels infinitely heavier. Now, when my departure from this realm is only a matter of days, they will take the one item they let me have upon entering it. From this moment on, one gloomy hour will be like any other, blurring into the next.

I have run out of time.

THIRTY-ONE

Carnations and Deprivations

One morning soon after, I awaken to see a strange woman sitting in my cell, watching me with the unwavering attention a mother bird bestows upon her fledglings. Her small eyes and Roman nose, a hawklike beak, only enhance this illusion. "Who are you?" I whisper anxiously. The woman does not reply, but continues to regard me as though I have in some way irritated her merely by virtue of my presence.

When Rosalie arrives with my breakfast tray, lowering it onto the little table by my cot, she murmurs, "I see you have met Madame Harel."

"Is that her name? She has not spoken a single word to me since I have risen. Why is she here?"

Rosalie sighs. "A representative from the National Convention came to the prison last night. They heard somehow that Madame Larivière has gone out of her way to make you comfortable. She has been relieved of her duties. Madame Harel has been assigned to look after you from now on."

Look *at* me would be closer to the truth. So, the newcomer is to remain seated in that chair night and day, her brief to observe everything I do, everyone I speak to, everything I say. For a moment I pity the homely Madame Harel, for she is as much a prisoner as I am. "But what about you?" I ask Rosalie.

She smiles coyly. "I am Madame Richard's personal maidservant, and I do what madame bids me. And Madame Richard has asked me to dress your hair today." She takes the length of white ribbon from her pocket and begins to arrange my coiffure, sprinkling my parted hair with a bit of scented powder, then binding the ends with the ribbon, firmly tying a knot before twisting my tresses and pinning them to the top of my head in a loose chignon.

Observing this procedure, Madame Harel scowls.

"I can dress myself," I say hastily, indicating the black silk dress draped over the other chair. Having taught myself to lace my stays and gown without Rosalie's assistance, I do so, then look for my plum satin heels. The cell is so small, they could not have gone far. Not finding them, I don a different pair.

The shoes are not located until Officers Gilbert and Dufresne relieve the gendarmes who guard my cell during the day. Citoyen Gilbert had begun to clean them for me, using his sword to scrape away the mold that, owing to the cell's dampness, had settled upon the satin. I humbly thank him, but when I feel Madame Harel's eyes upon me, I fear that the chivalrous gendarme may be removed from his post as well. I have no doubt that the woman is an informer.

I begin to settle into a routine, reading and tatting to pass the time. Rosalie has noticed that I have developed the habit whenever I grow anxious or bored of taking off my rings, rolling them about my palm, and then putting them back on my fingers again. Only to her do I confide my feminine distress: the unnatural bleeding. To help me stanch and conceal it, she rips up her own chemises and brings me the strips of fabric to hide under my bolster.

On the 28th of August, the prison administrator enters my cell with a round-faced man whose dark blue suit is splotched with mud. I wonder if it is raining outside. Apart from the stifling heat that gums my clothes to my body, I have no notion of what the weather is like beyond the prison walls. I cannot even hear when raindrops spatter the stones in the courtyard.

I recognize the Chevalier de Rougeville as the gallant soul who helped me to safety when the Tuileries was stormed last June, although he is aghast to see me so altered. "I am afraid I have aged considerably in the last year, monsieur," I say, making small talk. While Michonis converses with the guards, the chevalier removes his two boutonnieres and tosses the carnations toward the rear wall of the cell, near my bucket of slops. He arches an eyebrow. I answer with an uncomprehending look. We play this little charade for a few moments until finally de Rougeville draws closer and whispers, "Pick up the flowers; there is a note concealed within the petals of each of them."

In recent days Madame Harel has become weary of staring at me without surcease. As my activity has not been terribly entertaining to her, she has grown somewhat less vigilant, allowing herself to join the gendarmes' games of cards. To my relief, their assignments have been reversed and the sympathetic Officer Gilbert now guards me during the daylight hours.

Approaching him and interrupting his game, "Monsieur, I beg your pardon, but I think there is something in my vegetable dish." I point to my dinner tray. "I would not complain . . . but I think it is still alive." I make a dreadful face and he takes my meaning.

"That is indeed unpalatable. I will see to it right away, madame." Officer Gilbert rises from his chair to speak to Michonis, who is peering through the iron grille at the activity in the Cour des Femmes.

While Citoyen Gilbert busies himself with the complaint, I bend down to retrieve the carnations and read the messages on the scraps of paper secreted within them. *I am your faithful servant with a well-conceived plan of escape; I will come again on Friday,* says one. The other reads, *I have men and three or four hundred louis for bribes at my disposal.*

Color rushes to my cheeks for the first time in months; I start to tremble.

I have no pen and ink with which to write a reply. But I do have a scrap of paper. Using one of the pins I employ for my crude efforts at lacemaking I prick out a response: *Je suis gardée à vue, je ne parle à personne. Je me fie à vous. Je viendrai*—I am watched closely, I speak to no one. I place my trust in you. I will come.

Later in the day I slip the note to Officer Gilbert, who will pass it to the chevalier.

There is nothing to do now but wait and pray.

On the night of September 2, Michonis returns and my cell is unlocked. "Prisoner 280, we have orders to take you back to the Temple," announces the prison administrator loudly. The guards shoulder their muskets and flank our party. When they pause to open one of the wicket gates that punctuate the prison corridors, Michonis puts his finger to his lips and whispers to me, "The Chevalier de Rougeville is outside the prison with a carriage waiting to bring you to Jarjayes's home on the outskirts of Paris; from there you will be conveyed into Germany."

One by one, the padlocks on the wicket gates are opened. And suddenly—just one more set of bolts lies between me and freedom.

After we pass through the final gate, with the sentries' eyes upon us, Officer Gilbert halts abruptly. "Show me the order," he tells Michonis.

Michonis pales. "It—it comes directly from Citoyen Robespierre," he stammers.

"Then there will be a paper with Robespierre's signature on it. The head of the Committee of Public Safety is most methodical." I have never seen Gilbert so officious. What has come over him? Not only has he always been most solicitous of my welfare, but there was money to bribe him for his complicity.

"We—we only have his word," protests Michonis.

"I find that highly unlikely," the guard replies suspiciously. "When you show me the order with Citoyen Robespierre's signature affixed to it, I will release Prisoner 280 into your custody."

The plot has collapsed.

Michonis departs, ostensibly to obtain the "order," although none will of course be forthcoming and I know he will never return. I am escorted back to my cell. The following day I hear that the chevalier managed to disappear into the night, but Citoyen Michonis has been imprisoned right here in the Conciergerie.

I am visited by a pair of officials from the Convention. Their interrogation begins with a scrap of paper they confiscated from Michonis, peppered with pinpricks. My heart plummets. "The prison administrator tells us he was talked into conducting a man whom he had never before met into paying a call to your cell, and he gave you this," says one, handing me my own reply to the Chevalier de Rougeville. They have it wrong, but they still may know too much. "We took a rubbing of it with a pencil, but it makes no sense. Perhaps you understand it." Then they hand me their investigative efforts. Someone—most likely Michonis—added more pinpricks to the paper, completely obscuring my message.

I shrug, "I have no idea what this is, messieurs. The pastime of someone who was bored, perhaps?"

"Did you recognize the visitor who arrived with Citoyen Michonis?"

"No, messieurs, I did not," I say evenly. "I thought he was an officer of the guards, but if I ever knew his name I have forgotten it. There have been so many."

Their interrogation is uncomfortable, particularly when they divulge the chain of betrayal. The Chevalier de Rougeville's louis, however generous, were no match for the threat of the guillotine. The gendarme Gilbert showed the scrap of paper to Madame Richard, who, fearful of recriminations, brought it to the attention of the prison administrator, who took it from her but dismissed it as likely having little importance. Yet Gilbert did not wish to risk reprisals for not doing his job properly as it was already becoming known that he had done me a kindness by cleaning my shoe.

Within a few days I am deprived of anything the prison has previously deemed a luxury. The mattresses are destroyed in the search for contraband. Most of my linen is confiscated because they fear I will write and receive messages on the garments in invisible ink. They take my two rings, the last of my jewelry from Louis. At least I am permitted my caps and fichus. Never again will I be allowed any flowers in my cell, and I will be allotted no special privileges when it comes to my meals.

On the same day that Monsieur and Madame Richard are relieved of their duties, arrested, and themselves incarcerated, I am moved to a cell smelling of tinctures—a former pharmacy, I am told, with a new door two inches thick—and my guards are replaced with revolutionary zealots. The new concierge and his wife, Monsieur and Madame Bault, are grim and gruff, but from the way Madame Bault regards me, it is clear that she is too frightened to show me the slightest bit of kindness or humanity. She informs me that the Convention has warned her, she would pay with her life if I were not treated with severity.

Only Rosalie remains. Madame Richard would not allow her to join them in prison, and so she stayed on at the Conciergerie as a serving girl. She brings me her own chemises now because all but one of mine was confiscated in the wake of what the National Convention has dubbed the Carnation Plot. My candles have been taken, too, which means that I cannot read at night, or make my lace. The windows are boarded up.

Monsieur Bault is the very image of a *sans-culotte,* rudely bareheaded, and wearing the short red *carmagnole* jacket of the revolutionaries. The first time he enters my cell, he finds Rosalie about to coif my hair and, to my surprise, announces that the task is among his duties as concierge. I cannot imagine this coarse man touching me. "Rosalie, I wish you to put up my chignon today," I say, making sure that Monsieur Bault understands my preference.

"Leave it alone, citoyenne, it's my job," he says boldly, elbowing Rosalie out of the way.

"Non, merci, monsieur," I reply politely. I twist my hair myself and pin it to my head. Handing Rosalie the length of white ribbon, I murmur, "Take this, and keep it always, in memory of me."

She pockets the adornment and leaves the cell with the new concierge.

Yet Rosalie continues to risk her life for me. I shiver at night under my thin cotton coverlet but when Monsieur Bault refuses to provide a woolen blanket, insisting that Citoyen Fouquier-Tinville, the Public Prosecutor, has threatened him with the guillotine, she takes my nightgown and the large fichu that I wrap about my shoulders at night, and brings them to her own room to warm in front of the fire before placing them back under my bolster.

"Step lively. Don't push. She's not going anywhere!" Monsieur Bault chuckles, while a line of people parade past my cell as if I am a circus attraction. I can just imagine him printing macabre handbills proclaiming STEP RIGHT UP AND SEE THE *CI-DEVANT* QUEEN

OF FRANCE IN HER NATURAL HABITAT! As a snaggle-toothed man in wooden sabots passes, I notice Citoyen Bault pocketing a silver coin.

The new concierge's entrepreneurial enterprise goes on for days. Men and women of all stripes file past to goggle at me. Occasionally I see a former friend, a baronne or marquise in disguise who casts me a sympathetic look and whispers news of people we once knew.

The portraitist Alexander Kucharsky comes to paint me, and I am surprised that he is permitted to see me; surely sitting to a painter would be considered a luxury. But perhaps the National Convention will be pleased with the results because I hardly present the glamorous monarch limned so often by Madame Vigée-Lebrun in plumed headdresses and opulent, furbelowed gowns as wide as the canvas itself, or portrayed as a dairymaid in my straw hats and muslin *gaulles* with their pastel-hued silken sashes. Kucharsky's Antoinette is a shadow of her former self, her hair whitened, not with scented powder, but with grief, the Widow Capet of the nation's fantasies.

Most visitors to Monsieur Bault's lurid sideshow are *sans-culottes* who have come to gloat and *tricoteuses* who have taken a holiday from their front-row vantages at the executions in the Place de la Révolution as the hungry Reign of Terror claims its daily feast of blood. The hags cackle and jab at me through the bars with their knitting needles. My own were confiscated for fear I would employ them as weapons, and yet these red-bonneted harpies may carry them with impunity into the Conciergerie.

One day I spy a young woman amid the crowd bearing a different sort of weapon altogether—a chisel. I call out to my guards, for I fear she means to do some harm, forgetting for the moment the heavy bars that separate me from the rabble. Of course, she still might stab someone else. There is a scuffle outside the cell when a pair of gendarmes appear and pin the woman's arms behind her back, wresting the chisel from her grasp.

Immediately, the pretty young woman becomes hysterical. "Please, messieurs—I meant no harm! I am an artist. The tool you have taken from me is the only thing of value that I own besides my talent." She carries it everywhere, she says, because you cannot be too careful nowadays. With so many going hungry, people will steal anything in the hopes of selling it at a pawnshop for a sou or two that will buy half a loaf of bread.

At her mention of bread I begin to pay closer attention to the confrontation. Somewhere, in the dim recesses of my memory, I believe, perhaps, that I may have seen her before. Did she work at Versailles? In the kitchens, perhaps? Yet what cause would I have had to cross paths with a kitchen lackey? Nonetheless, I am certain I saw her at Versailles, although I cannot place the occasion.

"*Laissez,*" I command, and hope that someone will heed me. "Leave her alone. She means to do me no harm." *Unlike most of the rest of you,* I wish I could say.

Begrudgingly, the gendarmes relax their grip on the young woman, and return her chisel. She turns to me with a look of pure gratitude in her dark eyes, eyes that well with empathy and almost fill with tears; and because these days I am acutely aware of the value of a grateful expression, suddenly I remember that look and where I have seen it. She looked at my husband that way when each of them was in direst straits. If ever I learned her name, now would not be the time to use it. The last thing I should wish to do would be to imperil her life.

Autumn has arrived. The encroaching darkness is only one reason I begin to lose track of time. On the 5th of October the National Convention abolishes the Gregorian calendar, replacing it with the French Republican calendar. Weeks now have ten days, and the months have silly names redolent of weather or seasons of the year. Every day celebrates an animal, natural element, or aspect of vegetation. Roman numerals have replaced Arabic ones, so it is no longer 1793, but the year II, because the Convention has begun the new Republic with the year the idea of the calendar was first introduced. And it is not October anymore. I am told that this month, named for the time of the grape harvest, is Vendémiaire. From now on, the start of every month falls sometime between what had been the 22nd and 24th of the months on the old Gregorian calendar. I cannot imagine how most of France, people who can barely read, will commit all of this arcane nonsense to memory.

One night I have a dream that Rosalie is bringing me her white ribbon, but as soon as I take it in my hands it turns black. Then Rose Bertin visits my cell, bearing a stick full of ribbons in a panoply of colors—crimson, apple green, buttercup, royal blue, rose, violet, peach, lilac, and vermillion, but no sooner do I touch *them,* than each one becomes black, the color of death, and I dash them to the floor in horror.

They come for me on the evening of October 12. I have been expecting them. For the past several nights I have slept in my clothes, anticipating the summons to the guillotine. I intend to honor it in my widow's weeds.

The padlocks on my cell are opened to admit six armed guards, prepared to escort me across the cobbled courtyard to the building that once housed the Grande Chambre of the Parlement de Paris, the same hall where Louis had conducted many *lits de justice,* as well as the location of the sham trial of *l'affaire du collier,* the affair of the diamond necklace, where my nemesis the Cardinal de Rohan was exonerated by his peers and the clever confidence artist, the comtesse de Lamotte-Valois, was sentenced to branding and imprisonment.

With blue-coated soldiers in front of me and behind, I mount a winding stone staircase that leads to the hall with its High Gothic columns and black and white tiled floor. Only two candles illuminate the vast space, lending the home of the Revolutionary Tribunal, known nowadays without irony as the Hall of Freedom, the funereal glow of a crypt. There have been changes since I last entered it. In the niche once dominated by an enormous painting of the Crucifixion are busts of fallen heroes of revolutions past and present—Brutus and Marat.

Two men are seated behind a long table, the candlelight sculpting their faces with ghoulish shadow. I recognize one of them by his jutting chin and low forehead—the Public Prosecutor, Antoine Quentin Fouquier-Tinville. With exaggerated politeness he introduces his confederate, Nicolas Hermann, the examining magistrate. Like a pair of crows, both men are garbed entirely in black. Around each of their necks hangs a medal inscribed with the ominous words *La Loi*—The Law. They wear the round hats that are fashionable now, their brims turned up jauntily at the front, and embellished at the side of the crown with the fluffy black egret plumes I once used to adorn my riding *chapeaux*.

Fouquier-Tinville bids me take a seat on a hard bench opposite the table. In the shadows a stenographer sits with his quill poised. Regardless of what I say, I am condemned; before the Revolutionary Tribunal there is no appeal.

Citoyen Hermann commences the interrogation, explaining that our meeting is simply a preliminary hearing, meaning, I suppose, that this is merely the beginning of what we all know is a preposterous charade designed to be a sop to those who believe that the former Queen of France should at least have a trial before she is judged guilty of all the crimes against the Nation for which she stands accused.

Hermann begins by demanding whether I coerced Citizen

Louis Capet to affix his veto, despite the protests of the Minister of Justice, Antoine Duranton.

"Duranton was not yet the Minister of Justice," I reply calmly. "And in any event, my husband never needed anyone to persuade him to do his duty. Besides, these matters were decided in Council. As I expect you know, monsieur, queens of France are merely consorts to the monarch; as such, I was never a member of the Council and was never a party, nor even in the room, when such decisions were taken."

He does not like my answer. But I have no other. Citoyen Hermann changes the subject, certain that he will entrap me in a response that will condemn me.

"Before the Revolution, you had a relationship with the king of Hungary and Bohemia," he states.

I assume he refers to Joseph II, or perhaps Leopold. "Are you suggesting that it is unusual for a sister to be related to her older brother?"

Monsieur Hermann goes on to accuse me of ruining the nation's finances "in a terrible way" by sending wagonloads of gold to my brother. "You, Citoyenne Capet, have dissipated for your personal pleasures the fruits of the people of France, the sweat of their labors, in collusion with the ministers of state, sending millions to the emperor—funds to be used against the very people who have nourished you." Again I deny his charges. It is clear that he has believed a fiction perpetrated for years by my detractors.

"You were the maleficent one who taught Louis Capet that profound art of dissimulation which for so long he used to deceive the good people of France."

"It is true, monsieur, that for years the 'good people' of France were deceived—cruelly deceived—but not by my husband, nor by myself."

Citoyen Hermann leans forward, steepling his tapered fingers. His shadow looms upon the wall. "By whom, then?"

"By those with an interest in deceiving them. It was not in our interest to deceive them."

"Who then, in your opinion, are the persons who intended to deceive the people?"

I will not allow him to trick me by mentioning any of the architects of the Revolution or even its early blue-blooded adherents, such as the king's own deep-pocketed cousin the duc d'Orléans, who fooled the people only temporarily by changing his name to Philippe Égalité, for he may all too soon suffer the same fate as I. "I do not know, monsieur. Our own interest has always been to enlighten the people, not to mislead them."

My interrogator is becoming more exasperated by the minute. Growing red in the face, he raises his voice. "Never—never for a moment, Citoyenne Capet, did you and your husband desist from your plan to destroy the liberty of the French people. It was your aim to reign at any price, even if it meant you had to step over the battered, bloodied, and bruised bodies of dead patriots to reascend the throne!"

"We had no need to reascend the throne. We were already there," I reply, correcting his facts. "And we never desired anything but France's happiness."

"If this were true, citoyenne, you would not have incited your brother to make war upon France."

This time, the examining magistrate has utterly reversed the facts to suit his line of questioning. I gently remind him that it was France who had declared war upon Austria.

"But were you not interested in the military successes of France's enemies?" Citoyen Hermann has the relentless determination of a dog who fears that someone will confiscate his bone.

"I am interested in the success of the nation to which my son belongs."

"And what nation is that?" Hermann sneers.

"Isn't he French?" I ask rhetorically.

"I suppose you regret that your son has lost a throne that he would have mounted had not the people, awakening at long last to their rights of liberty, destroyed his opportunity."

"I shall never regret my son's loss of anything, if his loss proves to be his country's gain."

"Do you believe kings are necessary for the happiness of the people, citoyenne?"

"It is not for me to say. An individual cannot decide such a question."

Irked because he has not been able to trick me into making an incriminating statement, the examining magistrate continues to barrage me with questions, commingling fact with fiction by accusing me of "instigating Louis Capet's treason in June of 1791. It was you, citoyenne, who advised and encouraged—perhaps even persecuted—him into attempting to leave France."

For an educated man, his knowledge of geography is appalling— unless his intent is to perpetuate revolutionary propaganda. Montmédy, which had been our final destination, is of course within the nation's borders. "It was never the king's intention to leave France," I reply truthfully.

Hermann's frustration is written on his face.

Then he accuses me of entering into negotiations with foreign powers since the Revolution began. I steady my breath. "What proofs do you have?" I inquire calmly. Hermann's mouth twitches and he casts a brief sideways glance at the Public Prosecutor. I resist the urge to exhale with relief. They have nothing. And in soberest truth, this is the only treasonable offense I have engaged in. The rest of the charges are thoroughly invented. But that will not stop the Revolutionary Tribunal from convicting and sentencing me.

In all, the examining magistrate puts thirty-five questions to me during this preliminary hearing before demanding that I name an advocate to defend me at the impending trial. Perspiration beads upon my brow although the hall is cold. "I do not know anyone, messieurs," I admit.

"Then the court will appoint an advocate to represent you," the Public Prosecutor says. They are the first words Fouquier-Tinville has uttered in more than two hours.

The man chosen by the Revolutionary Tribunal is Claude Chauveau-Lagarde, already a distinguished lawyer from Chartres when he made his name by defending Marat's murderess Charlotte Corday. Her fate, too, was a foregone conclusion.

I meet Chauveau-Lagarde for the first time when he visits my cell in the Conciergerie the next day, bearing Fouquier-Tinville's eight-page indictment. My trial is scheduled to begin the following morning. I regard his earnest face, his large, intelligent brown eyes, and see a sacrificial lamb.

THIRTY-TWO

I Will Not Let Them Break Me

≈ OCTOBER 1793 ≈

"We don't have much time," Chauveau-Lagarde says. "I am sorry."

I see him glancing about the cell at the pair of guards, at Madame Harel in her stained mobcap, scowling as ever. "Do not expect us to be permitted any privacy," I tell him. He has the conscientious look of a man of genuine integrity who does not regard his commission from the Revolutionary Tribunal as a joke, but views it instead as a monumental challenge. Aware that the odds are insurmountable, he wishes nonetheless to build the best possible defense.

I study his face as he reads the indictment: Although Monsieur Chauveau-Lagarde is only a year younger than I am, time has been far kinder to him. "It is a matter of law that I read the indictment to you so that you may hear the charges in full," my advocate tells me, as if it were not a matter of life and death, or more accurately, death. Untying the scroll, he begins, "'An examination of the relevant documents,'" and then enumerates a list of queens of France to whom the indictment compares me, from Messalina to the Medicis—never mind that the first was an infamous Roman and that the other notorious women on the list (Brunhilda the Visigoth, and the ruthlessly sadistic Frédégonde, a Merovingian Queen), predate the kingdoms of Austria and France as we know them. "Please, madame, it is the law; I must read the full indictment to you." At my frustrated nod, he continues. "'Like these queens whose names will forever be odious and who will never be removed from the pages of history, the Widow Capet, Marie Antoinette, has, ever since her arrival in France, been to the French people a curse and a bloodsucker.'"

This is the preamble to a formal document?

The indictment reiterates the subjects I was questioned about yesterday: my political relations with the "King of Bohemia and Hungary," my brother Joseph, to whom I had allegedly sent millions; an "orgy" I had allegedly prompted when we entertained the Flemish regiment at Versailles shortly before the people stormed it in 1789; accusations that I have been responsible for the massacre of loyal patriots (they have corrupted the truth of everything!) and that I have betrayed France's military plans to her enemies.

"I would be an inept attorney were I to allow you to be surprised during the interrogation," Chauveau-Lagarde tells me, visibly uncomfortable, "but it pains me to know that the following charges will appall you. The accusation that follows is Jacques Hébert's. It reads: *That the Widow Capet is so perverted that, forgetting she is a mother, and ignoring the boundaries of nature, she has practiced with her own son Louis Charles Capet those indecencies avowed by the latter, whose very name invoke a shudder.*"

I scarcely dare to comprehend his meaning. Tangled as the verbiage is, can the vile Hébert be insinuating that I have physically violated my child? And that Louis Charles has confessed to it? My eyes sting with tears. "Of course this is untrue! How can anyone believe such a heinous accusation?"

"You must be prepared to fully rebut it at trial," Chauveau-Lagarde replies. "As well as the next charge in the indictment, which is no less ludicrous." Adjusting his spectacles he reads, *"That the Widow Capet pushed the bounds of dissimulation and perfidy to such an extent as to compose, print, and distribute pamphlets and caricatures in which she herself was depicted in a lewd and undesirable manner, in order to lay a false scent that would persuade the foreign powers that the French were grossly maligning her character. Moreover, it is Citoyenne Capet who is the true author of the memoirs and pamphlets allegedly written by the comtesse de Lamotte-Valois revealing the former queen's libidinous desires with persons of both sexes as well as the passionate Sapphic relationship between the queen and the comtesse."*

My hand flies to my mouth in horror. "That is an absurd fiction! Do they expect right-thinking men to swallow such nonsense?" But no sooner are the words out of my mouth than I have my answer. For so long the people have been willing to believe everything else: that I was solely responsible for bankrupting France, that I am sexually rapacious, that I controlled my husband's every breath, that I channeled wagonloads of gold to the Austrian emperor, even that I suggested that the starving people eat cake instead of bread when a harvest had been poor—a comment that makes no sense no matter how one looks at it, nor would it be my nature to say something so insensitive.

Chauveau-Lagarde has been shaking his head as he reads the indictment, shocked at its vitriolic tone. Sadly, I am unsurprised. "They hate me, monsieur, with a passion I believe to be unequaled in history. I am like the Biblical scapegoat, condemned to die for every ill that has ever befallen the nation."

The lawyer looks stricken. "Your trial is scheduled to commence tomorrow morning. And with regard to every one of these allegations there are sheaves of papers, mountains to be sorted and reviewed in order for me and my colleague, Tronson Docoudray, to mount your defense. Monsieur Docoudray is also a Parisian *avocat,* very well respected, but to prepare our case overnight is a Herculean task. There are so many different charges to refute and these documents—it would take weeks just to sift through them." Chauveau-Lagarde rakes his hand through his lightly powdered brown hair. "I urge you, madame, to demand an adjournment of three days. It would give me the bare minimum of time I will need to comb through all the documents and exhibits and prepare an adequate speech on your behalf."

"To whom would I make such a request?"

"To the Convention."

"No, never!" This I cannot do. These men already hold all the cards; I will not grovel before them.

"It must not be a point of pride, madame." He watches me struggling with my conscience. "If not for your own sake, then you must think of your son and daughter."

It has not taken him long to find my Achilles' heel. I am not permitted quill and ink but my advocate carries a portable writing desk, and so I put pen to paper, saying that I owe it to my children to allow my attorneys, who received their assignment only hours ago, to do everything in their power to justify their mother's conduct.

The appeal is delivered to Robespierre. But in the event that no reply is forthcoming, my defenders continue to prepare my case all through the night. It is fortunate for me that they have done so, for indeed, my plea goes unanswered; and at eight in the morning on the fourteenth of October, I am returned to the Grand Chambre.

* * *

Rosalie had helped me dress in the long black mourning gown that Mademoiselle Bertin had made for me, so lovingly patched by Madame Larivière. My white locks were tucked beneath a freshly starched white linen cap, over which Rosalie affixed my black crepe mourning veil. "You are so pale, madame," she murmured.

"I am bleeding quite a lot this morning." I confided. "For the past four days it has not stopped."

"Do you need more strips? I can rip up another chemise." She lowered her voice even further. "You do not know how long they will keep you and even though your gown and petticoat are black, you do not wish of course, to have"—she lowered her gaze and blushed—"any accidents." I could see she was mortified to discuss something so intimate, so humiliating, with the former Queen of France.

"How much time do I have? They took my watch, you know."

"I will be quick," she assured me.

And so my purse was stuffed with the sacrifice of Rosalie's own garments, to render me the slightest bit more comfortable during what was certain to be the most excruciating day of my life since the death of my husband.

I am escorted into the Grand Chambre by my two defenders. Chauveau-Lagarde wears a royal blue coat. Tronson's coat is green. I wonder whether their sartorial choices were made consciously; the blue is obvious, but green has become the color of counterrevolution.

The five judges and dozen members of the jury are dwarfed by the majesty of the room with its gilded Gothic vaulting. The revolutionaries have not bothered to paint over the gold fleurs-de-lis on the red and blue columns. Much of the décor is obscured, however, by the enormous crowd seated shoulder to shoulder, completely filling the two galleries of benches. I have never seen so many *bonnets rouge* in one room. The *tricoteuses* barely have room to spread their elbows; do they expect to knit throughout my trial the way they do during a full day of executions in the Place de la Révolution? A plain wooden balustrade is all that separates the area delineated for the trial from the lowest row of the gallery.

I am conducted to the witness seat, a hard wooden armchair. Louis had been permitted an upholstered chair with padded arms during his trial. I am keenly aware of the distinctions between the treatment they afforded to my husband (inasmuch as the perpetrators of the Revolution sought to eliminate him as the embodiment of the monarchy they believed had for centuries enslaved the people of France), and to me, whom they consider the scourge of the nation.

Monsieur Chauveau-Lagarde hands me a slip of paper upon which he has written the professions of the jurors, men of the people, just as they are in the American system of justice. A jury of one's peers, they call it in that new nation. Yet the members of this panel are hardly the social equals of an archduchess of Austria and queen of France. I glance at the paper while Fouquier-Tinville, the Public Prosecutor, reads the indictment. To a man, including the marquis d'Antonelle, a former representative in the Legislative Assembly and an early supporter of the Revolution, every juror is a devoted follower of Fouquier-Tinville and Robespierre. The other eleven jurors are comprised of members of the bourgeoisie as well as the laboring class: a surgeon, a bookseller, a wigmaker, a clogmaker, the proprietor of a café, a hatter, an auctioneer, a carpenter, a former prosecutor, and a journalist. In scanning the Grand Chambre for a friendly face, I am disappointed. I do spy a familiar one, however: the young sculptress who came to gawk at me in the Conciergerie. She peers at me intently as if she wants to draw my portrait.

I pocket the scrap of paper bearing the jurors' names. Pince-nez perched on his long hooked nose, Fouquier-Tinville is still reading the indictment. I sit rigidly, my expression impassive, while the charges against me, ludicrous and insidious, are announced to a bloodthirsty crowd. I catch Chauveau-Lagarde casting a surreptitious glance at my right hand and I realize I have been absent-mindedly running my fingers along the arm of the chair like it was the keyboard of a *clavecin*.

A hush falls over the hall as Nicolas Hermann, the examining magistrate, opens the interrogation. "Will the accused state her name, age, and occupation."

I speak clearly, but not loudly, and without emotion. I am cold and my lips are dry and chapped. "I was Maria Antonia of Austria and Lorraine, called Marie Antoinette when I came to France to wed. I am the widow of the former King of the French, the man you call Louis Capet. I am at present thirty-seven years old." Dare I hope that they will allow me to awaken on the morning of my thirty-eighth birthday on the second of November?

But before any more questions are put to me, the prosecution begins to present its case. Chauveau-Lagarde informs me that they intend to present forty-one witnesses against me and one by one we will have the opportunity to rebut their testimony. The interrogations and cross-examinations will undoubtedly last for hours. I can feel how heavily I am bleeding and am aware how weak and pale the loss of blood makes me, but I am determined not to appear frail or sickly during the trial. It is a Hapsburg, a Bourbon, who is in the defendant's chair, and at all costs I will maintain my dignity.

If it is some consolation to my defense, Fouquier-Tinville's case is surprisingly disorganized, with no regard to chronology, and his witnesses, who have not been vetted for credibility, testify to all sorts of nonsense, from hearsay at best, to utter fictions.

They depose a former serving maid from Versailles named Reine ("queen," of all things!) Milliot, a girl I barely remember, who tells the jurors that in 1788 she heard the duc de Coigny tell someone else—whose name she cannot recall—that I had sent my brother, the emperor Joseph, two hundred million louis. Two more witnesses swear under oath that they saw remittances for the money.

"When and where did you see them?" challenges Chauveau-Lagarde. Each witness mumbles that they cannot remember. My defender then demands that the remittances themselves or other tangible proofs be produced, to which Fouquier-Tinville admits that the prosecution has no such documents in its possession, nor, in reply to my advocate's next question, knows of any.

The Public Prosecutor then asks me directly, "Since your marriage, has it not been one of your chief aims to reunite Lorraine—which has been in the possession of France since before you were born—with Austria?"

"No, monsieur, it has not."

"But you are *Marie Antoinette d'Autriche-Lorraine,*" Fouquier-Tinville says emphatically, as if I don't know my own name.

Does the man know nothing about royalty? "Because, monsieur," I say patiently, "one has to bear the name of one's country."

Another lackey, a man I have never before seen, testifies that before the Revolution began, during the late 1780s, I carried a pair of pistols night and day with the intention of murdering the duc d'Orléans.

Fouquier-Tinville then commences a line of questioning about my purported extravagances. "Where did the money come from to build and furnish le Petit Trianon, the place where you hosted such lavish parties and where you played the goddess?"

"I did not build le Petit Trianon, monsieur. It was built by my husband's predecessor, King Louis Quinze, when I was a little girl, long before I came to France."

"But *you* spent massive amounts to renovate it," he sneers. "Where did you get that money?"

I notice the juror who I have decided must be the journalist scribbling down my answers in a little notebook. "The money came from a separate fund that was set aside for that purpose alone."

"It must have been quite a large fund, then, because the renovations for your little pleasure palace were both costly and extensive."

"I agree with you, Monsieur Fouquier-Tinville." The room inhales a collective gasp. "*C'est possible* that the Trianon cost immense sums—more than I would have wished. The expenditures were made incrementally. And no one would be more pleased than I to see the matter of the overages clarified and cleared up."

Out of the corner of my eye I see a glimmer of a smile on one or two of the jurors' faces. Or perhaps, buoyed by hope, I only imagine it. Nonetheless, the truth is on my side; all I need to do is utter it. If I do not dissemble, the Public Prosecutor cannot unsettle me. The calmer I remain, confident in honesty, the more frustrated Fouquier-Tinville becomes, conflating the allegations against me into a foul bouillabaisse.

"Is it not at le Petit Trianon where you first met the comtesse de Lamotte-Valois and where you subsequently trysted with her?"

"I never in my life met the Lamotte woman, monsieur."

"Wasn't she your unwitting victim in the notorious *affaire du collier*?"

"She could not have been, because I never met her."

"You *persist* upon denying that you knew her, madame?"

"I am not persisting upon denying anything, *monsieur le procureur*. I am only persisting upon speaking the truth."

Fouquier-Tinville gets nowhere with the charge that I wrote and publicized the comtesse's memoirs. I can see that the jurors do

not believe him. Nor has he any tangible proofs of such an allegation; and the same holds true for the charge that I was responsible
for writing, publishing, and disseminating the thousands upon
thousands of *libelles* that slandered me for so many years. The people may believe the pamphlets themselves, but they are not quite so
foolish as to think that I *wrote* them.

The day drags on. Owing to the vast crowd in the Great Hall
and the lack of ventilation, I grow hot and thirsty; finally Tronson,
my other defender, requests a glass of lemon water for me. Today is
the Feast of Saint Theresa, the name day of both my mother and
my daughter, and as such it is a day of fasting for me, but the court
takes a brief recess during the mid-afternoon so the jurors can eat
dinner. When I was a girl, the day was given over to celebrating
and rejoicing. What would Maman think to see me now? And
what of my poor, innocent Mousseline?

When the trial resumes, more witnesses are brought forward.
They attest to vast sums I am alleged to have paid to the duchesse
de Polignac and her family, including the furnishing of vouchers
that enabled her to draw upon the Civil List, which is funded by
the people's taxes. Under oath I state that I have had no correspondence with Madame de Polignac since my imprisonment. In reply
to the questions of the examining magistrate, Citoyen Hermann, I
clarify that "the wealth amassed by the Polignacs was due to the
positions they held at court. Should not people be paid a salary for
the work they do?"

Yet another witness, François Tisset, maintains that he had
seen my signature on vouchers authorizing sums to Gabrielle de
Polignac for as much as 80,000 livres, as well as vouchers signed by
the king for payments to various ministers.

"What was the date on those documents?" Chauveau-Lagarde
asks Tisset.

"August the tenth, 1792," the man replies confidently, smirking at the jurors. I realize I am holding my breath to avoid revealing my anger.

"All of them were dated August tenth, 1792?" my defender inquires.

"One was," Tisset amends. "I do not recall the other dates."

Chauveau-Largarde turns to me for a rebuttal. "I could hardly have dated anything on the tenth of August, 1792, nor could my husband, because that was the date the Tuileries was attacked and that morning we were taken into the protection of the National Assembly and incarcerated in the reporters' box behind the Great Hall for the remainder of the day. From there we were taken to the Couvent des Feuillants."

At this, my advocate asks Tisset if he still stands by his testimony. The witness darts his eyes to and fro, from the Public Prosecutor to the jurors, his face becoming paler by the moment. I wonder who has paid him to lie.

Chauveau-Lagarde then asks the Revolutionary Tribunal if they can produce the evidence of these financial transactions. Fouquier-Tinville squirms in his chair. Eventually he admits that the tribunal can produce no documentation in support of these allegations. Nor do they have any proof that corroborates the next prosecution witness's testimony that I sent the commanding officer of the Switzers a letter asking whether the monarchy could rely upon his men in the event of an uprising—presumably written sometime before the Tuileries was stormed either in June or August of last year.

"Where is this letter?" demands Chauveau-Lagarde, hooking his thumbs into the broad lapels of his coat, his habit, I have come to notice, when he grows confrontational. "Have you seen it with your own eyes?" The witness, the cousin of a former palace bootblack, who claims to have overheard someone else averring that I had written to the Switzers's commander, reddens and stammers his concession.

And on and on it goes throughout the long day, with each of the prosecution's witnesses being set up like pins and my defenders bowling them down one by one. The Revolutionary Tribunal has not one shred of evidence with which to convict me. If only this were a real court and not a sham. If only the truth mattered.

Not a single spectator has quit the hall, despite the late hour. Deep into the evening I am questioned about the royal family's flight to the frontier.

"Is it not true that you bent Louis Capet to your will and induced him to do whatever you wanted? You made use of his weak character to carry out your evil deeds."

"I never knew my husband to have such a character as you describe. And in any case, to advise a course of action and to actually make it manifest are two different things," I reply.

"That is not what your son told the Tribunal."

I suppress a shudder, imagining my terrified little boy uttering whatever the menacing, angry, frightening, threatening men coerced him into admitting, heedless of the truth, fearful that he would be beaten, or worse. "It is easy, Monsieur Hermann, to make a child of eight say whatever you wish him to."

"Who was the man who purchased the carriage you rode in?"

"It was a foreigner," I reply. Truthful, but evasive.

"From what nation?"

"Sweden," I say without hesitating, although my belly seizes with anxiety.

Hermann pounces like a cat upon a rolling ball of twine. "Was it not Count Axel von Fersen, who dwelled in Paris at the time?"

"*Oui,* monsieur."

And that, to my complete amazement, is the end of his inter-

rogation on this subject. Nothing further at all! Not a single question on where the money came from to depart, nothing on my
relationship with him. Perhaps they know nothing. I marvel how
the Revolutionary Tribunal can haul me before a jury on countless
charges, every one of which has been fabricated and for which they
have no legal proof, and yet they are blind, deaf, and dumb to the
facts of my life.

For a brief, pleasurable moment I feel as if I have just stepped
into a hip bath and my fear is melting away into the warm scented
water.

Finally, at eleven o'clock, Fouquier-Tinville's gavel descends
with a sharp crack. He announces that the remaining witnesses
will be interrogated tomorrow, beginning at eight in the morning.
It is after midnight by the time I am escorted back to my cell. Rosalie is waiting for me with a bowl of hot bouillon. "I have no appetite," I say as she unlaces me.

"You hardly took any nourishment today, and you need to keep
up your strength, madame," she replies with sweet solicitousness,
and for an instant I imagine that if she were highborn I would
make her a duchesse and commit my children into her care.

"You are too kind to me, Mademoiselle Lamorlière," I sigh.

A faint blush suffuses Rosalie's broad cheeks. "Only as kind as
you deserve, madame."

Morning comes too quickly. As I make my toilette before the
little mirror Rosalie had given me, I scarcely recognize the face I
see in the glass. The eyelids are swollen with weeping; the lids are
rimmed with red and shadowed with indigo demilunes of exhaustion and sleeplessness. My lips, even the famously protruding lower
one, are cracked and colorless. My skin, which the court painter
Madame Vigée-Lebrun once protested was impossible to duplicate
in oils because of its unique translucence, has lost its luster. My hair
is brittle and almost entirely white. I am not yet thirty-eight and I

surely look older than my mother did when she died at the age of sixty-three.

If it is possible, the Hall of Freedom, France's greatest contradiction, is more packed with humanity—another incongruity—than it was yesterday. My nostrils are assaulted as soon as I am escorted back to the unforgiving wooden chair; the Grand Chambre reeks of hundreds of malodorous armpits, unwashed garments, and all manner of rubbish from the *rues* clinging to the wooden soles of countless sabots.

The examining magistrate opens the second day of my trial by ordering a bailiff to empty the contents of the bag of "contraband" I had brought from the Temple to the Conciergerie. These are what remain of the personal effects they had not previously confiscated. Among the items tossed upon a table before the jurors are the locks of my children's hair as well as one of Louis's; two miniatures—one, a portrait of the princesse de Lamballe and the other of a childhood friend from Vienna, now the Landgravine of Hesse-Darmstadt; a notebook containing the names and addresses of Dr. Brunier and a laundress; and a piece of paper with "mysterious calculations" written upon it.

"That is my son's mathematics exercise," I tell the prosecutors. "Nothing more. It was the first time he solved every equation correctly. Proud mother that I am, I preserved it. I, myself, was an indifferent student at his age."

Jacques Hébert is then called to the witness box and sworn to tell the whole truth and nothing but the truth. He begins his testimony by boldly stating, "The accused is much more than a proud mother." His eyes glitter with malice. First, he claims that the Sacred Heart relic found among my possessions is a well-known counterrevolutionary symbol, proof alone of my perfidious, unwavering royalism. He adds that after the death of my husband I continued to adhere to royalist customs by placing my son at the head of the table to be served first as king.

"Did you see this yourself?" I demand.

Caught off guard, Hébert admits he was not an eyewitness. I am incensed, but I cannot show it. "We had no servants at the Temple after the king was executed," I say. "In fact, my son was seated at the foot of the table and I served him myself."

Hébert glares at me. "The prisoner and her defenders keep asking for proofs of each of the allegations against her. And on each occasion, the prosecution has had nothing to offer. I have provided to the Public Prosecutor and the examining magistrate a document signed by the accused's own son, Louis Charles Capet. It attests to the lewd and shameful *pollution indécentes* that his mother and his aunt, the *ci-devant* princesse Élisabeth, taught him to practice upon himself, and which they performed upon him, individually and collectively. This confession states that the child's own mother, and his aunt, made him lie down between them and on such occasions they forced him to pleasure them in unspeakable acts of debauchery." Hébert takes a document from his coat, unfolds and brandishes it. At the bottom of a few paragraphs written in a clearly adult hand is my son's signature in his childish looping scrawl, *Louis Charles Capet.*

The entire hall falls silent, rapt. I am literally made sick by this charge, the most heinous accusation anyone can level at a mother. But Hébert is not finished. "It is my belief that the accused wished to gain complete control over her son's mind because her plan was to one day regain the throne for him and become a regent as powerful as Catherine de Medici was in her day. To that purpose, she sought to gain control over the boy's body so that he could deny her nothing."

I need to vomit. I notice that even the demonic Fouquier-

Tinville is horrified at his deputy's allegation, because he, too, can read the shock on the jurors' faces. His famous eyebrows meet with worry. Hébert has gone too far. The men in the jury box are afraid for their lives if they do not render a guilty verdict—but they are not credulous fools.

Finally, Citoyen Hermann speaks. "What reply does the prisoner make to this accusation?"

I am trembling with rage and emotion. "I have no knowledge of the incidents Monsieur Hébert refers to."

This reply seems to be enough for the examining magistrate. I surmise from the look on his face that if he pursues it any further, things will only go hard for the prosecution. But then one of the jurors rises. "Citoyen President, I must ask you to draw the accused's attention to the fact that she has not answered Citoyen Hébert's allegation about what transpired between her and her son."

The examining magistrate glances down at his clasped hands and presses his lips into a grimace. A juror has demanded my response. He has no choice but to compel it.

I am hemorrhaging profusely. I have scarcely slept. But for the first time in two days of testimony, of absurd charges, calumnies, and abominations, I rise to my feet to refute the most lurid and pernicious of them all. "If I have not answered, it was because Nature herself refuses to answer such a charge against a mother," I reply, my voice filled with passion, with wrath, and with unimaginable pain. I turn to face the spectators—the *sans-culottes,* the *tricoteuses* who have paused mid-stitch, the young sculptress, the marketwomen and *poissardes,* nameless faces who hang upon my every word, and look them in the eyes, my own beginning to well with tears. "I appeal to all the mothers in this room."

For the second time today the Grand Chambre grows utterly silent. The hall crackles with tension. And then, as if a conductor has lowered his baton, the murmurs begin, most of them approving, but one voice carries above the others. "See how *proud* she is!"

I do not know whether this is a compliment or a criticism. "Was there too much dignity in my answer?" I whisper to Chauveau-Lagarde.

"Be yourself, and you will always do right, madame," he assures me. And before a livid Fouquier-Tinville can recall Hébert from the witness box, he cross-examines him. "From a review of the documents provided to me by the prosecution prior to trial, I understand that both the sister of Louis Charles Capet and his aunt were interrogated with regard to these allegations of incest between the accused and her son. Is that correct?"

"*Oui,* Monsieur Chauveau-Lagarde," Hébert concedes.

"And did they sign depositions?"

"They did."

"Do you have them and will you produce them now for public examination?"

Scowling, Jacques Hébert reaches into his coat. He hands two papers to my defender as if he desires the very touch of them to burn Chauveau-Lagarde's hand. My advocate unfolds the first paper. "Is this the deposition of Marie Thérèse, the older sister of Louis Charles Capet?" Hébert nods, his upper lip curling into a snarl. My defender asks him to peruse it, then says, "Doesn't Marie Thérèse state that she has no knowledge of any of the incidents you speak of? That she was never in the room when any such thing took place? That her brother never told her of any such events?" He shows Hébert the other document. "And is this not the testimony of Madame Élisabeth?" Once again the deputy prosecutor nods. "And does she not completely deny your allegations of incest, attesting that they are an utter fiction and never took place? That is the testimony above her signature—am I correct?"

Hébert has been beaten. Hermann and Fouquier-Tinville could

not appear more exasperated. I can see them wondering how they will regain the upper hand even as *I* comprehend that a guilty verdict is a foregone conclusion. Still, with the way things have gone for the past two interminably long days I continue to pray for a sentence of banishment with my children. The public thirst for a trial has been quenched. What more do they want?

Midnight has passed by the time the prosecution finishes presenting the last of their 141 witnesses. Finally, Fouquier-Tinville asks me if I have anything further to say in my defense.

I rise to my feet again. My legs wobble and I grasp the arm of the chair to steady myself. As soon as I stand I can feel the blood again. Seeping. I will myself to maintain my dignity for only a few minutes more. I cannot collapse now. Not here. After taking a moment to compose my thoughts, I say, in a clear, steady voice, "Yesterday, I did not know who the witnesses would be who would testify against me, or what they would say. Well, none of them has uttered anything positive against me. I will conclude by stating that I was only the wife of Louis Seize and I was bound to conform to his wishes by the ties of holy matrimony and the etiquette of the Bourbon court."

With this, the defense rests its case.

"You look tired," I whisper to Chauveau-Lagarde. He is afforded no time to respond to my solicitude. Fouquier-Tinville immediately orders his arrest as well as that of his colleague, my co-defender Tronson Docoudray. My hands fly helplessly to my face. Their death warrants may just as well have been written by my own hand.

I am not permitted to remain present while the examining magistrate reads his summation to the jury. Instead I remain in an antechamber, supervised by Lieutenant de Busne of the Garde Nationale while Citoyen Hermann puts four questions to the jurors, all of them related to a single charge of treason against the Republic of France, alleging that I conspired with foreign powers, France's enemies, despite the Revolutionary Tribunal's complete lack of documentary proof. Jacques Hébert's allegation of incest, as well as every other charge against me, has been dismissed.

I sip a glass of water while I await the verdict. It gives me something to do with my hands. A plump young girl I have never seen before brings me a bowl of soup. "Mademoiselle Lamorlière said I could take your bouillon to you because I told her I wanted to meet you," she blurts, as if I am still Queen of France. In her eagerness to serve me, she spills half the soup. It splatters all over the floor and a sepia-colored stain spreads across the front of her apron.

Rosalie herself comes to remove the tray. "I heard you answered like an angel," she says encouragingly. She presses her lips together and blinks back tears. "Perhaps you will only be exiled," she adds, before departing with the empty bowl.

At four o'clock on the morning of October 16, I am summoned back to the Grand Chambre. "The accused will be seated to hear the jury's verdict," intones Fouquier-Tinville. Their foreman, the marquis d'Antonelle, rises and speaks a single word: "Guilty."

I am strangely numb as the Public Prosecutor demands the death sentence. Citoyen Hermann rises and announces with triumph in his voice, "The proclamation of this verdict shall be printed and displayed across the Republic and the said Marie Antoinette, widow of Louis Capet, is to be taken to the place of execution in the Place de la Révolution where the judgment will be carried out by noon of this day."

At this pronouncement, my head is suddenly filled with sound. Everything around me is a blur. Seeing me falter as I rise from the chair, Lieutenant de Busne gallantly proffers his arm to lead me out of the Grand Chambre. In his other hand he holds his black bicorn; under the circumstances his bare head is a sign of humility in my presence.

As we reach the flight of stairs that spirals down to the court-yard, my vision suddenly darkens. "I can hardly see to walk!" I exclaim fearfully. A moment later my foot slips and I begin to pitch forward. The lieutenant grips me by the elbow.

"Do not be afraid, madame, I will not let you fall. I will save you."

"*Merci,* monsieur," I murmur. "But I am afraid nothing can save me now."

THIRTY-THREE

Adieu À *Tout le Monde*

※ OCTOBER 16, 1793 ※

They have left two candles burning on the table in my cell, a special dispensation for the condemned, I suppose. Enough to compose my farewells—the paper and ink being another concession from the Nation. I anticipated this moment—but even when the time comes, I did not expect it to be so soon. There is never enough time to bid adieu. And I will never be able to say good-bye to some of the people who have been the dearest to me, because they are gone already or else I dare not endanger them by sending a farewell: Maman and Papa. My siblings. Louis. Lamballe and Polignac. Axel.

I could chide myself for scoffing at the advice imparted by Papa, which Maman had given me during another good-bye, charging me to read it on my journey from Vienna to Versailles. Papa, who died too suddenly and too young, had prepared a copy of his advice for each of his children. *Take time out twice a year to prepare for death,* he urged us. How silly I found it at the time, as a girl of four-teen with a glorious future mapped out before me.

It is nearly dawn by the time I begin to write my last letter. I fear that it will never reach Mousseline or Louis Charles and so it is to Madame Élisabeth I convey the contents of my heart, my hopes for my children, my regrets, and my sorrows.

The quill moves across the paper as if God guides my hand. It is just as well because there are moments when I cannot see through my tears and the nib makes unsightly blots reminiscent of my girl-hood penmanship.

I have just been condemned to a death that is in no way shameful—that is a fate reserved for criminals—but to rejoin your brother. Like him, I am innocent. I hope I will show the same strength as he did in his last moments.

I am calm, as one always is when one has a clear conscience. My profoundest regret is that I must abandon my poor chil-dren: You know that I have lived only for them, as well as for you, my good and gentle sister. You have sacrificed everything to be with us and your friendship has always sustained me. In what circumstances have I left you! I learned through the pro-ceedings of my trial that my daughter was separated from you, *hélas!* The poor child; I dare not write to her; I doubt she would receive my letter.

I do not even know if this will reach you. I leave you with my benediction, for yourself and for both of my children. I hope that one day when they are older they will be reunited with you, so that they may fully enjoy your tender care. I have always endeav-ored to impress upon them that their principles and exact devo-tion to duty are the foundations of life and that their affection and mutual confidence in each other will constitute its happiness.

May my daughter feel that at her age she should always aid

her brother with the advice that experience has taught her; and let my son in his turn render his sister all the care and service that affection can inspire. May they both recognize that, whatever positions they find themselves in, they will never be truly happy without one another, and may they follow our own example. How often, in our own misfortunes, has our affection for each other provided us consolation! In times of happiness, we rejoice doubly when we can share it with a friend—and where can one find a friend more tender and more united than within one's own family?

May my son never forget his father's last words: that he should never seek to avenge his death.

I pause to consider how to address the most wrenching moments of my trial. Élisabeth was not present when the heinous allegations were made and I refuted them as gallantly as I could. Perhaps she does not even know that the charge was dismissed. But even though the law has erased it, the words cannot be unsaid and the damage to my son's mind and to his aunt's upright and noble character may never be completely undone.

I wish to speak to you about something that is painful to my heart. I know how much hurt my son must have caused you. Forgive him, my dear sister; remember his youth and how easy it is to make a child say whatever one wishes, especially when he does not comprehend what he is saying. The day will come, I hope, when he will feel only the value of your goodness and your love for him and his sister.

In a few minutes it will be time to make my peace with God. I want Élisabeth, always so devout, so correct, so good, to know that I have not left this earth unrepentant for my sins.

I die in the Catholic, Apostolic, and Roman religion, that of my fathers, that in which I was raised and which I have always practiced. Having no spiritual consolation to attend me in my final hours, not even knowing whether there still exist here any priests of this religion, and indeed knowing that I would expose them to danger were they to enter this place even once, I implore God for His sincere pardon for all the faults I have committed throughout my life. I hope that in His goodness He will accept my final prayers, as well as those which for a long time I have addressed to Him, and ask Him to receive my soul into His mercy. I ask pardon of all those I know, and from you, my sister, in particular, for all the pain that I have unwittingly and unwillingly caused you. I pardon all my enemies the evil they have done me. I bid farewell to my aunts and to all my brothers and sisters. I had friends. One of the greatest regrets I have in dying is the idea of being forever separated from them and from their sorrows. Let them know that right up until I drew my last breath, I was thinking of them.

Farewell, my good and tender sister; may this letter find its way to you! Think always of me; I embrace you with all my heart, you and my poor, dear children—my God, it is breaking my heart to leave them forever! Adieu, adieu! I must now devote myself to my spiritual preparation. As I have no freedom in my own actions, someone might bring me a priest, but here I will protest that I will not say a word to him and I will treat him as an absolute stranger.

~Marie Antoinette
La Conciergerie

It is an odd way, an abrupt way, to end a letter, I know, but they may come to take me away at any moment and I must pray before

I go. I write a few words in the prayer book I have carried since I was dauphine. Bound in olive-green Moroccan leather embossed with gold filigree, it was printed during the reign of Louis XV, in 1757, when I was only two years old. The frontispiece is stamped "Office of the Divine Providence for the use of the Royal House of Saint Louis at Saint Cyr and of all the Faithful." An anonymous schoolgirl, some daughter of an impoverished nobleman, would have first owned the prayer book before it became the property of the last queen of France. Who will carry it next? I wonder. Who will read the words I inscribe before I enter immortality?

> *mon dieu, have pity on me!*
> *my eyes have no more tears*
> *to cry for you my*
> *poor children; adieu, adieu!*
>> *Marie Antoinette*

After I have finished my devotions I take the opportunity to lie down and rest for an hour. Thisbe settles on my *poitrine,* and the soft rise and fall of her silky chest steadies my nerves. Perhaps it is not such an absurd thought, but I realize that it is the last time I will be able to lie upon my back, or my side, or curled up like an infant. It is the last time I will ever recline as a whole human being. The next time I lie down on my stomach, my head will be severed from the rest of me.

The bells of Notre-Dame de Paris toll ominously. At seven o'clock, Rosalie enters the cell, her eyes red and swollen. "Would you like any nourishment, madame?" she asks, choking on the words.

I long to ease her pain, to take her in my arms and tell her it will be all right, to transfer all the love I have for my precious children into the embrace I would give to this sweet young woman.

But I cannot touch her. To do so would seal her own warrant of execution. "I do not need anything, Rosalie. *Merci.* All is over for me," I answer quietly.

"It will make me happy if you just take a few spoons. For me," she says, trying hard to smile.

I have no appetite, but I manage a spoonful or two of bouillon. Rosalie offers to help me dress. My long chemise is soaked with blood. I must have a clean one. I do not want them to shed my blood on garments that are already embarrassingly stained. The guard is watching me haughtily. "*S'il vous plaît, monsieur,* for modesty's sake, permit me to change this one last time behind the screen."

He tells me curtly that it is forbidden. With a sigh, I don fresh linen, a shift that Rosalie had, I am now certain, been saving for this day. The dear girl tries to shield my body from his impertinent stare. Yet I cannot leave the blood-soaked chemise on the bed for my enemies to find after I am gone, to gloat over as some sort of macabre relic of my feminine infirmity. Weeks ago I noticed a crevice in the wall. During a moment when the guard's gaze is fixed upon something else, I crush the garment into a ball and wedge it into the gap.

Sitting upon the cot I roll my black silk filoselle stockings over my legs and secure them with embroidered garters. I am about to step into my black gown when the guard says "*Non!* It has been forbidden."

"What else am I to wear, monsieur? I am in mourning for my husband and the year has not expired."

"The Revolutionary Tribunal has declared that it may be construed as an insult to the people."

"To decently mourn my husband?" I repeat incredulously.

"To mourn a king."

The only other gown I have that is in tolerable condition was sent to me from the Temple by my *belle-soeur;* it is a simple dress of cotton piqué in purest white with long narrow sleeves and a small ruffle about the neck. In some ways it reminds me of my golden days at Trianon. And then, in a flash of clarity I recall a lesson from my girlhood with abbé Vermond about the medieval queens of France, whose formal mourning attire was not black, but white. With a secret smile I think, *I will indeed go to the scaffold in full mourning and the Revolutionaries are too ignorant to know it.*

I remove the black crepe streamers from my pleated linen bonnet and secure it upon my head, then Rosalie slides my feet into the plum satin shoes, the very pair that officer Gilbert had one day so kindly cleansed of mold and rust, using his sword to scrape away the filth and dampness. Rosalie drapes a pristine fichu of white muslin about my shoulders. "You look like I imagine an angel does," she murmurs.

I notice Thisbe nosing about the crevice where I hid my bloodstained chemise. "When I am gone, I want you to take her," I whisper to Rosalie. "She will need someone to look after her. Someone who will love her."

"Madame, you could give me no greater honor."

Someone thinks to send a *mignonette* from a nearby café to my cell. Closing my eyes I sip the bittersweet brew, inhaling its fragrant aroma, remembering how often I had begun the morning at Versailles with just such a cup of chocolate. My eyes sting with tears.

I am kneeling in prayer on the threadbare carpet by my bed when Monsieur Larivière, the turnkey, enters with Monsieur Bault, to inform me that it is now ten in the morning and the court clerk and two of the judges will be arriving momentarily to read me my sentence.

"I already know it. It is unnecessary to read it," I say, rising to my feet when I see Citoyen Hermann leading the delegation into my cramped cell. Rosalie slips past them as they enter, pressing her handkerchief to her lips. I will never reproach her for not being able to say good-bye.

"*N'importe,*" replies one of the judges. "It does not matter what you wish. The sentence must be read to you again. It is the law."

"Monsieur Larivière, please convey my thanks to your mother for her kindly care, and ask her to pray for me," I murmur to the turnkey.

The cell is suddenly thrown into shadow. The door has been darkened by Henri Sanson, the *bourreau,* a man well over six feet tall and as broad as the doorway. The post of Royal Executioner of France is the family sinecure. His father Charles Henri executed Louis. Henri has held the office since July.

"I am here to bind your hands," Sanson says, his voice as deep and rumbling as a bassoon.

So they intend to send me like a little white lamb to the slaughter. "Must you?" I ask, more plaintively than I had intended. "Louis Seize did not have his hands bound when he left the Temple. They were not bound until he reached the foot of the scaffold, I was told."

"I have my orders" is Sanson's succinct reply. He secures my hands tightly behind my back. I wince and blink at the pain. I did not imagine the shackles would fit so snugly, slicing into the tender flesh of my wrists. The *bourreau* then takes out his enormous pair of shears and with no acquiescence to vanity, removes my bonnet and lops off my snowy tresses in thick uneven hanks so the guillotine's blade—that "humane" instrument of death, that "social equalizer"—will strike true when it falls. If the knife is impeded, my demise could be a painful one indeed. Sanson pockets the hair he has shorn. I know it will later be burned. Secret royalists will be denied this relic of my martyrdom to the monarchy of France.

I don't dare glance at my reflection in Rosalie's red lacquered mirror. Perhaps my locks are not so different now from when Léonard restyled them after the first dauphin was born. I had lost so much hair then and the *friseur* transformed me from an unhealthy new mother into a fashionable woman once again.

Mon Dieu! My fear has suddenly gotten the better of me. "*Monsieur le bourreau,* would you kindly unbind my hands? I must attend immediately to a call of nature." I plead with the executioner to assist me before I have an embarrassing accident. Sanson looks to the guard for permission. He nods his head and I am released to the humiliation of lifting my skirts to relieve myself, emptying my bowels in the corner of the cell like a streetwalker in the shadows of the Palais Royal.

After I have smoothed out my skirts I request permission to redon my bonnet as well, then present my hands to Citoyen Sanson and once again he jerks them roughly behind my back. When I consider that he is the seventh generation of his family to perform the duties of official executioner and that the office was bestowed upon the Sansons by Louis XV, I would have hoped for a modicum of gentleness.

The *bourreau* attaches a rope to the shackles and I am paraded through the Conciergerie and into the courtyard. I blink several times. I have been confined so long in the dim recesses of my cell and the torchlit cavern of the Gothic Grand Chambre that my eyes are unused to the daylight. It is a misty morning, but the autumnal chill of the previous night has passed. I expect the sunlight to emerge by afternoon, but I will not be here to see it.

"Where is the coach?" I ask, expecting to see a closed unmarked carriage of the sort that conveyed Louis to the Place de la Révolution.

"You were not a king," Citoyen Hermann remarks. Instead, what awaits, drawn by a pair of *rosinantes,* sturdy drays, is a wooden tumbrel, one of the open-railed carts that conveys common criminals to the guillotine. The victims are usually seated shoulder to shoulder, facing each other around the inside perimeter of the wagon. Sanson instructs me to sit upon the hard plank with my back to the coachman, rather than face forward, the way the highest-ranking person sits in a carriage. I cannot see the direction in which we are going, which disorients me. I am not to face the future, but to look upon the past and what has led me to this jostling wagon ride toward eternity. A constitutional priest garbed in beige *sans-culottes* and a long brown vest climbs up and sits beside me but I remain determined to ignore him. He does not even remove his hat. Facing sideways is Sanson; his assistants take their places on the opposite bench.

The actor from the Théâtre Français, Grammont, mounted on horseback, holding aloft a naked saber as though he is leading a charge into battle, heads the macabre procession that conveys me from the Conciergerie through the crowded *rues* to the Place de la Révolution. Grammont rises in his stirrups, brandishing his sword and inciting the rabble to insult me as I pass. "Make way for the Austrian bitch! *Et voilà!* The infamous Antoinette! *Elle est foutoue, mes amis!* She is done for!" Shouts of *"À bas l'Autrichienne!"* and *"Vive la République!"* rend the air.

A sudden jolt nearly knocks me off the unforgiving wooden board, a mishap noticed by one of the gendarmes who make up my escort to the scaffold. "Those are not your silken cushions at Trianon!" he sneers at me as the tumbrel clatters past, spattering dozens of citizens with mud. Nonetheless, ecstatic at my humiliation, they toss their liberty caps in the air.

I am determined to maintain my dignity and hold my head high. I will die a daughter of Austria, a wife and mother of France. Soldiers with their bayoneted muskets balanced on their shoulders are everywhere I look. I have never seen so many guardsmen. Sanson tells me that thirty thousand reinforcements have been called into Paris today. Why? To keep the peace? Do they think the people will foment a riot after the embodiment of their hatred is dispatched? Do they think I will attempt an escape? That Count von Fersen will ride into the capital on a white charger and sweep me off the scaffold and out of the cold cruel arms of Madame Guillotine?

Axel, wherever he is now, could not get past the city gates even if he were to attempt it. They have been barricaded; cannon are mounted on every bridge and in every public square.

The tumbrel rolls into the rue Saint-Honoré, once the site of Rose Bertin's opulent emporium Le Grand Mogol. My memory flashes upon the first time I stepped across the threshold in the company of my friend Louise, the duchess de Chartres, who in those innocent days never could have imagined her husband would—as the duc d'Orléans-turned-Philippe Égalité—betray his kinsman and vote to kill a king. As the cart passes the Oratory, I catch sight of a mother struggling to lift her chubby infant high enough so that he can see above the crush of people clamoring for a glance at the former queen's final journey. Always drawn to the sight of babies, I cast a melting glance in the direction of mother and child and for the fraction of an instant the faintest smile crosses my lips. And then—as the baby brings his moist little fingers to his lips and blows me a kiss, a single tear courses down my cheek, despite my vow to show no weakness before the people. I lift my chin and square my shoulders. My posture will remain regal, as if I am wearing the unforgiving stays I always detested as a girl, when my refusal to abide such corsets nearly resulted in an incident of international proportions.

The crude open cart rumbles past the Tuileries Palace and Gardens and I recall the days I spent there with my family. How foolish I was to think only of our deprivations at first, how little we had compared to the splendor of Versailles and Fontainebleau. We had each other then. At the sight of the gardens littered with fallen leaves in shades of ruby, gold, and brown, and the façade of the Tuileries with its shattered windows and battered stone, I blink away tears.

As we near the Place de la Révolution, I am struck by the eerie silence that greets the arrival of my cavalcade. In June of 1773, Louis and I made our first formal entrance into Paris as dauphin and dauphine. How the people had loved us then! They greeted us with songs and dances and showered us with flowers. On the steps of the Hôtel de Ville the capital's mayor presented us with the keys to the city. We represented a young, bright hope for France's future. How much has changed in twenty years! The same people who once pelted the rosy-cheeked royals with blossoms and sugared almonds not only orchestrated but cheered for their executions.

The mist begins to lift, revealing patches of blue, punctuated by big-bellied white clouds. As the tumbrel rounds a corner, two monuments dominate my view, piercing the sky. The first is the enormous seated figure of the Goddess of Liberty who replaced the toppled and desecrated statue of Louis XV in the center of the Place. In one hand she holds the sword of justice; on her head is sculpted a triangular liberty bonnet. Her unseeing eyes look across the Place toward the other vertical shrine, the altar of the Revolution on which its victims are slaughtered, the trapezoidal blade glinting as it catches a ray of sunlight.

Two tall wooden uprights connected by a crossbar form this neoclassical sculpture. Suspended from the crosspiece is the fatal instrument, the great equalizer that dispatches baron and bootblack, princesse and petty thief, with the same reputedly painless alacrity. A pair of sparrows dips and wings above it as if they plan to build a nest upon the crossbar.

As we reach the foot of the scaffold, I realize, to my horror, that the stories I have heard of the circus atmosphere surrounding the executions are no exaggeration. I spy lemonade sellers, people consuming bags of nuts, and pamphleteers still hawking *libelles* and lewd caricatures accusing me of fornicating with Polignac, Lamballe, Artois, and anyone else the authors can invent. The *tricoteuses* are indeed seated around the perimeter of the scaffold, the incessant clicking of their wooden needles providing a percussive accompaniment to the daily parade of judicial murders.

"Two hundred thousand people have come here this morning," Henri Sanson tells me.

Why do they behave as though they are here to watch a Punchinello puppet show? I wonder. The notion that a fifth of a million people have come to witness my gruesome demise is enough to make me ill.

I refuse the *bourreau*'s assistance in alighting from the tumbrel, although it is no mean feat to descend with my hands tied behind my back. Before me looms the wooden platform, larger than I had imagined, high and broad enough to cast the yard below it into shadow. The scale is not human. I feel dwarfed by it; a grown man could almost stand beneath it without stooping.

I ascend a mundane wooden staircase. My spirit is strangely calm, now. There is supposed to be no pain. But even if there is, I have endured so much over the years that one instant more would scarcely trouble me. I am looking at the white clouds scudding across the sky, thinking of my family waiting for me just beyond them, when I hear the *bourreau* mutter, *"Sacré bleu!"* and I realize I have stepped on his foot in my haste to greet Madame Guillotine. "Pardon, monsieur," I murmur contritely. "I didn't mean to do it."

I do not wish to address the crowd, nor do I expect that the Nation would permit me to do so, as other queens about to lose their heads such as Anne Boleyn and Kathryn Howard did in their day. However, I have something to say to God and to my absent children, and raising my eyes to heaven I utter it simply. "Dear Lord, may you enlighten and touch my executioners. *Adieu, mes enfants.* I go to rejoin your father."

The *bourreau*'s two assistants, men with ummemorable faces wearing long brown vests and sand-colored *sans-culottes,* grasp my upper arms and thrust me roughly toward the guillotine, physically forcing me to lie facedown upon the horizontal plank beneath the shining blade with my throat resting in the lower section of the neckhole. I look out across the rabble below me, seeking a friendly face. Perhaps it is only my imagination but I think I spy the young woman who came to the Conciergerie with her chisel. Then the vast sea of faces begins to blur. Henri Sanson removes a watch from his pocket. It is precisely 12:11, he says. I have four minutes left to live. That is how much time it will take his assistants to secure me to the plank of the guillotine and to lower the board above my neck.

I feel a breeze upon my brow. The air shimmers before my eyes. My field of vision is reduced to a patch of purest blue October sky.

Out of the corner of my eye I spy something fluttering on the breeze and try to identify it but my head is immobilized. Yet then I see it again, dancing before my eyes.

A blue butterfly.

And on its fragile wings are borne the joyful memories of numberless carefree days: Louis's image floats before me—the husband I came to appreciate far too late, a man I fell in love with after twenty-two years of matrimony had come and gone, a benevolent autocrat born to a role he never wished for and overtaken by circumstances far greater than anything he could have imagined. I will always remember him as he was on the day we met—the shy, stocky, myopic boy whose diffidence and ungainliness eclipsed the kindness and intelligence that for so many years I was too blind, or heedless, to see. The first thing I will do when I meet him in Heaven will be to apologize for not having appreciated him for so long. I see him now as he was that day in the forest at Compiègne, too timid to speak to me, and then before the altar in the chapel at Versailles, perspiring profusely in his suit of blinding white satin, then in the Cathedral at Rheims baring his breast to receive the anointment of sacred oil from a vial as old as the French monarchy itself. I can picture him holding Mousseline right after she was born as though she were the most precious thing in the world to him and quoting his favorite poet to let me know how delighted he was that I bore him a daughter, even though a son would have ensured the succession of the realm.

The princesse de Lamballe merits my apologies as well. She died because an angry mob detested *me*. It was me they wished to punish by dismembering her. Her face swims before me, softening into a rare smile during a sleigh ride at Versailles. And then the gruesome image of her severed head dances before me, and I blink away the image, eager to quickly replace it with a happier memory.

I see my favorite brother Joseph, tall and elegant, and always teasing me. He emits a silent chuckle, no doubt mocking one of my outrageous coiffures, or the two-inch circles of rouge that were de rigueur for the highest-ranking ladies at the Bourbon court.

Mops, my beloved pug, bounds into view, playing with a length of blue satin ribbon. There must be dogs in Heaven! And then my little daughter Sophie appears. She gazes at me with unconditional love. Her face dissolves like a wisp of smoke as my older son's visage floats before my eyes—Louis Joseph with his fine brown curls and pure blue eyes, so frail, so trusting, too good for this world. With remarkable clarity I recall watching him roll his first hoop and play at bilbo catch, so delighted the first time he managed to land the ball inside the cup, our visits to the royal *ménagerie,* and our picnics of strawberries and cream on the verdant *tapis* at Trianon.

These memories elicit reminiscences of stolen moments of passion with Axel as well as innocent games of croquet and blindman's buff with my beloved Trianon *cercle.*

At this, Maman's disapproving expression shimmers into view and I see her kissing me good-bye, charging me to make the French think she had sent them an angel. *I will be one soon enough, Maman. But they are sending me back to you.*

I see Papa, his cheeks pink from the frosty winter air, hoisting me—bundled to the ears in white velvet and marten—onto his shoulders and tossing me gently over them into a snowdrift as I laugh until I am overcome with hiccoughs. How I recall our last embrace! As he was about to depart for my brother Leopold's wedding, overcome by a premonition of his own demise, he sent a messenger back to the Hofburg to fetch me so that he could embrace me one last time.

So many farewells at the Hofburg! My beloved sister Johanna, about to become a bride and the Queen of Naples, taken instead into death's icy embrace. I see her as she was on her last day of life, in a tightly boned gown of violet brocade, her gaze wise, gentle, and obedient, a follower, unlike my sister Charlotte who became Queen of the Two Sicilies in her stead. As girls, wherever one of us led the other would cheerfully go, but Charlotte cannot do that today.

I recall one sunlit afternoon when I had persuaded our governess the Countess von Brandeiss to hold our lessons out of doors, high above the Hapsburgs' summer palace of Schönbrunn. I had become distracted by the flight of a magnificent butterfly with wings of iridescent blue, and leapt up from the grass in my stocking feet to give chase.

The drummers' rhythmic tattoo crescendoes. The *bourreau* pulls the string and the fatal razor descends with a *whish* through its channels.

My ears fill with sound, at first like rushing water, and then as hollow as silence.

Yet I can still see the butterfly. I am laughing but no sound escapes my lips as I chase it into the clear blue sky.

Acknowledgments

I owe bouquets of fleurs-de-lis to my brilliant editor Kate Miciak for her belief in me and her enthusiasm for my work, and to the phenomenal Caitlin Alexander, who began Marie Antoinette's journey with me and shared my vision from the start; to the rest of my team at Ballantine, past and present: Randall Klein, Crystal Velasquez, Gina Wachtel, Ashley Gratz-Collier, and Lindsey Kennedy; to my agent extraordinaire Irene Goodman for whom I never have enough superlatives: her devotion to my career in macrocosm and to the Marie Antoinette trilogy in microcosm has never flagged; to Anne-marie von Eynern for help with German phrasing; to the historical fiction blogging community for being so supportive of the genre in general and my MA novels in particular; to my old pal Buzzy Porter; to Lucy and Andi for checking my French; *et finalement, à mon mari* Scott, for loving me so much and making my life a better place in which to create.

Bibliography

Although it is not customary to provide a bibliography for a work of fiction, my research for the Marie Antoinette trilogy has been so extensive that I wished to share my sources with my readers. I am indebted to the following fine scholars and historians.

Abbott, John S. C. *History of Maria Antoinette*. New York: Harper & Brothers, 1849.

Administration of Schönbrunn Palace. *Schönbrunn*. Vienna: Verlag der Österreichischen Staatsdruckerei, 1971.

Asquith, Annunziata. *Marie Antoinette*. New York: Taplinger Publishing Company, 1976.

Bernier, Olivier. *Secrets of Marie Antoinette: A Collection of Letters*. New York: Fromm International Publishing Corporation, 1986.

Boyer, Marie-France, and François Halard. *The Private Realm of Marie Antoinette*. New York: Thames & Hudson, 1996.

Cadbury, Deborah. *The Lost King of France: How DNA Solved the Mystery of the Murdered Son of Louis XVI and Marie Antoinette*. New York: St. Martin's Griffin, 2002.

Castelot, André (trans. Denise Folliot). *Queen of France: A Biography of Marie Antoinette*. New York: Harper & Brothers, 1957.

Cronin, Vincent. *Louis & Antoinette*. New York: William Morrow & Co., 1974.

De Feydeau, Elisabeth. *A Scented Palace: The Secret History of Marie Antoinette's Perfumer*. London & New York: I. B. Tauris, 2006.

Erickson, Carolly. *To the Scaffold: The Life of Marie Antoinette*. New York: St. Martin's Griffin, 1991.

Fraser, Antonia. *Marie Antoinette: The Journey*. New York: Anchor Books, 2002.

Haslip, Joan. *Marie Antoinette*. New York: Weidenfeld & Nicolson, 1987.

Hearsey, John. *Marie Antoinette*. New York: E.P. Dutton & Co., Inc., 1973.

Hibbert, Christopher and the Editors of the Newsweek Book Division. *Versailles*. New York: Newsweek Book Division, 1972.

Lady Younghusband. *Marie Antoinette: Her Youth*. London: Macmillan and Co., Ltd., 1912.

LeNotre, G. (pseudonym). (trans. Mrs. Rodolph Stawell). First-person narrative of Louis François Turgy, included in *The Last Days of Marie Antoinette,* Philadelphia: J. B. Lippincott Company, 1907.

Lever, Evelyne. (trans. Catherine Temerson). *Marie Antoinette: The Last Queen of France*. New York: Farrar, Straus & Giroux, 2000.

Loomis, Stanley. *The Fatal Friendship: Marie Antoinette, Count Fersen, and the Flight to Varennes*. New York: Avon Books, 1972.

Mossiker, Frances. *The Queen's Necklace: Marie Antoinette and the Scandal that Shocked and Mystified France*. London: Orion Books, Ltd., 2004. Originally published in Great Britain by Victor Gollancz, Ltd. in 1961.

Pick, Robert. *Empress Maria Theresa*. New York: Harper & Row, 1966.

Saint Amand, Imbert. *Marie Antoinette at the Tuileries, 1789–1791*. BiblioLife, LLC: public domain, originally published before 1923.

Thomas, Chantal. (trans. Julie Rose). *The Wicked Queen: The Origins of the Myth of Marie Antoinette*. New York: Zone Books, 2001.

Weber, Caroline. *What Marie Antoinette Wore to the Revolution.* New York: Picador, 2006.

Webster, Nesta H. *Louis XVI and Marie Antoinette During the Revolution.* New York: Gordon Press, 1976.

Zweig, Stefan. (trans. Cedar and Eden Paul). *Marie Antoinette: The Portrait of an Average Woman.* New York: Grove Press, 2002. Originally published in the United States by Viking Press in 1933.

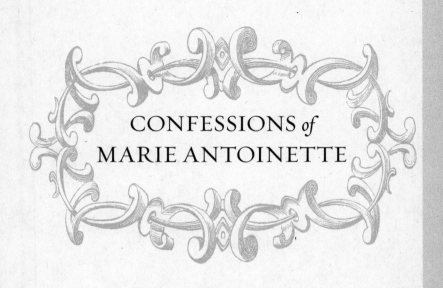

CONFESSIONS *of* MARIE ANTOINETTE

JULIET GREY

A READER'S GUIDE

About Marie Antoinette

Although Marie Antoinette's trial was in one respect the prosecution of a decade of sexual debauchery depicted in the countless *libelles,* despite having wasted hours of time during the trial on such fictitious allegations as a Sapphic relationship with the comtesse Jeanne de Lamotte-Valois and an incestuous one with her son, none of the more salacious charges against her were presented to the jury in the prosecutor's summation. The one charge that stuck was that of treason and conspiracy, and in fact, the Revolutionary Tribunal was right.

Marie Antoinette *did* correspond with foreign powers—and frequently—as well as those who communicated on her behalf, in an effort to enlist their aid to liberate the royal family from the clutches of the Revolution and to topple the fledgling French Republic. The only problem with the prosecution's case is that they lacked a shred of proof to back up this allegation. The documentary evidence of Marie Antoinette's desperate efforts to free her family and reverse the revolutionary tide only came to light much later. Lacking the physical evidence with which to convict her, *by law* the jury should not have found her guilty. But of course this verdict was a foregone conclusion long before the trial began. Even before there was a decision to hold a formal trial at all, men like Hébert were literally calling for her head and would not be denied.

After her death, Marie Antoinette's head and body were taken to the Cimitière de Madeleine for burial, but the gravediggers were so insensitive and disrespectful that, according to historian Antonia Fraser, they tossed her head between the legs of her corpse while they took their lunch break, affording a young wax worker, Marie Grosholtz (who in 1796 married a man named Tussaud), the opportunity to make a death mask of the doomed queen. However, Fraser is the only biographer I have read who makes this claim.

It was too costly to individually bury the numerous victims of the Reign of Terror, which ravaged France from September 1793 to July 1794, so the nation allowed the bodies to accumulate. Imagine the unhealthful conditions as a result of this decree. Not until sixty corpses were amassed could a collective burial take place. The corpses and coffins of all victims of the Revolution were smothered in quicklime to advance decomposition. After her death, Marie Antoinette's clothes were distributed to the female inmates of the infamous Salpêtrière prison. Rosalie Lamorlière gathered her few remaining possessions, including the little hand mirror with the red lacquered back, placing them into the cardboard box she had given the queen during her incarceration in the Conciergerie. Marie Antoinette's letter to Élisabeth never reached the princess. It made its way into the hands of the Revolutionary Tribunal and was eventually found under Robespierre's mattress. It remained in the Republic's archives for twenty-one years.

After the restoration of the Bourbon monarchy that followed Napoleon's 1814 exile to Elba, an effort was made to accord the executed monarchs a proper burial. On January 15, 1815, Marie Antoinette's bones were identified by scraps of her black filoselle stockings and the garters she customarily wore. The following day, the remains of Louis XVI were found. On January 21 (not-so-ironically the twenty-second anniversary of his execution), the royal spouses' remains were interred in the crypt at Saint-Denis, the traditional final resting place for France's monarchs.

Readers might be interested to discover what happened to several of the historical figures in this novel after Marie Antoinette's execution. Some survived the Revolution; others were not so fortunate.

Madame Royale, **Marie Thérèse,** the sole surviving daughter of Louis and Marie Antoinette, remained incarcerated for another three years, after which she was released in exchange for imprisoned commissaries of the Revolution. She eventually married her first cousin the duc d'Angoulême, the eldest son of Louis's youngest brother, the comte d'Artois. After their marriage in 1799, the couple, who would always remain childless, moved to Buckinghamshire, England, returning to France only after the restoration of the Bourbon monarchy in 1814, following the enforced abdication of Napoleon. Upon the death in 1824 of her uncle Louis XVIII (the former comte de Provence), her father-in-law Artois became King Charles X of France, which meant that Marie Thérèse was the dauphine. In 1830, during yet another revolution, Charles X abdicated in favor of his eldest son. But Marie Antoinette's daughter was Queen of France for less than an hour, because her husband was urged to immediately abdicate in favor of his nephew, the duc de Bordeaux. Marie Thérèse spent the remainder of her life in exile, first in Edinburgh, then in Prague, and finally on the outskirts of Vienna. She died of pneumonia in 1851.

Louis Charles, Marie Antoinette's only surviving son, who technically became Louis XVII upon the death of his father, died in the Temple prison on or about June 8, 1795, at the age of ten. He had become fat from a poor diet, yet had not grown much taller. His jailers left him to stew in his own filth for weeks on end. His sister described how his bed had remained unmade for six months, chamber pots went unemptied; and her brother, as well as the room's meager furnishings, were covered with fleas and other bugs. Because the windows were never permitted to be opened, the stench in the room was unbearable.

For many years after Louis Charles's death, it was suggested that he had been replaced with a hapless changeling and smuggled out of the Temple. Several young men came forth during the beginning of the nineteenth century to claim that they were the dauphin of France. Marie Thérèse refused to meet any of them. However, the boy's heart was taken away by the doctor who performed the autopsy on his body, and it finally came to reside in a crystal urn in the Cathedral Saint-Denis in Paris. According to the duc d'Anjou, a representative of the Spanish Bourbon royal line, mitochondrial DNA testing on the organ in 2000 proved conclusively that the DNA sequences were "identical with those of Marie Antoinette, two of her sisters, and two living relatives on the maternal side."

Madame Élisabeth was executed on May 10, 1794, the last in a group of twenty-five to be guillotined that day. She was seated on a bench with the other victims, but was placed nearest the scaffold, compelled to witness the executions of the other twenty-four people before it was her turn. It is said that she kept repeating the *De profundis* throughout this ordeal. Unlike the executions of her brother and sister-in-law in 1793, the people did not burst into rousing cheers of *"Vive la Nation!"* after the blade descended. By this time, they were becoming not only desensitized to the carnage of the Terror, but disgusted by it. The execution of the late king's thirty-year-old sister, a woman with no power or influence of her own, was, to many, an unnecessary afterthought. However, to the Committee of Public Safety Madame Élisabeth nonetheless represented a symbol of the monarchy and as such had to be eliminated.

Axel von Fersen never ceased blaming himself for the failure of the royal flight to Montmédy in June 1791. Because he had been one of the escape plot's masterminds and knew more about the plans and the route than anyone else connected with it, with the clearest hindsight he believed that if he had never left their party at Bondy as the king requested, and had instead insisted on remaining on the coachman's box, the royal family might have safely reached the frontier.

Fersen was in Brussels and did not hear the news of Marie Antoinette's October 16 execution until October 23. For a long while he felt utterly numb. He would see her face in his mind's eye. "It follows me wherever I go. Her suffering and death and all my feelings never leave me for a moment. I can think of nothing else. . . . That she was alone in her last moments with no one to comfort her or talk to her, with no one to whom she could give her last wishes, fills me with horror."

In the privacy of his diary he compared his devotion to Marie Antoinette to his passion for his longtime mistress Eléanore Sullivan (who was, at the time, the live-in love of a Scotsman named Quentin Craufurd, both of whom helped finance the royal flight that ended at Varennes). "Oh, how I reproach myself for the wrongs I did Her and how deeply I now realize how much I loved Her. What kindness, what sweetness, and tenderness, what a fine and loving, sensitive and delicate heart! The other [Eléanore Sullivan] isn't like that, although I love her and she is my only comfort and without her I should be very unhappy." In *Confessions of Marie Antoinette* I chose not to devote any page time to Axel's romance with Eléanore Sullivan as there was no place for it in my story line. Marie Antoinette, who narrates most of the novel, never seemed to have learned of this relationship, although others knew of it and warned Axel not to flaunt his affair with Eléanore in order to keep the queen in the dark about it.

Axel kept the date of October 16, "this atrocious day," as a day of mourning for "the model of queens and women." Marie Antoinette represented an ideal in his heart, and he was flooded with memories of her goodness and sweetness, her tenderness, sensibility, and loving nature. He confided to his sister Sophie that Eléanore Sullivan could never replace Marie Antoinette—"*Elle*"—in his heart, although he eventually asked Eléanore to marry him. But when it came to choosing between Fersen and Craufurd, Eléanore wed the man who for all intents and purposes had been her common-law husband for years, and settled down to a life of so-called respectability.

In the years after Marie Antoinette's execution, Axel von Fersen was heaped with honors in his homeland. He was created a Knight of the Order of the Seraphim, Grand Marshal of the Court of Sweden, and Chancellor of Uppsala University, and he was made Lieutenant Governor of the kingdom in 1800, 1803, 1808, and 1809. Yet he remained haunted by the events of the failed escape of June 20, 1791, and by the death of the Queen of France, commemorating the tragic anniversaries with heartrending entries in his *Journal intime.*

Seventeen years to the day after the ill-starred flight to Montmédy, Count Axel von Fersen, then Sweden's highest-ranking official after the king, was torn to pieces by a Swedish mob that believed he had poisoned Crown Prince Christian, the heir to the Danish throne. At Christian's funeral procession on June 20, 1810, to cries of "Traitor!" and "Murderer!" Fersen was kicked, stomped, and savagely beaten with sticks and stones while a battalion of the royal guard idly stood by. They would later claim that they hadn't acted because they'd received no orders to stop the attack. Severely battered, Fersen was helped to a nearby house, where he was allowed refuge in a small room. But the building's second story housed a restaurant whose patrons mercilessly attacked him again, ripping the ribbon with the Order of the Seraphim from around his neck and tossing it out of the window. A suggestion was made to similarly eject Fersen. Men began to beat him about the head with their walking sticks, and he lay on the floor of the small chamber, bleeding profusely, until General Silfversparre, no friend of his, arrived on the scene and established order. Silfversparre convinced Fersen that his only hope lay in placing himself under arrest and allowing himself to be imprisoned for his own security in Stockholm's Town Hall.

But the rabble followed Fersen and his escort inside the municipal building and dragged the count back outdoors, where the vicious pummeling continued. The fatal blow was delivered when a young man jumped on his chest, crushing his ribs.

Louis Stanislas Xavier, the **comte de Provence,** who, during the reign of Louis XVI was formally known as Monsieur (the title given to the king's next youngest brother), moved to the Palais de Luxembourg after the royal family was compelled to leave Versailles on October 6, 1789. But as part of the fateful flight to the frontier of June 20–21, 1791, Monsieur and his wife fled in their own coach for the Austrian Netherlands. They made it safely across the border and remained in exile for twenty-three years. Technically, the comte de Provence succeeded his nephew when Louis Charles died in the Temple in June 1795, becoming Louis XVIII, but at that time, the French Revolution remained in full swing. He was compelled to wait out both the Revolution and the Napoleonic era before the Bourbon monarchy was restored. Provence did return to France in 1814 after Napoleon was exiled to Elba, but had to slip back into exile himself in 1815 when the deposed emperor returned to reclaim his imperial throne.

Louis XVIII finally ascended the French throne on April 11, 1814, and again (after a hiatus due to Napoleon's return), on July 18, 1815, ruling until September 16, 1824, during an era known as the

Bourbon Restoration; but, for the first time in French history, his was a constitutional monarchy and not an autocratic one. Louis XVIII and his wife Marie Joséphine of Savoy never had children, and on his death the crown passed to the youngest Bourbon brother, Charles Philippe, the **comte d'Artois.**

Artois and his wife Marie Thérèse of Savoy, the younger sister of Provence's wife, fled France on July 17, 1789, three days after the storming of the Bastille. At the time, Artois was one of the most hated men in the nation. His extravagant lifestyle rivaled Marie Antoinette's; he had a cavalier attitude toward his staggering debts and was universally caricatured (although it was untrue) as the queen's lover. During the Revolution, Artois and his wife enjoyed a peripatetic existence. Émigrés had been declared traitors by the National Assembly, their titles forfeit and their lands confiscated. However, Artois eventually landed on both feet in England, where George III awarded him a generous allowance. After Napoleon's abdication, when the Senate declared Louis XVIII restored to the Bourbon throne, Artois arrived in France ahead of his older brother and acted as his regent, creating a secret-police force that reported directly to him. It was so secret that the king didn't even know about it! On September 16, 1824, Louis XVIII died and Artois succeeded him, reigning as Charles X. As a monarch he was as unpopular with the people as he had been during his verdant days at Versailles. A revolution during the summer of 1830 left him with no alternative but to abdicate. Another scandal erupted when Charles insisted on bypassing his oldest son the duc d'Angoulême, husband of Marie Antoinette's daughter Marie Thérèse, in favor of his grandson, the dauphin's nephew. After relinquishing his throne, Charles resumed his peripatetic ways, moving several times to various locales on the Continent and within the United Kingdom. He died on November 6, 1836.

In August 1792, the **marquis de Lafayette,** who kept shifting allegiances when the going got tough during the French Revolution, tried to escape to America via the Dutch Republic as the more radical factions gained ascendance. He remained an Austrian prisoner of war for five years. Although Napoleon negotiated his release, Lafayette refused to serve in his government. But as the governmental model shifted to a constitutional one, in 1815 Lafayette was elected to the Chamber of Deputies during the emperor's Hundred Days and served as a Liberal member of the legislative body during the Bourbon Restoration. During the Revolution of 1830, he was invited to become France's dictator. He declined, supporting instead Louis Philippe d'Orléans's bid to become France's next constitutional monarch.

In Lafayette's final years he was fêted as a hero in the United States for his contributions to the American War of Independence; and many parks, streets, and monuments still bear his name. Lafayette was made an American citizen during his lifetime (his honorary citizenship was reiterated in 2002), and when he died in May 1834, the soil that comprised his Paris grave came from George Washington's grave at Mount Vernon.

Antoine Barnave, the deputy of the Assembly who began as an enemy of Marie Antoinette but became an active sympathizer, was arrested on suspicion of being a clandestine royalist on August 19, 1792. Charged with treason he remained in prison for more than a year and was guillotined on November 29, 1793 at the age of thirty-two.

The vicious Jacobin extremist *"enragé,"* **Jacques Hébert** who attacked the Girondins as well as the more moderate voices of the Revolution, had his date with Madame Guillotine on March 24, 1794, as the Revolution continued to eat its own, bringing down the brief Hébertist regime eleven days earlier. One of the first wave of revolutionaries, **Georges Danton,** considered a moderate *"indulgent"* by the time the Terror was in full swing, was denounced by the more radical factions and went to the guillotine himself on April 5, 1794.

The architects of the bloody Reign of Terror, including **Maximilien Robespierre** and **Louis-Antoine de Saint-Just,** were executed in the Place de la Révolution (now the Place de la Concorde) on July 28, 1794, in an event known as the "coup of 9 Thermidor, year II," for the date of the uprising, per the new French Republican Calendar. **Antoine Simon,** the former shoemaker assigned to reeducate and care for Marie Antoinette's son, was also guillotined on July 28. He and his wife had been removed from their jobs at the Temple in January 1794. While many history books depict Simon as an illiterate alcoholic brute (a portrayal I was taught in school as well, just a few decades ago), this characterization has never been conclusively proven and may have been exaggerated in accounts left by royalist sympathizers. In any event, it is true that Simon was no rocket scientist. Nor was he the sort of guy you'd want to entertain for dinner (at least I wouldn't). But it's entirely possible that he was not a caricature of an archvillain either.

The deaths of Robespierre, et al., effectively ended the Reign of Terror. Although the Revolution's thirst for blood began during the summer of 1789, the "Terror" did not begin until September 1793, a month before the execution of Marie Antoinette. Nor was it confined to Paris. The Terror was responsible for some 25,000 summary executions across France, as well as the 2,639 people who were sent to the guillotine in Paris and the 16,594 who were beheaded with the "national razor" in other areas of the country. Charged with dictatorship and tyranny on July 26, the following day Robespierre attempted to avoid arrest by throwing himself out of a window. He succeeded in breaking both his legs, and, unable to flee, was subsequently arrested. He then tried to commit suicide by shooting himself, but the bullet lodged in his jaw and he was executed on July 28. It is said that the executioner yanked off the bandage that was binding the accused's bloody and swollen jaw, producing an agonized scream that was silenced only by the guillotine blade.

The Reign of Terror claimed approximately 50,000 victims. Of those who were condemned by Revolutionary Tribunals throughout France, only about 18 percent were aristocrats, 6 percent were clergymen (predominantly Roman Catholic), and 4 percent were bourgeoisie, or middle class. A whopping 72 percent were people from the lowest social strata: peasants or common laborers who were accused of petty crimes, hoarding, and issues related to military service such as desertion or evading the draft. This would put the lie to any assertions that the Reign of Terror was largely an act of class warfare against the aristocracy. Ironically, and tragically, a handful of demagogues perpetuating their new Cult of Reason to a populace that was predominantly impoverished, and too lazy, ignorant, or brainwashed to think for itself, managed to make an entire nation *lose* its reason entirely and descend into a civil war that benefited no one.

François Adrien Toulan, the former music seller and ardent republican-turned-royalist sympathizer, was eventually guillotined after the discovery of his complicity in one of the plots to effect Marie Antoinette's escape from the Temple. During the restoration of the monarchy, Marie Thérèse, Marie Antoinette's only surviving child, granted Toulan's widow a royal pension.

Jacques François Lepître was arrested on October 8, 1793, and condemned by the Commune on November 19 for conspiring to aid the royal family. Lepître was subsequently denounced by Monsieur and Madame Tison, the nasty republican couple in charge of minding the royal family at the Temple, along with ten others suspected of being actively sympathetic to the royal family, including the commissioners **François Adrien Toulan, Claude-Antoine-François Moëlle,** and one of the architects of the infamous Carnation Plot, the counterrevolutionary **Alexandre Gonsse de**

Rougeville. The self-styled Chevalier de Rougeville would survive the French Revolution only to be shot as a traitor for abetting the allied armies against Napoleon in 1814. Lepître also survived the Revolution, eventually becoming a professor of rhetoric in Rouen. He died in 1821.

After bringing the relics of Louis XVI to the comte de Provence, the **Chevalier de Jarjayes** was made an adjutant by the king of Sardinia and participated in the counterrevolutionary military campaign of 1793, fighting with the Sardinian army. He then became involved in the failed Carnation Plot to release Marie Antoinette from the Conciergerie. Jarjayes survived the Revolution and was awarded the rank of Lieutenant-General by Louis XVIII after the Bourbon restoration. He died in September 1822.

The **Baron de Batz** also survived the Revolution, although he was arrested following the 1795 coup d'état after he had fled to Auvergne and bought a castle there. However, the baron managed to elude his captors in the course of being transported to Lyon, fleeing to Switzerland. Eventually he settled in Auvergne and was awarded two distinguished honors—the rank of maréchal de camp and the Order of Saint Louis—for his prior service to the crown during the Bourbon restoration. He was also a distinguished military commander under Napoleon, although his command of the Cantal was revoked after the Hundred Days of the emperor's resurgence. In January 1822, Baron de Batz died in seclusion at Chadieu.

After royally botching his assignment during the ill-fated flight to Montmédy, Marie Antoinette's legendary coiffeur **Léonard Hautier** returned to Paris where he maintained a low profile throughout the rest of the Revolution.

Marie Antoinette's lady in waiting **Henriette Campan** and Louis's *premier valet de chambre,* **François Hüe,** both survived the Revolution and went on to write memoirs of their experiences in the last days of the *Ancien Régime*. Madame Campan's memoirs are often relied upon by biographers and taken as gospel, but many of the events she records took place before her time in service to the monarchs began and are also tinted with a rosy glow, intended to cast the sovereigns in a soft light that would rehabilitate their reputations in a post-Napoleonic world. For example, her famous attribution of the phrase "May God guide us and protect us, for we are much too young to reign," which she places in Louis's mouth at the moment he hears of his grandfather's death, falling upon his knees in prayer, is more than likely a fictional embellishment. For one thing, Campan wasn't there. For another, neither the emotion nor the expression is in keeping with the teenage Louis's personality. But generations of biographers have included it in their academic tomes as fact.

Hüe accompanied Marie Thérèse to Vienna in 1795 and when her uncle Louis XVIII eventually ascended the throne, was made a baron as well as Treasurer General of his household. Hüe died in 1819 and is buried in Père Lachaise cemetery.

After the Revolution ended, Madame Campan, finding herself penniless, eventually opened a school, which was patronized by, among others, the future wife of Napoleon Bonaparte, Rose de Beauharnais. This led to a position as superintendent of a school in Écouen founded by Napoleon for the education of the daughters and sisters of Légion d'Honneur recipients. Henriette Campan retired to Mantes after the restoration of the Bourbon monarchy in 1814 and died in 1822.

Louis's other faithful valet, **Jean-Baptiste Hanet-Cléry,** was arrested and imprisoned more than once following his master's execution. Finally sent to the horrific La Force prison on September 25, 1793, he was not released until the Terror ended, several days after the fall of Robespierre. He eventually ended up in Austria, where he joined Madame Royale's household, and then that of the comte de Provence, where he dwelled in exile in Verona. Cléry did not return to France until 1803. Though he was offered a position as Josephine's chamberlain by Napoleon, he refused it and went into self-imposed exile instead, rejoining Marie Thérèse, first in Warsaw and then in Vienna.

Cléry suffered an attack of apoplexy in 1808 and died the following year on his estate in Austria. His tombstone reads *"Ci-gît le fidèle Cléry"*—here lies the faithful Cléry.

Claude Chauveau-Lagarde, who defended Marie Antoinette at her trial, did survive the Revolution, dying in 1841. He also defended Madame Élisabeth as well as several of the moderate Girondins who were placed on trial during the Reign of Terror, including Madame Roland, **Jean-Sylvain Bailly,** and Jacques Pierre Brissot. He is buried in the Cimitière de Montparnasse in Paris.

During the September massacres the royal children's governess **Madame de Tourzel** and her teenage daughter **Pauline** were smuggled out of La Force prison by a mysterious man, possibly an aristocrat. The two survived the Revolution, but from time to time over the next several years Louis Charles's former *gouvernante* would be accosted by various impostors claiming to be Louis XVII. Madame de Tourzel was made a duchesse by King Charles X, the *ci-devant* comte d'Artois, and she eventually published her memoirs. In 1814, Pauline and Marie Antoinette's daughter, then duchesse d'Angoulême, were reunited. Pauline served as a lady-in-waiting to the duchesse until the abdication of Marie Thérèse's father-in-law Charles X in August 1830.

Florimond Claude, the comte de Mercy-Argenteau, who had long served as Austria's ambassador to the Bourbon court, and who in some ways was both a mentor and surrogate father to Marie Antoinette, was appointed ambassador to Great Britain in July 1794, another cushy posting. Unfortunately the sixty-seven-year-old diplomat died on August 25, a few days after arriving in London.

Rose Bertin survived the Revolution, traveling to Germany and later fleeing to London to ride out the storm. There she reopened her business, attracting as posh a clientele as she had in Paris. She returned to the French capital in 1795, briefly numbering the soignée Josephine de Beauharnais among her new customers. In the early years of the nineteenth century, as fashion's silhouettes became streamlined and simplified, Rose transferred the business to her nephews and retired from the fashion world. She died at her beloved country estate in Épinay-sur-Seine in 1813 at the age of sixty-six.

Rosalie Lamorlière, Marie Antoinette's devoted servant in the Temple, continued to serve the Richards at least until 1799. Twenty-five years old at the time she knew Marie Antoinette, she never married although she did bear a daughter to a man whose name appears lost to history. Rosalie's daughter erected a tomb in her honor in Père Lachaise cemetery in Paris.

As for **Louison Chabry,** although she is the "everywoman" of *Confessions of Marie Antoinette,* she is not a fictional creation. In 1789, she was a twenty-year-old sculptress who did in fact participate in the *poissardes'* October 5 march from Paris to Versailles, and she was indeed one of the half-dozen women chosen to form the little delegation that would present the people's grievances to the king in a civilized manner. Louison's fifteen minutes of fame came on that day when she met with the king and fainted in his presence, whether from hunger, exhaustion, awe, or some combination of all three. She witnessed Louis's kindness and solicitousness firsthand and I used that event as a springboard for the rest of her character, especially when it comes to her ambivalence about certain aspects of the Revolution, in contrast with her wholly fictional boyfriend Armand, whose beliefs are more in keeping with those of the young revolutionaries of the day. Nothing much is known about Louison Chabry. Her name is even spelled "Chabray" on occasion and some biographies refer to her as a seventeen-year-old flower seller rather than a twenty-year-old sculptress. My own research, as well as my gut hunches after living, eating, breathing, and sleeping Marie Antoinette's life for the past five years, have me leaning toward the latter age and vocation.

Having Louison as my alternate narrator allowed me the best of both worlds. She really existed, so I could keep the novel "honest" by not suddenly introducing a fictional narrator into the trilogy; but little enough is known about her that I could plausibly place her in a number of locations and at seminal events populated by hundreds or thousands of Parisians—Revolutionary events that Marie Antoinette would either not have been aware of at the time, or would never have attended, but which I felt my readers needed to know about in order to have a more complete picture of the age. Because Marie Antoinette was so insulated, her scope was more circumscribed, and this became even truer during the royal family's various incarcerations and their increased deprivations. The character of Louison also afforded me the opportunity as an author to create a more nuanced world. France was not either Bourbon white or revolutionary tricolor at the time, although the voices of the Revolution were doing their best to convince the people "if you're not for us, you're against us." Human beings wouldn't be what they are if there were not shades of ambivalence, doubt, and confusion. As a simple example, one could deplore the fact that the clergy paid no taxes and still be horrified by the National Convention's orders to massacre priests.

Readers always ask how much of this novel really happened. The Marie Antoinette trilogy is extensively researched and heavily based on the historical record. It's the novelist's prerogative to fill in the gaps with her imagination. It's my personal philosophy with historical fiction that if an event could plausibly have happened, then it's fair game to include it in the narrative, but if it plays fast and loose with dates or moves battles around (or invents them), those are lines I will not cross. Nor could I invent happy endings that simply did not take place just to satisfy some unwritten rule of commercial fiction. Any historical figure who lived more than two hundred years ago is dead by now. Sometimes gruesomely. Grab a Kleenex and get over it. I won't have Marie Antoinette survive the French Revolution and live happily ever after with Axel and the kids in Stockholm just because you don't want to cry at the end of the novel.

On the other hand, some things are so wonderful that even a novelist can't make them up. I am a proud history geek and a research junkie. I love discovering those little snippets of information that humanize a single moment in a distant time, those sparkling gems that make you gasp or cry, or laugh or shout, "I've got to use this!" I'll leave you with just a few examples of my favorite "wow" moments from my Marie Antoinette research.

Madame du Barry really did write to the queen after the October 6, 1789, storming of Versailles, placing her château, Louveciennes, at the royal family's disposal and offering them sanctuary there at any time. This heartfelt offer makes an exceptionally touching coda to the story line of the women's rivalry that began in the first novel of the trilogy, *Becoming Marie Antoinette*. Despite her humble origins, Jeanne du Barry, Louis XV's last mistress, was a royalist with every fiber of her being. Not only did she fund the escape of émigrés, but she allowed her home to be used for secret royalist meetings. Although she was genuinely touched by it, Marie Antoinette never answered her former rival's letter and the royal family would never know the extent of the comtesse's loyalty to the couple she once derided at court. Unfortunately, Madame du Barry survived the queen by less than two months. A victim of the Terror, she was guillotined on December 8, 1793.

The marquis de Favras was indeed summarily executed for

being a member of the nobility (although technically it was for plotting to sneak the royal family out of Paris—except that the royal family knew nothing about it!) years before the guillotine was put to use decapitating aristocrats simply for having blue blood.

The disastrous events of the family's ill-starred flight to Montmédy are as I described them. Louis really did get out of the hackney and wander about the outskirts of Paris to help hunt for the berline—imagine if he'd been seen! The party really did get turned around in the streets getting out of the city, the broken axle incident actually occurred, and Léonard Hautier really did tell the cavalry not to show up, although if the royal family hadn't wasted so much time getting lost in the first place, the *friseur*'s frazzled message might have been moot.

Some of what Louis's valet Hanet Cléry tells Marie Antoinette right after the king's death, conveying his last words to her, comes from Louis's Last Will and Testament, but I wanted the queen to be aware of them then and there, and they fit nicely within the moment. Louis did, however, give his wedding ring to Cléry to hand to Marie Antoinette, saying, "Poor princesse; I promised her a crown. Please tell her that I leave her with sorrow."

It is also true that the vendors in the marketplace provided the choicest meat and produce to the staff at the Conciergerie when they were informed that the food was for "the poor queen," putting the lie to the historical contention, as well as that perpetuated by the revolutionaries during Marie Antoinette's lifetime, that absolutely everyone from the lower social orders detested her.

And as Marie Antoinette was transported in the jouncing tumbrel through the rue Saint-Honoré en route to the guillotine, a baby in his mother's arms really did blow her a kiss. Even now I get a lump in my throat writing about it.

As for Marie Antoinette's last letter, written to her sister-in-law Élisabeth from the Conciergerie just hours before her death, I translated it from the original French and debated whether to include it in the novel. It is hardly a literary masterpiece, and from a levelheaded editorial perspective somewhat stops the forward momentum of the narrative at a time when we are hastening to the guillotine. Then again, it might be just the right moment to step back and take a breath.

Marie Antoinette's correspondence has been an integral part of this trilogy and her last letter is indicative of her final thoughts—a bit random and disordered—as well as her thought processes themselves. My interpretation of both the phrasing and the content is that despite her efforts to convey a certain level of tranquility, to convince Élisabeth that she was at peace with the inevitable, underneath it she was desperate to unburden herself of a few things and did not want to die without doing so. So, while her letter will never enter an epistolary pantheon, after she has so generously shared every detail of her life with me for the past several years, it seemed churlish not to give her the last word.

Vive la reine. Vive la reine martyre.

Questions and Topics for Discussion

1. It's almost axiomatic that History demands a scapegoat when something goes wrong. In Marie Antoinette's case, the "arrogant Austrian," the "selfish spendthrift," made the perfect target for the revolutionary demagogues. How often throughout history has the outsider, the "other," been blamed for the failure, for example, of a nation's economy? Discuss examples, past and present.

2. Historians have debated for more than two centuries as to whether Marie Antoinette had a love affair with Count Axel von Fersen, and if so, how far it went on a scale of platonic to sexual. Do you think they had a relationship? If so, how intense do you think it was? Do you think Louis knew about it? Do you think he forgave Marie Antoinette? Do you think she forgave herself?

3. During the ill-fated flight to the frontier on the night of June 20–21, 1791, why do you think Louis insisted that Axel leave the royal family at Bondy, even though Axel was the

mastermind of the plot to escape? Tragically, there was a domino effect of mishaps and screwups with the plans from that point on. Do you think that if Louis had allowed Count von Fersen to remain on the coachman's box, the family might have made it to safety?

4. The French nicknamed Louis XVI *"Le Désiré"* when he began his reign. He ended up deposed and executed. Do you think Louis was a good ruler? Why or why not?

5. If you had lived during the years 1789–1794 would you have been a revolutionary, a royalist, or more like the characterization of the young sculptress Louison Chabry, who was neither wealthy nor impoverished, and who struggled to comprehend what the massive social and political changes were all about and tried to make sense of them?

6. What do you make of the fact that some of the most bloodthirsty revolutionaries, specifically Jacques Hébert and Maximilien Robespierre, dressed not like the *sans-culottes* they identified with politically, but like the aristocrats they condemned? Discuss this in conjunction with the numerous condemnations of Marie Antoinette's ostentatious wardrobe and the accusations of her extravagant expenditures on it.

7. Biographers and historians have claimed that Madame Royale, Marie Antoinette's daughter Marie Thérèse, whom she nicknamed Mousseline, was as a child, very cold to her mother and as an adult extremely unforgiving of Marie Antoinette's character. Marie Thérèse's own memoirs are indeed not very charitable toward her mother. What do you make of this and why do you think Madame Royale felt this

way? Do you think her feelings are justified? Do you believe Marie Antoinette loved her daughter as much as she did her sons?

8. In August 1791, in a letter to the comte de Mercy-Argenteau, Marie Antoinette penned a remarkable sentence, which those who believe her to have been insensible of the turmoil around her might find to be surprisingly self-aware. She wrote, "Tribulation first makes one realize what one is." What does that statement mean to you in light of her life's journey and where it had led her by this point? How did tribulation both affect and change Marie Antoinette? If you were in her shoes, how might you have coped with the same tribulations?.

ABOUT THE AUTHOR

JULIET GREY has extensively researched European royal history and is a particular devotee of Marie Antoinette. She is also a classically trained professional actress with numerous portrayals of virgins, vixens, and villainesses to her credit. She and her husband divide their time between New York City and Washington, D.C.

www.becomingmarie.com

Chat.
Comment.
Connect.

Visit our online book club community at
Facebook.com/RHReadersCircle

Chat
Meet fellow book lovers and discuss what you're reading.

Comment
Post reviews of books, ask—and answer—thought-provoking
questions, or give and receive book club ideas.

Connect
Find an author on tour, visit our author blog, or invite one of
our 150 available authors to chat with your group on the phone.

Explore
Also visit our site for discussion questions, excerpts, author
interviews, videos, free books, news on the latest releases,
and more.

Books are better with buddies.
Facebook.com/RHReadersCircle